Purchased from
the Estate of
Mrs. Frances Kerlin Hanmer McMichael

THE COLOUR OF BLOOD

Emily Howard is nineteen years old, slim and petite, with a pale complexion and a red rose tattoo. She is also missing. She disappeared three days ago, and now her father has been sent photographs of her naked body. He is desperate to find her.

So he calls Ed Loy, a private investigator who knows the dark streets of Dublin better than most; a man who will find Emily within twenty-four hours.

But locating her turns out to be only the beginning. Within hours, Emily's ex-boyfriend is found murdered, and Loy finds himself in a race against time to catch a killer—and to unearth the many dark secrets the Howard family have kept long buried.

THE COLOUR OF BLOOD

BLOOD

Declan Hughes

WINDSOR
PARAGON

First published 2007
by
John Murray
This Large Print edition published 2007
by
BBC Audiobooks Ltd by arrangement with
Hodder and Stoughton

Hardcover ISBN: 978 1 405 61858 8
Softcover   ISBN: 978 1 405 61859 5

British Library Cataloguing in Publication Data available

Printed and bound in Great Britain by
Antony Rowe Ltd., Chippenham, Wiltshire

Grateful acknowledgement is made for permission to reprint the following material: Excerpt from 'This Be The Verse' from *Collected Poems* by Philip Larkin. Faber and Faber Ltd. Copyright © the Estate of Philip Larkin, 1988. Excerpt from *Sleeping Beauty* by Ross Macdonald. Vintage Books, Random House Inc. Copyright © 1973 Ross Macdonald.

To my mother

I

Halloween

We from the bridge's head descended, where
To the eighth mound it joins, and then, the chasm
Opening to view, I saw a crowd within
Of serpents terrible, so strange of shape
And hideous, that remembrance in my veins
Yet shrinks the vital current . . .
Amid this dread exuberance of woe
Ran naked spirits wing'd with horrid fear,
Nor hope had they of crevice where to hide,
Or heliotrope to charm them out of view.

Dante, *Divine Comedy, Inferno,*
Canto 24, trans. H. F. Cary

1

The last case I worked, I found a sixteen-year-old girl for her father; when she told me what he had done to her, I let her stay lost. The case before that, I provided a husband with evidence of his wife's infidelity; that night, he beat her to death, then hanged himself in the marital bedroom. Now I was calling on a man who by nightfall would be the prime suspect in two murder cases. Maybe one of these days, I'd get a better class of client. Maybe some day. Maybe not today.

The late-October sun hung low in the grey morning sky, a silver glare behind the mist that had blown in south of Seafield. At Bayview Harbour, I swung sharp right up a steep lane and parked by a double-fronted stone Victorian house with a brass plaque on the wall that read, 'Shane Howard—Dental Surgeon'. I opened the low gate and walked along a cobbled path bordered by glistening rowan trees, their berries flaring blood-orange through the mist. Crows on the roof beat their wings and made their low tubercular moan. At the heavy green front door, I looked back and breathed in air that was dank and clogged with salt and the musk of rotting leaves. It was the cleanest breath I'd draw until it was all over.

The hall was dimly lit by a dust-stained chandelier with only two working bulbs. Framed photographs of green-shirted Irish rugby players in action hung from the picture rail. The receptionist had snow-blonde hair, high cheekbones and midnight-blue eyes and an engagement ring with

3

red stones that made me think of a crab claw. I gave her a card with my name and what I did for a living printed on it and her eyes widened with anxiety; she compressed her lips and nodded at me gravely and reached for the phone.

'It's all right, Anita, I'll deal with Mr Loy.'

The speaker was a swollen man in his mid-forties encased in a charcoal three-piece wool suit that bulged like a bull's pelt. He had a port glow to his full jowls, a plume of dark grey hair swept back from his oily brow and a complacent expression in which boredom and self-satisfaction vied for supremacy. He inclined his head to one side and flexed his protuberant eyes and fleshy mouth in a brisk rictus of acknowledgement. The gesture made him look fleetingly like a gigantic oriental baby. I looked at the floor, and noticed his feet: like those of many fat, self-important men, they were very small.

'Denis Finnegan, Mr Loy. Mr Howard's solicitor. I wonder if I might have five minutes of your time.' His voice was like the quiet, oily purr of an expensive car.

'Mr Howard spoke to me himself,' I said. 'He didn't say anything about a solicitor.'

Finnegan did the oriental thing again with his face, this time with a lot of blinking and sighing, as if to deplore the free will with which his client had unaccountably been gifted.

I raised an upturned palm towards him and nodded; Finnegan turned on his heel and, beckoning with a nod of his huge head, began to climb the stairway halfway down the hall. Through a glass door, three patients sat around a large mahogany table, leafing through magazines. I

4

followed Finnegan up the stairs and into a small dark sitting room off the first-floor return. A bare yellow bulb hung from the cobwebbed ceiling; there were concertina files and drug company cartons piled against the ochre walls and a dusty three-piece suite arranged around a low table. Finnegan sat on the couch; I took one of the creaking chairs; it was the kind of antique furniture you felt might break if you shifted in your seat.

'I assume my client has told you everything,' Finnegan said, and waited for me to reply. I waited for him to continue. We sat for a while in the ensuing silence. Finnegan crossed an ankle over one knee. His socks were red silk, and his tiny polished brogues gleamed in the yellow light. He raised his eyebrows expectantly, as if it was only a matter of time before I told him what he wanted to know. I stood up and made for the door.

'Mr Loy, I understood we were going to talk,' he said, his voice yelping a little.

'So did I. But you're not talking.'

I opened the door. Finnegan stood up surprisingly quickly and waved his hands at me. They were pudgy hands, and they matched his socks.

'Please sit down, Mr Loy,' he said. 'I won't take up too much of your time, I assure you.'

I shut the door behind me, but stayed standing. Finnegan crossed the room, handed me a business card, then retreated to his seat and nodded briskly, ruefully, as if conceding his ill-judged choice of tactics.

'Mr Howard didn't ask me to, ah, intercede with you today.'

'No kidding. I guess he hasn't told you why he wants my *intercession* either. Well, if he hasn't, I'm not going to.'

Finnegan pursed his lips and raised his eyes, if not quite to heaven, at least to the dirty yellow bulb above his head, and steepled his index fingers together; after an interval of meditation, or silent prayer, he exhaled loudly through his nose and began to speak.

'My client's mother recently passed away. She leaves a substantial property on several acres adjacent to the Howard Medical Centre. That property, and the lands surrounding, are currently the cause of some contention between my client and his wife.'

'And between your client's wife and your wife. You are married to Shane Howard's sister, Sandra, aren't you?'

Finnegan nodded slowly, thoughtfully, his eyes vanishing momentarily into the folds of his crimson jowls.

'You do your homework, Mr Loy.'

'This is Dublin, Mr Finnegan. I just keep my eyes and ears open.'

'Yes, I am Mr Howard's brother-in-law, but I have no interest—no *beneficial* interest—in his mother's estate: the property and lands were left solely to Mr Howard; his sister is not named in the will.'

'So what do you want?'

'My client's wife, Jessica Howard, is, ahm, a highly spirited personality. If she were to discover that her husband had, for example, hired a private detective to spy on her, in the hope of gaining evidence that might be used against the lady now

6

or at some future date, in proceedings intended to undermine her entitlement to what she is legally and morally entitled to consider her due . . .'

'She wouldn't see the funny side.'

'She might pursue a litigious course which in the short to medium term would probably benefit no one except my colleagues in the legal profession. And while strong collegiate impulses are not alien to me, the bonds of family are more tightly drawn; for my late mother-in-law's estate to dwindle while disputatious solicitors spar, Jarndyce and Jarndyce-like, would, for the family, be to find ourselves in a very bleak house indeed.'

Finnegan unleashed a salvo of self-approving mews and yaps as a coda to his painfully forced literary reference, and his thick lips quivered with near-delight at his own facility, and for an instant I could see him back in the university debating chamber, basking in the braying regard of his peers, the legislators and judiciary of the future.

He opened his great maw to continue, but I beat him to it. It was a little after nine in the morning, and I hadn't had breakfast, and another of those ornate sentences that showed how much his father had paid the Jesuits for his education and I was going to have the kind of headache only gin would cure, and it was too early for gin.

'It's about his daughter,' I said.

'Emily?' Denis Finnegan said.

'That's right. She's gone missing.'

'And he wants her found?'

'Or wants to talk about it, anyway. She's nineteen, so there's a limit to what I could do, if she'd prefer to stay lost. What I'd be prepared to do.'

7

'I see. I see. I was under the impression . . . or rather I made, in the circumstances, the understandable assumption . . .'

'You thought he was hiring me to dig some dirt on his wife.'

'I certainly suspected he had something of that character in mind.'

'Is there any dirt to dig?'

'Let's just say I believed it expedient to inquire a little further into the potential veracity and, so to speak, *density* of any such allegations before deeming it appropriate to conclude that an operative such as yourself might properly be charged with the task of investigating further.'

I had the headache now. My left eyelid was flickering like a light bulb about to blow. I put my hand on the door and opened it, all the while keeping contact through my right eye with Denis Finnegan, who had narrowed his eyes and bared his teeth in a grimace of farewell. With the bare bulb directly above his head, his great face suddenly resembled a skull swollen and distorted by water.

'We'll speak again, Mr Loy, I have no doubt,' he oozed.

The words hung in the air like an emblem beneath a death's head. I stepped backwards through the door and pulled it shut and went downstairs.

A broad-shouldered sandy-haired man in a white linen tunic had his face bent close to Anita's pale head. His voice was working in a low rumble, then hers gushed forth in a flow of easy, throaty laughter. It was the kind of laughter that makes a man feel like his luck is in, the kind of laughter you

8

hear in bars and on street corners late at night. When my leather-soled black wingtips hit the tiled hall floor, their heads sprang apart and the man raised himself to his full height and turned to face me. He was about six three, heavily built like the rugby forward he had been, with a scowl on his open face.

'Mr Howard,' I said. 'Ed Loy. We spoke on the phone.'

Howard nodded slowly and looked at his watch.

'You're late,' he said, his tanned brow frown-ridged, bushy eyebrows shading his eyes.

'Your solicitor thought he needed to speak to me,' I said.

'Is Finnegan here again?' Howard said.

He glared at Anita, who flushed and nodded quickly. Howard flung a meaty hand in my direction.

'What did he want?' he said.

'I don't know,' I lied. 'I don't think he knew himself. To listen to the sound of his own voice, it felt like.'

'That sounds like Dinny all right,' Howard said, nodding. The huge planes of his face slowly began to shift into a smile. Then he laughed, an astonishingly loud, crashing sound, like the engine of a tractor flaring into life. As suddenly as it had started, the laughter sputtered out and he stared down at the black and white tiles and cleared his throat. He lifted his head, leant across the reception counter and patted Anita's hand.

'I'll be in the study, Anita. I'm not to be disturbed,' he said, nodded to me, and unlocked a door across the hall from the waiting room. I followed. As I passed Anita, she was caressing her

9

ring between finger and thumb. In the faint light, the uncut stones had the dark glow of arterial blood.

'Nice ring,' I said. 'When's the big day?'

'It's not an engagement ring,' she said. Her accent sounded Eastern European. Colour seeped across her pale cheeks like red ink on a blotter. 'It's for protection. A talisman.'

'Protection against what?' I said.

She shrugged.

'You know. Whatever. My sister gave it to me.'

She tried to smile, but it didn't come out right. She looked down and fussed with some papers on her desk. As I opened the study door, she had pushed her left hand to her mouth and was gnawing on the ring like an anxious child with a pacifier.

*　　　*　　　*

Shane Howard sat behind a dark wood desk, lit by a green-shaded lamp. The long room was otherwise in gloom: heavy velvet drapes hung over the windows. There were more rugby photographs hanging on the walls—Howard had been a second-row international when I was at school, and one spectacular shot showed him bursting across the line through a shambling disarray of English forwards. Above the white-marble mantelpiece hung a portrait of a handsome silver-haired man in tweeds and flannels with a stethoscope around his neck; a plaque at the base of the gilt frame identified him as Dr John Howard, 1915–1985. All over was an airless fug of dust and old upholstery and cigar smoke; Howard's desk was strewn with papers and framed photographs, used cups and glasses, an almost empty bottle of Bushmill's and two overflowing ashtrays. I sat across the desk from him, refused his offer of a cigar, and shook my head quickly when his hand strayed towards the whiskey. He nodded, cleared his throat, and then took an envelope from the desk, passed it to me and said, 'My daughter.'

Emily Howard was about nineteen, slim and petite, with a pale complexion and black eyeshadow around her large brown eyes and full red lips and short spiky hair dyed candy-apple red and piercings in her ears and nose and on her tongue. She also had a red-rose tattoo high on one thigh and her nipples were pierced and her pubic hair had been shaved into a tiny heart and dyed red. I could see this because in the photographs she was naked, and having sex with a boy and another girl, in most of the usual ways and a few that weren't so usual, except in photographs like this. The other girl wore a sequinned eyemask and her blonde hair was tied in a shiny scarf; the boy wore wrap-around shades and a black baseball cap; the only one you could get a clear look at was Emily. I looked up at her father. His bloodshot eyes were fixed on one of the framed photographs on his desk: a sandy-haired big-eyed girl of about six with no front teeth, biting into an apple.

I looked at the photographs again. When I worked in LA, at least once a month I was asked to find a girl who'd gone missing, and she'd almost always turn up having sex on camera in the San Fernando Valley, and in the movies she did, she always had this smile that didn't reach her angry eyes, a smile that said fuck you to someone, usually her father, or her stepfather, or her uncle; to some man who had taken everything from her before she was old enough to understand what it was. And she'd always say the same thing: that she was never going home again. And if letting a bunch of strangers ejaculate on your face is preferable to going home, then home must have really been something. So I'd go back and tell the client—the father, or stepfather, or uncle—that she didn't want to see him, and usually I'd give him a tape, or a magazine, so he could understand for himself what he had done. But he rarely did; more often than not, he'd ask me if I could get her autograph.

'Will you find her?' Howard said.

I looked at him. He didn't look the type, if there was a type, which there wasn't, and this wasn't that kind of porn. Still, it was hard to tell from the photographs: in most of them, Emily Howard looked detached, ironic even, as if to indicate a distance from what she was doing; but in a few of the shots, there was a glint in her eyes that could have been anger.

'How did you get these?' I said.

'They were hand-delivered. I didn't see who by. And there was a message.'

He passed me a sheet of white A4 with a note typed on it: *Next stop the Internet, where your daughter's ass will live forever—unless you cough up fifty grand by midday on Thursday. We'll tell you where and when.*

'They don't say they're holding her against her will,' I said.

'What are you suggesting—that she's in on it?' Howard said. 'How dare you!'

'Could she be?'

'Get out of my house.'

Howard's voice was loud, but it lacked conviction; he clutched the edges of the desk with his great hands.

'Has she new friends, or friends you don't know about? Has she become secretive about who she knows or where she goes?'

Howard's hands slapped down hard on the desk, sending papers flying and raising a cloud of ash. He stared to one side and to the other, opening and closing his mouth as if, in his rage, he didn't trust himself to speak, or he couldn't figure out who he was angriest at. Then he tried another laugh, but it didn't catch, and left him breathing hard and blinking back what looked like tears.

'Maybe you'd better tell me all about it from the beginning,' I said. 'When did it go wrong between you and Emily?'

Howard flung his head towards me as if I had accused him of something, chin thrust out, jaw set, eyes ablaze, ready for the fray; then as quickly the fire left him; he nodded eagerly, exhaled loudly, and in a low, deliberate voice that sounded as if it was only allowed out on special occasions, began to speak.

'That's just it,' he said. 'We had always been very close, all the while she was at school—great pals. More. I suppose she was Daddy's little princess, you know? That's what her mother always said, anyway. But we were the best of friends. Always came with me to see Seafield play rugby, even the away games. Picking her up after dates and clubs and so on, like her own personal driver I was. Then she went to university, and all that stopped,

13

overnight, it seemed. Didn't want to know me. First cheek and smart answers, then the silent treatment. We'd always kept her hair long, and one day she came home with it all cut off, spiked up and bleached blonde. Broke my heart. I mean, look at her.'

Howard plucked one of the framed photographs off his desk and passed it to me.

'That's Emily the day she got her Leaving Cert results. A real lady she was growing into.'

I looked at a pretty girl with long blonde hair and too much orange make-up and fussy designer clothes and intelligent eyes blurred with boredom and premature cynicism. There were fifty-year-old women all over the city traipsing from beauty parlour to hairdresser to designer store trying to maintain that look. At least Emily'd had the spirit to tear it up.

'Once she did the hair, we didn't know what to expect next: a pierced nose, a tattoo, God knows. She dropped all the girls she'd been to school with, girls she'd known all her life, girls whose parents are *our* friends. Her boyfriend since fifth year, David Brady, had just made the Seafield first fifteen—smashing guy, one of the best full-back prospects in the country, good career ahead—and she dumps him for one of the club barmen, he's in her class at college, some scrawny clown who plays in a band. Broken up about it, poor David was. Then she started staying out, night after night, wouldn't tell us where.'

'Drugs?'

'No. I don't know. Drink maybe. Hangovers. She spent enough time in that bed. But she's nineteen, half of them get sleeping sickness that age. Seems

14

to go to all her pre-med lectures.'

'She's doing medicine?'

Howard gestured to the portrait above the fireplace with a wry smile.

'She's going to make her grandfather proud. He didn't think dentists were top drawer. At last, a doctor in the family.'

'How long has Emily been gone?'

'This is Wednesday. I haven't seen her since last Friday. The photographs arrived yesterday.'

'And *do* you think she's in on this?'

'She's always had everything she wanted. No girl could have been better looked after.'

'Maybe she's tired of being looked after. Maybe she's decided it's time she looked after herself.'

Howard shook his head.

'No, I . . . she has seemed angry at us . . . but I don't believe she would do this. Not unless she was being forced in some way.'

'Why was your daughter angry, Mr Howard?'

'I don't know. I don't know. She had no cause to be. No cause.'

Howard shook his head, his damp brown eyes gaping, seemingly bewildered at the thought that his daughter might not be his best friend for life, or that at nineteen she might want her own life, rather than the one he had fashioned for her.

'Will you find her?'

'Mr Howard, why haven't you taken this to the Guards?' I said.

'Because I don't want any more people knowing about this than have to. In my experience, once the Guards know about something, so does everyone else. I can depend on you to be discreet, I assume.'

I said nothing. My job was getting people to tell

15

me their secrets, not swearing them to secrecy. Discretion rarely came with the territory.

'Anyway, if I send the Guards after her, I have little chance of winning her back.'

'Maybe she's a bit old for her father to win her back,' I said.

'Maybe,' he agreed wistfully, staring again at the photograph of his daughter as a six-year-old, as if that was the image of her that had taken permanent root in his mind. 'But she's never going to be old enough to have her body splashed across the Internet like a cheap whore.'

I couldn't argue with that.

There was a knock on the door, and Anita appeared.

'Dr Howard, there are six in the waiting room. And Miss O'Kelly is . . . well, you know how she gets.' A phenomenally loud over-elocuted female voice could be heard bellowing something about consumer choice and the need for a patients' charter.

'It's not her fault,' Howard said. 'I've kept them waiting. Thank you, Anita. Give me a minute.' The receptionist shut the door behind her. Howard stood up.

'Mr Loy, I have patients to treat. If there's anything else—'

'I'll need phone numbers for Emily's boyfriends and friends, past and present, I'll need to look at her room—'

'I was about to say. My wife is waiting in the house. She'll fill you in on all that.'

'I'll need to know immediately they call, and what they say. I'll need your mobile number to key into my phone, so I'll know when you call. And I'll

16

need a cheque.'

I told him how much I wanted, and he said I should invoice him, and I said I preferred to get paid up front, and he asked would I settle for half, and I asked him if that's how he ran his own business, and he said that was completely different, and by this stage Miss O'Kelly's fluting cries were loud enough to be heard through the closed door, so Howard wrote the cheque, smiling, as if he found the little people's need for money quaint and amusing, and flung it at me, just so I'd remember how completely different we were. He went out to rescue his patients, and as I heard his loud mechanical laugh defuse Miss O'Kelly's ire and I got down on my knees to retrieve the cheque from under the desk where it had fallen, I wondered, not for the first time, why it was that the richer the people who hired me, the more reluctant they seemed to pay me. Maybe it was an attempt on their part to recapture the control they felt they had lost by revealing so much about themselves. Or maybe it was just that they hadn't become that rich by parting easily with their money.

2

When Shane Howard said his wife was waiting in the house, it turned out he didn't mean the house we were in: that was only used as a dental surgery these days. Anita directed me downstairs through a stone-floored kitchen piled with boxes of drug-company samples and calendars and laundered white tunics and out into a sodden, half-wild back garden. Through the thickening mist, I walked along another damp cobbled path flanked by rowan trees until I came to a dark-green-marble pond about fifteen feet in diameter. The low walls formed a hexagon, and each side and angle was inlaid with a greenish crystal flecked with red the size of a child's fist. Orange and yellow leaves floated on the surface of the cloudy water. The whole thing looked beautiful and grave and strange, like a memorial without a dedication, and I wondered what its purpose was, what puzzle it was asking me to solve. Then I reflected that a downside of my job was the habit of searching for mysteries where there were none; sometimes a pond is just a pond.

At the bottom of the garden a tongue-and-groove door in a whitewashed roughcast stone wall opened into the garden of what Anita had rather loftily called 'Howard residence'. (Anita had also scrupulously avoided mentioning Mrs Howard by name.) Howard residence was a seventies-style L-shaped dormer bungalow with great floor-to-ceiling plate-glass windows. The garden was tended to within an inch of its life, with snooker-table lawns and tightly sheared borders of bay and box. At the front of the house, a black Porsche lurked on the gravel drive, sleek and feline; the garden there dropped steeply to another white stone wall, shielded by a row of mature eucalyptus; a hundred feet below the wall, the railway tracks vanished into a tunnel; beyond that, a shroud of grey where the sea spread out towards the sky. What sounded like gunshots snapped in the damp air, and then the crackle and hiss of fireworks

18

sparkled through the gloom, and I remembered it was Halloween. I rang the doorbell and Jessica Howard answered it and led me into a room the depth of the house with walls of glass back and front.

Jessica Howard was maybe a little too blonde for her age, and the skirt of her dark suit was maybe a little too short, and another woman mightn't have worn heels so high or a top cut so low or perfume so musky, not this early in the morning, or at all, but another woman might have looked tarty, or cheap, or desperate, and Jessica Howard didn't: she looked bold and direct and careless. Or at least, that's how it seemed to me, at first; then again, I wasn't another woman. While she made coffee I looked around the room, which was sparsely furnished with a couple of long couches and a round glass table with four metal chairs. On the walls, there were framed posters advertising theatrical productions: *Juno and the Paycock* at the Abbey, *An Ideal Husband* at the Gate, *Shopping and Fucking* at the Project. Above the fireplace, two photographs hung: one showed a younger version of Mrs Howard in Restoration costume with cleavage fit to bust; in the other, she sat naked on a rug with her back to the camera, her head turned around to smile, heavy-lidded, into the lens. Between them, a portrait of the lady in pop-art oils, big-haired and glowing like a trophy bride. I began to see where at least some of Emily's anger might have come from.

Jessica Howard brought a tray with a pot of coffee, a jug of hot milk and two mugs to the table and I joined her there. She offered me a cigarette, which I gladly accepted, poured coffee, which I

19

took black, blew a fine jet of smoke towards the ceiling and smiled at me. I shifted in my seat and said, 'Mrs Howard—'

'Jessica. Call me Jessica. And I can call you Ed, can't I?'

I said she could. Her blue eyes flickered, as if registering a victory, and I noticed how cold they were; the sex that animated every curve of her body didn't seem to touch her soul.

'Well Ed, did my husband manage to tell you anything of worth—in between banging on his desk and shouting his head off?'

'He gave me the basic outline,' I said, laying the photographs and the note on the table between us. She leafed through the shots, shaking her head and sighing heavily, but her dismay seemed more aesthetic than maternal.

'That hair is such a mistake,' she said. 'Not to mention the tattoo, and the piercings. Emily has a good body, and fine features, but she seems determined to make the worst of herself. Still, if these photos do end up on the Internet, the consolation is, no one will ever recognize her.'

'Provided she reverts to being an orange-faced south County Dublin blonde,' I said. 'Maybe she's frightened no one will ever distinguish her either.'

'Not everyone can stand out from the crowd,' Jessica Howard said. 'Now, what do you need from me? I have to show a house later this morning.'

'I thought you were an actress.'

'So did I. Not enough people agreed. Of course, when theatrical fashion swings towards the more *homely* type, one begins to feel foolish for having hung on to one's looks. And sometimes, sleeping with all one's directors can be as bad for one's career as sleeping with none of them. But that's the way it goes. And selling houses in the current market is like catching money in a bag—not a comparison one could ever make with working in the theatre.'

She smiled, and passed the photographs of her daughter back to me, taking care to brush her hand against mine as she did so. She licked her lips and widened her eyes in a 'what are we going to do next?' kind of way. I tried not to take her flirting personally, but I was the only man in the room, and I was a man, and I still hadn't had any gin.

'You don't seem too anxious about what's happened to your daughter, Mrs Howard,' I said. Jessica Howard didn't exactly roll her eyes, but she came close.

'Do you know what's *actually* happened to Emily? *I* don't,' she said. 'Shane wants to keep treating her like a child. She's nineteen years old, for Christ's sake. When I was nineteen, I was living in Paris with my boyfriend; I'd had an affair with a married man, an abortion; I'd taken cocaine, acid, heroin; I'd had any *number* of threesomes,' she boasted, gesturing dismissively towards the photographs of her daughter, as if they presented some kind of threat, as if mother and daughter were rivals. Maybe they were.

'And would you wish all of that for your daughter?' I said. My voice rang pinched and priggish in my ears, but I intended the reproof.

'What I'd wish for her is that she'd get out into the world and live. And it looks like, at last, that's what she's doing.'

'Your husband believes she's being held against her will, that she was forced to have sex on camera—that's abduction and rape, Mrs Howard.'

'I don't believe that for a second. I think this is some scheme the girl's dreamt up to squeeze more money out of Shane. And to give him two fingers as well, let him know she's not Daddy's little girl any more. That's what I would do if I were she.'

'Why would Emily need to blackmail your husband? Surely he's always given her whatever she wants?'

'Only as long as she does what he wants. That's the Howard family motto: do what we want and we'll tolerate you. The code of the Howards.'

She drew hard on her cigarette and exhaled in a long sigh of rancour and discontent.

'They wanted me to give up my career when we had Emily. Sandra, and the mother. Said it was unfair to the baby, and to Shane, who had his rugby and was building the surgery and needed support at home.'

'And what did you say?'

'I said Shane wouldn't have married some *frau* whose only ambition was to raise his children and keep his house, and I had no intention of turning into one. In retrospect, I think that's precisely what Shane did want. But he didn't get it. His mother hated me. Always had, hated me even more then. Wouldn't even come to see me on stage, not once in twelve years.'

'And the father was some kind of famous doctor?'

Jessica Howard rolled her eyes and said 'Ye-ah' with two syllables, like a character in an American sitcom.

'Dr John Howard. Professor of Gynaecology and Obstetrics at UCD, Master of the Rotunda

22

Maternity Hospital, Knight of Columbanus, senator, adviser to four successive ministers for health, the power behind the Howard Maternity Centre, where the sons and daughters of the comfortable are born, the Howard Clinic, where they go for repairs, and the Howard Nursing Home, where they die. Famous enough for you?'

'Kind of.'

'It's refreshing there's someone who doesn't know the Howard legend, chapter and verse.'

'I lived in LA for twenty years.'

'Well, if you didn't know what a great man he was, you'd quickly learn: his children keep his memory alive like he was a saint; they practically light candles to him.'

'And Shane's sister, Sandra, is she a doctor too? It tends to run in families.'

'A doctor? Sandra Howard was a *teacher,*' Jessica Howard said, using 'teacher' in the sense of 'failure'. Her voice had darkened, curdled with bitterness and smoke.

'She was deputy headmistress at Castlehill College. The youngest deputy headmistress in the country, no doubt you heard about that in LA, her mother certainly regarded it as of international importance. Now she runs the whole medical set-up, all the clinics and trusts and funds and chairs and so on. The keeper of the Howard flame.'

A foghorn sounded in the bay, harsh and prolonged. Jessica Howard looked out towards the gloom and shuddered. It was such a theatrical gesture that I almost laughed out loud, but something—a flash of rage, and then a dark shadow in her cold eyes—made me stop. I didn't know what the shadow meant, and I wasn't sure I wanted to, but it was no laughing matter. When she spoke again, it was in a completely different register, as if she had conceded her facade had been too brittle for the situation.

'I'm not an uncaring mother, or indifferent to my daughter's safety. On the contrary—it's because I care that I want her to break free, to gain her independence. I don't want her in thrall to the Howards, you see.'

'You make them sound like a cult.'

'Sometimes I think they are. The confidence and security of believing you're part of a natural elite, that your family has some great mission to accomplish, that you're *entitled*, by reason of your birth—all that is pretty seductive. Certainly seduced me. The power, the prestige, the charm of the Howards. But the way they want to control people's lives—it didn't succeed with me, so now they're trying with Emily.'

'When you say "they"—'

'Oh, the mother played her part before she died, but Sandra and Shane, mainly—they speak as one voice, usually Sandra's. Don't get me wrong, Sandra is in many ways a great lady, and she's had her share of troubles: her first husband died, and she had to look after her awful mother on top of her own kids. It's just weird when it feels like the man you married's a stand-in for his sister. Eventually, it's beyond weird.'

'So what are you saying, it was Sandra's idea that Emily should do medicine, she'd be carrying on the family line, so to speak?'

'You pay attention, Ed. It's rare in a man, almost unheard of in an Irish man. Yes, despite the fact neither of Sandra's kids is going to be a doctor, the burden of family destiny came to rest on Emily's shoulders.'

'Against her will?'

'I thought so. She seemed happy enough, but she always did. She liked to please, she was a dutiful daughter, that was the role she played. And now that's exploded, hasn't it? The centre wouldn't hold. I should have protected her. I should have been there more.'

She slumped in her chair, suddenly looking awkward and ungainly, like an adolescent herself, exhausted by the passions that surged through her without warning.

I shook my head.

'We don't know. Maybe your daughter is as angry and resentful as you say. Maybe she engineered all of this. Or maybe she's being held against her will. We need to find her, and find out from her what she wants.'

'If it means being returned to her father—'

'She's nineteen years old, Mrs Howard, as you pointed out. She's free to go wherever she pleases. Is her father really such a monster?'

'No. No, of course not. I just think what Emily needs now more than anything is her independence—'

'And what do you mean, "returned to her father"? Do you not live together any more?'

'I don't know that that's any of your business. But no, is the answer. We're in the process of separating. Solicitors are drawing up papers. All that good stuff.'

So Denis Finnegan had more than one reason to be concerned about Jessica Howard's highly spirited personality. I watched her now, talking

25

into a mobile phone whose insistent ring had rescued her from any further interrogation. As she spoke, her shoulders eased back and her chin lifted, as if her relief at escaping the demands of her family was warming her blood. She closed the call and shook her hair back and moved her teeth against her pouting lips, like a thoroughbred in the show ring.

'That's work. I've another client who wants to view the house. I need to go now. Shane can take you through anything else you need.'

I looked at her, unable to conceal the astonishment I felt.

'What?' she said.

'You sure you're not too busy to be bothered with all of this?' I said. 'Your ex-husband-to-be passed me over to you because he wouldn't keep his patients waiting; now you want me to go because you can't postpone an appointment.'

'It's work—'

'What are you, chasing the mortgage here, two houses on the top of Bayview Hill?' I said. 'I'm being paid to find your daughter, so I have to take it seriously; it would be nice if her mother did as well. Maybe you're right, she's just letting off some steam, going through a wild phase to shock you all. But if she's not—if she's been kidnapped, and raped, and abused and degraded, and is trapped somewhere, frightened and alone—it would be nice when I find her if I could say with confidence that you're worried about her; nice if you could promise to be here for her if she needs you.'

Jessica Howard reddened with anger and started to shout.

'How dare you? Who the hell do you think you

are, that you can talk to me like that? I run my own business, it took me time and energy and goodwill to build up, I've worked bloody hard, I can't just jeopardize it all for the sake of . . .'

Shock spread across her face as she realized what she had been about to say, hung there for seconds in the quivering 'O' of her lips and the horrified stare of her eyes and the now all-too-visible lines in her brow, and then dispersed with the tears she began to shed.

'I need to see Emily's room,' I said quickly. It was exhausting trying to keep up with her shifts in mood, and not a little unnerving. I needed some space to remember what her behaviour reminded me of.

Through sobs, she directed me down the hall to the last door on the left. It looked like she was going to accompany me, and I was about to reassure her that there was no need when her phone rang again and she composed herself and wheeled about and headed towards the living room, laughing brightly, back in business.

Emily's room hadn't been painted black or scarlet; she didn't have a pentagram on her floor or a coke spoon in her jewellery box; there were no whips in her underwear drawer, or vodka in her desk. But you could tell the occupant of the room was someone in the process of change. The furniture was antique French, white-stained with gilt trim; the bed was brass, the bedclothes plain white. A desk sat by a window with a sea view that would have been spectacular if you could have seen through the mist, which was thickening. On the desk was the outline in dust of a laptop computer and a white telephone without caller ID.

There were lecture notes and textbooks in pathology, anatomy and microbiology; no diaries or personal notebooks. There was a CD player and a few CDs: Britney, Christina and a clutch of boybands quaked before Deicide, Sepultura, Slayer and System of a Down. On the bookshelves, brightly coloured chicklit squared off against the two Naomis, Wolf and Klein, and a handful of volumes by Alice Miller, the psychotherapist who reckons we're all abused children one way or another, and it's all our parents' fault. There were dictionaries of mythology and phrase and fable, and several books about the supposed properties and applications of crystals. Her wardrobe and chest of drawers told the same story her father had: three-quarters of the clothes were preppy suburban, then suddenly there were red-satin dresses, leather jackets, fishnet stockings, spike-heel boots. In her jewellery box, there were little gold chains and charm bracelets and a few swimming medals; on her dressing-table mirror hung an array of Gothic crosses, chains, beaded-and-jewelled necklaces and bracelets. I picked up a silver wristband that had greenish stones with red flecks. They looked like smaller versions of those I had seen set into the walls of the garden pond. Against the light, the red in each stone looked like veins in a tiny green skull.

Under the bed, I found a beautifully made doll's house: it had castellations and a turret and a tower. The back doors opened to reveal the usual furniture and a random assortment of toy figures; neither side of the roof opened. The house stood on a broad wooden base; to the front there was a drive lined with plastic trees; at the rear there was a lawn sloping down to a circular pond; the perimeter of the pond was made of tiny pebbles glued together. A fine coat of dust clung to it like age; I guess it hadn't been played with for a long time.

I went through every item of clothing that had a pocket, but there were no scraps of paper or tickets; there was nothing else under the bed, no boxes of letters or mementos or photographs. I flicked through the pages of the books, but all that fell out, from the very oldest, were dried autumn leaves. Had Emily taken everything with her that bore a personal trace, or had she simply not kept any of it to begin with? I heard Jessica Howard calling my name. I did the only other thing I could think of: I pressed 'Redial' on the telephone. After a dozen rings, a male voice answered.

'Woodpark Inn?'

I thought for a few seconds.

'Hello?'

'Have you a late extension tonight?' I said.

'Halloween party, ten till two, battle of the bands, tickets twenty euro,' he said.

'Thank you,' I said, and hung up. The Woodpark Inn. Not Emily Howard's style, I would have thought. But then, what would I know? As much as anyone, it seemed.

In the living room, Jessica Howard sat at the table, her hands folded across her breast, her head slightly bowed, her crossed legs tucked beneath her chair. She looked exhausted, about ten years older than the woman who had greeted me. The way she sat seemed intended to minimize her body space, and I remembered at last what she reminded me of: the swings between sexual

29

exhibitionism and physical awkwardness, between rage and carelessness, cold objectivity and tears. She reminded me of the lost girls I tried to rescue from San Fernando Valley porn sets, or rather, the way they'd be in twenty years' time, eyes still bright but hard, souls cold as the dead.

She brightened up when she saw me, and pointed to a sheet of paper on the table.

'David Brady was Emily's boyfriend for two years. This is his address and mobile number. Here's a photograph of the two of them together. Absolute ride, I certainly would have, thighs to die for. The guy she's going out with now is called Jerry . . . blank, I'm sorry. He was a barman at the rugby club, not sure if he still is. Oh yes, and his band is called—what's the other name for Calvary? You know, where Christ was crucified?'

'Golgotha,' I said.

'That's right. His band is called The Golgotha Pyre.'

A smile creased up through her beautiful, sad face.

'You can only *imagine* what they sound like.'

She got a bag and an umbrella and saw me to the door. Outside, as she was locking up, I thought of the Alice Miller books.

'Jessica, was Emily in therapy of any kind?'

'No. At least, not that I know of. But I wouldn't be surprised if . . . no, actually, Shane wouldn't have kept that from me. No, she wasn't.'

'Are you?'

Her slender figure crooked against the cold rain that had started to fall, Jessica Howard flashed a grin at me as she walked towards her car.

'I'm beyond therapy, Ed,' she said, without

30

turning around. 'I'm out the other side.'

She got in the Porsche, pointed it down the hill and vanished into the mist.

I walked back up to my car. I drove a racing-green '65 Volvo 122S. It had been my father's, and although we had never seen eye to eye, I somehow felt driving it was keeping faith with his memory, though I'd be hard put if called upon to explain exactly what I thought that meant. Beneath the windscreen wiper someone had left a white envelope which was now damp with rain. I pulled it out, sat into the car and opened it. Inside was a mass card. The name on it was Stephen Casey, and the date of the requiem mass was set as All Souls' Day 1985. All Souls' Day was November the 2nd, two days from now. I put the card in my jacket pocket. Before I had a chance to turn the car, a black Mercedes the width of the road swept past me with Shane Howard at the wheel.

3

Tommy Owens had given up booze and dope and coke and E because he was broke because he couldn't hold down a job because of all the booze and dope and coke and E he'd been doing, and his ex refused to let him see his daughter until he cleaned up. Being sober all the time wasn't easy for Tommy, and Tommy being sober wasn't easy for me either, since he'd asked me to act informally as his sponsor. I explained that, since I had no intention of stopping drinking, that mightn't be the wisest idea, but he insisted,

31

maintaining that having to put up with some sanctimonious bastard thrilled with himself for having given up booze would drive him to drink. In practice, it didn't mean a lot more than my letting Tommy hang out at my house, sleep on my floor and generally make himself at home whenever it suited him, as well as helping him out of whatever scrapes he inevitably found himself in. All of which I'd been doing anyway. The new development was Tommy wanting to be involved with the cases I worked, to talk them through and offer me advice.

At first I resisted this because my work was complicated enough, and depended a lot on instinct and intuition, capacities that were easy to undermine, especially if exposed to the chaos of Tommy's mind. Not to mention client confidentiality. But his thinning, wispy hair and tufty straggle of beard weren't the only ways in which Tommy resembled a beady old lady: he knew everyone in Seafield, Bayview and Castlehill and outlying areas, and everything about them, always had, since we were kids, who lived where and who lived there before them; who was rising, who falling, everyone's business but his own. So when I checked my phone and found three messages from Tommy asking what the deal was with Shane Howard, I called him and gave him the bare skeleton—it was always a fine line, because I had the persistent suspicion if he heard something juicy enough, he'd trade it in for a night in the pub and a gram of coke. Not this time though. Immediately he heard David Brady's name and the word 'porn' he said I should meet him at once at my house in Quarry Fields.

Although I had grown up in the house, I hadn't

been back in it long enough to get used to calling it mine, despite a hefty standing order on my bank account reminding me that I was the only one paying the mortgage my mother had taken out to fund the old age she didn't live to see. A fifties semi-detached, it had seen better days, and I had done nothing to the exterior to improve it, other than have the side garage demolished and a gated wall built to connect the back line of the house to the perimeter. The earth had been turned where the concrete was lifted, and I scattered some grass seed for want of any better idea of what to do with a space I still considered haunted. Tommy was outraged, and accused me of wanting 'a businessman's lawn, like a fuckin' snooker table'; he had worked for my father once, and restored the Volvo in the garage, so he felt he had a claim on the space. He got busy with paving stones, cobbles, recycled tiles and anything else he could steal from the day-labouring jobs he occasionally worked, laying them in a loose path and planting herbs and heathers in the gaps between them. The hedge at the front of the house was of holly, yew and cypress; Tommy flanked the path with these, adding bay to give richness; the result was a secluded, tranquil path running south towards a gate of spiked black palings that let in the afternoon light. It was a good job, and I was grateful to him.

Inside, I had done little other than sand, stain and varnish the floorboards and paint the walls and ceilings white. I didn't have much in the way of furniture, but I bought a brown leather couch long enough to pass out drunk on without waking with a deformed spine. Tommy Owens was sitting on the couch now with two remote controls in his hands. I sat beside him, reached out a hand and he passed me the DVD remote control.

'Why d'you still wear your wedding ring, Ed?' Tommy said.

It was a good question, one I'd been asking myself. My marriage had fallen apart after my daughter Lily died, days short of her second birthday; I have the vaguest memory of signing divorce papers, drunk, like everything else I did in the aftermath. My ex-wife had recently been in contact with me for the first time since then. She wanted to be the one to tell me that she was getting married to the man she had gone out with before she met me, the man she had never entirely gotten over or indeed separated from while we were married, although of course I didn't know about that until it was too late. She wanted me to know that she would soon have this man's child, and she wanted me to hear it from her, not someone else. I thought it unlikely in the extreme that anyone who knew me in LA would ever mention my ex-wife to me again, but maybe she was acting out of sensitivity. Maybe she wanted to tell me that she grieved too for what we had had, for what had been lost. It didn't feel that way, however. The way it felt was that she had held our shared past, our child, our history, held it aloft in one hand, and then set fire to it, and she wanted to make sure that I had seen the flames. I didn't say that though. I wished her luck, and hung up before I said anything else, before she could hear the bitterness and anger in my voice, the grief that had never entirely abated, and that felt sometimes like it never would. I still wore my wedding ring

34

because I didn't want to forget the flames that burned me, or the past that binds.

'Saves me beating them off with a stick,' I said. Tommy rolled his eyes.

I'm not sure if there are ideal conditions to watch porn, but sober before midday doesn't even come close. On the screen, a blue-eyed blonde in her early twenties was going at it with a pale, blond-haired bloke about the same age or younger on someone's living-room floor. The woman wore a black-satin eyemask; the man wore black wrap-around shades. I looked at the photographs of Emily's threesome. It looked like the same guy in the film. Something about the blonde looked familiar too. They were joined by a plumpish, dark-haired woman wearing a lot of complicated black underwear, most of which she left on. There was no attempt at a story, no dialogue other than moans and groans, the camerawork was shaky and amateurish, and there was no lighting, so the action was enveloped in shadow and murk.

'Tommy, where are we going here?' I said.

'Hold on, hold on.'

Scowling, for Tommy had always been puritanical about anything to do with sex, he fast-forwarded until the scene cut to one where the threesome was shot against two full-length mirrors.

'Now, there.'

He froze the disc. Visible in one of the mirrors was the hand-held camera, and the forearm, of the cameraman. On his wrist, the man wore an identity bracelet with a series of letters and numbers in relief where a name would usually go.

'That's David Brady,' Tommy said.

'How can you tell?' I said.

'What can you see?'

'2 J S 2,' I said. 'What's that?'

'2JS2. When David Brady was at Castlehill, the school won the Junior Cup two years running, and then the Senior Cup the same. David Brady was the only one to play on all four teams.'

'Rugby, Tommy? It'll be golf next.'

'Fuck off. There's practically a fuckin' shrine to the guy in the Castle Inn sure.'

'Since when do you go to the Castle Inn? Thought that was rugby all the way.'

'I get around man. I get around.'

I showed Tommy the photographs, and he quickly matched the skinny guy with the one in the film by means of an eagle tattoo on his left shoulder blade.

'The background's the same too, carpet, cushions, sofa,' Tommy said, nodding seriously, thoughtfully, like we were partners. I wasn't ungrateful for his help, but still.

'Where did you get this, Tommy?'

'This what?' he lied. His eyes flashed quickly to his end of the couch and back. Old Pokerface.

'This porno DVD we're watching. Where did you get it?'

I got up and stood over him. I could see his green-canvas backpack tucked away on the floor by the side of the couch. Tommy held my gaze, tapping with his right hand on the arm of the couch.

'I just picked it up, you know man?'

An I-can't-think-of-a-lie lie.

'In actual fact, David Brady gave it to me himself,' Tommy said hopefully.

In actual fact. I hoped he wasn't going to make a habit of using that expression. I made a move towards the bag. His right hand formed a fist and he brought his left shoulder around, as if to say he was ready. I nodded and moved in just slowly enough to give him time to get out of the way. He got, sliding to his left with a hangdog expression on his flushed face.

There were about two hundred DVDs in cardboard sleeves, each one with the legend 'Threesome Porno' written on it in Tommy's surprisingly polished hand. Tommy wouldn't meet my eyes. I was starting to get angry. I turned off the television and removed the disc from the DVD player and shut off the power and none of it made me feel any calmer.

'Tommy. Explain this to me,' I said.

'It's nothing man, I'm just holding it, know I mean?'

The accent thickened the more he stalled, as if the right blend would be truly impenetrable.

'You're going to sell them for what, a tenner a go? Two grand, door to door on the estates, in the right pubs. And what do you keep?'

'Three-quarters.'

'Bullshit. Two euro in ten.'

'Five.'

Spots of anger erupted all over Tommy's taut rodent face.

'It's all right for you, you have all these rich cunts paying you all the time,' he said.

'Yes, being paid money for work I do, it's called my job.'

'Well how come I don't have a job? Been clean three months now and I still can't get regular work.'

What could I say? That it was going to take more than three months' sobriety to convince garage owners to take a chance on a man who had proved himself a legendary fuck-up in substance-abuse, work-rate and time-keeping terms? Not to mention everyone's aversion to employing a former associate of the Halligan organized crime gang.

'You're getting a few days a week on building sites.'

'Ah yeah, they put me with the Poles and the fuckin' Latvians on piss money man. I mean, fair play, nice lads an' all, even if I don't know what the fuck they're going on about half the time, but it's easier for them, they don't understand they're being ripped off. I do.'

'Anyway, that's not the point, the deal was, nothing dodgy if you're hanging out here. I already have Dave Donnelly's new sergeant popping in often enough to keep tabs on me. I don't need any shit, Tommy.'

'There's nothing illegal about this. Not really. I mean, it's not like dealing, is it?'

'Home-made porn for sale door to door? It's a church fund-raiser. Tommy, who did you get these from?'

Tommy looked like the bold child he had never entirely stopped being. It wasn't a good look on a man in his forties. But what he said took me aback.

'Brock Taylor.'

'Brock Taylor? The guy who bought the Woodpark Inn?'

'Yeah. That shook you, didn't it?'

Brian Taylor—nicknamed Brock (the Irish for

38

badger) because of the lock of naturally growing white hair that flared in the midst of his luxuriant black bouffant—led a gang out of the north inner city in the nineties that pulled three of the biggest bank and security-van jobs the country had seen. There was no forensic evidence, no witnesses and none of his gang would give evidence against him. And he did himself no harm by continually lobbing hefty cheques at local charities. Eventually, the Criminal Assets Bureau confiscated half a dozen houses and two pubs from him because he had no explanation for how he had paid for them; although they were worth a total of five million, Taylor's sole declared income for the period was 90 pounds a week in social welfare. But no one ever got to his bank accounts. He did eighteen months for intimidation of a witness, then came out, spent a few quiet years laundering all his remaining cash through two betting shops and an amusement arcade and watching the value of the properties he had managed to hold on to soar, then emerged suddenly, living in a house in Fitzwilliam Square and as the new owner of the Woodpark Inn, a sprawling 'car-park pub' that stood at the junction of Seafield, Castlehill and the once notorious Woodpark Estate. He'd been busy with his chequebook as well, to drug-rehab and homeless centres, charities for sick and disabled children and so on, and a couple of tame journalists had been enlisted to build a Robin Hood anti-hero image: the hood with the heart of gold who only did what, let's face it, we'd all do given a chance: take back some of the money the banks robbed from us over the years. As a result, and because he was a hail-fellow-well-met type of guy and because he seemed to lack entirely the whiff of cordite, he was being made welcome in all sorts of places you wouldn't have expected before, including Seafield Rugby Club, whose grounds lay adjacent to Woodpark.

Tommy looked at me with a defiant smile.

'All right, you took me by surprise, well done. What's Brock Taylor doing peddling amateur porn?'

He shook his head, his expression relaxing into its usual pasty combination of suspicion and anxiety.

'I think he's after Brady in some way. I don't know how. He told me to take the DVDs, but to wait for the word before I started hawking them. Said if I sold any before that, he'd want to talk to me.'

'Did he mention Brady by name?'

'No. It was all a certain party this, a certain party that.'

'And was there a deadline? A cut-off point, after which you could go ahead?'

'Tomorrow afternoon.'

I could hear him say it, but there was a reverberation, a kind of psychic echo to it, as if I had heard it many times before. As of course I had: not this specific detail, but the connection, the way on a case nothing is accidental, everything forms a pattern, and what you thought you were looking for marks only the first step along the path. Tomorrow was Thursday; the deadline for Shane Howard to pay his daughters' kidnappers the ransom was midday Thursday; now a porn movie directed by her ex-boyfriend was ready to flood on to the market after that time—if the ransom wasn't paid?

Or despite that?

Not the detail, but the connection.

'He did say one of the places to sell was outside Castlehill College. Which is where David Brady went to school. So that maybe says there's some kind of threat going on.'

'And how did he hook up with you?'

'You mean, me being such a fucking loser an' all?'

'If the cap fits. What I meant was, Brock having his own boys to do the necessary.'

'I don't know that he does. Or at least, not on the street, you know? He doesn't want to be associated with any of that now. He's a member of Seafield Rugby Club and the Castlehill Lions Club and the fund-raising committee to buy a new dialysis machine for St Anthony's and all this.'

'And it didn't occur to you to wonder about the wisdom of working for Brock Taylor? Did you not learn your lesson with Podge Halligan?'

'Ed, nobody knows what Brock is up to. I mean, he never dealt drugs, he's not robbing, he owns the pub and a few houses and apartments scattered around. That's all he looks like he's doing, property development.'

'And a little hardcore porn.'

'All right, I don't know why he called me, and I didn't expect him to be into all this.'

Tommy gestured disgustedly at the TV and his bag of DVDs.

'He said there was some kind of underage scene going on, and he was trying to get to the people behind it.'

'Child porn?'

'Not children, young teenagers. Thirteen,

41

fourteen.'

'Your daughter's age.'

'I'm not the only one with a daughter. So I thought, if that's what's going on, and if Brady's involved, and if Brock is after him—for whatever reason—and he can't get the evidence, and he wants to shame him around town, and there's a few bob in it for me, why not?'

I looked at Tommy, who was lying about at least some of it, of course, but who had worked himself into believing that he had told the whole truth and nothing but. The problem was, it didn't add up.

'Shane Howard told me David Brady was one of the most promising full backs in the country. What's he doing still playing club rugby for Seafield? The best players are all professional now: why isn't he playing for Leinster, or any of the Celtic League sides? And what's he doing making hardcore porn films and . . . I mean, if he shot the photographs of Emily, we have to assume he's in on the blackmail attempt as well.'

Tommy looked at me and shrugged.

'That's where you'd earn your money, by doing your job. Boss.'

If he had grinned, I might have slapped him, but his face was a mask of earnest and diligent apprenticeship. I gathered the DVDs together and put them in a paper carrier bag.

'I hope you're being straight with me, Tommy. Because this is serious business, and if you're fucking around, I won't take it lightly.'

'On the level man, on the level,' Tommy said, as usual looking far from. 'I swear on my daughter, on Naomi man.'

And he held my gaze, and I felt he understood

42

how serious it was, and I knew if anything had meaning for him, it was his child, and I believed him.

We all make mistakes.

4

David Brady had an address in the Seafield Waterfront apartments. I stood outside the security door to the complex with my car keys in one hand and my phone in my ear, nodding and saying 'Absolutely' and 'No problem' and 'Monday at the latest' until a short man with his hair gelled into the spiky fin that for some reason was the current style of choice for young male estate agents appeared in the lobby, a sheaf of apartment specifications under his arm. The Waterfront had sold off the plans eighteen months before; now the complex was finally open, half the apartments were on the market again as investors sold up for sixty or seventy grand more than they had paid. I pointed at the door, still nodding into the phone, and Spiky Fin, who I noticed had acne, and possibly short trousers, opened it and extended an apartment spec to me. I waved my keys at him, too busy by far, and slipped around to the elevators.

As the elevator rose, I inspected myself in the mirrored doors. I wore a black suit, a white shirt and black shoes. I wore a black overcoat in deference to the season. I had a black knit tie in my pocket, but it was rarely necessary these days. I had fallen into dressing like this partly by accident: I got off the plane from LA in a black suit and the

43

airline promptly lost the rest of my luggage. I couldn't think of anything else to wear, so I simply bought more of the same. It meant I rarely had trouble with a doorman, a maître d' or a corporate PA, quite the opposite in fact. And if it also meant in certain situations I was a shade conspicuous, well, that can work to your advantage too, provided you don't mind leading with your chin. After an October off the booze and working hard at the gym, I was a few pounds below fighting weight, clear-eyed and ready for action. I went for a reassuring smile. Then a look of reliable authority. Neither worked. The darkness in my eyes and the drawn clefts in my cheeks seemed to anticipate what I would find in David Brady's apartment. I was trying to sell my reflection an impression of life, but it was no good. I was calling on death, and my face knew it before I did.

I knocked on the door and it gave against my fist; it had been left on the snib. The apartment was eight floors up, and looked out over Seafield Harbour through one wall of glass; if the mist hadn't been so thick, you'd have seen right across the bay to Howth; as it was, you could see about as much as David Brady, who was lying on his tiled kitchen floor with a halo of blood around his head and a Sabatier carving knife stuck in his chest. He had been stabbed a number of times in the stomach and chest, and the back of his head looked like it had been smashed repeatedly on the glazed terracotta tiles. I took a pair of surgical gloves from my coat pocket, put them on and gave the body a quick once-over. Brady's flesh was still warm to the touch, even around the hands: there was no visible lividity, no evidence of early rigor in

44

the eyelids or the jaw; he could have been killed ten minutes ago.

I looked at the photograph Jessica Howard had given me, of Emily and her boyfriend David Brady. It must have been after a match: Brady jubilant, red-faced and mud-smeared in a striped rugby shirt; Emily, all blonde highlights and orange tan, gazing adoringly at her prince. My tongue felt swollen and dry in my mouth, and sweat suddenly sparked in my hair and on my brow. I crossed to the glass wall and slid the balcony door open and stepped out into the clammy cold air. Petrol fumes mingled with the salt tang from the sea; behind the roar of buses and trucks, the foghorn sounded, a dark bass note of mourning beneath the traffic's metallic clamour.

I went back in and began to search the apartment. The living-room-kitchen-dining area was one open-plan space; off the kitchen ran a short passage with doors to a small bathroom and the only bedroom. Neither of the porn shoots had taken place here. There was a white G5 iMac on a desk in the living room. I booted it up and went into the bedroom. There were two televisions; the one in the bedroom was cabled for PlayStation, and games lay in piles on the floor. There were other gadgets: Gameboys and MP3 players, and a mini hi-fi system on the ledge behind the bed; no sign of camera equipment. There was nothing else of interest, except to note that David Brady had a mirror on the ceiling over his bed and a bunch of sex toys and a stack of porn DVDs in his bedside locker. A man who brought his work home with him. None of the porn was homemade; the DVD collection outside was all store-bought—action

45

adventures and teen comedies, horror and sports. There didn't appear to be any books in the apartment at all.

I sat in front of the computer and searched for any file containing the words 'emily', 'howard', 'threesome' or 'porn'. As I did, I heard sirens outside. There was a folder with some photographs of Emily as she used to look; that was all. I tried searching for Brian Taylor under his own name and the nickname 'Brock'—nothing. I opened Entourage and sorted the 'Sent Items' folder by 'Attachments'—and finally came up with it. It was called 'emho', and it had been sent as an attachment to the email address 'maul@2ndphase.ie'. There was nothing in the subject line or body of the mail to indicate who it was being sent to. I found the original 'emho' and opened it. Inside were the photographs of Emily's threesome. The sirens reached a climax and stopped. I looked out quickly over the balcony. Two white Garda cars with blue-and-yellow markings were outside. I didn't have much time. I deleted the email, deleted the contents of the 'Deleted Items' folder, trashed the 'emho' folder, emptied the trash and shut the Mac down.

I finished back at David Brady's body for one last look. He had patch pockets on his shirt, but they were soaked in blood; the pockets to his low-slung jeans were easier to get to; one had a handful of change, which was no use; the other had a mobile phone, which was. The light by the side of the elevator showed the Guards were on the fourth floor; I reckoned there'd be four of them, two in the lift, a uniform to watch the foyer, another for the fire stairs; I jammed the apartment door wide open and made it to the stairs as the elevator left seven. There was no sign of a Guard on eight or seven; I flashed a look over the balcony and saw him about a third of the way up; I went down to six and ducked inside. I summoned the elevator and went down to the first floor, then got off, sent it down, and made for the stairs again. The Guard above me had vanished: checking one of the upper floors, I guessed. On the ground floor, I took a squint through the small window into the foyer. The uniform, a blonde with hair cropped short and long legs, was looking into the empty lift. She looked towards the fire door and I pulled back. I didn't want to go through the back exit into the yard in case it tripped the alarms. I looked back: the elevator doors were closing, the uniform presumably inside. I kept my head down and pushed fast through the door and along the foyer on to the street.

*   *   *

I sat on a stool in the Anchor bar for a while going through the text messages on David Brady's phone and savouring my first alcohol in a month. Strictly speaking I should have waited until midnight, but since I had never before interfered with and altered a crime scene, or tampered with and stolen vital evidence, I figured I was entitled to an early drink. Two actually, a double Jameson and a pint of Guinness. The Anchor was its usual hushed, devotional lunchtime self. No food was served, or even contemplated; men did their dreaming and praying over pints and shorts, working their newspapers like beads; Silent John, the barman, kept a gruff distance. Hard to blame him: the Anchor was full of people who started drinking at ten thirty in the morning; when I wasn't working, I was sometimes one of them; why would a barman want to be friends with a bunch of alcoholics? On the other hand, why run a pub like the Anchor if you didn't want to spend your life among drunks?

It didn't take me long to find the message I was looking for: '452 Pearse Avenue, Honeypark', plain and simple. Not a rugby-playing address, but not far from Seafield Rugby Club. I thought about David Brady, dead at twenty, and wondered what had taken him from the Waterfront Apartments to Honeypark Estate, and finished my drinks and went to see if I could find out.

Honeypark and Woodpark are sprawling local-authority estates on the southern borders of Castlehill and Seafield. Woodpark dates back to the forties, and many of the houses have been bought out by their tenants and subsequently sold on to young middle-class families; many have been through the three generations they say it takes for a council estate to be tamed. Although it still has an edge, the estate no longer possesses the fearsome reputation it had in my youth, when news that the Woodpark lads were on the prowl gave the dullest of evenings out a sense of danger, often realized. That honour now belongs to Honeypark, built during the eighties in the expansive grounds of a tumbledown Anglo-Irish 'Big House' south across the main road. Someone told me they took all the tenants who'd been evicted for antisocial behaviour for ten miles around and dumped them in the improbably named Honeypark. The buses had stopped going in early on, not only because

48

they'd attack and rob the drivers, but because they'd tear down the bus stops and attack the buses with them. You could find any drugs you liked in Honeypark, but no one wanted to go in there to get them, so the dealers drifted up into Woodpark in grey hoodies and Burberry baseball caps, frightening the mothers with the three-wheel buggies and the old ladies with the two-wheel shopping trolleys alike. It's not as bad as it used to be either, but no one could say Honeypark had been tamed.

I stopped off at the Woodpark Inn to check the list of bands scheduled to play there that night. Workers from the nearby industrial estates and retail warehouses were sitting down to soup and sandwiches and carvery lunches; balloons that looked like Halloween pumpkins and luminous plastic skeletons hung above their heads. The smell of food made me queasy; I wanted another drink, but I had work to do first. I found the posters advertising the night's line-up: The Golgotha Pyre, Emily Howard's boyfriend Jerry's band, were third on the bill.

I walked back out into the mist and fading light and drove down into the sprawl of Honeypark. Every house had been painted white twenty years ago, and very few of them had been painted since, so the whole estate had an eerie sheen to it; dirty and wan, and furled in white cloud, it felt like I was driving into a grimy snowdrift. Pearse Avenue was a long meandering road that twisted and forked like a maze; I got lost two or three times until I took my bearings from the three sets of lads who were building bonfires on the paltry scraps of green the council had allocated for the tenants' recreation and parked not far from the biggest of the three. The boys building it were excited, throwing the occasional banger at each other as they piled car tyres and burst mattresses on top of packing crates and builders' pallets.

Pearse Avenue curved in a horseshoe oval on the far side of the green, and 452 was the centre house of the five houses that made up the oval. As I put my hand on the gate, someone threw a banger that exploded a few feet away from me. I twisted my head, startled by the explosion, and heard the baying laughter of the boys who had thrown it; when I turned back, there was a short fat man with greasy black hair and a black tracksuit and heavy black shoes standing in the doorway of 452, flanked by two lads of about twenty in grey hooded tops and grey track pants, one tall and bulky, one short and slight. The hoodies started to approach me. It looked like I was in the right place. I preferred not to carry a gun, but I was wondering whether I should have overcome my scruples for Honeypark's sake. On the other hand, these boys did not exactly look officer class. I vaulted the gate, reached in my breast pocket and pulled out an ID card. No one reached for a weapon when it looked like that's what I might have been doing.

'Seafield Garda,' I said in a very loud voice, moving towards them, 'investigating the murder of David Brady.'

The two grey hoodies looked at each other, then back at me. I said David Brady's name and the word 'murder' again, and the hoodies turned and nodded and ran fast in separate directions, leaping over the walls of the neighbouring houses; the greasy fat guy looked like he wished he could join

50

them, but now I was standing in his way. He backed towards the house, but I moved quickly to put myself between him and the door.

'Is this your house, sir?' I said.

'No. Yes. No,' he said, his voice ragged with tension.

'Which is it?'

'Yes.'

'Name?'

'Sean Moon.'

'What can you tell me about David Brady's murder, Mr Moon? What do you know about the disappearance of Emily Howard?'

His pale-green eyes burned red; I could smell the whiskey in his open pores; sweat coursed down his acne-ravaged brow.

'I don't know, I . . . I don't know anything.'

I heard muffed sounds from upstairs: thumping on a floor or a plasterboard wall, then a muffed scream.

'They made me, I didn't have any choice,' Sean Moon said.

I pushed past him and went straight up the stairs. The back bedroom door was shut, but it wasn't locked. I opened the door to find two people locked in a struggle on the bed. One was Emily Howard, and the other was the skinny blond boy who'd been in the film and in the photographs, the one with the eagle tattoo on his shoulder. I could see it now; he was bare-chested, wearing only a pair of jeans; Emily wore a short red kilt and a black bra. They didn't notice me for a few seconds, and I didn't announce myself. Their struggle wasn't much more than a playfight; in fact, it looked like foreplay; either Emily was stronger than the boy or he was letting her dominate; she had straddled his chest and pinned his arms behind his head when she saw me.

'Who the fuck are you?' she said.

'My name is Ed Loy,' I said. 'Your father hired me to find you.'

Using a hand flat on the boy's hairless chest for balance, she swung a bare leg over his head and stood in front of me, head back, chest thrust forward. Her pupils were dilated until they seemed to stain her brown eyes black; her lips were so engorged they hung open; I could feel her hot breath in my face.

'What are you, some kind of private dick?' she said, her voice a sustained jeer on the edge of a laugh. I nearly laughed myself, her derision was so incendiary.

'That's right,' I said.

'Well you've found me. Now fuck off. Oh, no, wait, there's one message you can take back to Daddy: tell him his nephew Jonny is here.'

The boy flinched when she said this, and turned away towards the window. Emily either didn't notice, or didn't care. She didn't look like she was on drugs; or rather, she did, but I didn't believe she was. Her eyes had the recklessness I had seen in her mother's, but none of the coldness; they were aflame with passion and young-girl bravado; something about them looked not entirely sane.

'That's right, Mr Loy. I've been fucking my cousin Jonathan, Aunt Sandra's pride and joy. Tell Daddy, tell Jonny's mummy. Let them incorporate that into the illustrious fucking chronicle of the Howard family. Maybe then they'll leave us both the fuck alone.'

52

Emily's voice was quite high by the end of this, teetering on hysterical. In the olden days, I suppose I would have slapped her across the face. It would probably've been easier for her than having to hear what I did say.

'Emily, I've got some bad news. Your ex-boyfriend David Brady was found dead this morning. He was murdered.'

Emily's face went perfectly still and her eyes rolled back in her head. The blood left her face and she began to shake. I thought she was having a convulsion, so I reached my hands out to steady her. She slapped them away and began to pummel me with her fists, raining blows on my chest and face. I caught hold of her arms above the elbow until she stopped and stood still for a while, her breath coming in quick bursts until she went limp and dropped her head on to my shoulder and let the tears flow.

Jonathan leaped to his feet and came around the bed towards us. I held out a hand to keep him at bay. In a voice that sounded like a shrill, highly strung version of Denis Finnegan's, he screamed, 'This is all your fault, you devious whore, you filthy fucked-up bitch!'

5

I thought I had Jonathan calmed down, and then Emily started up at him and the two of them let fly and it was you always you never your dad your mum fuck the Howards for a while, with Emily decidedly having the upper hand. It was an

53

oppressive little room to share with two half-dressed cousins having a bitter lovers' quarrel. Finally they subsided again. I suggested they put some clothes on and said I'd see them downstairs.

Sean Moon was waiting in the living room. I looked around the kitchen first: full of pizza boxes and microwave meals, it looked like people had been camping there for a while. When I went into the living room, the first thing I noticed was that it matched the room the porn had been shot in. The second thing was that Sean Moon appeared keen to talk, but anxious that he might be overheard.

'It's OK, they're still in the room,' I said. 'What's on your mind?'

'I've never been in trouble with the police,' Moon said.

'Well, tell me what happened and maybe you won't be,' I said.

'They paid me to let them use the house.'

'Who paid you? The grey-hoodie boys?'

'The Reillys. They're . . . I don't know. Their da has a paving business across in Woodpark, but the Reillys are into everything. Anyway, I was in the Woodpark Inn and they asked—said it was just for a few days, couple of blue movies, I could watch and everything, thousand euro.'

'And who all was there?'

'The two upstairs, and another girl called Wendy in the first one, and then Wendy and Petra in the second. And the Reillys.'

'And David Brady.'

Moon looked at the floor. The carpet had originally been a pale shade, ivory or vanilla. It was difficult to say what colour it was now, such was the variety and texture of the stains and sheens it

54

had accumulated. I wouldn't have touched it, let alone had sex on it.

'Why was he murdered?'

'Good question. Any ideas?'

Moon shook his head violently.

'I've never been in any trouble—'

'You told me that. But the Reillys have. Are they killers?'

The headshake again.

'No. Just . . .'

'Drugs?'

'I think so. But I don't—'

'I know, you don't. What do you do?'

'I'm on disability. Chest. Inhalation of fumes.'

I looked around the room. By the TV there was a stack of videos and DVDs: Manchester United, *Star Wars*, *Star Trek*, *Lord of the Rings*, a lot of cartoons. And a PlayStation and a bunch of computer games. What Sean Moon did was watch TV, by the looks of things.

'Do you go to the Woodpark Inn much?'

'Just when there's a match on. I don't really drink. Don't like the taste.'

'What about the porn films, Sean. Did you like them?'

He looked up at me from beneath his pocked brow, a furtive leer on his overgrown child's face.

'They said they'd give me the DVD. But they haven't. Do you think they will?'

I heard footfalls on the stairs.

'I don't think so, Sean. I don't think so.'

*   *   *

Emily and Jonathan were silent on the drive back

to Shane Howard's surgery. There was nobody there except Anita, who told me Shane had called her at lunchtime to cancel the afternoon's appointments. Of course, there were two patients she couldn't contact, so she had to stay here to face them when they showed up. She didn't look very happy, and although she smiled and blessed herself when I told her I had found Emily, she seemed like a woman with a lot on her mind.

I swung around the harbour and up the steep drive to 'Howard Residence'. The Porsche wasn't there, but Emily had a key. When we got inside, Emily announced she was going to bed. I said I didn't think that was a very good idea and she erupted again and said she didn't care what I thought, I was just another flunky bought and paid for by her father and now I'd done my job I should crawl back down beneath the stone I'd slithered out from. Jonathan had helped himself to a brandy from a drinks table, and was sitting on the sofa watching us. He was very skinny and his eyes were red and his expression flickered from a disdainful glare to an eye-rolling smile, as if at the appalling comedy of the situation. I wondered that he could find comedy in what had happened, but evidently he could: occasionally he would laugh, as if remembering an especially amusing moment, and then his eyes would narrow and his hand would flash up to cover his mouth, as if he was afraid he might suddenly give the game away.

'I don't know that I've done my job yet. I need to get your side of the story,' I said to Emily.

'I don't *think* so,' she said, and walked out of the room. I followed her down the hall.

'In that case, I'll have to ring the Guards and tell

56

them that you and your cousin participated in pornography that may have been filmed by the recently murdered David Brady. I have the photographs, and the other film Jonathan was in, and it's starting to look like I'll have no option but to turn them over,' I said to her retreating back.

She stopped, but didn't turn around.

'There's also the question of whether you were being held against your will, or whether you were willing players. If the latter, there might be charges of blackmail and extortion to consider.'

'I'm really really *tired,* Mr Loy,' she said in her best sulky-spoilt Daddy's-girl voice.

'I'm not feeling too chipper myself, but since neither of us is three, or eighty, I think we can probably make it through another hour or so without needing a nap,' I said.

Her shoulders began to shake. More tears, I thought, but when she turned around I saw that she was laughing.

'All right, fair enough, you're not like the usual twats Daddy sets on me,' she said. She shook her red hair, then nodded at me with those deep dark eyes, her sullen pout fully restored.

'What are the usual twats like?' I said, as we went back into the living room.

'Big ex-cops in anoraks with beer bellies. They're supposed to be inconspicuous, I mean, hello? In a pub full of scrawny students, and a fat culchie with a big red face trying to blend in? I don't *think* so.'

Emily sat down beside her cousin, slapped her hand on his knee and ran it up his thigh. Jonathan rolled his eyes back in his head as she did this; when she reached his crotch, she squeezed and he shot his tongue out. I went to get a brandy for myself. The house was cold, and what the kids were doing was annoying, and what I feared lay behind it was disturbing me. There was Jameson, so I had a glass of that instead. It was suddenly dark, dark the way it gets at three thirty on a dull misty Halloween, darker than night it seemed.

Emily was poking Jonathan in the side now and he was juddering and grimacing and giggling. I sat down opposite them and waited for them to stop, and after a while, they did.

'Whose idea was the porn?' I said.

There was silence for a while, then Jonathan pulled his hand from his mouth.

'David Brady's,' he said.

Emily hit him in the face so quickly that it was difficult at first to take in what had happened. She was wearing several rings, and they raked across Jonathan's cheek and temple drawing needle sprays of blood. He yelped in pain and cowered away from her, but quickly tried to retrieve himself, shaking his head and contorting his grimace of pain back into the mask of detached amusement he seemed to wear for protection. Just as quickly he was on top of Emily, his hands around her neck, and she was writhing beneath him on the sofa, her motorcycle boots kicking in the air. I grabbed his head by the hair and tugged him off her, then hauled Emily to her feet and clasped her flailing wrists in one hand. Jonathan recoiled on the couch, hands up, head bowed, cowering, a dog who'd been beaten too often; Emily was kicking at my shins, dragging me across the room.

'That's enough now, enough, do you hear me?' I shouted. Emily's face was flushed with rage, her

58

lips compressed, her breath coming hard through her nose. She bent down and sank her teeth into my hand, and I had to use all my will not to slap her face. I put the flat of my hand against her chest and pushed her hard across the room. She fell back on to the couch, winded. There was blood on my torn hand; it tasted of metal, and of fear.

Emily was staring at me in astonishment.

'No one pushes me around,' she said. 'No one treats me like that.'

'No one bites my hand unless I ask them to,' I said. 'But here's the thing: if you take a walk on the wild side, be prepared for the unexpected.'

'Do you—*actually*—know who I am?' Emily Howard said, with all the contemptuous hauteur a private education and an exclusive south Dublin address afford.

'I'm scared to find out, sweetheart,' I said.

We sat in silence for a while after that. Jonathan drained his brandy, and Emily clicked the rings on her right hand against the rings on her left. Somewhere across the bay, fireworks crackled and shot their plumes of light through the murk; like a relief diagram of nerves and synapses in the body, they seemed to give the falling night scale and dimension. I felt like there was a gulf between me and these damaged, spoilt, feral kids; feared that if I asked the wrong question or said a word out of place, it might tip them over an edge they were clearly teetering on. I could call Denis Finnegan and leave them in his charge. That would possibly have been the smart play. But I knew I wasn't going to let any of this go until I got to the bottom of it.

'All right,' I said. 'For starters, neither of you was forced to do anything against your will, is that so?'

'You mean, fuck?' Emily said with a big leering grin.

I nodded.

'No, we weren't forced. Were we, Jonny?'

Jonathan shook his head, his smile back in place, his eyes in his lap.

'We did it all for love, Mr Loy,' Emily said, and waggled her tongue at me.

'Why was David Brady shooting pornography? How did that come about?'

'How do you know it was David?' Emily said.

'Jonathan told us,' I said.

'Jonny is mistaken, aren't ya babe?' Emily said.

Jonathan pushed a kind of spluttered laugh through his nose.

'I make many mistakes,' he said in an arch, ironic tone, as if he was quoting a line from a movie.

'Also, there's a shot of his wrist in the movie Jonny made with, what's this they were called, Wendy and Petra?'

'Kylie and Stacey more like,' Emily said in a bad Dublin accent. 'Hayley and Kelsey.'

'And on his wrist was his 2JS2 bracelet—no one but David Brady has one. And he had the photos on his home computer. So we all know it was him. What we don't know is, why.'

'Are they still there, on his computer, for the Guards to find?' Emily asked, her tone suddenly urgent.

'You first. Why were you making porn films with David Brady? And why were you doing it in Honeypark?'

Emily looked to Jonathan, down the corridor that led to her bedroom, and then towards the door, but there was no way out. She sighed

60

laboriously and began to speak.

'Back when DB and I were going out, during the summer, we went through this phase of doing E and kind of like, getting off with other people in front of each other. It was like, we'd give each other marks out of ten, don't think much of yours, total minger total babe type of thing. And then sometimes, we'd bring someone back to his. It was a bit of crack, a bit pervy, a bit fucked up. And we'd be in control of it all, so the next morning, or even the middle of the night, if we decided we'd had enough, we'd just throw them out. Anyway, we were at this Saturday-night bash in Seafield Rugby Club and the usual parade of sluts were flaunting themselves at DB, honestly, they'd feel him up right in front of me. So we fix on this cute little one with porn hair, you know, dead flat, snow blonde? And we get it together back in David's. Didn't think much more about it really.'

'Until when?'

'Until a couple of weeks ago, I get a call from David—we broke up last month, when I was going to Trinity, totally my call, just that thing of girls dragging their boyfriends from school to college is a bit tragic, isn't it? Anyway, got this call, and he's in a major fucking *zone.* Seems Miss Porn Hair took some shots on her mobile, seems her old man found them, seems she was only thirteen when she got with us. So he's up in arms—but he's also a bit of a dodgy geezer, the father.'

'Did you get a name?'

'I assume David did. But he didn't tell me. What he said was, this guy and his daughter would press charges against both of us, which would be like, a whole child-abuse paedo trip, unless we did what

61

he wanted. And what he wanted was, first off we'd do this porn thing, and then we'd blackmail some money out of my dad.'

'And where did Jonathan come into it?'

Emily looked at Jonathan, her eyebrows raised.

'Ve haf alvays been, how you say, kissing cousins,' Jonathan announced in a stage German accent, then curled up with his head in Emily's lap.

'And did David Brady know that?'

'Sure,' Emily said. 'It was his idea that Jonny be involved. Easier for me to handle.'

'Keep it in ze family, ja? Unt also, ze question I am alvays asking myself is, Fot vould Jesus do?'

'And the answer you got was, Jesus would make some porn?' I said.

'Jesus vould do fot he could to help his cousin,' Jonathan said, and they both howled with hysterical laughter. I felt like I was minding a couple of tots who'd broken into the booze cabinet and scarfed some Bailey's: it was bound to end in tears; I just had to wait it out.

'It's not a major deal, *daad*,' Emily said, increasingly irritated that I couldn't see the funny side. 'I mean, everyone's done home-made these days. I used to do it all the time with DB: we'd watch it, then tape over it. The whole scenario this time was, it would never go public.'

'But that would be the threat.'

'To Dad? Sure. But like, fifty grand, so what? That's like fifty cent to anyone else. All that old Howard lolly. Why not give someone else a suck?'

'And the idea that he might be upset, or anxious, that he might think you had been kidnapped and raped—the distress you might cause him: none of that was a worry to you?'

Emily's expression shifted in an instant from the bad-girl bravado of her mother to the blank implacability of her father; she stared at me as if I understood nothing, and when she spoke, it was with deliberate, glacial force.

'Of course it was a worry. I'd never want to hurt my father. Or at least, not like this. But what else could I do? You think he'd've been happier if I was up on some child-rape charge? The crucial thing was it was never going to go public.'

'Except it may well have. The film Jonny made?'

'Mit Vendy unt Petra, ja?' Jonathan said, still skittish, almost hysterical.

'I have a few hundred copies of it, ready to be sold in pubs and door to door,' I said. 'So whoever you were dealing with wasn't to be trusted.'

'Jonny's in shades, no one will recognize him.'

'Anyone who spots his tattoo will. I think the blackmailer could make a case to Jonny's parents that Jonny's identity could be easily uncovered by anyone who's seen that tattoo.'

Jonathan sat up abruptly, his antic mask replaced by a cold stare he directed first at Emily; when he turned it on me, it was accompanied by the curling of his lips into a sneer.

'Is that what you think, Mr Loy? Your "professional" opinion, is it?' he said, his reedy voice shaking but stoked with the insolence of entitlement. Emily put a calming hand on his arm, but he shook it off.

'If my mother . . .' he hissed at Emily, and then stopped, and turned away from us both like a sulky child. Emily looked cautiously at his back, and then turned to me.

'So who were we dealing with?' she said. 'Who is

this blackmailer?'

More than likely Brock Taylor, if Tommy Owens wasn't lying. Always a big if.

'I don't know,' I said. 'Someone who still has *both films* in his possession. Someone who wants to put the bite on your father, and is likely to come back for more. Someone we can't rule out for David Brady's murder.'

'Are the Guards going to find the films on DB's computer?'

'Not now,' I said.

'So we're not connected to that?'

'As long as they don't send the hard drive for technical examination. But if they don't come up with a suspect fast, that's what they'll probably do. They've found a body that's been beaten and stabbed to death. They'll pull all out all the stops to find his killer.'

Emily's eyes suddenly filled with tears. She looked up to the ceiling, as if gravity might stem their flow, but they overspilled.

'Beaten and stabbed to death,' she said. 'Oh Jesus, this is such a fucking nightmare. Poor David. I can't believe it. I can't believe it.'

She cried for a long time, her legs drawn to her chest, howls that dwindled into sobs. Eventually Jonathan climbed down off his perch and put his long skinny arms around her and they clung together on the sofa. It was pitiful to watch, but it was also a relief: one of the first signs either had exhibited of a normal human emotion.

There didn't seem a lot more I could do here. Denis Finnegan's card had his home number added in ink; I went out into the hall and rang it and a Filipina or Latin American voice answered.

'Sandra Howard, please,' I said.

'Who is calling?'

'My name is Ed Loy. I'm calling about Ms Howard's son, and her niece.'

I heard muffed voices in the background, then a crisp, tense Irish voice came on.

'Mr Loy, this is Sandra Howard.'

'I'm a private detective, Ms Howard. Your brother hired me to find Emily, and I have; she's here in Bayview, in your sister-in-law's house. Your son is with her, but Shane's not here. I don't think they should be alone now.'

'Don't let them leave. I'll be there in minutes.'

Fifteen of them, in fact; on the sofa, the kids sat in the dark, huddled together, asking for nothing, like infants asleep in the back of a car after a long journey. I paced the hall, smoking. The knock came on the door and a tall, green-eyed woman with a black cowl-hood over her dark-red hair stood in the porch, silhouetted in the shimmer of the approach light; out in the bay behind her, fireworks flashed and crackled, sending plumes of red high in the sky and making her look momentarily like a creature from myth, a rebel angel with red wings, or a saint captured in stained glass.

'Mr Loy? Sandra Howard,' she said.

'They're inside,' I said.

She walked down the hall and smiled sadly at the sight of Emily and Jonathan curled up together on the couch. Thanking me, she put her cold hand on mine and drew me out to the front of the house, where we stood in the rain and mist, like the last mourners in a deserted churchyard. A volley of bangers crashed out like gunshots; after a hissing

65

silence, the voices of dogs were raised in response; their barking and howling echoed through the hills.

'Poor dogs,' Sandra Howard said. 'Halloween is always a bad night for them.'

I nodded.

'Denis told me you were searching for Emily. I hadn't realized Shane was so worried about her.'

I nodded again, and told her a little about where I had found her son and her niece, and what they had been doing, and the part David Brady had played in it, and how he had ended up. She took it all in without seeming surprised or ruffled by anything except Brady's murder. While I waited for her to respond, I looked at her milky skin, the laughter lines around her green eyes and her full red lips, the unlined brow and the fine high bones and I thought, *Even in distress, this is the most beautiful woman I've ever seen.* I probably fell a little in love with her there and then. Maybe if I hadn't, we'd've got to the truth a lot quicker. Then again, maybe if I hadn't, we wouldn't have got to it at all.

Sandra Howard had been looking out in the dark towards sea, towards where she knew the sea to be; you could hear the roar in the rising wind. She turned back to me and took my hand again and began to speak.

'I've been trying to find Shane all day, ever since Denis told me he'd hired you. He's not been answering his phone.'

'He's not at the surgery either. His receptionist hasn't seen him since this morning.'

'What did he hire you to do, exactly?'

'To find his daughter. And to bring her home, if

66

she wanted to come.'

'What about the people behind this? Did he not want you to put a stop to them?'

'Since the main man I understand to be behind this has photographs of Emily in a threesome with his thirteen-year-old daughter, I don't know that we have a great deal of leverage. I mean, we could try and nail him for blackmail, but the reason Emily took it on herself to go along with the porn film in the first place was to avoid underage-sex charges, and all the attendant disgrace for her and the family. That hasn't changed.'

'But those films are still out there. That means Shane is still susceptible to blackmail.'

'As are you,' I said. 'Jonathan's in both films.'

Again, there was no reaction that I would have expected from a parent: no expression of disgust, no shudder, no sense of disappointment. Just a shrewd, appraising glimmer in those flashing green eyes, and a toss of her dark-red head as she came to a decision.

'I'd like to retain you, Mr Loy—as long, that is, as you're still available. I want you to sort this out. If that means getting hold of the tapes, or films, or negatives, or whatever they are, fine. If you have to pay for them, I'll make a deal. But we can't have that waiting in the long grass for us. Not for the children, and not for the Howard family.'

She looked at me full on then, and smiled, as if to apologize for the rhetoric, and I smiled back, mostly because I found it impossible not to, impossible to refuse what she had asked. I nodded, and she went inside to the children, and I stayed outside and smoked a cigarette. They were normal kids, I told myself; troubled, sure, a little

67

oversexed, maybe, but normal. I said it to myself again: normal kids, a normal family. Above the noise in my head of first cousins having three-way sex at all, let alone on camera, and their aunt and mother barely registering either fact, it was hard to make out exactly what I was saying.

6

I checked my mobile phone, which I was in the habit of leaving turned off. There was a message from Detective Inspector Dave Donnelly of Seafield Guards, saying he looked forward to talking to me about my most recent client, Shane Howard, and his daughter's ex-boyfriend. That hadn't taken long. So Dave had the case. I still didn't feel right about removing evidence from the Brady crime scene. Last time we had spoken, Dave had accused me, only half in jest, of becoming part of the luxury service industry: someone who carried rich people's bags for them and eased their burdens. He had finished his pint, so he used it as an exit line, which was just as well, as I couldn't think of much to say in reply. 'Rich people have their troubles too' sounded kind of lame, even if it was true. 'Rich people pay my bills' was closer to the truth, though I didn't like admitting it. Had I compromised a murder investigation just so I could keep Emily Howard's life tidier than she took any care to make it? Maybe. But I took that risk because I knew I would get to the truth faster than the Guards did. If I didn't believe that, then I would be as bad as Dave had painted me. And if it involved serious criminals from Honeypark, even Brock Taylor himself, I could make those connections before anyone else. And Dave wasn't above taking my help when he needed it.

Meanwhile, here I was, smoking a cigarette on top of Bayview Hill, waiting for a woman who drove a black '06 reg Mercedes-Benz S500 to tell me what to do. She came out of the house with Emily and Jonathan, whom shock continued to age in reverse: they looked like a pair of frightened children, bloodless and numb. Jonathan had retreated behind iPod headphones; Emily carried an overnight bag and a worn stuffed dog. Sandra Howard opened the car for them, then came across and stood beside me. Her hood was down, and her red hair glistened in the thick damp air; it hung in a fringe that kissed her kohl-ringed eyes. She was wearing black, some combination of cape and cowl that came to her ankles. She took the cigarette from my hand and drew hard on it.

'Jesus, this is such a mess,' she said. 'Mr Loy—'

'Ed,' I said.

'Ed. I'm bringing Jonny and Em up to Rowan House, that's the family home. Would you come with us?'

'Of course,' I said. 'I'll follow you there.'

She held the cigarette up as if to give it back; I gestured to her to keep it; she caught my hand again and held it in her cool grip. Her red nail polish was chipped, and her nails were bitten to the quick; she wore a red-and-green braided band on her wrist; she smelt of smoky salt earth and the sweet tang of spice. She looked straight at me, and I looked straight back; I thought I could feel her green eyes searching mine, like she could see inside my thoughts, see my doubt, my suspicion, see how little I really trusted her, or anyone else. But I wanted her to believe I could trust. Looking in her eyes, I wanted to trust her.

Lord, I believe, oh, help my unbelief.

She brought her hand up to my face. I wasn't sure what she was doing, but I wanted her to keep doing it. Her crooked finger rested cool in the hollow of my cheek.

'Something is happening to us, Ed. Emily vanishing, David Brady—the Howard family is under threat. You'll help us, won't you?'

I nodded. I felt at that moment as if I were under her spell, as if I would have done whatever she asked me. A firework raked across the sky like a searchlight in the dark and caught us for a split second, frozen in its glow. I sometimes thought of it later as a strobe flash that captured Sandra Howard as she had been, before the fall—but of course it was no such thing; the high saga of the Howards was plummeting to its close, and whether she knew it or not, Sandra wasn't just caught up in its descent, she was fanning the flames that sped it down.

*　　*　　*

I followed the roll of the great black Merc, feeling dragged in its imperious tide, as our cortège made slow progress through the rush-hour traffic on the narrow roads south of Castlehill. Once we joined the M50 northwards we picked up speed against the flow. The Merc turned west on Exit 13 and climbed south through Sandyford and Kilgobbin, then cut up through narrow twisty roads to the foothills of the mountains. I followed along a road bounded now on one side by a high stone wall; on the other, gorse and ferns gave way to marsh and shallow bog. At a junction high above the city, great iron gates within the wall marked the entrance to Rowan House; I waited while they swung open, and then followed as the Merc crunched up a track lined with ash and rowan trees to a house I had seen already that day, in miniature, on a plinth beneath Emily Howard's bed.

Rowan House looked like a Victorian merchant's idea of a baronial castle: cut from pale granite, it had castellated bay windows, battlements, a small octagonal flag tower at one end and a much larger corner tower at the rear with a slated conical roof. A weathervane spouted from the flag tower, atop whose pointer a spotlight picked out a metal 'H'; another spot found the plain cross on the round tower's peak.

The entrance hall was a great white rotunda with a sweeping circular staircase in pale wood to the right and a corridor at left that served the ground-floor front rooms; assorted portraits of Dr John Howard hung at every turn; ahead, an arch through which Sandra Howard had already swept led to another, slightly smaller hall, with stairs down to the basement level and a further corridor for the back rooms and yet more paintings of her father; at the far end of this hall stood double doors that might once have led down to the garden; now they opened on to a windowless corridor whose ceiling was only about twelve feet high, whose walls were crisp white and unadorned by portraits of any kind, a corridor that emerged

71

into a modern, rectangular open-plan living space with great plate-glass walls and no hint of baronial grandeur: the corridor and living room of a house built maybe in the 1970s, seemingly grafted on to the rear of the fake castle. There was a fire burning in a big open grate, with a brushed-steel vent to take the smoke; the flames drew everyone to huddle in their glow.

Two maids in black and white uniforms had materialized when we first entered the house; after brisk instructions from Sandra Howard they'd vanished; now they were back with drinks and cold cuts and salads, which they set on a long table at one end of the room. The sudden pang in my gut reminded me I hadn't eaten all day; Jonny fell on the food like a starving man, and, once I had reassured myself that Sandra and Emily were OK, I followed suit. Sandra sat on a long couch at the end closest to the fire; Emily lay curled up with her head in her aunt's lap, her stuffed dog pressed to her cheek and her left thumb in her mouth. The maids, who were both tiny Filipinas, swirled around collecting coats and filling cups and pouring glasses of water and setting out bottles of spirits and mixers and tubs of ice and asking if there was anything further before silently dispersing. I ate smoked salmon and rare cold roast beef and tomato and avocado salad and potato and hazelnut salad and drank a cup of coffee and halfway through my second bottle of Tyskie, a very strong Polish beer that I had pined for during my month on the dry, I began to feel faintly human again.

Jonny had put steel-rimmed granny glasses on; he kept flashing anxious glances through them at his mother before looking at me and gulping air through his mouth; finally, his mother rose and led Emily out of the room, and he got his chance to speak.

'You won't tell, will you?' he asked. 'Tell Mummy, I mean.'

'Tell her what?' I said blankly.

'About, y'know. The porn. And the whole thing with Emily.'

He had one of those voices that sounded as if it hadn't completely broken, and was always struggling to find its correct register, like a radio station that isn't fully tuned in. Combined with pale stubble that looked like thistledown and gangling limbs that seemed not to fit him properly, he could have passed for fourteen.

'Emily's father thought she had gone missing. Did your family not worry?'

'I don't live with Mummy; I have rooms in Trinity.'

And an old-style Trinity accent to go with them. *Rums in Trin'ty.*

'What age are you, Jonny?'

'Nineteen. Same as Emily. I got Schol—a Foundation Scholarship—in mathematics. Which confers all sorts of perks. I can eat in the Dining Hall, and wear an academic gown—'

'And graze your sheep in College Park?'

'They didn't apprise me of that privilege, but if it's available to me I shall certainly take it up. As soon as I get the sheep.'

He gave a sniffing, snorting, yelping laugh, the kind of sound teenage boys who learn Monty Python routines by heart make: maybe the kind maths geeks make too; then he blinked unhappily

73

at me, his anxious eyes enlarged by the powerful lenses.

'I need you to tell me a few things first. How did you get mixed up in all this?'

'Emily rang me. Asked me if I wanted to be in a threesome with two girls. Said that it would be filmed, but that I could wear a mask.'

'And you said no problem?'

'Mr Loy, mathematics scholars are not exactly coming down with offers of twosomes, let alone, ah, exponentials thereof . . . and the offers we get—well, those *I* tend to get are generally from the kind of girls who hope I won't be too interested in sex. So it was hardly something I felt I could pass up.'

'And the offer coming from Emily, that didn't surprise you?'

Jonny stared at his plate.

'No. We've kind of . . . from a youngish age, sort of . . . experimented. Not so much in the last few years. Since Emily had boyfriends. But before, well . . . it was always her idea—I mean, it would have had to be, she being the girl . . . I suppose she tried stuff out on me . . . before doing it for real.'

'When you say youngish?'

'Thirteen, fourteen.'

'And then she dropped you. Did that hurt?'

'Maybe. A little. But we'd still, occasionally— Christmas, or at a family party—she'd give me . . . a treat.'

'So there was no great problem for you when she suggested you make a movie with her?'

'On the contrary.'

'And this whole thing about her and David Brady being blackmailed—'

74

'They didn't tell me about that until afterwards. And I wasn't too happy. I mean, whoever was doing it was going to try and get money out of Uncle Shane, it was clearly some kind of lowlife scumbag. But when Emily explained the situation, that they were implicated in a whole underage thing, I had to go with it.'

'You didn't think you were being sucked into it?'

'I didn't. But with the tattoo, I don't know what to think.'

'When did you get the tattoo?'

'About a month ago. And it was Emily's idea. She asked me to come along with her when she was getting hers, part of her whole new look, the hair, the piercings, all that. And while we were there she persuaded me to have one done. I'm sure she didn't . . . I'm sure it was just in fun.'

'I'm sure it was. But do you think . . . might Emily have lied about the whole situation with the thirteen-year-old girl? Might she have set you up?'

'No.'

'Jonny, was she with you all day today? In the house in Honeypark?'

'She was in the house, but not always in the room. We had our own rooms. It was a weird set-up. I mean, that creepy guy, Moon, and the Reillys, total little skangers but decent enough actually, they'd get us food and drink and whatever, it didn't feel like we were there against our will. I was just waiting for Emily to give me the word on when we were getting out. And to be frank, given the amount of sex we were having, I didn't care when that would be.'

'She was in the house, but not always in the room. If she wasn't in the same room as you, could

75

that mean she might have left the house?'

'I suppose so,' he said, then shook his head quickly, took his glasses off and stared at them.

'Why would she have left the house?' he said, his voice shrill. 'What are you implying? That she killed David Brady?'

'I'm not implying anything. I'm asking questions. That's my job.'

'Well, I think I've had enough of your questions, Mr Private Detective. It's a grubby little job, don't you find?'

His Trinity manner had become grander, his voice a fluted drawl; I could feel the class boundary rising to divide us.

'It certainly has the habit of uncovering a lot of grubby secrets,' I said.

'So there's no point in asking you not to tell Mum—'

'I've already told your mother everything. I'm working for her, as well as for your uncle. She didn't appear particularly surprised.'

Jonathan stood up abruptly, and his metal chair fell back with a crash against the hardwood floor. He looked down at me, his lips compressed, his hands clenched into fists.

'If you think trying to pin a murder on Emily is going to help anyone in this family, you must be out of your fucking mind,' he said, in a low voice thick with passion. 'But I wouldn't expect someone like you to understand a family like ours.'

Since Jonathan himself had raised the possibility that Emily had the opportunity to kill her ex-boyfriend, I was a little taken aback by his sudden rage. As he stalked off, his mother approached from the passageway and tried to stop him; he

76

backed away and waved his unwieldy arms at her, then ran down the corridor and a door slammed.

Sandra Howard replaced Jonathan's chair, sat in it, a pale smile on her face, and began to assemble the ingredients for a gin and tonic. She was wearing a dark suit, black shot with some kind of green; the hem of her skirt brushed her knees; her legs, in black stockings, looked long and slender.

'The teenage symphony: tears and tantrums, and the slamming of the bedroom door. Don't take it personally, Ed.'

'I think he meant it personally.'

'What were you talking about?'

'His relationship with his cousin. Among other things. Where is Emily?'

'Resting. She has a room here. She was starting to freak out. A doctor is coming up from the Centre to see to her.'

Sandra flashed an uneasy look at me, the first time I'd seen her furtive or defensive. She took a long hit on her drink, which was heavy on the Tanqueray, and brandished the green bottle at me. I took it and made my own. When Sandra looked up again, her gaze was steady.

'They've had a rough time of it over the years, Ed, both Jonny and Em. I know, silver spoon, everything money can buy, everyone should have their troubles, but really, they shouldn't.'

'Why shouldn't they? Tell me their troubles.'

'Jonny's father died when he was eleven. Richard O'Connor was my first husband. He was a doctor—he was the one who helped me believe in myself, in my father's legacy—because I hadn't gone into medicine myself, I felt unworthy, I had been teaching in Castlehill College, drifting, really,

77

but he gave me focus—he reminded me I was my father's daughter. And I took over the running of the Howard Maternity Centre, and I founded the Howard Clinic and the Howard Nursing Home, assembled the investors, saw them built and open and running successfully.'

Sandra got up suddenly and turned all the lights out and beckoned me across the room to the great window.

'You can just about make the three towers out through the mist, see? I hope one day to see a fourth.'

Three great blurs of light were discernible, shimmering in the murk. I looked at Sandra, straight-backed, regal. Her eyes were shining with pride, and something that looked like defiance, or triumph, and something else, a shadow, a sudden darkness that appeared from nowhere and was just as briskly dispelled.

'He said I did it all myself, but of course I didn't, it was Dr Rock—that's what everyone called him, Richard O'Connor, R-O-C—he inspired me, Ed, just like my own father had inspired me, and Rock inspired Jonny too, he—you know when Jonny was eleven, he played rugby, played very well, he was a prospect, insofar as you can be at that age, but to look at him now, well, you couldn't imagine it, could you?'

I shook my head.

'Rock had played, and he coached at Seafield and even in the school. And I'm not like Shane, I'm not saying rugby is some kind of universal panacea, but—sometimes a father can be so important, so inspiring, that when he dies it's like the air has gone out of the world. I think that's

78

what happened for Jonny. And Denis didn't get to know him until later. In fairness, Jonny's started to get along really well with Denis since he went to college. He really goes for the whole legal-Caesar bit. It's me and Denis who don't get along so well any more.'

'Is that right?' I said. 'Are you separating?'

'I think so. Mutually. Amicably. We've just . . . run out of . . .'

She exhaled, smiling, and shrugged, and waved a hand in the air. I didn't smile back.

'I don't think it's having an effect on Jonathan, if that's what you meant,' she said.

'It wasn't. You were going to tell me about Emily. Her troubles.

'Emily—oh Jesus, Emily.'

She walked across to the fire, where she stood, staring into the flames. I stayed by the window. I could see the fire reflected in the glass, flickering red in the black.

'Emily's mother, Jessica—you met her, didn't you?'

'This morning, yes.'

'How did she strike you?'

'Initially, very sexy, maybe a bit too flirtatious, a bit blatant. A bit much. And then . . . I don't know, like she was at one remove from herself . . . like she was damaged.'

Sandra stared into the fire and breathed out slowly.

'Damaged . . . damaged is a good word. Jessica's mother died of ovarian cancer when she was six. She was an only child. Her father was a not terribly successful actor, and the heavy drinking that usually goes along with the theatre got much worse

79

after his wife's death. And Jessica looked after him. Made his breakfast, ironed his clothes, made sure he was on time for rehearsals. She was his little wife. Her periods started early, when she was about eleven; at twelve, she'd reached full sexual maturity. At least, her body had. And her father noticed. And Jessica noticed him noticing, and began to use make-up, and to dress so he'd go on noticing. And one night when he lumbered in from the pub after whatever play he was in, or wasn't in, drunk again, she was waiting for him in the marital bed . . . his patient little wife, all ready for love . . . and he tried to resist, but, as with the drink, and the failure, he didn't try hard enough.'

Her voice had thickened with emotion; now it faltered. The fire crackled and hissed. I stood dead still, as if moving might break the spell, as if we were at a seance and Sandra was communing with the departed. She glanced quickly over her shoulder at me and I saw her eyes were glistening. There was nothing I could say, and before I had a chance to think of something, she turned back to the fire and continued.

'She told me all about it one night, early in the marriage. She'd had a row with Shane—over sex, how she wanted it more than he did, or how he had accused her of cheating with her leading man: young love, high drama, and she arrived up here and we drank brandy, and she told me all about it. How it lasted eighteen months or so, until she was fourteen. By then she had started sleeping around—older boys at school, a couple of her friends' fathers. And her own father had fallen apart under the strain, the shame of it all. Spent time in mental hospital. And drying out, though as soon as he'd get out, the drinking would start again. Whiskey, at the end. And Jessica running wild now, expelled from school, and no one to care for her—there was an aunt, on her mother's side, in Clontarf, but she didn't want to know. And the father died, pancreatitis, I think, or maybe liver, a drink death anyway, and Jessica was left, sixteen, all alone, desperate, afraid. Taken into foster care, ran away, one, two, three families. And finally the social worker in charge of her case, despairing, took a flyer, had the inspired idea of encouraging her to act. She got in touch with some of Jessica's father's former colleagues, the employable ones, and they were all stricken with guilt and there-but-for-the-grace-go-I sentimentality and they got her some walk-ons and a few auditions and she turned out to be a natural. I suppose you could say the theatre saved Jessica's life.'

Sandra turned and faced me, and I could see the glow of the fire in her red hair, and the pity in her green eyes.

'But those eighteen months, Ed . . . herself and her father, and Jessica just twelve, thirteen years old . . . alone in the house, her father's little wife . . . I don't think she ever moved on from there. From what Shane said—and I know she's been unfaithful to him throughout their marriage— she doesn't much enjoy sex, but she likes the power it gives her.'

'And Emily . . .' I said.

'And Emily,' she said. 'Her mother's daughter. Emily and Jonathan. Shane didn't know, and Jessica didn't know, but I knew, I think I've always known. Is that what Jonny was so excited about, that I might find out?'

I nodded.

'The weird thing is—the awful thing, maybe—I never felt it was wrong. I mean, kids are going to do it, thirteen, fourteen, you can try and delay, but by sixteen most of them are having sex, and as a parent what are you going to do? Tell them not to? Or pretend they aren't? I mean, it's good, isn't it? If you do it right? And if they experiment together, if it's not an older person taking advantage of them.'

'I think some people might feel a little uneasy at their being cousins.'

'It's not brother and sister. It's not an incestuous relationship. The taboo about cousins marrying, reproducing, is based on the fear that they'll keep doing it, and that the children of extended families of married cousins will marry each other. Then you have a problem.'

'I doubt if your brother would be so sanguine.'

'I don't know that I'm sanguine about it either, Ed. I'm just saying I never felt it was wrong. Maybe that says as much about me as it does about anyone else. I mean, Jonny's been in therapy since shortly after Rock's death. And Emily—this is something else her father doesn't know—Emily has been seeing the same therapist for years too. She came to me, I set it up for her. So . . . and no, I don't believe there should be a stigma attached to it, but I'm old-fashioned enough to wish our kids didn't need it. So sanguine isn't close to how I feel.'

'When I spoke to Jessica Howard, she said it was your idea that Emily do medicine. She suggested that you were anxious one of the children be the keeper of the Howard flame. That that burden came to rest upon Emily.'

A flash of rage creased her brow, and stained her cheeks like wine spilled on white linen.

'It was not a *burden,* that's so typical of the way Jessica twists everything, Emily wanted to do medicine, wants to still, she . . .'

Sandra caught herself, and gave a rueful little laugh, and twisted her mouth in acknowledgement of her flash of temper.

'I'm sorry, Mr Loy. Sisters-in-law. Jessica is . . . not always the easiest person to get along with. I'm sure it is difficult to marry into a family like ours. But her own insecurities, her need to be the centre of attention, haven't helped matters. She wouldn't even come to my mother's funeral this year. Said they'd never got along, and to pretend otherwise just because she was dead was hypocrisy. Never mind that it was her husband's mother, the self-obsessed fucking *egotism* . . .'

'Did Emily go to the funeral?'

'Of course. She and her granny were close. But look, I don't . . . I didn't really want to get into all this . . . I don't necessarily believe that's at the root of Emily's issues . . .'

'I think family is central,' I said. 'She seems very angry at the Howards. That there's some great tradition, some grand example she's expected to live up to. She wishes you'd just all leave her alone.'

Sandra nodded.

'She's nineteen, just started at college, a new life. Maybe that's as it should be. Jonny's gone the other way, he talks about the Howards like we're an empire on the march, superior beings all. Probably healthier at that age to want your family

83

on the sidelines. Make your own name.'

I was relieved at what she said. It didn't mean the blackmailer had gone away. But it suggested that the source of Emily's troubles was not as grave as it might have been.

We stood in silence for a moment. The fire, reflected in the black glass of the walls, seemed to wash the room in its red glow; logs spat and hissed in the grate. Sandra smiled, and this time I smiled back. She came close to me; I could feel her breath on my face, her wood-spice scent, her sudden need. I swallowed, and took a step back, and put my hand in my jacket pocket, and fingered the mass card that had been left beneath my windscreen wiper outside Shane Howard's surgery, and played a hunch.

'All right then, Sandra,' I said. 'Do you remember someone called Stephen Casey?'

I must have really fallen for Sandra Howard. Because when she looked at me, and looked away and as quickly back, and said, 'Who?', and then, when I had repeated the name and she, having given herself time, having made a thinking face and taken a thinking walk, shook her head emphatically and said 'No', not only did I realize instantly that she was lying, I was *surprised.*

'He died on All Souls' Day 1985,' I said.

Her eyes cast around the room, and up at me, and away again. It was almost painful to watch. The telephone rescued her. She left the room to answer it, and I stared at the fire and tried to remember the last time I had been surprised that someone was lying to me. I looked in the flames and tried to remember my ex-wife's face. I found that I couldn't.

84

7

I went through a door that led down to the front of the new house and stood outside and smoked a cigarette. There was a sloping garden and a gravel drive that seemed to lead down to the road, and I wondered why Sandra Howard had not approached the house this way. But, since I was already wondering whether anything she had told me was the truth, it didn't seem the most pressing detail. I wondered also whether I should feel pleased with myself that I had caught her in a lie, thereby breaking the spell she had cast over me, or dismayed by my easy susceptibility to a beautiful woman who paid me some attention. Maybe it was Jessica Howard who had got under my skin; maybe it was her daughter's lurid adventures in pornography. Male lust is a tenacious and comical affiction, immune as it can sometimes be to feelings of compassion or understanding; at times it reduces us all to the lunatic in that Italian movie, sitting in a tree hollering 'I want a woman.'

I checked my phone and found that Dave Donnelly had called again. I walked down the drive a pace, intending to ring him, when I spotted a circular pool halfway down the garden. Security lights lit the grass as I approached it, and I realized it was a match for the pool in the back garden of Emily's doll's house. It was bigger than the one in Shane Howard's back garden, and less ornate: a low, roughly packed granite wall, maybe three feet of water, a rough sandy bed. No marble, no crystal gems, no sense of it being a memorial or a deliberate feature. I looked back up the hill: the turrets and castellations of Rowan House loomed up behind the new extension, ghostly in the mist, like a phantom castle from a Gothic romance.

When I walked back up to the house, Denis Finnegan and Shane Howard were in the living room with Sandra. Shane was attempting to fix himself a drink he evidently didn't need; when he saw me he came across and wrapped his arms around me, pinning my hands to my sides, and lifted me off the floor in an embrace. He smelt of whiskey, and of rain.

'You found her! You boy ya! You found my princess!' he roared. His voice was hoarse, ragged with emotion; he looked like he'd been crying. He set me down and batted me on the shoulders with his forearms; I raised my hands to prevent him picking me up again.

'Have you seen her?' I said.

'I looked in,' he said. 'She's woozy. Sandra had a doctor in to give her something. Best to sleep it all off.'

Shane nodded then, as if his daughter's difficulties could be dispensed with like a hangover, and went back to his drink. Denis Finnegan raised his eyebrows and beamed conspiratorially at me; Sandra looked anxiously around at us all.

'Where did you get to today, Shane?' I said. 'We were all trying to get hold of you.'

Shane thrust his chin out and shrugged, like a bored and dismissive primate.

'Just needed to get some air, you know? After talking to you, got rattled. Couldn't sit still. Drove around a bit; parked up near the old pine forest on

Castlehill. Turned the old phone off, so I wouldn't be waiting. The waiting is the worst. Tramped around there for a while. Stopped off for a few drinks, little place in the mountains. Then turned the phone back on, and got the good word.'

Shane delivered all this in a burly rugby-club drawl that brooked no further interrogation. Maybe that was all he had done. And maybe I was bought and paid for. But I wasn't going to be treated like the help.

'This case is not closed yet, and for as long as it runs, I'll need access to you at any moment; I don't want you to vanish like that again, do you hear me?' I said. 'That's if you care a damn about your daughter's safety.'

Shane was ready to blow at that, but I didn't give him an opening. Instead I gave him what I had given Sandra: the sexual relationship between Emily and Jonathan, the two porn films and David Brady's involvement with them, the threat of blackmail over underage sex leading to Emily's part in the extortion attempt on Shane Howard, the uncertainty over just who was behind it all, the murder of David Brady. I left out the detail of my having been in David Brady's apartment, and I left out Tommy Owens and Brock Taylor; I gave them everything else.

Shane Howard had been on his feet when I recounted the history of his daughter's sexual relationship with her cousin, his hands balling into fists, his eyes blurring with rage; but the news of David Brady's murder hit him the hardest. Sandra went to him and wrapped her arms around his great shoulders and pulled his head to her breast and they subsided to the floor, Sandra whispering

87

to her little brother and stroking his sand-coloured hair. It was touching and pathetic, a grotesque pietà that was moving and disturbing. It was a pity there *wasn't* a fourth tower, the Howard Psychiatric Hospital: then the entire family could walk down the hill and check themselves in. I realized then that I wanted, as much as anything else, to *understand* this family in their houses on the tops of hills, to uncover their secrets, to see the Howards plain. Once I had admitted that to myself, I knew there was no way on earth I was stepping off this train until the end.

Denis Finnegan stood by the fire in a black chalk-stripe suit and a canary-yellow and royal-blue striped tie with a face that seemed to have attained a deeper shade of red as the day wore on. With a Scotch in his hand, he looked like a clubman from a bygone age.

'Sandra has advised me of her intention to retain you on the family's behalf,' he said.

'The problem is blackmail, and it hasn't gone away just because we've got Emily back,' I said. 'In a way, her absence was never the problem, seeing as it was voluntary. Chances are, whoever's behind this has copies of the films and photographs that can be rolled out again. Not to mention testimony and photographic evidence of underage sex. Chances are also, this individual won't be content with fifty grand the next time.'

'Do you have an individual in mind?' Denis Finnegan said.

'It's too early to say.'

Finnegan checked his watch and turned the TV on; it was nine o'clock and the main evening news on RTE was just starting. David Brady was the first

88

item in the bulletin, with an exterior shot of the body being wheeled on a gurney through the entrance to the Waterfront apartments. There was some archive footage of one of his schools-cups performances; Shane Howard detached himself from his sister after this, and took himself off to a corner by the window, where he sat on the floor and looked alternately out at the night and down at the floor, his great head tipping between his bent knees.

'I'll need to talk to Emily again tonight,' I said to Sandra.

'She may already be asleep,' Sandra said. 'Dr Hoyle gave her something.'

'Then I'd better see her now,' I said.

I followed her down the white corridor to Emily's room. She knocked on the door, then opened it cautiously. The bedside light was still on.

'Emily? Emily, it's Sandra. Ed Loy needs to talk to you again.'

Emily moaned and grunted a little, then said, 'OK.'

Sandra went in, and I followed. She sat down in a chair in the corner of the room, and I stayed where I was and shook my head. She looked up at me quizzically, and I shrugged. She got up and said, 'Emily, I'm going to leave Ed here. I'll be outside.'

Emily didn't say anything until Sandra left. Then she said, 'I suppose she looks sexy, but she's a nun, deep down. Deep deep down, she's a nun.' Her voice was a Valium blur. 'Do you like sexy nuns, Ted?'

'Ed,' I said. 'I'm not sure if I would. I don't think I've ever met one, but then again, I've never been in the habit of checking nuns out for their sex

89

appeal.'

Emily considered this for longer than it deserved. Free of make-up, her eyes were red and swollen; blue veins lined her pale face.

'Well, maybe you should,' she said. 'Her and Denis don't live together any more. Maybe she wants a man who doesn't have a head like a boiled ham. A man like you, Ted.'

'I'm not in the market for marriage.'

'Neither is anyone in this family, haven't you noticed?'

'I need to ask you a little more about the threesome you had with David Brady after the rugby-club party, about the underage girl. Did you get her name?'

'No names, that's the way to do it. Except, if they turn out to be thirteen, it obviously isn't the way to do it.'

'You must have called her something.'

'Called her c'mere. Called her c'mon. Called her see ya.'

'What was she like? Older than her age, obviously, was she clever, educated, what class was she?'

'She was smart. A smarty-pants. She made us laugh. And her accent was middle middle, could have been anything, working class reaching, upper middle relaxing, hard to know. Snow-blonde porn hair though, make-up a bit on the skang side, but not a pram face.'

'What about her father? How did that happen? Did he approach David Brady directly, or did the girl do it?'

Emily pulled the covers over her face.

'Why don't you ask him, Ted?'

'Ask who?'

'David, of course. Ask him what happened.'

I didn't know if it was the Valium, or if she was affecting some kind of mental confusion, or if she was genuinely disturbed, but I felt I couldn't take the time to find out; the Howards seemed to be falling apart, and I was going to have to work hard and fast to stop the entire family from going under. I pulled the duvet cover away from Emily's face.

'David Brady's dead. You know that. Stop messing around and tell me what else you know.'

Emily flinched, as if the narcotics of shock and tranquillizer were wearing off and grief was finally seeping through.

'I don't know,' she said. 'I don't know that David knew either. Jerry Dalton must have known. He told David . . . he was the go-between, I suppose you'd say. He told David what the threat was, what he had to do.'

'Jerry Dalton . . . is that your new boyfriend?'

'My new boyfriend? Jerry Dalton's not my . . . who told you Jerry was my boyfriend?'

'Your mother.'

'What the fuck would that fucking whore know? What does she care who I'm going out with, except to shove her tits in his face and try and fuck him like she does with every man she meets?'

Emily's eyes were spilling tears; her face was twisted with bitterness and grief, red raw and swollen ugly. She looked better than she had all day.

'But you know Jerry Dalton.'

'He's a barman in SRC. Seafield Rugby Club? And he's in my class at college. And he has this

91

metal band. Everyone knows Jerry. He's a really nice guy. A friend. At least, I thought so, but if he's hooked up with whoever is doing all this—is it the same guy who killed DB?'

'Could be.'

Jessica Howard had called Brady an absolute ride, and said she certainly would have.

'Emily, might there have been anything going on between your mother and David Brady?'

She shook her head, but didn't look very convinced.

'Is that why you broke up with him, Emily? Because he was having an affair with your mother?'

'*No*, Jesus . . . whatever was going on . . . and I'm not saying anything was, but whatever . . . the whole thing with DB just got to be too much . . . too much E, too much porn . . . just too fucking . . . greedy . . . it wasn't about love at all any more, if it ever had been, it was just about us *gorging* ourselves . . . too fucking gross.'

She put her head in her hands and a convulsion of weeping surged through her, like a great wave. When it had crashed, she tipped her head back and shook it, as if she could dispel grief the way a dog shakes off salt water. I ploughed on, trying to get as much as possible from her before she went under for the night.

'Sandra told me she fixed up some therapy for you. Do you still go?'

Emily looked at me cagily, then smiled.

'I do go. I go to Doctor Dave. Who says, I'm not a doctor, and don't call me Dave.'

'What does he call himself? And where does he live?'

'David Manuel. He works from his house in Rathgar. But there's no point. He won't talk to you.'

'Maybe I'll talk to him. Isn't that the idea?'

I smiled at Emily, but she didn't smile back. She had laced her fingers and was working her rings together, grinding the stones in an insistent rhythm. They were the same stones I had seen on a bracelet in her room, the same green-hued, red-flecked stones that were inlaid in the pool in Shane Howard's back garden.

'Nice rings,' I said. 'What jewel is it?'

'Bloodstone,' she said.

'Bloodstone? What's that?'

'Heliotrope is its other name. Bloodstone sounds better. It's a mythological stone, Ted. It possesses magical properties. *Man.*'

She looked up at me, her eyes suddenly twinkling, as if aware of the hippy-dippy nature of what she was saying, but willing herself—and me—to roll with it. Suddenly, I saw all her intelligence and wit being used in aid of herself for once. At last, I found myself liking her enormously. I smiled back, and she scrunched up her face as if she was embarrassed, and unused to people liking her for herself, or at all.

'Aunt Sandra gave me them, years ago. They say . . . "they say" . . . they never say who *they* are, but . . . *they say* if you soak the bloodstone in a certain kind of water, for a certain amount of time . . . it can turn the clouds the colour of blood. The other thing is better though . . . *they say* . . . if you clasp it in the right way, it can make you completely invisible.'

And with that, Emily slid back down in the bed

93

and pulled the cover right over her face, but not quite so fast that I didn't see a quiver in her lips, a glisten in her eyes, the bloodless pall of fear in her cheeks. I stood there a moment, and she poked one hand above the covers, just far enough to show the rings, and gave me a little kid's closed-hand wave.

Sleep well, I thought. Whatever the hell it is, it seems to be coming down hardest on you.

I shut the light out before I left.

＊　　＊　　＊

In the living room, Sandra and Shane Howard and Denis Finnegan were sitting around the big table, talking in murmurs; they went quiet and looked up at me as I approached. Sandra made an expectant face, as if waiting for a report. I nodded to her in reassurance. Then I took the mass card out of my pocket and laid it open on the table and said, 'Who was Stephen Casey?' There was a satisfying reaction: Shane's jaw fell open, and Denis flashed an urgent look at Sandra, who was staring at the table. Each of them knew. None of them would answer. I leant my hands on the table. I didn't have to fake it.

'You people are living in a dream if you think I can do anything for you,' I said. 'I found Emily without your help; keeping her safe—and your precious family's reputation intact—isn't going to be as easy. A case like this, it tends to shine its light into corners you thought would never be exposed. But if you're hell-bent on keeping all your secrets, fine, just be prepared to take your chances with blackmail, maybe even jail time for

94

Emily. Let me know what you decide—I can't hang around—and neither will our good friends the Guards.'

8

I was halfway across the white rotunda of Rowan House when Sandra Howard caught up with me. She grabbed my sleeve and pulled me around and I shook her hand away. She looked at me as if I had slapped her.

'What gives you the right to talk to us like that? Who the fuck do you think you are?' she said. She stepped in and raised her hand to slap me. I caught her wrist and held it.

'I thought I could trust you,' I said. 'I don't like being lied to.'

I let her wrist go. She held her hand in space for a moment, then reached for the back of my head, and her eyes widened and her lips parted as she pulled herself close to me and pushed her face at mine, and her smell was all salt earth and spice, and I could feel the blood in my chest, in my throat, and we were kissing, her hands in my hair, pressing my mouth to hers, her tongue on mine. She put my hand on her breast, and ran hers between my legs; we were pulling at each other's clothes, biting each other's lips. 'Come on,' she said, and maybe she had a room in mind, but we didn't get further than the stairs; she turned on the wide steps and pushed me down and lowered herself on me with a moan, and we fucked beneath a portrait of Dr John Howard, and our cries echoed around the hall like memories, and when we finished, her eyes were wet on my brow.

'What is it?' I said.

She shook her head and put a finger to my lips and smiled.

'I'm sorry, Ed. I'm sorry Shane has drawn you into all this. Drawn you in here.'

She wouldn't say any more. We fixed ourselves up and stood in the hall, not looking one another in the eye. I had a metallic taste in my mouth; I drew my knuckle across my lips and it came away smeared with blood; Sandra laughed and did the same. It was the kind of sex you spend your life dreaming about and doing your best to avoid, the kind that, even if you almost always regret it, makes you feel like you're truly alive. There was a sound from across the hall, as if someone was approaching; when no one came, I thought it more likely that someone had been watching and then slipped away.

Sandra came out with me to my car. The mist seemed to have cleared a little, at least enough to make out bonfires south towards the mountains; the damp night air was thick with smoke. Sandra leant against the roof.

'You don't have to know everything, Ed,' she said. 'What happened twenty years ago may not be relevant today.'

'You thought it was in the case of Jessica. You think it is for Jonathan and Dr Rock.'

'And what—we should share everything with you and let you decide what's important?'

'That's right,' I said, smiling because she was— smiles as steady and false as masks.

'And what does that make you? More father

confessor than detective.'

'Call it what you will,' I said, 'I'll find it out anyway. What happened here didn't start last week, and it's not going to stop overnight. All you can do is slow it down. Once it's begun, you can't stop it. Unless you want to sacrifice Emily and Jonathan. Because they're the ones who are suffering for your silence.'

This time I let the slap come. Sandra Howard hit me full across the face, and stared at me, trembling, blinking back tears, and then turned and walked back up the steps and inside the pale granite castle and closed the great doors of Rowan House behind her.

*　　　*　　　*

I got a number for David Manuel from directory inquiries, and rang him on the drive down to Woodpark. Manuel's wife answered, and was reluctant to hand the call over—I could hear conversation and laughter in the background—but I kept insisting until he came to the phone.

'David Manuel.'

His voice was quiet and precise.

'My name is Loy, I'm a private detective, employed by the Howard family. I found Emily Howard—I believe she's a client of yours.'

Manuel said nothing.

'I'd like to talk to you about her, and about Jonathan.'

'I can't tell you anything about what they've told me, that's privileged.'

'Of course. But you might be a help in other ways. In what you know about the Howard family, for example.'

'I told you, that's confidential—'

'Not all of it may be. Not all of it has to be. You're not a doctor, or a priest; you're not bound by any real laws, after all. And they're both in danger, you know, Emily and Jonathan.'

'In danger? Are you trying to scare me, Mr Loy?'

'Maybe just a little. I'm certainly scared on their behalf. And I don't scare so easily. They'd both be in jail if I told the Guards what I know. Can I come and visit you now?'

'Now? I have people here, I can't just . . . no, that's out of the question.'

'Tomorrow then.'

'I have a client at nine.'

'I'll be at your door at eight.'

I ended the call before he could object.

*　　　*　　　*

The Woodpark Inn had a bar with lino on the floor and tables and chairs laid out and some unspeakable celebrity talent show at maximum volume on the television and fluorescent lights glaring and a dartboard and fifty or so people who wouldn't see fifty again drinking pints and whiskey-and-lemonades and arduously not smoking. They looked like they'd been coming here all their lives, and they probably had. The lounge was relatively quiet: couples with nothing to say to each other and subdued groups of ill-assorted women in their forties sat beneath the skeletons and pumpkin balloons like adults in their children's bedrooms, wondering how they'd grown too old to enjoy the action but not old enough to feel relaxed about

98

missing it. There was no sign of Sean Moon, or the Reillys, or Brock Taylor. The action—the Halloween Battle of the Bands—was taking place in a hall that must originally have housed dances, maybe bingo nights. The bouncer had a shaved head and a big black moustache; he looked at me and smiled and said 'Too old' in an Eastern European accent. I said, 'Record company.' He inclined his head towards the racket that was emerging, looked back at me in a sceptical kind of way, then shrugged elaborately, as if human folly was beyond his control, and let me pass.

I paid twenty euros to a bored-looking girl in white baggy sportswear with lacquered hair tied tight in a topknot and went inside. The bouncer was right: I was too old. The hall was full of goth kids and surfpunk kids, metal kids and indie kids, kids who were trying to look like all of the foregoing and failing, groomed and styled OMIGOD girls in party frocks and burly-looking rugby boys with their hair gelled into fins. There were a few older faces, casualties from the culture wars, the type you see at rock gigs everywhere— plump, bikerish alcoholic women with purple hair and tattoos, tiny wrinkled men with dirty grey ponytails—but basically it was a room full of kids, and I was a forty-three-year-old man in a suit among them. I felt pretty sleazy, but then, I'd been feeling pretty sleazy the whole day, ever since Shane Howard had shown me pornographic pictures of his daughter and, amidst the pity and indignation I felt on Emily's behalf, I hadn't been able entirely to suppress the rather less noble feeling of lust, or subsequently to banish the lurid images from my heated brain.

I got a pint of Guinness at the bar and found out from an elfin barmaid with enormous eyes and short plum-coloured hair whom I also let believe I was from a record company that The Golgotha Pyre wouldn't be on for a while. The band on stage were dressed in ruffes and lace and floppy white shirts and wore a lot of make-up; I couldn't work out if they were impersonating the New Romantic bands from the early eighties or the current wave of bands who impersonated them. I finished my drink and got a second; the barmaid pointed Jerry Dalton out to me across the hall, and told me they'd already had a lot of interest, but that no one had done a deal yet, and that whoever signed them was going to be very lucky; her great eyes glowed with passion as she spoke, as if she were more than a little in love with Dalton herself; I asked her if she knew if Emily Howard was Dalton's girlfriend and she shook her head and smiled pityingly at my middle-aged literal-mindedness, and said all she cared about was the music.

Jerry Dalton was tall and lean with a dark mop of wavy black hair that came to his shoulders and a goatee that failed to disguise the clean line of his lantern jaw; he wore a black T-shirt with GOLGOTHA PYRE written on it in letters of flame, black jeans and black boots with thick metallic soles. An inverted crucifix hung around his neck, and he had a lot of rings and bracelets with skulls and serpents' heads on them. He was standing at a tall circular bar table with a bottle of Budvar, talking to a faintly insane-looking guy with very long ginger-blond hair cut in a fringe and black-rimmed glasses who vanished when I introduced myself.

'A private detective? Woh, deadly,' said Jerry Dalton. 'What can I do for you?'

'I want to ask you about your girlfriend, Emily Howard.'

'She's not my girlfriend.'

'Is she not? I thought she was.'

'You thought . . . what business is it of yours anyway?'

'Emily went missing. Someone was blackmailing her father. I found her. She said you were the connection through which the blackmail threat came to David Brady. Now Emily is home, and David Brady is dead, and I want to find out who's behind it all.'

Jerry Dalton looked stunned.

'David Brady is dead? Dead how?'

'He was murdered. Beaten, then stabbed, whoever did it wanted to make sure. So Jerry, on whose behalf were you giving David instructions? Brock Taylor?'

Dalton drank some beer and shook his head.

'Brock Taylor? I don't think so. I don't know, to be honest.'

'How could you not know? Emily said you were the go-between.'

'Well, that's not exactly true. I work part-time at Seafield Rugby Club, yeah? Well, I come on shift last weekend—Friday night, about ten to seven. And Barnsey, Tony Barnes, the manager, tells me there's a letter waiting for me behind the bar. I open it, and there's a sealed envelope inside, and a note asking me to make sure David Brady gets it.'

'What kind of note?'

'Handwritten. No signature. I still have it, I

101

think.'

He pulled up a long black leather coat from the floor, searched in the pockets and came up with a fistful of paper; amid receipts, flyers and ticket stubs he found a folded piece of grimy cream notepaper. I unfolded it. In a neat hand that looked strangely familiar, in ink, was written, 'Jerry, please see David Brady gets this.'

'Did Barnsey say who left it?'

'He didn't see.'

'And what happened then?'

'There was a match that night. David Brady was in after, with all the rugby guys, big night on the beer. I gave him the envelope, a little while later he came back up and asked me if I knew who dropped it in. He was pretty agitated, I suppose.'

'What do you mean, you suppose?'

Dalton put the flat of his hand against his mouth, as if he was about to say something against his better judgement, then lifted it above his head.

'Well, David wasn't the most . . . don't want to speak ill of the dead, but he was kind of an abrasive guy, you know? And he had a lot of people who'd laugh at his jokes, which were usually at someone else's expense . . . and he was pretty aggressive with the bar staff, he'd stand at the bar, wouldn't speak, would expect you to know what he drank, then when you gave him his drink, he'd go, "And the guys?" So you were also supposed to know what *they* drank, and if you didn't he could be pretty obnoxious . . . ah, it sounds a bit petty, all I'm saying is, I don't remember registering whether he was freaked out about the letter in particular, 'cause his general manner was so hostile, I kind of let it flow past me,

102

you know?'

'Tell me about Emily. You're in her class in college?'

'Yeah. We met up about a month back. Freshers' week, all the new kids. We went out, hung around, couple of times, I was into it, she was casual, I didn't push it. We'd've seen more of each other if it was up to me. But she's not the kind of girl you boss around.'

'You were out to her house?'

'I met her mother. She's pretty full on.'

'Tell me what you know about Brock Taylor.'

Dalton looked around uneasily.

'I don't mean his record, we all know that. Just, current form.'

'He owns this place, but he's not here much. He's around Seafield Rugby Club a fair bit. In a suit, being a hale-and-hearty rugger kind of guy when he's not quite born to it. But he's getting his feet under the table there 'cause he's so much bread, which he's happy to donate to their building fund and so on. So whatever he did in the past is forgiven, or forgotten.'

'What about the Reillys? Have you seen them around?'

'Around SRC? They're officially barred. You see them in the car park, dispensing their wares.'

'Coke?'

'And E, a little dope. Mostly coke. As if the guys needed any assistance in being obnoxious.'

'David Brady a good client of theirs?'

'Oh yeah. That's why his game was for shit. Brady was the only one would bring the Reillys right into the club. No one would say a word to DB.'

103

The band on stage finished in a synthesizer crescendo. Applause drifted across the room in gusts. The lights came up harsh and unforgiving on even the youngest faces. Jerry Dalton stood up.

'We're on next, Mr Loy. But if there's anything else, get in touch with me. I really like Emily, and I'll do whatever I can to help.'

I took his phone number. The ginger guy with the fringe was onstage, assaulting a drum kit. I guess that helped explain his insane look. Jerry Dalton picked up his coat and gave me his hand. I gestured to the cross hanging upside down from his neck.

'What's that about?' I said.

He fingered the cross, looked around the room, and made a sweeping pass with his hand.

'It's all about hypocrisy, Mr Loy,' he said.

I wasn't about to argue with that.

The Guinness was good, so I had another pint and waited for the band to start. The Golgotha Pyre were a metal trio. Jerry played guitar and sang, and a guy with a ZZ Top beard wearing a black overcoat played bass with his back to the audience. They sounded like seventies heavy metal and nineties grunge, very doomy and tortured, and they could play a bit; they had songs called things like 'Lake of Fire' and 'Judgement Day' and 'Blood on the Wind'. At first they made me smile, but soon, they just made me feel old. I had lost the facility for listening to music when my daughter died; so far it hadn't returned; when it did, I doubted whether heavy metal would be the form it took. But they were sincere, and Dalton's voice was at the lower end of the balls-in-a-vice scale. When I finished my drink and left, there were kids headbanging into the speaker bins.

I came out through a different door to the one I had entered by, and the air seemed suddenly to intensify the strength of the beer I had drunk, so that I had trouble getting my bearings in the vast wrap-around car park. It was still overcast, starless in the black, but the mist had lifted, and my eyes kept getting snared by a spider's web of fireworks in the sky and bonfires in the hills. The Reillys came quietly, grabbing me just as I spotted my car, the bulky one behind me to grab my arms and pin them, the smaller one walking quickly up, sniffing and panting and pushing the blue-grey Sig Sauer pistol to my chest and pulling the trigger before I saw a thing. There were cracks in the sky, and bangs from afar, but nothing from the gun, just a series of clicks, each one deafening to my ears.

The gun must have jammed. Small Reilly lifted the Sig to my eyes and grinned, his vivid blue eyes gleaming, and said: 'Keep out of the David Brady thing, righ'?' and slashed me down the right side of my face with the blade front of the gun barrel. I felt a smart of pain as Small Reilly raised the Sig again and brought it round to my left. I ran Big Reilly into the car behind me, braced back against him, swung my legs up and kicked Small Reilly full in the chest, heels out, so he went over and his head hit the tarmac with a smack. I came down hard on top of Big Reilly and heard the gun skittering beneath a car and elbowed Big Reilly a couple of times in the stomach. I was on my feet now and blood was coursing down my face; I could feel it hot in the fold between my neck and collarbone. Big Reilly was coming at me now with a knife. Small Reilly was still on the ground, fumbling to get up, one hand on his head.

'Shank the cunt, Wayne,' he spat. 'He's out of fuckin' order, man.'

Wayne may have been trying to do just that; he was swiping, slashing the air, jabbing at me; or maybe he was just trying to get to his brother; I should have just backed off and let him get away if that's what he wanted to do, but it wasn't what I wanted to do; I wiped the blood off my face with the palm of my right hand and I blocked Wayne's path between two cars, and he lunged at me and I sidestepped and grabbed his blade wrist with my bloody right hand and twisted it behind his back, up and up until he dropped the knife, and slapped his face down on the hood of the parked car, once, twice and again, until it was a bloody mess, and smashed his blade hand on the hood, once, twice and again, and smashed it some more so he couldn't hold a blade in it any time soon, or ever, and flung him at his brother, who still hadn't made it up, and the two went down in a heap, and I picked up the knife and moved in, wiping another flush of blood off my face, a roar like the beating of wings in my ears now, ready to keep going, to shank the Reillys myself, to atone for the shame of having been caught unawares; even if they hadn't meant to kill me, they could have, and I wouldn't have them thinking they could try it again, and then I heard a voice.

'Fuck sake, Ed, you don't want to kill the fucking *Reillys*. That'd only give them ideas above their station.'

9

Tommy Owens, in an olive-green snorkel coat and a black fleece hat, with the Reilly brothers' gun in his hand, looking like I hadn't seen him in a long long while: grinning, head bobbing with adrenalin, or speed, probably both, all of a swagger, ready for the fray.

I walked over to him and took the gun. It was a compact Sig Sauer, the P225, barely more than seven inches in length, grey-blue and slick with my blood. As I trained it on the Reillys, it weighed surprisingly light in my hand.

'Besides,' continued Tommy. 'As a gun, it makes a good set of brass knucks.'

'What do you mean?' I said.

'Check the clip,' he said.

The Sig was chambered for 9-mm Parabellum, the magazine was eight shot, and it was empty. The Reillys had come to throw a scare into me, not kill me. Now I was going to find out why.

Tommy looked at my face.

'You're gonna need stitches for that, Ed,' he said.

'What are you doing here, Tommy?'

'I'll tell you after. Sketch, sketch.'

I looked around. A few punters were watching from the pub door. It was only a matter of time before we'd have bouncers on the scene, and then cops. I took a clean handkerchief from my jacket and pressed it to my face to staunch the blood flow.

'I want to talk to the Reillys.'

'Talk to Darren, he's a slimy little cunt, but he's

the brains. Such as they are. Anyway, Wayne's fucked, isn't he?'

Tommy took the knife from me and advanced on the Reillys as he said this, separating them with a few flashes of the blade. Darren Reilly looked dazed from the crack his head had taken, still winded from the blow to the chest; Wayne crouched against a car, his good hand cradling his wounded one, clutching both to his bloodied face, as if afraid it might fall off if he released them.

'Stay down, all right?' Tommy said to Wayne.

'You won't have Loy with you next time,' Wayne Reilly honked through his fingers. Tommy aimed a kick at him, and Wayne cowered beneath the car. Tommy reached inside Darren Reilly's grey hoodie, grabbed him by the hair and dragged him squealing towards me.

'Shut the fuck up,' he said, looking towards the pub door, where more people had begun to gather. 'Car?' he said to me.

I pointed towards the old Volvo, and Tommy led Darren Reilly towards it. Tommy's limp was still there—his ankle had been stomped to shreds back when we were kids—but his energy had changed; now it resembled the kind of go he'd had when we were in our teens, and every trip to shoplift or rob an orchard or a bike or hotwire a car had been led by Tommy Owens, with me his willing accomplice. I'd thought disappointment and failure had sucked that kind of verve out of him long since, but here he was, bundling Darren Reilly into the back seat of a car and taking his phone away from him and tying a scarf around his eyes: alive and kicking.

'Down at the corner of Pearse Drive and Pearse Rise, Ed,' Tommy whispered in my ear. 'There's a place there that's just the job.'

The place was a lock-up garage on the outskirts of the Woodpark estate; two metal up-and-over doors were chained and padlocked; graffiti said 'FUCK THE POLICE' and 'HONEYPARK RULES' and 'MARIA AND CHRISTY 4 EVER'.

Tommy produced a bunch of maybe a hundred keys and passed it to me.

'Right-hand door should be good, Ed. One of them fits, can't remember which. I'll mind young Darren here.'

After trying a dozen or so keys, I found one to open the door. There was a space directly inside. I got back in the car and drove it in. Tommy got out and shut the door and flicked a switch and fluorescent lights came on. My face had started bleeding again, but slower this time; I refolded the handkerchief and used it as a pressure pad. There were three other cars in the garage, all covered with tarpaulins; the rear of the concrete building had aluminium doors that matched those we'd entered through. There was an office partition with fibreglass windows and dusty, empty shelves; the desk and chair within were tattered and filthy. I looked at Tommy for an explanation.

'Garage owner in town. Used to do a little work for him, fitting up hot cars. He has lock-ups all over, moves the motors between them, so if one is raided, there's no connection made with the others. I made copies of the keys when I was doing a job for him. Checked this one the other day, it had a free space. Always come in handy.'

I nodded. Had Tommy gone back into the hot-car business? Had he ever left? Catching Tommy in a lie was as difficult as it had ever been, particularly since he often wasn't sure himself, trusting in the one true faith of Make It Up As You Go Along.

Tommy got Darren Reilly out of the car. The journey had restored his spirits. He lifted the tarpaulin and inspected the navy hood of a Mercedes saloon with no licence plates.

'This is what I'm talking about, Tommy.'

'No way, Darren,' Tommy said.

'Nothing you can do about it, when fuckin' Wayne gets after yiz—'

'Fuckin' Wayne is gonna need a doctor for his *face* before he does anything else,' Tommy said. 'And even if he does get after us, he doesn't know where we are, does he?'

'I meant, after, when you're out and about. When you're on your own man.'

'I wouldn't be thinkin' about after if I was you, Darren. Who says there's gonna be an after?'

Darren laughed, a clattering football rattle of a laugh.

'What are you, hard men all of a sudden? Sure your man Loy there's in with the cops so he is.'

'He may be, but I'm not.'

Tommy suddenly hit Darren Reilly a backhander across the ear. Reilly squealed, but I could see Tommy wince; the blow had hurt his hand, and he was trying not to show it; I winced myself at the sight of Tommy hitting anyone: violence had never been part of his rogue's repertoire.

'Tommy,' I said, as sharp as I could make it. Tommy looked up guiltily and almost blushed, and I had to turn to hide my face; I thought I might burst out laughing. I walked to the doors at the far end of the lock-up. Tommy followed me, trailing

110

one eye back towards Reilly, who was rubbing his ear and swearing.

'What the fuck is going on here, Tommy? In a lock-up, slapping people around? What are we, going to torture the guy?'

'He owes me money.'

'He owes you money how? Low-rent drug dealer skangin' round the Woodpark estate and he owes you money, and you unemployed and looking for work on the level, now how could that be?'

Tommy's lower lip protruded from his reddened face, his brow all furrowed in a schoolboy frown. That was how it went with Tommy and me: first I had to be his older brother, then his father, then his headmaster. And having to be anybody's headmaster was a bolt-upright three-a.m. nightmare at the best of times, and it never seemed to be the best of times any more. My face smarted, and the blood was still flowing; I nudged Tommy in the ribs to start talking.

'Those porno DVDs,' he said. 'I got them from the Reillys.'

'Not Brock Taylor.'

'No. So anyway I paid in advance.'

'Why did you tell me you got them from Brock Taylor?'

' 'Cause I thought it would shut you up goin' on about what a fuck-up I was, if I was in with Brock. Anyway, a fiver each I gave the Reillys, reckoned I'd make ten, come out a grand ahead.'

'And Brock Taylor?'

'What about Brock Taylor? He has nothing to do with anything, I told you, I just . . . thought of him.'

'How did you "just" happen to show up tonight? Right place, right time? You following me, or the

111

Reillys there, or what?'

Tommy looked away, exhaled loudly through his nostrils, shook his head.

'Just coincidence, Ed. Thought I'd go up the Woodpark Inn for a pint. Came out, spotted you in the—'

'Come on, Tommy. At least the Brock Taylor lie had a certain amount of class.'

'I swear on my daughter's life.'

'I don't believe you. Tommy—'

'I was following the Reillys.'

'Thank you. Why?'

'I owe them money. Borrowed it for, just, you know. The usual.'

'And?'

'And I can't afford to pay it back, and the interest is fuckin' mounting, so I was trying to get something on them I could use.'

'What kind of thing? Use how? Catch them dealing coke, or loan-sharking, then threaten to give witness evidence to the Guards? Not your style. I don't believe a word that's coming out of your mouth, Tommy, not one fucking word.'

'I was hanging round the Woodpark, waitin' there for them. The Reillys are in and out all night so they are. I didn't know they were going to attack you, didn't even know you were there.'

But I had stopped listening. My face was aching, and blood had seeped into my right eye, tearing it up. I spat on the handkerchief and wiped it clean. At least the flow of blood had subsided. I was cold and tired; I needed a drink and a hot shower and a decent night's sleep and a case that didn't involve first cousins fucking each other. Instead, here I was in a lock-up with a torn face and my best friend the compulsive liar and a little scumbag called Darren Reilly, who had threatened me and pistol-whipped me and who was now leering through the window of a stolen Mercedes at himself, or at the image of his idealized self behind the wheel. I thought I'd better give Tommy some time to make up whatever it was he was going to say next. I walked up fast behind Reilly and grabbed him by the collar and tapped his face firmly against the car window a few, maybe half a dozen times and dragged him to the front of the lock-up and pushed him at one of the aluminium doors. He saved himself any further damage by bracing his hands against the support struts on the door. There was blood on his face, and he was whimpering.

'All right, all right,' he said. 'Fuck sake. What do you want?'

'Who told you to warn me off?'

Darren Reilly didn't answer immediately, so I pulled him off balance and stamped on his foot, near the ankle, hard. He screamed and fell to the ground and lay there moaning.

'Who told you to warn me off?' I said again.

'Sean Moon,' he said. 'Jesus fuck!'

'Sean Moon? Don't make a clown of me here, Darren.'

'I swear. Paid us an' all. Like when we were minding the young ones.'

'What young ones?'

'The Howard kids.'

'Sean Moon paid you to mind Emily Howard and Jonathan O'Connor?'

'Sure. Brady organized it with him. We just done

113

what we were told. Take the money and run.'

Reilly wiped some blood from his face, and put a tentative hand to his nose. It didn't look broken to me. Maybe I was losing my touch.

'So David Brady was in charge of it all then?'

'Moon isn't the gobshite you think he is. Bit of a fucking brain, could've gone to uni an' all. Two of them working together, looked like to me. They organized the whole blackmail thing with your one's oul' fella, Howard.'

'They organized it?'

'Yeah. I think your one was in on it, though. I didn't care one way or the other. They paid us well, is all I know. Even if they wouldn't let us watch the riding.'

'And who blackmailed Brady into making the porn in the first place?'

'Sorry? Lost me there man,' Darren Reilly said. He worked his foot around in a circle. 'At least it's not broken. I wouldn't give much for your chances once Wayne gets his nose sorted out, he's a tendency to bear a grudge so he does.'

'David Brady was blackmailed into making the porn by someone whose daughter he had sex with when she was underage. Do you know who that was?'

'The dirty fucker. No, I don't know.'

'I do,' a voice said.

When I turned around to look at Tommy, his head was bowed and he was shaking. He lifted his head and swung an unsteady finger at me, and I was taken aback to see tears in his eyes. He said something, but I couldn't hear what it was. I went closer, and he spoke into my ear.

'My daughter, Ed,' he said. 'Naomi.'

And suddenly, it all made sense. I took the note that had been passed to Jerry Dalton in Seafield Rugby Club out of my pocket and looked at it. 'Jerry, please see David Brady gets this.' That was why the handwriting had looked familiar. Because it was Tommy's surprisingly elegant hand, not quite copperplate, but not far off. The first time I'd had a note from him, aged about nine, it read, 'You are dead at breaktime.' Best joined-up writing in the class. We fought in a ring of shouting boys, huddled against the granite wall at the far end of the schoolyard, and I was winning when Tommy sidestepped, and I slapped a right hook into the rough granite and my knuckles exploded in crimson. Smarter than he looked, often smarter than me. Underestimate Tommy Owens at your peril.

Tommy subsided on to the tarp-covered hood of another German saloon at the far end of the garage, a BMW by the shape. I left Darren Reilly and walked across to Tommy.

'Tell me,' I said.

'She stayed over, that time you were on that bar-fraud thing in Wicklow. We'd been getting on well, you know, even if her mother has done her best to turn her against me. Not to mention letting her run wild, the mouth on her, fucking this, fucking that, thirteen years old. And make-up, and hair bleached blonde, wearing this pink-velour tracksuit with "Juicy" on her arse, and a black thong sticking up over it, and a tattoo at the base of her spine, you know, a fucking tramp stamp, two bolts of lightning it looked like, pointing down towards her hole, I mean fuck sake, is Paula on drugs letting her get that done? But I said nothing.

I mean, she's doing well at school, she's a good laugh, and she's always stuck up for me with Paula. Even when there wasn't a lot to stick up for.'

I turned to check on Darren Reilly, who looked away quickly; he had come closer to us since Tommy started talking.

'Let's dump head-the-ball here before you tell me any more, Tommy,' I said.

Tommy tied the scarf around Darren Reilly's eyes and I opened the door to the Volvo and reversed out. The lights went off and Tommy and Reilly emerged on to the street, and as Tommy reached up to pull the door down, I saw Reilly tugging at his blindfold, and the scarf fell down around his face, and once he clocked where he was, he pushed the blindfold back over his eyes and tightened it again. Tommy snapped the padlock shut on the aluminium door as if he hadn't noticed what Reilly had done. He pushed Reilly in the back seat and I drove back to the Woodpark Inn and Tommy pushed Reilly out of the car and Reilly walked away into the car park swearing several varieties of revenge on us both. Tommy got back in the car beside me and I drove up on to the dual carriageway and joined the northbound flow of traffic for the city.

'Anyway,' Tommy said, 'we're sittin' there watchin' Buffy or something on the telly and there's a knock at the door, shave-and-a-haircut, ten-bob, like that, y'know, and Naomi's on her feet in a twinkling, "That's for me, Da," and out the door. Some young fella she was expecting, I can hear them in the hall. I'm saying nothing, don't want to blow it. Anyway, she's in such a rush to see your man she's left her phone there on the arm of the couch, one of the camera ones, you know, and there's all giggling and hissing coming from outside the door, and I just have a quick look at the phone, see who's ringing her, what's what. Bit nosy, but . . . whatever. I'm still her da, amn't I? Thought I'd say I was thinking of getting one myself if she came back in. And I'm scrolling through the photos. Her friends in school uniforms, spotty young fellas, Paula, my ma, even one of me in there. And then there's one of Naomi and the Howard young one, and they're both sucking this lad's prick. Fuck sake, I nearly threw up, I'm not coddin' you. And back I go, and there's more, all riding each other, doing everything, and filming each other doing it, fucking disgusting now, and I can see your man is David Brady. In one of them, he's winking at the camera while Naomi . . . Ah fuck. *Fuck.*'

Tommy stopped talking, and I could hear his breath coming deep and slow as he tried to compose himself. The mist had blown up again; the world had shrunk to four streams of traffic, flowing relentlessly to and from the city. I lit two cigarettes and passed one to Tommy; he took it and the car filled with smoke.

'I heard the front door slam, and she comes back in, all smiles, beautiful, you know, still my little girl. And I thought, *Just leave it, talk to Paula, don't . . . don't fuck things up here.* I mean, I thought that, but how could I not say anything? Thirteen years old, and that fucker smirking like a cunt . . . anyway, I just blurt it all out, and she goes mental of course, calls me a snooper and a pervert and a scumbag and all this, so she's storming out and I say, does Paula know about it? That stopped her in her tracks. 'Cause OK, the tattoo and the clothes and all, but Paula isn't gonna be impressed by those pictures, not one little bit.'

Tommy's ex-wife had dyed red hair and coarse good looks, and her voracious appetite for men was matched by her utter disdain for them; Paula slept with men *before* the first date, thus ruling out the likelihood of there ever being one, and endlessly reconfirming her low opinion of the sex. She had made several contemptuous passes at me recently, after hours in a bar full of people with no homes they wanted to go home to; I had evaded her, but with a woman like Paula, in a bar like that, you felt it was only a matter of time. But when she caught a bloke who had moved in with her for a few months putting the moves on Naomi, she stabbed him in the hand with a screwdriver. 'I was aiming for his balls,' she told Tommy. The guy went to stay with his brother in Copenhagen, which is probably far enough away, although I would have gone further.

'So what happened, Tommy?'

'She told me she was on E, up at Seafield Rugby Club, and she got off with Brady, and then he talked her into the whole idea of a threesome. Seems to be a thing now, girls snogging each other and all, even when they're not lezzers. Fucking disgusting, so it is. She was trying to keep a brave face on it, what a great time she had, how I'm out of touch, but I went through the photographs with her, and by the end she was in bits she was. I felt bad, like I was bullying her, but it was for her own good. It was like, someone else seeing them— me seeing them—the whole thing of it came through to her at last . . . the *shame* of it, know I

118

mean?'

We were stopped at a red light in Donnybrook; across the street, loud music and flashing lights came from a rugby-club Halloween party; drunken teenage girls dressed in short skirts and skimpy tops tottered along on high heels, arm in arm, primped and groomed and sheened like footballers' wives, or drag queens, or third-world hookers; two girls sat on the kerb, one getting sick, the other holding her friend's hair out of the vomit's path. Sugar and spice.

'So I had to think about what to do. I didn't want to tell Paula, for the same reason I didn't want to go to the Guards: because that would only land Naomi in the shit. I mean, she probably looked eighteen, she was on E, she was in a club with a full bar . . . it wasn't as if Brady had snatched her in an alley. On the other hand, couldn't let the smirking cunt away with it. In the shots, he was holding a camcorder, filming it all himself, he was. That's where I got the idea.'

'Give him a taste of his own medicine.'

'Something like that.'

'With a view to . . . what, exactly, Tommy? I mean, given that you find it all so disgusting, why would you want more porn to be made?'

'As an insurance policy. Against Brady. He could sell it to anyone, put it out on the Internet, my daughter. Fuck knows what Brady does with the films he makes.'

'Did with them. He's not going to be making any more.'

'I didn't have anything to do with that, Ed.'

'*I* believe you.'

'It was in my head . . . I probably wasn't thinking

119

straight, I was in a fucking rage. In my head to make a show of Brady, to humiliate him—'

'Why didn't you make him perform then?'

'What?'

There it was: the stalling-for-time 'what?', the catch-me-out-I'm-lying 'what?'

'The only proof Brady was involved in making the porn films is the shot of his bracelet in the mirror, which must have been accidental. So what insurance was involved in having him behind the camera? No, Tommy, you were in on it, weren't you?'

'In on what, Ed?'

'Don't do this, Tommy, don't be lying to me now. In on the blackmail attempt on Shane Howard. Just tell me, was it your idea or Brady's?'

Tommy rolled down his window and threw his cigarette butt out on to a Leeson Street thick with refugees from a fancy-dress ball: skeletons and witches and vampires weaving in a band along the pavement, dodging the less elegant drunks and Halloween revellers. A thunderous fusillade of fireworks cascaded across the sky. Tommy rolled his window back up.

'It was Brady's,' he said.

My heart sank in my chest.

'What was the connection with Sean Moon?'

'I don't know. Brady just seemed to know him.'

'And the Reillys were in on it too?'

'No.'

'Yes. Who brought them in? I know they supplied David Brady with drugs. But maybe they were connected with you too, Tommy. Maybe you brought them in because you did owe them money. Or maybe you suddenly owed them because the blackmail deal was off. I was on the

120

case, and you didn't want to go through with it any more. And then David Brady was dead, and you couldn't go through with it. But the Reillys weren't happy, they thought they were stepping up a gear. Blackmailing someone like Shane Howard with porno pictures of his daughter, that's not a one-off payment, that could be a fucking salary. A job for life, buy a lot of Mercs that way.'

'No.'

I pulled the car up against the railed park on the south side of Fitzwilliam Square. My cheek was still burning, but when I put my hand to it, it came away dry; if it had stopped bleeding, it could knit together without stitches.

'Come on Tommy. Don't you think I didn't see through that pantomime you were acting out tonight? How you just happened to bring Darren Reilly to a lock-up full of stolen cars you had worked on; how he looked at them like he'd had advance warning; how you tied his blindfold loosely enough on the way out, and turned your back to lock the door, so he could have a quick look around to see where it was. Surprised you didn't slip him a key while you were at it.'

'Ed, it wasn't that way—'

'The second he was inside, he was gawping at a Merc, and he said, "This is what I'm talking about, Tommy." And you hitting him on the ear, you think that took me in? The truth, Tommy.'

'Darren Reilly . . . all right, I said I'd show him the cars, but . . . he'd know it wouldn't be wise to go breaking into them. Because he'd know who owns them.'

'And who would that be?'

'Brock Taylor. I swear, I know I lied before, but

121

I'm telling the truth now, Brock owns them, all over the city, it's big business, hot cars, do them up, reconditioning, new plates, all this. I used to . . . years ago . . . the one in Woodpark was the first. Near where your da's garage used to be.'

'What's that supposed to mean? What's my da got to do with it?'

'When I worked for your da, well, Brock used work there too. That's where he started, robbing cars. *You* remember—'

'I don't remember, and I don't care, Tommy. My father's dead and gone, he has nothing to do with any of this.'

Tommy was ready to come back at me, but he thought better of it; he shook his head and grimaced.

'All right, all right. I'm sorry, Ed, I know I fucked up here, big time.'

'What did you think was going on with Emily Howard? I mean, after the grief with your daughter, did you not stop to think about what the other women were going through?'

Tommy, shamefaced, made his best attempt at a shrug.

'I suppose I thought they were over eighteen. I wasn't around for any of the filming.'

'You were just going to get your cut of the ransom money and pay the Reillys off.'

Tommy nodded.

'And then what? Hardcore pornography, blackmail, murder, and then what? Live happily ever after?'

Tommy bit his lip. He looked as if he was about to cry.

'It was for my daughter, for Naomi. I'd nothing

to do with the murder, Ed, you know I could never—'

'Don't hide behind your daughter, Tommy. Naomi didn't borrow money from thugs. Naomi didn't force other women to have sex on camera. Get out of the car.'

'Ed?'

'You know where we are?'

Tommy looked around.

'Town somewhere. Near Baggot Street?'

'Fitzwilliam Square. You know who lives across the road?'

I pointed at one of the red-brick four-storey Georgian houses across the street, their sash windows reducing in size as the floors reached the roof.

'No.'

'You sure?'

'No, I told you.'

'Your old friend Brock Taylor lives there. They had his house in the *Irish Times* property supplement, he's a prominent resident of the square, apparently. Maybe he'll be able to solve your problems. I can't do it any more, Tommy. By rights I should turn you into the cops. You're a liability I can't afford. Give me your key. I want you out of the house. Out of my sight.'

'Please, Ed,' Tommy said. 'The Reillys would have killed me—'

I pushed a fifty into his hand for cab fare and leant across him and opened his door, and when he didn't move, I pushed him out. He threw his key in the window and limped across the street, and came briefly to a stop in front of Brock Taylor's house, triggering a security light. For a moment he twisted and turned on the spot, like a moth drawn to the beam of a lamp. Then he shook himself loose, shook an angry two fingers my way, scuttled down a lane and vanished into the shadows.

10

I drove back along the coast roads and tried not to think about Brock Taylor and Tommy Owens and my father. By the time I pulled into my drive, I had succeeded: I was thinking about a cold Jameson and a warm bed when my phone rang. It was Shane Howard, and he didn't sound good.

'I'm here,' he said. 'The Guards will need to be called.'

'Why is that, Shane?' I said.

'Because Jessica . . . my wife is dead. I think she's been stabbed. I'm here.'

'You think she's been stabbed?'

'Yes. I need to call the Guards.'

'Just before you do, Shane, tell me where "here" is. Are you at home?'

'No. I'm at the . . . house. The showhouse. I don't know the address. Somewhere in Bayview.'

Jessica Howard had been on her way to show a house when we parted. I rolled down the window. The night smelt of sulphur and the ooze of rotting leaves. I tossed the Reillys' Sig Sauer into a holly bush at the side of my house, pulled out of the drive and headed south towards Bayview.

'All right, Shane, look around the room, Jessica's bag, there'll be a prospectus, a leaflet with pictures

124

of the house somewhere, can you have a look for that?'

I heard some background sounds, and then Shane's voice again.

'I have it,' he said, his voice cracking. He made a long low sound, a sigh, or a moan, then he said, 'There's hardly any blood. I'll have to ask the Guards about that.'

'Just read out the address, Shane.'

He gave me the address of a house in a cul-de-sac off Rathdown Road.

'I'm nearly there, Shane; just sit tight till I reach you.'

'I have to call the Guards,' he said again.

'I'll call them for you,' I said.

I owed Dave Donnelly a phone call anyway.

*   *   *

I parked on the road and walked carefully through the darkened cul-de-sac: nine detached seventies bungalows in a U shape set around a raised oval of well-maintained green space. The showhouse was fourth on the left. I didn't have to count; Shane Howard had parked his Merc right up on the pavement, so the neighbours could take note of the registration; already someone had left a pink slip of paper beneath the windscreen. It read, 'This is not a public car park. Residents' cars only. Please do not park here again.'

The smart play would have been not to disturb the crime scene. But Shane was already in there. And besides, being an estate agent was as smart a play as you could make in Dublin these days, and all it got Jessica Howard was dead. She lay on the

125

maple floor of the large living room with two puncture wounds beneath her left breast. There was very little blood, the merest filigree on her blouse; rather more on her hands, where she must have tried to defend herself. Her legs were twisted and splayed, and her skirt was up around her thighs, but her stockings and underwear were intact; there were no obvious signs of sexual assault. Livid patches stretched across her chest and face; they were turning purple, which meant she probably had been dead for six hours or more. Around the time when Shane Howard claimed he had been rambling around the pine forest in Castlehill. I thought of Jessica Howard's beautiful, sad face that morning. 'I'm beyond therapy,' she had said. 'I'm out the other side.'

'Where's all her blood?' Shane said.

Last time I'd seen him, he'd been hunched in a ball on the floor in Rowan House; now he was sitting crouched on the steps that led from the hall down into the living room; it seemed like his great frame was buckling under the strain, like the earth was dragging him down.

'It looks like she was stabbed in the heart. When that happens, the bleeding is mostly internal. It probably means she died quickly, and without much pain,' I said, the latter without much conviction: I couldn't imagine any pain greater than knowing you were about to die.

Shane nodded blankly at me, then attempted a brave smile. I couldn't hold his gaze.

'We were about to separate. Already separated, really, about to start the old divorce thing. I held out. Hoped she'd come back. But she wanted to be free. Always did. No one could ever capture her.'

126

'Shane, why are you here?'

'She always told me where she was showing a house. In case she got into trouble. There was that one, in England, years ago, young one, just vanished, showing someone a house. And Jessica's on her own, no back-up, no office. Even though we were separated, I'd still look out for her. She'd call, or text, to say she was home. It was how we started really, she was always ending up in a jam with some lad, out on the street, or a gang of fellas at a party. Shane to the rescue. That's how she . . . and then throughout the marriage, she'd go off on a wander . . . lost weekend with some actor who'd end up thumping her . . . or some situation in a hotel, she crying down the phone . . . Shane to the rescue. Each time I'd forgive her. She made an awful fucking clown of me, I know that. But sure, what can you do?'

'Tell me you didn't kill her.'

'I didn't kill her. I remembered, up at Rowan House, that I hadn't heard from her. So I drove down to check. This is what I found.'

'The Guards will make you chief suspect, you know that.'

Shane looked at his dead wife, and nodded.

'Sure I have you, don't I? You can find the fucker who did this to her.'

'I can try.'

'Good man,' he said. 'And there's Dinny Finnegan. Let Dinny earn his fucking money for a change, the fat bastard.'

With that, he let his head sink back on to his chest.

*　　　*　　　*

I couldn't raise Dave Donnelly on his phone, so I rang him at home and got his wife, Carmel.

'Hey gorgeous. He can't talk to you. He's asleep.'

'It's only half-ten. What is he, getting old?'

There was a muffled growl and a shriek of laughter, and a crash, as if the phone had fallen on the floor. Carmel came back on the phone, her voice hoarse and breathy.

'For fuck's sake, Ed, it's a date night, our first in ages: now kindly fuck off and call him in the morning.'

'I'm sorry Carmel darlin', but it can't wait. Tell Dave Shane Howard's wife is dead, and I'm here with Howard at the crime scene.'

My voice must have carried across the bed. Dave came on the phone immediately. As I gave him the address I could hear Carmel wailing in frustration in the background. I ended the call and we went outside and sat in Shane Howard's Mercedes until the cops arrived.

*   *   *

Superintendent Fiona Reed got the case. She was a hard-bodied woman in her thirties, with short red hair and a constant air of irritated disapproval which I had never managed to dispel. She took a quick look at the body, and then, as the crime-scene examination team from the Garda Technical Bureau went to work, with photographers and fingerprint and mapping and forensics officers in their white protective suits streaming under the blue-and-white tape that secured the house, and the State Pathologist

128

expected, Fiona Reed leant in through the car window and told me to get out.

'I want to talk to Mr Howard. And Dave Donnelly wants to talk to you. Seafield station.'

I was distracted by a flashbulb, and turned to see a press photographer across the road and a camera crew arriving. I turned back to Superintendent Reed, but before I had time to formulate the thought, she had a defensive finger in my face.

'I don't know where the fuck the leak is, but it's not coming out of Seafield. It could be the Technical Bureau, it could be the NBCI, but when I find the fucker, I'll have him gutted and spayed. Answer your question?'

'Yes ma'am,' I said, grinning at what I took to be a minor victory.

She turned to summon a couple of uniforms to deal with Shane Howard, then turned back and gave me a big grin.

'By the way, you're fucked, Loy. And Dave agrees. This time, you're fucked, once and for all. And not *before* time.'

As I walked down towards my car, Denis Finnegan was sailing up the cul-de-sac in another vast black Mercedes. The Howards must've bought them by the fleet.

*   *   *

In Seafield station, I was led to a draughty interview room with faded yellow walls and threadbare grey carpet tiles. There were several televisions on the wall with VCRs and cameras, presumably for filming suspect interviews: new

129

since the last time I'd been hauled in. I was expecting Detective Inspector Dave Donnelly; when Detective Sergeant Sean Forde came in, I knew Dave was really pissed off at me.

Forde was about thirty, with one of those fake country accents guards from Dublin often affect; he had the grave dignity and self-importance and feeble wit of a provincial bishop; and since he had been appointed to the area, it appeared that he had taken it upon himself personally to give me a hard time, perhaps at Fiona Reed's behest. In appearance, Forde was a red man; there was no way around it. He had the remnants of carrot-coloured red hair tufted in a seemingly random arrangement on a small pink skull; his face was an alarmingly high shade of burgundy, like a whiskey tan, or severe sunburn; his hands were mottled with port blotches and spots.

'Well Mr Loy, in the wars again, hah? How'd you get that on your face, carving knife slip, did it?'

Carving knife. David Brady. They didn't give that out on the news. This is a fishing expedition. Keep your cool, Loy.

And then Dave came in.

There was a book once about a guy who took to making every decision in his life on the throw of a dice. I never read the book, because I figured the idea was so brilliant that any mere recounting of it could only be a disappointment. But it haunted me down the years, and there were times in my life when it seemed to me that I might as well have been that guy. I thought those times were done. Not so, to judge from what emerged from my mouth next. Dave Donnelly sat down at an angle to Sean Forde, just as I leant across the table

130

between us and told Forde to fuck himself.

'Ah, would you ever go fuck yourself,' I said.

The effect was, predictably, instantaneous: Sean Forde leapt up and came over the table at me, his astonished eyes burning with fury; I was on my feet when Dave flashed his great hand between us and brought Forde's flight to an abrupt stop; he turned to me and yelled, 'Sit down, Ed.'

Maybe if Dave had worn clothes that fitted him, he wouldn't always have looked like he was about to explode in some awesome fit of rage. But for reasons best known to himself, and even when he hadn't been dragged out of bed, he invariably dressed like he had tonight, in a pale blue shirt straining at the chest with its flaps hanging over his belt, flat-fronted grey trousers skintight on his huge thighs and a fawn sports coat that barely covered his waist. Still, he was right to be angry. Forde may have been on my case, but he was only Reed's monkey; the fact that Dave Donnelly and I were friends rankled with her, and I knew she gave Dave a hard time over it too. And I was tired, and wondering whether I had treated Tommy too harshly, and my blood felt like there wasn't a drop of alcohol left in it. Still, none of that was any excuse for acting like a gobshite.

'Don't be acting the bollocks now,' Dave said to me. Was it my imagination or did I see a flicker of amusement in his eyes? I knew he couldn't stand the sight of Forde. If there had been a flicker, it was gone in an instant, replaced by a heavy-browed glare. I glared right back. Go in like a gobshite, maintain like a gobshite.

Forde was up and inserting a video cassette into one of the VCRs and turning on a TV and

131

pressing a remote control. I arranged my face so it looked expressionless, which wasn't easy, as the tape was showing CC footage of the foyer of the Waterfront apartment complex and the time was lunchtime of the day just gone. You could see the estate agent with his stupid spiked-fin haircut opening the door. And then you could see me walk in, wave my keys and head straight for the elevator. Sean Forde freeze-framed it on me as the elevator doors opened and I stepped inside; then he turned around and set his boiled-lobster face in a victory leer.

'Would you like to explain what you were doing there, Mr Loy?' Dave said.

I looked blankly at him. Maybe they had footage inside the elevator, or in the corridor outside David Brady's room, in which case lying now would be a bad move. On the other hand, if they had anything better than this, Dave wouldn't have been on a date night with Carmel; he would have had uniforms outside my house.

'Me? Doing where?'

'The Waterfront apartments. Where David Brady's body was found today.'

I nodded, then looked puzzled.

'You think that's me?' I said.

The camera must have been positioned inside the door, facing the elevator. Because the only visible part of me throughout the shot was of the back of my head.

'That *is* you,' Forde said.

I shrugged.

'It looks like a man in a dark coat. I know I look like a man in a dark coat too, but I'm not sure there aren't a lot of us about. More and more as it

132

gets into winter.'

'Your client, Shane Howard. Brady was his daughter's ex-boyfriend. Did you find her?'

'I did.'

'Good for you. Now, what were you doing at the Waterfront apartments on the day he was murdered?'

I shook my head, as if there was nothing I could add to what I had already said. I was trying to work out whether the camera could have caught me in the corridor outside the apartment, or on my way down in the elevator. In theory, CCTV is an exact science, but in practice management companies install the equipment and then frequently skimp on running it properly by only inserting tapes or discs in random cameras, or by disabling the recording equipment altogether, in order to save money. Dave said nothing either. Silence wasn't usually his interview technique of choice, but I got the feeling this interview was Fiona Reed's set-up; silence wasn't often my favoured option either, but after the day I'd had I was too wrecked to do much other than sit there. It might have helped if Sean Forde had something to offer. As it turned out, he had quite the opposite.

'The timing is 12.45 p.m.,' he announced excitedly. 'Time of death has been confirmed as being no earlier than 12.50 and no later than 1.45. This puts you securely in the frame for the murder, Loy. What do you have to say to that?' His voice had built to a shrill little toy-dog bark; his face was like a neon beetroot.

I looked at Dave, but he had found something of great interest to study on the floor by his chair. I could only assume Forde had dreamt this nonsense up himself, on the off chance half my brain had slipped out my ear at some point during the day.

'Is that all?' I said.

'You haven't answered me,' Forde said.

'Of course I haven't. A, I wasn't there. B, if I had been, I wouldn't have killed my client's daughter's boyfriend. C, even if I had, unless he was blown up, or shots or screams were heard, or the murderer broke the victim's watch and you know for a fact he broke it in the act, you have no way of estimating time of death to that narrow a time slot—and no way of *confirming* it at all. We all know that, apart from the people who make the TV cop shows so we can all get a decent night's sleep. Which is what I want to do, so can I go home now, please?'

Dave Donnelly rolled his eyes at Forde; it was quick, and easy to miss it, but I didn't; neither did Sean Forde. It was hard to say whether he blushed or not, but he mopped his brow, and it wasn't a hot night. He stood up and fumbled with the VCR and rewound the tape and played it from about an hour earlier that day. This time a large man with sandy-coloured hair and an unmistakable lumbering gait ploughed through the lobby. As if to ensure that there should be no doubt, when he reached the elevator doors, he turned around to see if anyone was following him. It was clear, even on the blurred CCTV image, that it was Shane Howard.

Someone once said about Hollywood that if you can fake sincerity there, you've got it made. I didn't have to fake surprise after seeing the footage of Shane Howard on his way up to David Brady's apartment; nor did I think anything other than that he could easily have been guilty—the

134

body had been warm to the touch when I got there, no rigor, it all fitted. But what kind of day was he having, rushing out to murder David Brady, then dashing across town to kill his wife? What had possessed him? My brain wouldn't process it. Dave Donnelly was saying something, but I didn't hear what it was.

'I'm sorry,' I said.

'Can you help us with any of this?' he said.

'I can not,' I said. 'When I spoke to Shane Howard this morning, he identified his daughter splitting up with David Brady as one of the possible causes of what he saw as her personal decline. He seemed to hold Brady in high regard.'

'Maybe after you left, he got some news?'

'Maybe he did. After I spoke with him, I saw his wife for about an hour, then I came back up to his house to collect my car, and I saw him taking off at high speed. His receptionist said he didn't come back all day.'

'You should have told us that before.' Dave stood up.

'I was busy with other things,' I said. It sounded lame, even to my ears. 'Later on, I saw Shane Howard at his sister's house. When he saw the news reports of David Brady's murder, he was very upset.'

'Did he say where he had been in the interim?'

'He said he went for a walk, and had a few drinks in a pub. He said the stress of his daughter's absence was getting to him.'

'Don't talk to one of my officers like that again, Mr Loy. Or things will get very complicated for you around here.'

'Are you—'

135

'We're following a definite line of inquiry,' Dave said. 'Sergeant Forde. Maybe best to employ language the man understands. Tell Mr Loy to go and fuck himself.'

*　　　*　　　*

My car was parked on the street; I waited there in case Dave wanted to talk to me, or give me a full-scale bollocking; five minutes later I saw his car tearing out of the station at speed. Maybe there'd been a third murder. Or maybe he was hoping Carmel might still be awake.

*　　　*　　　*

I had a brief phone conversation with Denis Finnegan. Shane was arrested under Section 4 of the Criminal Justice Act, which entitled the Guards to hold him for six hours. They could extend this by another six hours before any charges were brought, but Finnegan was hoping they could avoid this. He said he'd be in touch in the morning. There was a message from Sandra asking me to call her, but I didn't. I'd had enough of the Howards for one day.

When I got home, I poured an absurdly large Jameson and opened a bottle of Guinness and drank them standing in the dark of my kitchen. The back garden was washed in the ghostly spray of a neighbour's security light. The male and female apple trees were bent beneath their weight of ripe and rotting fruit. I knew how they felt. On the up side, I had found Emily, and I had identified at least some of Shane Howard's

136

blackmailers, even if one of them was a friend of mine; on the down side, my client was in police custody, being questioned over two murders, and I wasn't at all sure he didn't deserve to be charged with them. I wondered whether Shane Howard had suddenly discovered his wife had been having an affair with David Brady and killed them both. I wondered who David Brady had emailed Emily's sex film to. I wondered if Brock Taylor had anything to do with any of it, and if Sean Moon really had paid the Reillys, if he was a major player and not the overgrown child he appeared to be. And I wondered who had sent me the mass card for Stephen Casey, and who he was to the Howards, and how he had died.

I sent Dave Donnelly a text message reading:

1. Sorry about that, Chief.
2. Stephen Casey RIP All Souls' Day 1985. Any bells? Loy.

There was a blinking light on my home phone. The message was from my ex-wife's new husband. She wanted me to know she had gone into labour. She wanted me to hear the news before anyone else. I didn't want to know, and I didn't want to hear the news, and I didn't drink to her or him or the child they would have together or the happiness I didn't wish for them. I just drank, until finally the whiskey made me think there was almost something funny about it all. Then I almost laughed at it. Then I remembered I had tossed the Reilly brothers' gun in a holly bush, and went outside and retrieved it. Then I lay on the living-room couch that was long enough to pass out on

137

without fucking up your back, kicked off my shoes
and went to sleep.

II

All Saints' Day

When there's trouble in a family, it tends to show up in the weakest member. And the other members of the family know that. They make allowances for the one in trouble . . . because they know they're implicated themselves.

Ross Macdonald, *Sleeping Beauty*

11

The beating of wings woke me at six; there had been crows on the chimney stack and on the window sills the past few mornings. I lay there for a while listening to the asthmatic sound of their breath, waiting for the cawing to begin, but they kept their counsel. I undressed, showered and, with some difficulty, shaved; my face bled a little, but it was in one piece, although the wound did make me look a little like the bad guy in a black-and-white movie. I dressed and cut two oranges into quarters and ate them while I scrambled three large eggs with butter and chives and had them with a few slices of smoked salmon and two cups of coffee. I took two Nurofen Plus for my hangover and another two for my face and for the ache in my hand where Emily Howard bit me.

Outside was dawning the kind of day I always remembered All Saints' Day as having been: the overcast morning after, grey and gloomy and precarious, as if the world was a smoke-filled globe made of fragile glass that could shatter at any moment. The pungent smell of fireworks lingered, like cordite after a shoot-out. Above the low rumble of traffic I heard the brisk rustle of crows in the holly bushes; black and grey against the glistening red berries; they took my appearance as a cue to begin their arrhythmic dirge. The newspapers had been delivered; I picked the pile off the doorstep and put them on the passenger seat of the car. The phone rang as I left the house; it was Denis Finnegan to say the Guards had extended Shane's period of detention for another six hours. At lunchtime, they could either charge him or release him. I had a lot to do before then. Grey dawn bled imperceptibly into day as I got the Volvo on the road.

The stop–start motion of cars on the N11 to Ranelagh gave me plenty of time to scan the headlines, which, in the tabloids, were dominated by the two murders. Jessica Howard took precedence, of course, and a couple of the tabloids printed her photograph alongside a shot of Esther Martin, a woman who had been killed in her home a year or so back. The Guards had arrested her husband several times but had been unable to bring charges: placing the photographs of the two murdered women side by side made it clear, not only that the Guards believed Shane Howard to be guilty, but that they had no qualms about leaking their belief to the media. Amid the appropriately pious tone of the reports, there was considerable leeway for a more salacious emphasis: Jessica had played Sally Bowles in *Cabaret* some years back, and the *Irish Times* was the only paper that didn't find an excuse to feature a photograph of the actress spilling out of tight black 1930s underwear. Instead, the *Times* led with stories about a public-sector pay rise and a European trade directive, relegating both murders to page two, where Jessica Howard was noted as the daughter-in-law of Dr John Howard; the photograph they used showed her peering primly out from beneath a shawl in *Riders to the Sea*.

There was an ostensibly sympathetic account of Jessica's career in the *Irish Independent* that read as if written in code, with references to the 'exceptionally close professional relationships' she had formed with her directors.

David Brady's rugby achievements were recorded and several ex-players—including some of Shane Howard's former international teammates—pitched in with their eulogies; a couple suggested that perhaps latterly, Brady was beginning to see his future outside full-time professional rugby, a tactful way of saying that he hadn't lived up to his youthful promise—or that he had blown his talent up his nose.

I turned left on Appian Way and cut up through Ranelagh village and stopped at the corner of a leafy square on the way to Rathmines. David Manuel lived in a Victorian three-storey red-brick house with stained-glass panes in the front door and a tangle of bicycles and rucksacks and trainers in the wide hall and a wife with salt-and-pepper curls and purple dungarees who directed me up the bookshelf-lined stairs to his attic floor office, which was decorated in cream and oatmeal tones with floor-to-ceiling bookshelves too, and roof windows that would have let in all the morning light if there had been any.

David Manuel, waiting, in his fifties, wore a three-quarter-length cardigan in assorted shades of green and a pale-green collarless linen shirt and matching trousers and olive-green Birkenstocks; his silver hair was shoulder length; his tiny face was lined but soft and unmarked, like a nun's; he steepled his fingertips and smiled thinly at me through silver-framed glasses. I mopped my brow with the back of my hand; the sweat stung the teeth-shaped wound Emily Howard had left there.

'Dr Manuel, Ed Loy.'

'I'm not a doctor—'

'I know that,' I said. Sweat smarted in my eyes, and I wiped them with my sleeve. Manuel looked at me quizzically.

'Maybe you need a doctor. Are you ill?' he said. His voice was high-pitched, querulous and amused. 'You look too fit to have a heart condition.'

First rule with therapists: don't get caught in a lie you can't conceal.

'I probably had too much to drink yesterday. Last night.'

'Don't you remember which?'

'Both.'

'And the face wound, that was a fight?'

'Yes.'

'And all of this, the drinking, the fighting, it has to do with Emily Howard? Or is it just how private detectives behave, or how they think they're meant to behave?'

'The drinking just has to do with me. The fighting, yes, that had to do with the case.'

'And this case: is it the same one the Guards are investigating, the murders of Jessica Howard and David Brady?'

'I think it's connected to those murders, yes.'

'Are you a fully licensed private detective?'

'I was. In LA. When the licensing system kicks in here, I'll apply for one.'

'And Shane Howard hired you?'

'Initially. Now his sister Sandra has. I suppose I'm working for both of them.'

'But you're more concerned with Emily Howard.'

'I'm concerned with all the Howards.'

Manuel looked at me, nodded, and sat back. I

144

took him through Emily's disappearance, the porn, the relationships with David Brady and with her cousin Jonathan. When I had finished, he sat still for a while, then shook his head.

'I can't tell you anything she hasn't already told you.'

'But you can tell me what you *think*.'

David Manuel angled his head from side to side, as if weighing up his options.

'I think Emily, to use a not very technical term, has been acting out. And acting out is not inconsistent with anger at her parents. And that anger may have many causes.'

'Might one of the causes be sexual abuse?'

Manuel said nothing, so I went on.

'Her aunt told me Emily's mother was abused as a child. She certainly seemed to have an extremely competitive attitude to her daughter when it came to sex. And the fact that Emily let herself be photographed and filmed having sex, well, I've dealt with girls who've gone into that world. You could say the porn industry is based on a whole bunch of angry, abused women "acting out". And we ignore their pain and pretend to believe them when they say they're reclaiming the control that was stolen from them, that they're "empowered". Already degraded as children, we become complicit in their further degradation as disturbed, malformed adults; we're like the keepers in an asylum, raping the patients over and over again and insisting they're in charge.'

'You're a moralist, Mr Loy.'

'Aren't you? Or can you not tell me about that either? Was Emily Howard sexually abused?'

'I don't know, is the truth.'

145

'Do you know what she *thought*?'

'That, I certainly can't tell you.'

'This is a serious business.'

'And I assure you, I'm taking it seriously. I intend to talk to Emily as soon as possible. Depending on what she feels free to share—'

'What about Jonathan?'

Manuel put a hand up to his mouth, then instantly removed it; an echo, conscious or unconscious, of Jonathan O'Connor's inhibited mannerisms.

'I would say, that in many Irish families, going back through the years, the children who were abused and the children who weren't in many respects often resemble each other. They exhibit similar symptoms and vulnerabilities. And so it is very dangerous, even when a child—I'm talking about adult children, you understand, the child–parent relationship—it can be dangerous even when a tale of past abuse is raised, for the therapist automatically to assume that what is being recounted is the literal truth. Or alternatively, to believe someone's ferocious denials that no abuse took place, particularly when you've heard from that person's siblings that it most certainly did.'

'Why is that? Why would people believe they had been abused when they had not? Why would they deny it when it had occurred?'

David Manuel took off his glasses and polished them on a corner of his linen shirt.

'I believe it stems from . . . from a cultural legacy in this country, a legacy of deep-rooted worthlessness that was inculcated in the individual, and handed down through the generations. "Man hands on misery to man. It deepens like a coastal

146

shelf," as Larkin put it. The English enforced the idea that being Irish was an inferior state. The Catholic Church instilled a sense of fear and shame, not just about sex, about everything, about our very existence: work and pray, work and pray. Poverty, of course, a history of poverty played its part in undermining any sense we might have of our worth, of our personal identity. And the crawthumpers and bogtrotters who replaced the Brits, the pious fools and gombeens and Irish-language fanatics who told us we couldn't all expect to live in our own country, and then made sure half of us had to emigrate by their insularity and sheer bloody incompetence. All internalized by our parents and grandparents, always the same message: we're worth nothing, and we deserve less. And now, of course, we have money, and the Church is no longer a force, and we're still hiding behind the lies, we keep insisting nothing bad has happened, we live in determined, alcoholic furies of denial. "We're grand now," we laugh, with our legendary sense of humour. But you can't shake off all that . . . what is it the Catholic Church used to call its teaching?—"formation". You can't just get rid of it. It's, ah, "part of what we are".'

I wasn't sure I followed everything Manuel said, but I nodded just the same.

'I wouldn't have thought Larkin was the most inspiring laureate for a therapist,' I said.

'It depends what you think a therapist is,' Manuel said. 'People think therapists are all about dredging up what your parents did to you and then blaming them for it and feeling better about yourself as a result.'

'Isn't that what they *are* about? I see you've a

147

row of Alice Miller books there on the shelf. Emily had a bunch of them in her bedroom. Isn't that her M.O.? It's all Mummy and Daddy's fault? Every child a damaged child?'

'Well of course, in a way she's right. But that doesn't mean the parents are *to blame*.'

'You're speaking in riddles. Either someone is to blame or he isn't.'

'And now you're speaking like a cop. Look, in regard to the Howards, I think . . . I think if you want to know about what's going on in that family in the present, you need to be investigating the past, Mr Loy. It's not what Emily and her cousin did last week, or last year. It's what happened twenty, *thirty* years ago that counts.'

'Is that what Emily has been talking to you about?'

'As I said, I need to speak to Emily. If she agrees to what I ask . . . is it to you or the Guards I should talk?'

'Talk to me. I'm not just a cop. The Guards only care about the killer.'

'And what do you care about, Mr Loy?'

'Oh, I care about the killer too. But most of all, I care about the truth.'

*   *   *

I didn't know what to make of David Manuel. On the one hand he sounded like a columnist for a Sunday newspaper, with his elaborate theories and historical justifications for why the Irish are the most unhappy nation on earth; on the other, he seemed like he wanted to help, and was genuinely concerned about Emily Howard.

I had some more coffee in Ranelagh in one of those uncomfortable little shops with tiny metal tables and chairs and high stools all packed too close together. None of the serving staff was Irish. David Manuel might have said that something in our collective psyche prevented us from working in cafés, a post-colonial superiority complex that didn't permit us to wait on people without being obnoxious to them, perhaps. Whatever the reason, it was all to the good; the European staff were friendly and pleasant and didn't make you feel you were burdening them with your custom, or detaining them from more important pursuits like text-messaging their friends and rolling their eyes.

I leafed through the rest of the papers. Two things caught my eye: one was a follow-up item about a recent report into clerical child sex abuse in a rural diocese. It highlighted the way in which, time after time, when the original allegations had been made against priests who had turned out to be guilty of abuse, the local communities had automatically closed ranks—with the priest and *against* the accuser, ostracizing them within their own villages for daring to speak out. The other was an article about obstetricians and gynaecologists who had worked over the years in hospitals bound by a Catholic code of ethics, and detailed a number of incidents in which obstetricians had performed hysterectomies on women who might have had complications with future pregnancies; sterilization was against the Catholic 'ethos', and so removing the womb was seen as preferable. It also outlined a practice called 'symphysiotomy', which involved cracking and widening the pelvis of women who might require repeat Caesarean

149

sections. I couldn't work out if or why Caesarean sections were against the Catholic 'ethos' in themselves, but they were considered high-risk procedures in the past; the fear seemed to be that women, rather than take the risks, might employ some form of artificial contraception, or undergo sterilization. In practice, symphysiotomies gave women crippling bone injuries and permanent bowel and bladder problems; those who gave birth to further children were often left bedridden. Again, these barbarities were prescribed by the Church, but enforced enthusiastically by its many willing lay helpers.

Across the road, a mass was giving out; All Saints' Day was a holy day of obligation, but that didn't carry the force it had in former times; even though it was early enough for workers to attend, none of the people streaming out of the church was under sixty; most looked eighty. Maybe the good old days were coming to an end at last.

The article about medical practices named several obstetricians, most of them either dead or struck off; the list of names included Dr John Howard. The other name I noted was the writer's: Martha O'Connor.

*   *   *

Dave Donnelly phoned as I was driving south, and told me to meet him in the car park of the Castlehill Hotel. I parked beneath the aching trees and crunched across the gravel, through horse-chestnut shells and sycamore mulch, to his blue, unmarked car. I got in the passenger side, Dave flexing his massive neck right and left to make sure

150

no one was looking. Then he turned on me.

'You're some bollocks, Ed. You know what that kind of shit looks? Like you think you can do as you please because I'll protect you. Telling a DS to fuck off. Who the fuck do you think you are?'

'I'm sorry. I was tired.'

'Don't think Fiona Reed hasn't heard either. The word's gone out. That's everyone gunning for you, Ed, any excuse, speeding, drunk and disorderly, vagrancy—'

'Vagrancy?'

'Yeah. Walking while Loy. I'm telling you, you better have something to offer in all this or you're fucked. And I can do nothing. And even if I could, I wouldn't. And they're having the CCTV footage enhanced, so you're probably fucked anyway. You were there, weren't you?'

Instead of answering, I gave Dave everything I could on the Emily Howard kidnap. When I finished, he said, 'Were you at David Brady's place? Did you interfere with a crime scene?'

'How's it looking with Shane Howard?'

Dave looked at me hard, then waved a meaty hand in the air and snorted like a horse bothered by flies he knows he's bigger than but has to put up with.

'The killer was someone she knew,' he said.

'Or someone she was showing the house to—she was going to get close to strangers too, especially if they were men.'

'What have you got?'

'Her phone calls. I spoke to her about half-ten yesterday morning.'

'You were one of the last people to see her alive.'

'She took at least two business calls while I was

151

there, at least by her manner I assume they were business.'

'Her phone wasn't at the scene. We're waiting on the service provider to give us the details. Anything else?'

'Classy move, sticking Jessica Howard beside the Martin woman in the papers today.'

'Fiona Reed's call.'

'So Howard's the prime suspect then.'

'Of course he fucking is. Why? Because he's the *husband.*'

I once worked a case in LA for a husband the Hollywood cops were convinced had killed his wife who had been photographed in San Francisco's Chinatown signing a business deal at the moment his wife had been shot dead: neighbours heard the shots, and heard a car screeching away minutes afterwards, so the TOD was firm. The detective in charge of the case explained to me that even if the husband had been photographed signing a business deal *in China*, they'd still make him their prime suspect. When I asked him why, he told me if I'd ever been married, I'd understand the guy with most reason to kill his wife is always the husband. As it turned out, my client was guilty; he had killed his wife that morning and hired a petty hood to fire a gun in the air and drive away at the moment he was establishing his alibi. But someone had spotted the driver, and as soon as the cops caught him, he gave the guy up. Moral of the story, for the cops at any rate, and I was more of a cop than I was anything else: it's always the husband, even when it can't be.

'We know Jessica Howard liked to play away. She was a regular in the Sunday papers sure, in some nightclub with some racing driver or footballer. Maybe she pushed Howard too far. Maybe David Brady was the last straw, his daughter's ex-boyfriend. That's not right, is it? His blood is up, he has to do it. He's over to Brady's flat, does him, then charges back up to Castlehill and kills his wife.'

'You haven't enough, have you?'

'That would be an operational matter.'

'In other words, no.'

'In other words, fuck away out of the car before someone spots me talking to you,' Dave growled.

'Anything on Stephen Casey?' I said.

He handed me a three by five index card with a name and number on it.

'That's the man who worked the case.'

'What case?'

'You can find out. Now get out of the car.'

I shut the car door and Dave started the engine. As he was about to pull away, I leant in the passenger window.

'Dave, get Brady's hard drive on his computers analysed. His emails, who he sent attachments to.'

'Why?'

'Just do it. Look for home-made porn films, and follow who he sent them to.'

'Ed, were you there? You were fucking there, weren't you?'

'Thanks Dave,' I said, and meant it. 'I'll give you what I get as soon as I can.'

'I can't keep looking out for you if you're hell-bent on acting like a cunt,' Dave said, and drove away without meeting my eye.

12

I walked quickly back to my car beneath the lowering sky. My first idea was to brace Sean Moon. I drove slowly through Woodpark. Waiting at the lights by the Woodpark Inn, I saw Jonathan O'Connor crossing the main road and entering the car park towards the lounge. He wore a long black overcoat and a black baseball hat, and he walked with a swagger I hadn't seen in him before.

I drove on down into Honeypark as the mist was blowing in again. At least mist was what I thought it was first. Then I amended it to fog, thick and grey, belching across the sky. I passed the three massive bonfire sites, two of which were still smoking; some of the houses nearest the bonfires had blown-out windows; a couple had scorched walls and melted drainage pipes. The fog was gusting through the air, dark, almost black, and there was a heat to it, and then, as I rounded the corner for Moon's house, a red glow behind it, I saw it wasn't fog at all, it was smoke: Sean Moon's house was ablaze, and a ring of onlookers shielded themselves from the heat as it went up. I could hear sirens. I parked and approached on foot as a Garda car, an ambulance and the fire service arrived. A round man with no neck in a round-neck pullover with a newspaper rolled beneath his arm on the edge of the crowd was pulling ferociously on a short, squat cigarette and making a succession of knowing faces and noises, all of which seemed intended to indicate that nothing he was seeing came as a surprise to *him*.

'Just go up, did it?' I said.

'If you want to believe that, you're welcome, bud,' No Neck said.

'What do you mean, it was started deliberately?'

'And if you want to put words in my mouth, that's another thing.'

He took a step towards me, scowling, his eyes watering. He smelt of stale smoke and fresh booze and despair at nine thirty in the morning. I fronted off a little, turning my head so that he'd notice the wound on my face. He noticed it, and stepped back.

'Was there anyone in there?' I asked. 'Was Moon there?'

'Moon? Why would Moon be there? Fuckin' runner-in.'

'I thought he owned the house. I was talking to him there yesterday.'

'Were you now?' No Neck suddenly sounded interested. 'What about, bud? The blue movies, was it?'

'What do you know about the blue movies?'

'I heard they were shooting them in there. Young ones, in the nip. And they were going to be selling them. Is that true?'

'It might be,' I said. 'But listen, if Moon doesn't own the house, who does?'

No Neck's face went blank, as if a switch had been flicked to close it down. I found a five-euro note in my pocket and wafted it at him. His eyes clicked on like two balls of a fruit-machine jackpot.

'No names. But it's well for some who can be buying pubs and houses all round here, and drinks on the house up the rugby club for all the nobs. Well for fuckin' some, isn't that right bud?'

Brock Taylor again. You couldn't keep him out of this. I gave No Neck the five. He grabbed my arm to thank me but I shook him loose, gave him a wink and a thumbs-up and doubled back to my car. I could hear No Neck calling after me as I walked through the smoke, a series of chants whose alternate refrains were 'Young ones in the nip' and 'Well for fuckin' some'.

I parked outside a semi-detached house within view of the Woodpark Inn. I had only been gone fifteen minutes; chances were Jonathan was still in there. After an hour I began to doubt it; after two I was ready to give it up as a bad job. It was just as well I didn't; about fifteen minutes later he came out, followed by Darren and Wayne Reilly. Wayne had a bandaged nose, I was happy to see. The three of them stood in the car park and nodded in a congratulatory kind of way at each other for a few minutes and then dispersed. The company he keeps.

*   *   *

On my way out to visit Dan McArdle, the retired Garda detective, I called Sandra Howard and apologised for not having been in touch sooner.

'That's all right. No one got much sleep here last night.'

'I can imagine. How is Emily faring?'

'She's very upset, as you can imagine. David Manuel is with her. He always has a calming effect. Ed, Denis said you were there. You saw the . . . body. Do you think Shane . . . ?'

'I don't know, Sandra. Is the answer. I don't know. But I'm working on the basis that he didn't.'

'You're still with us then. Thank God for that. Denis says he doesn't think they have enough to charge him.'

'That's probably right,' I said.

'Ed, I owe you an apology. For last night.'

'Which part of last night?'

'The slapping part.'

'Good. Because I'm not sorry about the other part.'

'Neither am I.'

We let that hang for a while.

'Ed?'

'I'm here.'

But not for much longer. The traffic was getting busy as I took the Tallaght exit off the M50, and I needed to concentrate on the road.

'I'm going to have to hang up in a minute, Sandra.'

'Stephen Casey,' she said.

'Yes?'

'Richard O'Connor, my first husband. He was married before. His wife was killed, stabbed to death by an intruder. Rock was injured. The man—boy really, he was only seventeen—the boy who killed her—'

'That was Stephen Casey?'

'Yes. He killed himself. Drove a car off Bayview Harbour. They found him on All Souls' Day, 1985. I couldn't . . . I should have told you, but with everything that had happened I just . . . didn't want to go back there. Do you understand, Ed?'

What was it David Manuel had said about the Howards? 'It's what happened twenty, *thirty* years ago that counts.'

'Of course I understand. I'll see you soon.'

157

I broke the connection as she began to ask me when. I didn't trust myself with Sandra Howard. I was glad she had told me about Stephen Casey, but I wasn't sure if she had told me everything. It was my job to find out, and it was probably wiser if I kept my distance while I did. I didn't want to keep my distance though, and I doubted very much that I would.

I drove out through a series of industrial estates and drive-in shopping parks. Housing developments fanned back towards the hills, and gleaming new apartment blocks were dotted along the main road, some with cranes still hovering above them. Between Tallaght and Jobstown, I turned off the road and pulled into a new apartment complex called Sycamore Fields. It had some desultory strips of landscaping around it, and about a dozen spindly sycamores wilting under the burden of the name; to one side there was a petrol station, to the other, a DIY warehouse. Dan McArdle buzzed me in, and was waiting on the eleventh floor when the elevator doors opened. His apartment was not as high-end as David Brady's—the fixtures and fittings were cheaper, and the furniture was basic and functional—but it was more like it than not; there was a dormitory feeling that this was a roof beneath which to sleep, not a home in which anyone would want to live, or certainly not for any length of time. Dan McArdle, steel-grey hair gleaming, in a brown three-piece suit, shirt and tie and carpet slippers, told me to take a seat at the dining table, itself a mere step from the kitchen and living areas. While he was making tea I hadn't asked for, through the walls I could hear a shower

158

running, a TV tuned to a news channel and a woman having a tortured telephone conversation with an errant boyfriend. The neat, clean room smelt of smoke and fried food and pine air freshener. McArdle presented me with a mug of tea and a digestive biscuit and sat opposite me with the same.

'Nice place,' I said.

'Fantastic, isn't it?' he announced heartily, in a rich old buttermilk-thick Dublin accent. 'The wife died, and I was roaming around the semi, no kids, so I sold the thing, got a great price, bought three of these yokes, live in one, rent out the other two, great investments, on top of the Garda pension, not too bad at all.'

He dunked his digestive in his tea and sucked at it. He was maybe seventy, silver-thatch eyebrows, dark-grey eyes, jutting chin smooth and glowing with aftershave; his jacket sagged on his big frame, and his shirt was loose around the folds of his shrinking neck: a physically powerful man getting used to the diminution of his powers, or to something worse. As if he could read my thoughts, he produced a packet of Major cigarettes and pulled an ashtray between us.

'Lung cancer. They can do shag all, excuse me French, except tell me to stop. They can shag off, am I wrong?'

He lit a cigarette, took a long drag and then coughed for a few minutes. I went to the sink and got him a cup of water—I couldn't find a glass. He drank the water and put his cigarette back in his mouth, I lit a cigarette of my own and we sat for a while, smoking. The noise from the other apartments was so loud and clear it seemed to be

159

coming from the very room we were in, but McArdle seemed inured to it, maybe even grateful for it, occasionally tapping his fingers to TV jingles or raising an eyebrow in mock sympathy if the girl on the phone yelled or cried especially plaintively.

'I was hoping you might tell me something about Stephen Casey.'

'So the bould Dave said. You were buddies from way back, is that so? Well, Dave was the first man to the house that time, hadn't been a wet day on the job and I didn't think he'd last after seeing what he seen, that's the God's honest truth.'

'Which house was this?'

'Doctor O'Connor's up in Castlehill, in a cul-de-sac there, just down from the hotel. The lad knocked on his door late, about nine it would have been. It was just getting dark, early autumn, August, September. Maybe they shouldn't have opened it at all. But sure, it was a doctor's house, used to callers, and anyway, who wouldn't've answered the door back in those days? It's only today we think like that.'

'So they opened the door,' I prompted. Like many lonely people, when he had a chance to speak he was eager to take full advantage of the opportunity by cramming in as many digressions and editorials as he could.

'The wife opened the door—Audrey her name was—and there was this lad in an anorak with a balaclava on, and he must have stabbed her there and then, straight through the heart, two or three times, nice clean job, very little blood, forcing her back into the hall and kicking the door shut behind him. From what he told us, the husband came out next, and tried to save the wife, getting in front of

160

her. He got slashes to the hands for his trouble, and a wound on his right side. The lad forced him back into the cupboard under the stairs and locked the door, then he went through the front rooms and filled a bag with silverware and ornaments. That was it really. Oh, and all O'Connor's rugby medals, mounted on a board.'

'That was it? No jewellery, no safe?'

'He didn't stay around long enough. Don't know why. Only thing we could think, he was put off because the O'Connors' ten-year-old daughter woke up and came down the stairs.'

'So Casey could kill a woman no bother, baulked at killing a man and bungled the robbery rather than harm a ten-year-old girl? He couldn't even tie her up?'

'That was all we could come up with, son.'

'Did the girl say anything?'

'She tried to call us, after Casey had left. But he cut the phone lines. She had to go out, in her nightdress, smeared in her mother's blood, because of course she tried to wake her mammy up, across the road and get the neighbours to ring the Guards. God love her.'

'And then what happened?'

'And then, nothing: no witnesses, no leads, nothing. And a month or so later we found young Casey dead at the wheel of a stolen car. Drove off the harbour wall at Bayview. At the deepest part. He'd been missing all that time. And in the boot of the car, all the stuff that had been stolen from the O'Connor home. Apart from the rugby medals, they never showed up.'

'Very neat.'

'That's what we thought.'

161

'Autopsy? Was he dead before he hit the water?'

'Post-mortem putrefaction had been speeded up too much for any satisfactory examination to be carried out.'

'Very neat part two. And you got the glory.'

'All tied up in a nice neat bow. Stepped up to inspector. End of story.'

'And was it the end of the story? Or was there more that got brushed under the carpet?'

McArdle pressed his lips shut, plumped up his bird's-nest eyebrows and looked at me through eyes that still glowed with quiet menace. That must have been a pretty intimidating look back in the day.

'You did what you had to do. Open and shut. No sense bringing in a lot of for instances. Especially not given the people involved. And it was only later that you really began to wonder about them.'

'For instance?'

McArdle lit another cigarette, hummed along briefly to the piercingly loud theme tune of a sitcom from a neighbouring apartment, then stared at his hand and began counting off on his fingers.

'For instance, Stephen Casey was a pupil at Castlehill College and was in Sandra Howard's French class, where he was considered a favourite of hers. Where some of his classmates thought there was more than a teacher–pupil relationship between them.

'For instance, Dr Rock was a part-time senior rugby coach at Castlehill, and Stephen Casey was prop forward on the first team.

'For instance, Sandra and Dr Rock, who survived the attack which saw his wife slaughtered with

162

relatively and mysteriously minor injuries, wed a mere two years later.

'For instance, Stephen Casey was the son of a single mother named Eileen who had been a servant for Dr John Howard and family up in Rowan House until the doctor's death; the Howards paid for Casey's education.

'For instance, after Stephen Casey's death, his mother Eileen—a servant as I say—suddenly had the money to buy a house in Woodpark, and married shortly after.'

Having used up the fingers and thumb of one hand, McArdle made it into a fist and drove it into the palm of its twin, showering cigarette ash above us like funereal confetti. Then he stood up and went to a cupboard and took a bottle of Jameson and two glasses and brought them to the table.

'I usually have my first around about now,' he said. 'Will you join me?'

It was twenty-five past twelve, but I nodded immediately: my heart was pounding and adrenalin was coursing through me, my brain racing at the implications of what McArdle had just told me.

'Dave D told me you were a sound man for the gargle,' he said approvingly.

He had poured two straight shots, and we both lowered them in one. McArdle leant across the table then, his dark eyes flaring red and watery.

'See now son, what I told you there. I don't even know if there's anything to it. Compared to some of the things I seen. Say nothing, isn't that right? They should've had it embroidered on the uniform.'

He poured another for himself, picked up a

163

remote-control handset, and pointed it at a widescreen television, flicking through the channels until it arrived at an old western starring James Stewart, one of those fifties ones where his face looks twisted with hatred and fear, haunted by the past, by what he did, or failed to do. He turned the volume up so that it dampened out the spectral manifestations from the neighbouring souls.

'Ah, the bould Jimmy. This is me now. Good luck there son. God bless.'

I got up and went to the door, then thought of something.

'Just one last thing. The ten-year-old girl who saw her mother killed. Do you remember her name?'

McArdle frowned, muted the sound on the TV.

'Say again, son?'

I repeated the question.

'Mary, I think. No. Marie? No, Martha. Martha O' Connor. She does be on the television now, sometimes, making documentaries, sticking it to the Church and all. Fine big girl. Mouth on her. Writes for some paper or other, I don't know, these days I just get them for the telly. But that was her name all right, Martha O'Connor.'

13

I bought an *Evening Herald* at a set of traffic lights coming out of Tallaght from a vendor weaving between the lanes. Its headline didn't need much deciphering: above shots of Jessica Howard, Shane Howard and David Brady blared the words

'DEADLY TRIANGLE?' The phrase was prime tabloidese, as banal as it comes, yet it set off a geometrical ricochet in my head, resonating across twenty years to the deadly triangle that haunted Dan McArdle to this day. I tried to remember what I had seen in Sandra Howard's eyes the first time I mentioned Stephen Casey's name: fear, or grief, or deception? I wondered whether she had acted on her attraction for me to quash her own sad memories, or whether she had fucked me on the stairs to tame me and draw my sting, whether, having run the Howard family for twenty years, she thought she could run me too. And I wondered, at some base level I didn't much like thinking about, which of those motives I found the greater turn-on.

Nearing Seafield, the Jameson started setting off chemical explosions in my stomach. I parked below the Seafront Plaza, got a roast-beef-and-pickle bagel and a bottle of beer and took them back to the car. Fog was rolling in now; I couldn't see either of the great piers, let alone the water in the bay. I made some calls between bites: leaving a message for Martha O'Connor at her newspaper to call me on the subject of Dr John Howard, and asking David Manuel to check in with me once he had spoken to Emily Howard. There was a message from Denis Finnegan waiting when I hung up: Shane Howard had been released. I drove through Bayview and up the hill by the harbour, and parked a little way down from the surgery. I navigated the narrow road with difficulty; there were two Mercedes S-series saloons and a BMW parked outside. Irish people loved announcing their newfound prosperity through bigger and wider cars; it was a pity they hadn't spent a few shillings building roads for the cars to fit on, or wondered whether, if they wanted to live in old houses on quaint, windy roads, they should consider sizing their cars accordingly.

I walked up between the borders of rowan trees. Their gleaming berries seemed swollen, fit to burst. Before I knocked, Anita opened the door, her face rigid with fear; the red gems in her ring seemed a link with the berries, and I felt I followed them rather than her, the stones glowing, arterial, blood the sunken trigger to it all. At reception, Denis Finnegan appeared, and I began to reel slightly at the parallel to the previous morning's events. I showed him the cover of the *Evening Herald*, and he rolled his eyes and shook his head.

'It says a file is being prepared for the DPP,' I said.

'They're in no position to press for a prosecution. They can place him at both scenes, but there is no physical evidence so far, and, despite tabloid tittle-tattle, no motive, and therefore, in my opinion, from the Latin, fuck all case,' Finnegan said. 'I'm afraid Shane—'

Shane Howard emerged from his office. He wore a tweed jacket and brown cords that looked like he had slept in them; his face, drawn and pale, announced that he hadn't slept at all.

'Speak of the devil!' Denis Finnegan announced brightly, as if Howard's appearance was a delightful if unexpected surprise; his face registered irritation.

'Come in, Mr Loy. Denis, wait here.'

'Shane, I think it would be prudent if I were in the room—'

'Denis, you're giving me a pain in the hole. I

166

trust Loy. Come in, man.'

'If it's all the same to you, I'd prefer to talk outside. In the back garden?'

'Oh yeah?' Shane Howard said dubiously.

'Walls have ears,' I said. He smiled and tapped his nose.

'Right you be. Just find a coat.'

Shane Howard went into his office. Denis Finnegan came close to me.

'I take it what Shane tells you doesn't find its way into the ear of a certain detective inspector in Seafield,' he said.

'Take it how you want,' I said. 'You do your job and I'll do mine.'

Finnegan's face lost composure momentarily and a flash of dark rage creased his brow and glowed in his bulging little eyes. I pulled away from him as Shane Howard emerged from his office wearing a tan suede car coat.

'Let's go then,' he said.

I followed him downstairs through the stone-floored kitchen and out into the garden. He shut the back door behind us, turned to me and laughed.

'Dinny's face! Fucking priceless. Seen too much of that bollocks the last twenty-four hours.'

'I'm sure he's only trying to look out for you.'

'Are you? I'm not so fuckin' sure, not so fuckin' sure at all.'

'What do you mean? Do you think he's more interested in Rowan House, in your mother's will?'

Howard looked at me in astonishment. His large face had a tendency to pantomime his emotions: anger, surprise, amusement, all vivid as a cartoon character's.

167

'How'd you know about the will?'

'That's why he was here yesterday morning. He thought you wanted me to spy on Jessica, get something on her to maybe coax her into accepting less of a settlement. I told him the truth: I didn't know anything about the will.'

'Rowan House all comes to me. And you know something, I wish it didn't. Sandra's being very good about it, but I know how I'd feel if it all went to her.'

'Why don't you split it then, yourself?'

'That's what I might do, you know? I mean, how many houses can you live in? Jaysus.'

'Did Jessica have a plan for it?'

'She thought it should be razed to the ground, build apartments and houses there. Yield a fortune in this climate.'

'And Sandra disagreed?'

'We all know she wants to build a fourth tower. That's the dream. And the only place for it is where the house is. I just wanted to avoid the whole issue, to be honest, I wouldn't discuss it with anyone.'

Howard turned to me suddenly.

'Listen, I didn't kill them, all right? David Brady, Jessica. I didn't kill either of them. Not saying I didn't want to. Not even saying I wouldn't have, if I'd caught them together, if it had been true. But someone got to them first. I swear that's the truth.'

'Tell me what happened. You bolted out of the surgery like a madman.'

'Someone called me—'

'Man, woman?'

'Couldn't tell. Low voice, but light. Odd.'

'As if they were trying to disguise it?'

168

'Could have been. Tell the truth, *what* they said put out of my mind any thought of the *way* it was said.'

'And what did they say?'

'Your wife's sleeping with David Brady. She's at his flat right now.'

'And what did you do?'

'What I was supposed to do, I suppose. Someone's played me for a right cunt in all this—'

'What did you do?'

'Got in the car. Blemmed round to Brady's place. Up in the lift. And there he was, brains on the floor, great fucking knife in the chest.'

'So what did you do then?'

Howard exhaled, a massive sound, like a sleeping horse in the still night.

'Nothing. I was upset. I made a run for it. And then . . . like I told you. Wandered around Castlehill forest. So on. Got to Rowan House.'

'Did you not worry about Jessica's safety? Ring and see if she was OK?'

'I should have. I don't know why I didn't. I just panicked, you know? I couldn't think straight.'

'But the person who called you—they were trying to put you in the frame, right?'

'It looks that way.'

'Who do you think killed David Brady?'

'I don't know. Now I know what he got up to with Emily, I think I could have killed him myself.'

'Could Emily have done it?'

Howard shook his head.

'Not the girl I know.'

But, as we were finding out, that left a lot of room for manoeuvre.

'Who killed your wife, Shane?'

169

'I don't know. I don't know.'

We had reached the ornamental pond. I looked at the stones embedded in its walls.

'Do you know about those,' I said. 'Bloodstones?'

'Ah, that's that oul' crystals shite. Sandra put them in.'

'Sandra? Not Jessica?'

'No. Sure Jessica wouldn't spend a night in the surgery after we were married. She thought it was creepy. She insisted on the new house.'

'So this garden—'

'When I opened the surgery, Sandra had the pool set in. Mid-eighties, after the old man died. Said it was some kind of memorial.'

'To whom?'

'The old man, I assumed. Truth? I was playing rugby and trying to get established, get some patients, I didn't have the time to worry. In other words, I didn't give a shite.'

'And the stones?'

'I told you, it's some kind of New Age malarkey. Sandra was big into it. There was a while there, they'd all be going on about it, crystals with healing powers, and aromatherapy and all this. Terrible shite. In the chair, had to argue a few around, the women of course, how this or that natural healing gemstone or potion was all well and good but the old local would still be her best bet if she didn't want to pass out with the fucking pain.'

'Sandra told me Jessica had been sexually abused as a child. And Emily wears rings on her fingers with these bloodstones. They're supposed to make the wearer invisible. That's what people who've been abused say: either they feel invisible, like

170

they're not real, or they wish they *could* feel that way.'

Shane Howard's face had shifted completely: his reddening face was a mask of aggression, mouth and eyes bulging, like the second row he had been hurtling into a maul.

'What are you saying?'

I braced myself and kept on talking. 'I'm not accusing you of anything. I'm asking: the apparent lack of sexual inhibition, the full-on exhibitionist relationship with David Brady, the casual sex with her cousin, the precarious emotional and psychological state your daughter is in: is there a possibility she was abused too?'

Shane Howard came at me big but slow, full of rage, but with no strategy; his arms were spread out and flailing at my head; I ducked and grabbed his left forearm as he slapped my head with his right; I bent his left at the elbow and drove it hard behind his back and up, fast and hard until he dropped to his knees and tried to scream but couldn't, he was in such pain, held it just before the break.

'I've had just about as much as I can take on this case, I've been slapped and bitten and pistol-whipped and all because I'm trying to help you and your fucking family, so don't think about coming at me again, because you're too slow and you're too old and I'll have you, do you understand? DO YOU UNDERSTAND?'

He grunted a yes.

'Are you going to try and answer my questions?'

He nodded. I released his arm and shoved him away. He half walked, half ran to the rowan-tree border and hung on one of the trees, shaking a hail

171

of blood-red berries through the cold misty air, then turned, head bowed, massaging his left arm and shoulder. I looked back at the house, and saw Denis Finnegan's face looming out from an upstairs window; we locked eyes briefly, and then he vanished like steam on a pane. Shane Howard loped back towards me, almost grinning, like we had just clashed on the rugby field and he wanted to reassure me there were no hard feelings.

'Fair play. Lost it, understandable enough. Know you're only doing your job.'

'Answer the question, please.'

'Jessica abused, I never heard that. She never told me that. Why she'd tell Sandra and not me I don't know, unless it was one of those women's things. I mean, I knew she started early, thirteen or fourteen. She was always boasting about what she'd got up to as a teenager. And maybe that was an example for Emily. Started her off early too, the way her mother used to talk about . . . men, sex, all that. Pushed her into all this stuff she was doing with Brady, films and so forth. But in terms of . . . well, I never laid a finger on the child. And if someone else *did* . . .'

Howard shook his head, his body quivering with anger and unhappiness at the thought. I put a hand on his shoulder to signal that line of questioning was over. I was as relieved as he was. I believed him when he said he hadn't killed his wife, or David Brady. And I thought he was telling the truth about Emily, at least as far as he knew it. Before I had a chance to say anything else, he produced an envelope and handed it to me. Inside was a sheet of white A4 paper, on which was typed:

172

In sympathy for your time of trouble, we extended the time allowed to you to pay the fifty grand. But we still have the film, so be outside the main door of St Anthony's church in Seafield at six with the money in a shopping bag. No cops—and that means Ed Loy. Or watch your little girl become a worldwide porn star!

'How did this arrive?'

'By hand, just like the last one. Anita said it came this morning. She didn't see anyone.'

There were only two possible candidates stupid or reckless enough to keep pushing a blackmail attempt on a murder suspect; I thought it was the Reillys; I hoped it wasn't Tommy; either way, I felt I could handle it.

'Right. This is all right. Provided you can stay out of jail. It's about three now. Can you get the cash?'

'I arranged it the day before yesterday, it's ready to be collected today.'

'All right. Take it out, and we'll make a plan. The bad news is, I don't think these people are the real threat. The good news is, I think we can take them down.'

Howard nodded.

'Just remember, though, I don't care about the money,' he said. 'I just want to help my little girl.'

'Well, you just might start to care about the money when they ask for it once a week. But I'll figure something out on that side of it too.'

He patted me on the shoulder. It hurt.

'There's one other thing,' I said. 'Sandra told me about Stephen Casey. Who he was, what he did. It's very sad. I can understand why none of you wanted to dredge that particular memory up. It's

173

just that I'm worried about his mother. Eileen, I think her name was. Sandra told me she was in service at Rowan House, then she left to get married.'

'Why are you worried about Stephen Casey's mother?' Shane Howard asked. His voice was careful and clear, and I was conscious that he was very wary of the subject.

'I think she might have something to do with all this. Just a hunch. That she might blame you—the Howards—for her son's death.'

'That's . . . why would she?'

'Chances are she doesn't. I'd just like to make sure. Eliminate her from my inquiries, as your friends the Guards say.'

Howard almost smiled at that.

'I don't really know much. As I say, I had the rugby, and the practice . . . it was one of those times, Sandra ran the show. What do I remember? She wasn't bad looking, say that. Very upset about the son, we all were, tragic for her. And then she got married . . . she moved to Woodpark, somewhere . . . Pearse something, Drive or Villas or whatever, everything's called Pearse there. Married to a bloke she'd been going out with a while, once got a backer on his motorbike, what was his name?'

Like an old vinyl record, I seemed to hear Shane Howard's next words in my head split seconds before he spoke them, like a ghostly premonition of worse to come, or the deadbolt realization that, deep down, you knew the worst all along.

'Dalton, chap's name was. Some kind of nickname, don't remember that. His second name though was definitely Dalton.'

174

14

Sandra Howard rang; her voice was high and urgent.

'Ed, Emily's gone. I went down to the Clinic to take care of a few things, and when I got back she had gone.'

'Is there any sign of forced entry, or of a struggle?'

'No. Oh my God, she's been kidnapped again.'

'I don't think so. Shane has just had another ransom demand. It used the film as a threat. Why risk taking her when they have the film as a bargaining chip?'

'You're right, I suppose.'

'She probably just wants some time to herself,' I said, wishing I were as confident as I sounded. When I ended the call, I had to go through it all again with Shane; by the time I had him reassured that Emily was in no danger, I was convinced she was.

Denis Finnegan was gone when we got back inside the house. I asked Shane Howard to use a mobile phone with an earpiece and to wear a hat so that I could contact him when he was waiting outside the church with a bag full of money. He said he didn't have a shopping bag, so I looked around and finally found a silver-and-blue bag advertising some drug company's latest product. Then I asked him to give Anita the rest of the day off, so I could follow her. He was offended that I didn't trust her; I reassured him that I didn't trust anyone, including him, that not trusting anyone

175

was my job. He thought I was being funny. I wish I had been. I didn't tell him I thought she looked far too frightened to be trusted, or that she bore a striking resemblance to the blonde in the porn film with his nephew Jonathan.

Shane Howard told me Anita had come into work today driving a blue '98 reg Fiat Punto—he hadn't noticed the car before—but he wasn't sure where she lived, or what her second name was. I waited in my car while he found her address in his files; by that time she had taken off and I was on her tail. I hoped I wouldn't have to follow her all the way to the North Circular Road, as that's where Shane Howard said Anita Venclova's flat was. I didn't. She went through Bayview and along Rathdown Road straight on to upper Seafield Road, then took the third exit off the roundabout by the DIY retail park, straight down into the Woodpark Estate. I was hanging back, keeping my distance, but I misjudged the roundabout; two buses crunched in front of me and a stream of traffic followed them, and by the time I'd reached Woodpark, I'd lost her.

I drove around for a while, aware it was most likely a futile exercise; trying to find a nineties reg Punto in a council estate was like trying to find someone in a grey and navy tracksuit, or a girl with snow-blonde hair, for that matter; I was on my third car and my fourth blonde when I decided to give up. And then I saw a small terrace tucked away in a corner between the church and the high wall the council had built to placate the residents of the adjacent non-local-authority houses, and I glimpsed a flash of blonde hair and a blue car, and I pulled into the church car park and got out and walked across to the sycamores and beech trees and the low three-bar metal fence that marked the boundary between church and houses, and slipped among them and saw Anita Venclova knock on the front door of a two-up two-down grey-pebbledash mid-terrace house, and look over her shoulder as a man opened the door and smiled in what looked like surprise and Anita looked in my direction and I tucked my head in behind the broad fungus-flecked beech trunk, and then looked out again to see her talking intensely to the man in the doorway—the man I had last seen in the Woodpark Inn, singing about 'Blood on the Wind'. Jerry Dalton, who was the right age to be Eileen Casey's second son, the right age to be Stephen Casey's half-brother, the right age to return and claim his inheritance.

He stepped aside and looked at the traffic and the cars in the car park and Anita went into the house and someone else approached the door and spoke to Dalton. Dalton half turned and said something over his shoulder, and the person moved fully into the doorway to continue the conversation. She had dyed her hair black, and she looked very pale, but there was no question that it was Emily Howard.

*   *   *

I walked back through the churchyard. An early-evening Mass had finished and a straggle of old ladies was emerging, the fleet helping the lame down the church steps; they grabbed their shopping trolleys or their walking frames and trundled off unsteadily into the falling night. A board mounted in the porch told me it was the Church of the Immaculate Conception, that the parish priest—and the only priest—was Father James Massey, and that tonight there would be Exposition of the Blessed Sacrament in an all-night vigil leading into dawn Mass on All Souls' Day. Years ago, a parish this size would have had two or three priests; now they were probably doing well to have one to themselves. I went around to the side chapel entrance at the rear of the church and knocked on the sacristy door. It pushed open under my hand, and I went in. To my right was a small office area with a desk and chairs and a filing area; ahead, stretching around the corner I could see Formica counters, a sink and shelves with church ornaments and hangings.

'Father Massey?' I said.

A tall, stooped, balding man of about seventy appeared, drying his hands and face on a towel. He had removed his vestments and was wearing the black shirt priests favoured for day wear; without the clerical collar it looked incomplete, and so did he.

'What is it?' he said, his voice sibilant, slightly high.

'I was wondering if you remembered a parishioner of yours, she would have had a son here maybe twenty years ago. Eileen Dalton, her name was. She may have been married here too. Her maiden name was Casey.'

'It wasn't, but no matter. Yes, I remember her. What connection have you with her?'

His manner wasn't unfriendly, just direct, guarded, maybe even protective.

'My name is Edward Loy. I'm a private detective,

178

working for the Howard family. Eileen Casey was the mother of a boy who was thought to have murdered Audrey O'Connor, the first wife of Sandra Howard's husband Richard. Eileen was in service with the Howards at that time. Stephen Casey then was believed to have killed himself. Not long after, Eileen was in a position to buy a house in Woodpark, where she married a man called Dalton.'

'And what do you want to know?'

'Where Eileen Casey, or Dalton, is now. And what she can tell me about her son.'

Father Massey looked at me appraisingly.

'When you say you're working for the Howards . . .'

'It means Sandra Howard is paying me. But I'm bound by the laws of the land. Her money doesn't buy her family a free ride.'

'Because I saw the awful news about Jessica Howard on the television last night. Are you saying what happened twenty years ago has something to do with that?'

'I'm almost certain that it does. I don't know how yet. But anything you can tell me could be vital.'

Father Massey turned and disappeared from sight. When he returned, he had put his collar on and a black jacket over his shirt; he carried two heavy, leather-bound books under his arm. He laid them out on the desk and opened one to December 1985.

'This is the marriage-register entry: you can see here, December 12th, Eileen Mary Harvey married Brian Patrick Dalton, their signatures there.'

He passed me the marriage register, and opened

the second book and quickly found the page he was looking for.

'Now, here it is, after what we are no longer allowed to call a positively indecent gap, 28th March 1986, a son christened Jeremiah John Dalton.'

He passed me the second volume. I took it, glanced at it and set it down.

'That was very easy,' I said. 'If all information was that simple to obtain, I'd be out of a job.'

Massey's wan face warmed to pink.

'What do you mean?'

'I mean, I come in out of the blue asking about a marriage and a christening from twenty years ago and you just happen to have the registers at hand, and find the entries in seconds. Surely you can't remember everyone you marry, every child you christen, off the top of your head.'

Massey had flushed red now. He turned his face away from me, and when he spoke his light voice wavered.

'Ah but poor Eileen was a special case. None of us could forget Eileen.'

'And why is that?'

'Because young Dalton ran out on her a month before the baby was born. And a month after the birth, Eileen herself couldn't take any more. She left the baby in the porch you entered, then slipped back home, sealed up the kitchen, turned the oven on and gassed herself. The strain of it all, the son dying, the young husband leaving, she may have been depressed after the birth . . . God only knows what darkness haunts one of His children when they feel driven to take that decision.'

Massey turned to me, and I saw that there were

180

tears running down his smooth, unlined face.

'Such a beautiful girl . . . too beautiful now, too trusting, too quick to sit on a handsome lad's knee, too much life in her, more than she could manage, and no one she could trust to help her cultivate it, help it grow. Such beauty . . . such a waste.'

He shook his head and wiped his face with a large white handkerchief.

'Forgive me. You're absolutely right, there are people I married last year and I would probably not recognize them if they walked through that door this minute. But you couldn't forget Eileen Dalton.'

'What happened to the child?'

'Oh, the Howards took care of everything. They paid for the funeral, such flowers, and they arranged adoption for the child with a family they knew.'

'How'd they manage that? I mean, didn't they have to go through some kind of agency?'

'In theory. In practice, John Howard was chair of the board of the Adoption Authority, and two of the board members were ex-students of his, and another was the chaplain at the Howard Medical Centre, and the adoptive father was a senior colleague of Howard's, so the whole thing went through on a hush-hush little nod. A nice respectable family the baby went to though, a very *good* family.'

There was something sardonic about the way Massey said this which, combined with the obvious affection he had had for Eileen Dalton, made me like him immensely.

'Did they take the house too?'

'Oh no. The Dalton fellow's name was on the

deeds, you see. And there was no mortgage. After a while, the council boarded it up; kids were having cider parties and all sorts up there. It's only this last eighteen months it's been done up; I heard it was sold, and the new owner has rented it out. Which I suppose means Dalton was out there all along, the blackguard.'

'The house,' I said. 'Is it the second in the terrace just past the church?'

'That's right,' he said. 'Pearse Terrace. How did you know? But you're a detective, I forgot. I suppose you dug it up, Mr Loy.'

I rose to leave, and he gathered the register together.

'By the way, you were absolutely right about something else too,' he said.

'And what would that be?'

'Deducing that I had shown these books to someone recently.'

'Was it a young man, slim build, long black hair, good looking?'

Father Massey laughed and said, 'Oh dear me no, I'm afraid not,' in almost a camp way. 'Quite the opposite, old and red and fat. Solicitor for the Howard family, he said he was. Nice person, just not at all easy on the eye. I'm sure you know him. Denis Finnegan.'

*   *   *

In the churchyard, there was someone standing by my car. As I got closer, I saw that it was Jerry Dalton, and that he was putting something beneath my windscreen wipers. I walked a little slower then, trying to creep up on him, but the

182

blare of a car horn alerted him to the danger; he looked back at me, then bolted for the road; I chased him, but he had too much of a lead, and twenty years, on me; Anita was waiting across the road in the Punto; Jerry Dalton got in beside her and they took off. No sign of Emily. I jumped the three-bar fence and knocked on the door of the Dalton house, once, twice, three times. No reply. I opened the letterbox and shouted through it.

'Emily? Emily, it's Ed Loy.'

'Go away.'

'Emily, your father's worried about you. Sandra too. I'm just checking that you're OK.'

'My mother's just been murdered and the cops think my dad did it; of course I'm OK.'

'Can you open the door? Can I talk to you?'

'No. Please, just leave me alone.'

'We have to believe Shane is innocent.'

'Why? I'd've killed her if I were him. They hated each other.'

'I don't know that that's true.'

'Who the hell are you? What do you know about any of it?'

'As much as you'll tell me. I know about Stephen Casey, and Eileen Dalton being Jerry's mother. I know you and Jerry are trying to get to the bottom of it all. That's what I want too. But I need your help.'

There was a long silence, and then the sound of sobbing.

'Emily?'

'All right. I'll ring Daddy. But please don't tell him where I am, I just need some time alone. I'm safe here.'

The sobbing continued. I let the letterbox close.

I walked back to my car, picked the envelope from the windscreen and put it in my pocket; I didn't have time for it now. Shane Howard was going to be outside St Anthony's church at six with a bag of cash, and I needed a partner if I was going to track whoever was going to make the grab.

*　　　*　　　*

The fact Tommy Owens went to great lengths to hide—you could say he'd dedicated his entire life's work to its concealment, if the phrase 'life's work' was one you could fit alongside Tommy with a straight face—was that his mother was a teacher, his family owned their own semi-detached house, and, while his father had drunk himself to death by the age of forty-three, he was an alcoholic *civil servant,* not some drunken labourer. In other words, Tommy grew up lower middle class, or what passed for it in Ireland in those days (it didn't always have much to do with money). But from the word go, Tommy wanted to be with the kids who were trouble, with the troubled kids, and his teachers went from telling him that they expected much better to being eventually relieved that his behaviour wasn't a lot worse. Everyone liked to say there was no real harm in Tommy, but that wasn't true; he did his fair share of things to other kids that, looking back, were as vicious and mean as it gets; so did I; so did a lot of us. But Tommy always did stuff that seemed guaranteed to backfire, to land him in even greater trouble: when it comes to the various working definitions of a loser, Tommy Owens fitted the bill in this regard: you always felt that, deep down, Tommy *wanted* to get caught.

Not a man you needed on your side in a crisis. On the other hand, I hadn't made enough friends since I'd been back to have many—all right, *any*—alternatives. Except for a few Guards, and they weren't what I needed for a ransom grab, or, after last night, for anything else right now.

Sadie Owens greeted me with a hug.

'Ah Ed, the boy. I hope you've come to take him out of this,' she said. 'The rages at least provide entertainment; the sulks are the worst thing.'

Sadie had looked about fifty when she was thirty-five, with paint flecks in her hair and colourful 'ethnic' skirts and an absent-minded air that never quite concealed how sharp she was; now she was seventy, she still looked fifty, but the paint flecks were grey hairs now, and the skirts were just a little wider at the hips. She rolled her eyes behind the thick Nana Mouskouri glasses she had always worn, opened the living room door, whispered 'Light blue touch paper,' and disappeared into the kitchen.

It usually took a long time to talk Tommy out of a sulk, even when—especially when—the bad blood had been his fault. In that respect it was like having a girlfriend, but without any of the advantages. But I didn't have a long time. So I turned off whatever quiz-show bollocks Tommy had been watching, sat down in front of him, put the sports bag I was carrying on the floor and said: 'Tommy, I think the Reillys, working with Sean Moon or independent of him, have pressed ahead with an attempt to blackmail Shane Howard. They've set a pick-up for six tonight, outside St Anthony's in Seafield. I want to follow them back to wherever they go once they've got the cash. Will you help me? And we'll call it quits.'

Tommy's valiant efforts to keep his sulk in place dispersed on the words 'pick-up'. He was grinning in anticipation, and nodded eagerly.

'Sure, Ed, what do you want me to do?'

I guess the fact he was here at all, and still wearing pyjamas and a dressing gown, ruled him out of the latest ransom bid. Another last chance for Tommy Owens.

'Two things, really. I need you to have a haircut and a shave, and then I need you to steal a car.'

*   *   *

St Anthony's is an old Victorian church set in off the main road near a crossroads; there's a big yard in front which is either open or closed to cars, depending on whether there's a coffin being brought to the church or just a regular mass. Tonight, the mass was at six, and all the dead were saints in heaven, so the yard was sealed off to traffic. Shane Howard stood in the church porch, pacing back and forth, his suede car coat on and a racing trilby on his head. He looked like a caricature of a south County Dublin rugby buffer, and as such, blended straight in to an area where the oval-ball game was a religion. I had passed by earlier, and was waiting near the crossroads in the '98 Punto Tommy Owens had stolen about half a mile from his house. ('Easier to leave it back if you know who you've stolen it from,' he said—some eighteen-year-old girl who had been given it for getting good exam results, apparently.)

When I'd called Howard on his mobile a few

minutes earlier, he was still raging about the difficulties he had had getting out of his house.

'Some Garda fuckers must have told the press, a whole pack of them had gathered. Garda car there too, I think. I had them out in fucking Bray, thought I'd have to head up the mountains, but I lost them up Enniskerry way, cut back down here with fucking minutes to spare.'

'You're all right now. Just hand them the bag, don't worry about getting a look at them or anything: I have someone watching. I'm going to go now; I need to talk to him. Don't lose the head now Shane, all right?'

'All right. Be sure and get these cunts now.'

'I'll do my best.'

Tommy Owens, clean shaven, with hair newly cropped by his mother and slicked back from his forehead (Sadie said, 'He looks like his father did when he only drank at weekends,' which, given the way Tommy lived, I thought was good going) and totally unrecognizable in a duffel coat, clear-lensed glasses with thick rims and grey desert boots, stood outside St Anthony's handing out eccentric religious pamphlets which I'd robbed from the porch of the Church of the Immaculate Conception in Woodpark about the spiritual benefits that would accrue from a special devotion to someone called Mother Meera, and also from the talismanic properties of Padre Pio's mitten. Tommy was anxious that he hadn't had the time to establish who or what these were, but I said the only people who might want to know would be as evidently mad as he was claiming to be. Beneath the duffel coat, Tommy had the Sig Sauer the Reillys had used to scare me off, only this time it was loaded; I had Parabellum 9 mm at home, and now they were chambered and ready to go. I wasn't armed. I figured if by some chance the Reillys made Tommy, he had the right to defend himself; giving him the gun wasn't easy, but the sober look in his eyes when he realized how much trust I was placing in him gave me hope he wouldn't fuck up. Not much hope, but some. What I really needed was some higher-quality back-up, or some less complicated cases.

I called Tommy, and he answered while handing out his wares.

'Mother Meera, God bless! Padre Pio, his dripping wounds, his blood-soaked mitten.'

'I thought the miracle was it *wasn't* blood-soaked,' I said.

'Fuck do *you* know?' Tommy hissed. 'God bless, terrible night, isn't it?'

He had a lisping, almost whistling voice he was using, one I hadn't heard since it had nearly got him expelled at school, when he reduced a very timid student teacher to hysterics by convincing her that the voice, which he only used when her back was turned, was the ghostly emanation of a dead child.

'Fuck Darren, they took the Merc,' was the next thing Tommy said, very low, followed by 'Mother Meera, Padre Pio, thanking you!' back up in the lisp again. I waited a few seconds, and then, 'Darren Reilly picks up bag, Wayne in midnight-blue Merc S-series Padre Pio, Mother Meera God Bless! '06 reg G67Y. Bag in car, Merc signalling to pull out. Mother Meera, Sacred mitten! Merc barges into traffic, heading your way Ed.'

'Good work. Thanks, Tommy. Keep your phone

188

on, I'll call you when I'm done.'

The traffic was a slow rush-hour drift in both directions. I looked in the rear-view, which had two mini-Bratz dolls hanging from it, waited until the Merc was passing, then signalled—and no one would let me out. A blue Mercedes could slide into any line of traffic, but a Fiat Punto? If a grown man was such a loser as to be driving a chick's car (and a teenage chick's at that)? Forget it my friend! I tried to keep one eye on the Merc up ahead; the lights were still red, but I had lost sight of it. And then there was a loud crash on my roof: Tommy Owens, waving his pamphlets in the middle of the street, horns blaring at him, giving me enough room to pull out, and him enough time to hop in. The lights went green, and Tommy flashed two fingers at the boy racer behind us with his hand on his horn, and leant out the window to keep tabs on the Reillys ('Left, Ed, left, the Woodpark Road'), and we were still in the game.

I had long been used to Tommy saying the last thing you expected him to say, so it should have come as no surprise when he said, 'I think we should call the Guards.' But it did.

'We have them with the money. Shane Howard can give his side of it, yous have the ransom note, what's the problem?'

'The problem is, we have a gun, we've set this up and we didn't tell them . . . the problem is me, Tommy. Unfinished business. Anything less than the whole thing tied up with a ribbon and they'll do me for something, anything. And I am going all the way on this one.'

'You always do, Ed. All right man. Just thought I'd say it. First time for everything.'

189

There is indeed. Within the hour, I'd be wishing for the very first time that I'd taken Tommy Owens's advice.

15

We followed the blue Merc up towards Woodpark, but then they swung right and drove towards the city for a while. I called Shane Howard, and told him we were on their trail.

'Fair enough. Little skanger in a hoodie it was.'

'We know who it was. Are you all right? Where are you?'

'I'm still here.'

'You should go home.'

'With all those jackals outside the house? No way.'

'What if Emily wants to come home?'

'Emily's fine. She called me, said she's with friends. Last thing she needs is to be splashed all over the newspapers.'

'Don't go missing now, Shane.'

'I'll tell you where I'm going. For the next half hour. To mass.'

He ended the call. The Reillys had changed direction again; they crossed the N11 and were heading west into the mountains. Tommy took the Sig and offered it to me.

'Here. Make me nervous, fucking things.'

I put the gun in my coat pocket.

'Thanks. You did well tonight, Tommy.'

He looked at himself in the rear-view mirror.

'I look like a fucking looper.'

'That was what you were supposed to look like. So you got it right. You made up for fucking up. What more can anyone do?'

I nodded at Tommy, and he nodded back, and that was almost that.

We followed the Mercedes through industrial estates, then climbed through dense pine forests and along narrow roads thicketed with bramble and fern; finally a road stretched out along foothills of granite and shallow bog, low clumps of heather and marsh grass. It ran about a mile at a slow incline; I thought about pulling in in case we were spotted, but I had no idea whether the Reillys were meeting someone at an outdoor rendezvous or calling at a house, or whether they'd just taken it into their heads to bowl out for an evening spin and count their money. I kept them in our sights, and then lost them as the Merc crested the incline; when we made it to the top, I saw the road drop and cut right against the side of the mountain; far below us the city lay, an irregular blur of lights in the mist and cloud. There was a lay-by halfway along, used as a viewing point; the Reillys, having slowed down near the lay-by, picked up speed again and then turned off to the right about half a mile further on. I kept the car moving slowly, wary of running into them if they were doubling back, wary of blundering about in the dark.

'I know where they are,' said Tommy. 'Pull into the lay-by.'

I did as he said. There was a grass verge with picnic tables and purple Hebe and St John's wort and a framed guide to the flora and fauna and a wooden gate across a rutted lane that led up into a forest of pines. Tommy hopped out and opened the gate, and we ran the car up and off the side of the lane.

'Used to bring a girl up here. There's a quarry about half a mile along. That's where they turned in.'

'Wait here,' I said.

Tommy shook his head.

'No way man. I may have made it up to you for getting involved with these cunts. But I haven't made it up to me yet. Anyway, I know the way.'

Before I had a chance to argue, he set off up the lane, dragging his ruined foot as if it was weightless; I followed. We climbed a couple of hundred feet and then bore left through the trees, picking our way over uneven ground. I kept my balance by hand, steering my way along the densely packed pines; resin clung to my fingers and the pungent smell burned clean in my lungs.

At the sight of light ahead, Tommy began to sidle gradually down the hill; when we began to hear the rumble of voices, we made our movements slower and more deliberate; finally we reached the edge of the pines, dropped to our knees and moved carefully between clumps of gorse and tangled bramble and fern for about twenty feet, until we were almost at the edge of a quarry. The sheer face, silver-grey and orange slashed with purple and white, was to our right; opposite and beneath us a slope of mud and heaped stone fell to a dust floor of shale and rubble. There was an orange digger at rest, and an unlit grey and green Portakabin with 'Norton Excavation' written on it; the lights came from the Reilly brothers' Mercedes and a navy-blue

Bentley. The Reillys were standing by the Merc, the silver-and-blue drug-company bag full of money between them. A man sat in the front seat of the Bentley, smoking, but I couldn't make out who it was. Standing near the Bentley was Sean Moon, or someone who looked like Sean Moon might have if he'd had a shower and put on a suit and a dark coat; he was still pretty fat, but he didn't look like a down-and-out. They were talking, but I couldn't make out what they were saying; Tommy turned to me and put a finger to his ear to say he couldn't hear them either.

Darren held up the bag, but when Sean Moon stepped forward to take it, Wayne moved between them. There was another set of exchanges, then Sean Moon called 'Maria!' to someone in the Bentley, and a very nervous-looking woman with snow-blonde hair got out. At first I thought it was Anita, then I realized it wasn't, but that I had seen her before and she had reminded me of Anita then too. It was the woman who had been in both porn films, the woman Moon had called Wendy, and was now calling Maria.

Maria was shaking, and didn't want to go to the Reillys, but Sean Moon was insisting, dragging her across the gravel; she stumbled, and broke a heel, and he held on to her and swore, and she stood straight, crying now, and he laughed and made an expansive gesture and said, 'Women! Jaysus!' and the Reillys laughed too, and Wayne took hold of Maria's other arm and dragged her across towards the Merc, and Darren handed the bag to Sean Moon, who quickly turned and tossed it in the front seat of the Bentley beside the smoking man, and as quickly shouted 'Maria' again, very loudly,

193

and she hit the dirt as quickly and when Sean Moon turned back he had a compact sub-machine gun, the kind you can fire in one hand, and two or three bursts of automatic fire sang out and echoed around the hills, and when it was over, the Reillys lay dead, and all you could hear was the sound of a woman crying.

The man in the car got out. He had a large head of hair in a bouffant style and a moustache, and wore a long, pale-coloured wool coat; he knelt down to comfort the weeping Maria; after a minute she rose to her feet, seemingly unharmed, and he walked her back to the car. Tommy turned to say something to me, but I didn't hear what it was because in the act of turning he dislodged a clump of earth or a pile of stones and whatever it was skittered down in a trail, right down to where Sean Moon stood. He trained the SMG in our direction and before I could do a thing, Tommy said quietly to me, 'One man, in the back lane,' and was on his feet, shouting, 'It's OK, Tommy Owens, it's all right.' He began to walk unsteadily down the slope, hands up, repeating the same words over and over, like a prayer.

'Who else is with you?' Sean Moon said when Tommy was about halfway down. I had the Sig in my hand and the slide pulled back, but unless I wanted to take Moon out now it was useless, and even if I did he'd still most likely be able to rake us both with a single burst.

'Nobody,' said Tommy. 'I'm on my own. After those fucking Reillys.'

He stumbled down to the bottom and walked towards Moon, who gestured first at his clothes. Tommy pointed at the Reillys and then at himself;

194

I guessed he was saying that part of the ransom belonged to him. The bouffant-haired man appeared above the low roof of the Bentley and Sean Moon went around and explained the situation to him. He nodded Tommy into the back of the car, then pointed up in my direction and whispered an instruction. I eased back on my hands and knees as quietly as I could before Sean Moon pointed the SMG up where I had been and sprayed a few more bursts of automatic fire around.

I jammed myself low behind a charred gorse bush; my irrational prayer was that the more the needles hurt my head and face and ears and neck, the less likely I was to catch a stray slug. The musk of the gorse flowers had long gone; in its place was the smell of charcoal and ashes.

The gunfire stopped. In the silence following, I heard the liquid purr of the Bentley and the crunch of gravel as it pulled away. I shinned down the slope and watched it slide majestically down the narrow road like a great sleigh on ice. I flashed on Denis Finnegan: the same luxury class, the same ooze through life. The Punto was well hidden above the lay-by; I decided to take the Merc; it would be better suited to what I had in mind. Even if the Guards found the Punto, chances were the owner had reported it stolen by now. I was halted momentarily by the Reillys' massacred bodies, bleeding on the shale. Their deaths probably wouldn't make the front page, or cause the people of Dublin more than a moment's pause: just another gangland killing, another pair of dead hoods.

I got behind the wheel of the Merc and lorried

195

it down in the Bentley's trail; I almost drove off the narrow roads a few times until I adjusted to the power of the engine. A waft of cheap aftershave and hash smoke and body odour clung to the interior: human traces that now evoked the sickly sweet smell of death. I became aware that I was shaking, and sweat was prickling at my scalp; I found the switch that rolled all the windows down and let the cold damp air into the car. I didn't catch sight of the Bentley for a while, but I didn't need to; I was pretty sure I knew where it was headed; I finally caught sight of it ahead of me on Templeogue Road; when I saw it was going on down through Rathmines, I cut right through Ranelagh, running a couple of red lights and piling along Leeson Street, then down Fitzwilliam Place and left along the lane to the rear of the south side of the square, where residents could park their cars if they hadn't built mews houses in their back yards. Brock Taylor hadn't. I parked right up against his barred electric gates and cut the engine and got out the passenger side and crouched below it and let the slide back on the Sig. 'Brock Taylor' was what Tommy must have said to me, what I hadn't heard above the sound of the rubble he kicked down. And then 'One man in the back lane.' I thought of the boy who cried wolf. Tommy had invoked Brock Taylor so often, and it had almost all been fantasy. I hoped, for his sake as much as anyone's, he had it right this time.

The gates swung open and a large uniformed security guard appeared and rapped on the driver's window of the Merc. I stood up and let him see the gun, and said 'Hands' and walked around and frisked him. His big pink face was round-eyed with surprise. He didn't have a weapon, which made sense; this wasn't some gangster's ranch in the mountains, this was Fitzwilliam Square, where the big rich kept town houses and solicitors had their offices. No one got shot around here. I took his phone and walked him through the gates and into a little booth on the left of the yard with a heavy metal door and a console and a CCTV screen and an armchair, and I gave him a tap or two on the back of the head with the Sig and pushed him into the armchair. There were no lights on in the house.

I went out and reversed the Merc into the yard and around the corner so it wasn't visible from the street, then I went into the little booth and consulted the console and flicked the switch that shut the gates. I waited for long enough to worry that the Bentley was going to dispose of its extra cargo first. Then lights appeared in the lane and the gates swung back to admit the great car. Brock Taylor was driving, with Maria in the passenger seat; Sean Moon was behind Taylor, Tommy beside him. Moon pushed Tommy out and walked him towards the house; the machine pistol was loose in one hand, the money in the other. I stepped out between Tommy and Moon and had the Sig in Moon's neck before he saw what was happening.

'Hold the sub out,' I said. 'Slowly.' I dug the Sig deeper into his neck as he extended his arm. The gun was a Steyr 9-mm TMP (tactical machine pistol), compact, dark grey, with an angled handgrip and a rotating barrel. It hung in a sling off Moon's right shoulder, beneath his coat. Tommy went to take it from him, and he started fumbling with the sling.

'Hold up,' I said. 'Tommy, step away. Moon, let the sub down and take your coat off, right arm first.'

Moon let the pistol hang by his side. I pressed the Sig in behind his ear. He began to wriggle out of the right sleeve of his coat. As the sleeve came off he raised his right fist up by his ear and smashed it back into my wrist.

'Ed, watch it! He's going for the sub!' Tommy called.

I kept my balance, and before his arm had dropped, I hit Moon on the back of the head with the butt of the Sig, twice, three times, not taps like I'd given the security guard. Moon collapsed in a heap. I detached the machine pistol from him and handed it to Tommy. Brock Taylor was out of the car, but he just stood, watching me. His hair and moustache were dark, except for the streak of white that flashed through both. When Tommy went to frisk him he gave a weary smile, as if he was too grown-up for all this child's play. He was unarmed.

The gates were closing automatically; I went into the hut and hit the switch to open them again. Maria still hadn't moved from the passenger seat. I opened the door.

'Maria,' I said. 'Come with us.'

She got out of the car, looked at Tommy, and spat in his face.

'Not with him. Pig!' she said.

'Not with him. You can go where you like now. To Anita?'

She looked at Brock Taylor in panic, then back at me, her eyebrows raised.

'You know where?' I said.

She nodded.

I wanted to ask her what had happened, or rather, how it happened. But all that could wait. I pulled some money from my pocket and gave it to her.

'Go on then,' I said.

She looked around the yard and almost smiled, then walked towards the opened gates. Her heel was broken, so she walked lopsidedly, then on her toes, then she pulled her shoes off and threw them in the dirt and ran barefoot into the lane and disappeared.

I took the Steyr from Tommy and told him to get the money. Then I tossed the Steyr on top of Sean Moon where he lay, blood seeping out of the back of his head. An all-in-one package for the cops. Then I looked at Brock Taylor, who hadn't taken his eyes off me.

'I don't much care about the Reillys. Don't mess with the girl again.'

'I was helping the girl,' he said, in one of those Americanized Dublin drawls that turned 'the' into 'de' and 'girl' into 'gurrl'.

'Don't help her then,' I said. 'And don't fuck with me either, do you hear me?'

'I hear you. Edward Loy,' said Brock Taylor.

I looked at him then, heard the threat, implied if not real, and realized this wasn't over, that there was no possibility, having witnessed the Reillys' murders, Tommy and I could just walk away as if nothing had happened. I went into the security hut and closed the gates again, then I came out, retrieved the SMG and showed it to Brock Taylor, who hadn't moved.

'Tommy, help me get Moon into the hut.'

We dragged his body in and heaved him on the floor beside the security guard; Moon's head was oozing slowly, but I'm afraid, right at that moment, I simply didn't care. I pushed the heavy door to and walked over to the Bentley.

'Keys,' I said to Taylor. His face fell.

'You're not taking this on me,' he said, his accent thickening in panic.

'That's right,' I said. 'We're all staying here. Keys.'

He handed me the keys. I gave Tommy the Steyr and told him to keep it trained on Taylor. Then I sat in the Bentley, reversed it as far as the gates and jammed it in alongside the door of the security hut. I got out and nodded Taylor towards the house. Tommy kept the SMG trained on him as we walked.

'Is he safe with that?' Taylor said.

'Guess you'll have to hope so,' I said.

What looked like a restored kitchen lurked at basement level; at the bottom of the metal steps that led up to the ground floor, I stopped Taylor.

'Lights are on. Is anyone home? Anyone expecting us?'

'No,' he said. 'There's always lights, for security.'

'Because if we're going, you're going with us,' I said, showing him the Sig.

'There's no one. I'm not working like that any more.'

'You're not? What was tonight? All you forgot was to make them dig their own graves.'

I nudged him in the back with the Sig and he climbed the steps, pressed a security code on a panel by the high four-panelled door and pushed through into the house. We followed, shutting the door behind us and walking through a room that had been stripped down to plaster and boards and not yet refurbished, along a narrow passageway and through into a high-ceilinged hallway with a flagstone floor. Paint and paper were peeling off the walls, and cornices and centrepieces were crumbling; oilcloths and tarpaulins covered furniture and woodwork; paint colour charts and pattern books for wallpaper and upholstery lay strewn about. Fitzwilliam Square, the last of the great Dublin Georgian squares, being bought up by the likes of Brock Taylor. However much the Criminal Assets Bureau had taken off him, it wasn't enough.

'I haven't got the restoration work fully under way yet lads,' Brock Taylor said, like an excited wife showing some pals round her new house. He led into the front reception room, which was carpeted deep blue and wallpapered in a tatty lavender-and-violet Regency stripe. 'This is still from the previous owner. I'm going room by room, want to live here too. Let the builders in when you're not around, fuck knows what they get up to.'

Heavy wine-coloured velvet curtains were drawn; Tommy and I sat in armchairs of a burly three-piece suite the same shade; Brock Taylor took the couch. Having sat down, Tommy immediately stood up again, and began to pace the floor with the Steyr. I found it a little irritating, but from the alarmed looks Taylor was casting Tommy's way, it was evidently irritating him rather more, so I let it roll.

'Now lads,' Taylor said, 'what can I do for you?'

'You could start by telling us why you had Wayne and Darren Reilly murdered tonight.'

Taylor laughed in an expansive, bogus manner he must have practised at Seafield Rugby Club. He stood up as he was laughing, wriggled out of his biscuit-shaded overcoat, which on closer inspection looked like it was made of cashmere, and sat down again. He wore a pale-grey linen suit and a charcoal polo neck and tan Italian loafers with transparent grey silk socks; his backcombed black hair sat high on his head; the white streak through it seemed to glow; there was a plastic sheen to his tanned face, to his groomed appearance, that gave him the embalmed look of a cabaret entertainer from the 1970s.

'Well, don't work up to it or anything, barge right in there with the leading question.'

He laughed some more.

'I don't want to stay here any longer than I have to,' I said. 'I'm just trying to figure out how long I'd have to spend giving a witness statement to the Guards, and when I'd be likely to get out. See, I've a lot of things to do tonight.'

Taylor looked at me coolly, appraisingly, trying to weigh up whether I was bluffng or not.

'We've got the murder weapon. We've got Moon's prints on it. We've got two witnesses. I think that's open and shut. What would you say, Brock? 'Cause it's nothing to me, in fact, it's about time I did myself some good with the guardians of the peace. Not that I had any special affection for Wayne and Darren, quite the reverse, but even they deserved better than what they got tonight.'

'Well, I wouldn't agree with you there, Ed. And you might not agree with yourself when you hear

202

the whole story.'

'Well tell it to me then. The whole story.'

There was a sound from the room above, a floorboard creak, a door slam. I went out to the hall and looked up the stairs.

'There's no one here,' Brock said. 'These old houses, they make all sorts of noise. Especially at night. It's like they're alive and breathing. Put the fear of God into you if you're on your own.'

I came back in and nodded at him. Brock looked anxiously at Tommy, leant forward in his chair and said, 'Your friend Tommy's making me nervous there, with the pacing and all. And since he's a major part of the story, I wouldn't like to feel . . . inhibited while I was telling it.'

I looked around.

'Tommy, stand still, will you?'

Tommy stopped pacing, and instead stood, swaying, the energy converted but sustained. I don't know how much calmer that made Brock feel, but he began to speak anyway.

'As I say, Tommy there starts the whole thing off, there's been some shenanigans between his daughter and Brady and the Howard one. Now I have nothing to do with this, my connection comes through Sean Moon.'

'Tell us about Moon.'

'Sean Moon is a character. In fact, he's a bunch of them. That's his whole thing, he can be a hard man, an earnest office type, round Honeypark he was like a big kid really, wasn't he, a bit sad, a bit of a loser? That's a useful one, get into all sorts of situations that way, no one takes him seriously until they have to. He's the son of an old, of a late . . . *colleague* of mine, I always took an interest in

203

him. Had a little bit of spark, of brain, of wit . . . no surprise to you I'm sure, but that's so rare as to be unique in my business . . . my *former* business. Anyway, I've been buying up houses around Honeypark, Woodpark, and I asked Sean in to just keep an eye on them, pick up the vibe in the area, who's dealing, who's paying off who, the usual, and I own the pub there now of course, Moon's a way of . . . he's another eye.'

'So what happens, Brady gets hooked up with Moon—'

'Through the Reillys, who are dealing coke there and looking to build, and fair enough—better them inside pissing out than the reverse but you want to keep them at a distance, which is why Moon is there. Brady has to make this blue movie for head-the-ball here, but he needs a location—doesn't want to do it in his own place, or the family home, or anywhere people might recognize. Now Brady's getting his coke from Darren Reilly, and he mentions that he needs somewhere, and Reilly brings it to Moon, who has a few options, houses I've bought. He runs it past me, I'm, whatever, don't draw attention to yourselves, keep the curtains shut and all.'

'And where does Maria come into it?'

'Now, I don't like this any more than you do. Moon's weakness is for women—'

'You're telling me Maria Venclova went with Moon . . . I mean, did you notice she's a beautiful woman? And he's a fat fuck.'

'Ah now, way of the world boys, Moon scrubbed up in his Armani and a roll of bills, you'd be surprised the calibre of trim he can snag. Not saying they're only in it for the money, but a

204

certain type of bar, a certain type of girl, they're out for a good time right now.'

'She didn't look like she was having a good time tonight, did she?'

'Well. That just got out of hand there, that was something that shouldn't have happened—'

'It was set up to happen. What, did you promise to swop the Reillys Maria for the blackmail money?'

'The blackmail . . . it should never have gone that far.'

'Blackmailing the Howards, that was Brady's idea.'

'Right. I think he used it with Moon as an incentive. I said don't use it, the power lies in not using it, in *not* making the threat. It's something to hold down the road, in case you need it. But when the Reillys heard about blackmailing Shane Howard, it was like all their Christmases had come at once, you know, they could screw this rich cunt until the end of time. And Moon strung them along—you know, send Howard a note, all this, careful not to name a place to dump the cash.'

'He named a time: Thursday at noon. What was he going to do?'

'He was getting to it. He was stringing the Reillys along, because of course they got into the whole porno thing themselves, they wanted to be making dirty movies, so Moon was filling them full of all that, he was going to divert them—'

'Using Maria as bait.'

'Yeah.'

'Maria, who he was holding captive. Where was she though, she wasn't at the house in Honeypark? Was she here?'

'She wasn't a whatdoyoucallit, a sex slave or anything.'

'In the porn film.'

'She went along with that. I can only tell you what Moon told me. I can't be certain.'

'She was here and then you brought her out last night, up the mountains—'

'Darren Reilly wouldn't let the blackmail thing drop, so he sent his own demand, he let Moon know he was doing it, he told him he'd split it with him fifty-fifty, or Moon could have it all if they could have Maria no questions asked. I wanted Moon to take them out on the street, arrange a hit, motorcyclist at the lights, bang bang and back in the local for last orders. Moon said no, too many leaks. But he wanted me to come too. Impress the Reillys, he said, put them at their ease, make them think they were stepping up in class.'

'And Maria . . . no wonder she was scared. You told her what to do?'

'That's what made me nervous, that she'd get caught in the crossfire if the Reillys started shooting. Moon said that's why he packed the sub, they wouldn't have time to draw, time to think.'

'Your only concern was Maria, was it?'

'I'm just telling you what happened. I mean, it was one of those fucking situations, suddenly you're sniffing around, David Brady's dead, the Howard woman, the whole malarkey. The Reillys had to go, but lesson learned, don't let the wrong kind of people in on anything. Don't need that. I'm a publican, and a property developer, and a businessman.'

'If that was true, you'd need to stop hanging around with the likes of Sean Moon. Who could probably do with a trip to Accident and Emergency, that little head wound of his.'

Taylor suddenly became more animated than he'd been all evening.

'Fuckin' A&E, fucking four- and five- and ten-hour waits, fucking government. You know the real scandal? No matter what you can afford to pay, you have an accident and you have to go to A&E, you end up with all the mucksavages and lepers and scum who don't have an arse to their trousers. How can that be fair, that even if you have the fucking cash, they won't let you jump the fucking queue?'

The chandelier above him gave his hair a sculpted, artificial appearance, as if it were a wig, and he were channelling the spirit of some elegant, grasping ghost who once bestrode Fitzwilliam Square with imperial entitlement. I got up and looked at Tommy; he grimaced at me, still shamefaced. I gave him a wink, then turned back to Brock Taylor.

'Are those your cars? The lock-up in Woodpark, and around the city? Hot cars made over for the less fussy type of client?'

Taylor grinned, as if I'd touched on one of his roguish but endearing foibles.

'Tommy tell you that, did he? Heard about that. I knew he remembered me. That's how I knew you too, Edward Loy. I used to work for your da, Eamonn, that garage he ran between Woodpark and Seafield. Years ago. Worked alongside head-the-ball, when he was just out of school. Did he not tell you?'

'Is that where you're from then, Brock? Woodpark?'

207

'Nah. Blessington Street. Northside boy me. Come up in the world, haven't I?' And he beamed expansively around at the beautiful elegant old room he now owned.

I paused at the door.

'Eileen Casey. Name mean anything to you?'

Not a flicker.

'No. Should it?'

'Eileen Dalton.'

He shook his large head.

'But you did ride a motorcycle, right?'

'A Norton Commando,' Tommy said.

'It speaks,' Brock said, and laughed his rugby-club laugh again. 'A Norton Commando is right. Cross the county in twenty minutes back then. Happy days, lads, happy days.'

*   *   *

Before we left the house, I had Tommy put the Steyr in the bag with the money. We didn't speak until we were down on Stephen's Green. Then he said, 'I didn't know she was, you know, being forced. I swear, Ed, I didn't. And I didn't take a go myself.'

'OK,' I said. His face looked like it had taken a few blows. I tried to think of something else that would make him feel better about it all, but nothing came to mind. I gave him something to do instead.

'I need my car,' I said, passing Tommy the keys.

'No problem,' Tommy said. 'What about the money? Should I drop it up to Mr H?'

'Nah, just stick it in the trunk. The press are camped up around his house. But get a cab. You don't want to get caught on the street with a sub-machine gun.'

'Where are you going to be?'

'Call me when you're on the road and I'll let you know.'

Tommy rested a hand quickly on my forearm, then turned and walked away.

16

It's not difficult to find someone with rooms in Trinity College; the names are listed outside each door. And it didn't take long to find Jonathan O'Connor, because he lived in one of the first buildings on the right in Front Square, which is where I started looking. I did have to lean on the bell for a while to persuade him to let me in, but that didn't take very long either. After about ten minutes he clattered down the stairs and opened the door.

'What do you want?' he said, attempting to block my path.

'I want to talk to you, Jonny. Ask you a few more questions.'

'Anything you have to say, you can say out here. I'm very busy at the moment, I've an essay to finish.'

A couple of female students had come in Front Gate and were heading in our direction. 'All right then,' I said in a much louder voice. 'I want to ask you about your use of prostitutes in the pornographic films you made, and whether you feared some of them were having sex in those films under duress: being raped, in other words?'

Jonathan looked at me in shock, then at the approaching women, then withdrew and said, 'Come up. Second floor.'

I followed him up two flights of stairs and into his 'rums', which consisted of a kitchen the size of a telephone kiosk, two tiny bedrooms and a living room with the kind of furniture junk shops no longer accept. There was a gas fire and no other form of heating; the bathroom was in the hall.

'Wow,' I said. 'Where do you have to live if you don't win Schol? On the street?'

'The privilege resides in living on campus,' he said, his little accent at its snootiest. 'And I don't have to share; one normally would. And of course I could fix it up and buy all sorts of furniture and so on, but how vulgar would that be?'

I nodded, impatient already with the idea of teasing him any further. I sat down on a steel-frame sofa and nearly fell through one of the cushions; Jonathan perched on an orange plastic chair in his expensive jeans and his expensive sweatshirt and looked at me with a supercilious grin. A silver laptop computer lay open on the table beside him. The walls were decorated with pictures of airbrushed, orange plastic women in and out of their underwear cut from the pages of *FHM* and *Loaded* and *Maxim*; the women looked as if they were all dying for sex; none of them looked like they came fitted with the flesh you need to do it properly. There were two portraits of Dr John Howard, and an aerial photograph of the three towers of the Howard Medical Centre. I was cold, and I had just seen two men killed; I needed a meal and a drink and a good night's sleep. One

210

out of three would do.

'Do you have anything to drink?' I said.

'I'm not running a pub, you know,' Jonathan said in an exceptionally spoilt and shrill voice. It took every ounce of self-control I possessed not to smack him in the head. At some level, I think he may have picked up on this. He trudged off to the kitchen and came back with a bottle of Absolut vodka and a carton of orange juice and two glass tumblers. I ignored the juice, poured off a slug of Absolut and threw it back.

'The blonde girl in the second sex film you made,' I said. 'What was her name?'

'Wendy. At least, that's what they called her. She was in the film with Emily too.'

'Was she Eastern European? And if you say you didn't check her passport I'm going to toss you out the fucking window.'

Jonathan looked gratifyingly frightened at my threat. I kept looking at the window, not because I was going to throw him out of it but because through it, you could see straight up Grafton Street; you were right in the heart of the city. I was starting to see the point of these 'rums'.

'I think so,' he said. 'She didn't really speak very much, but when she did it was with an accent. Polish, or Lithuanian, I don't know. And no, in answer to your next question, it didn't seem like she was being forced. She wasn't wildly enthusiastic either, but . . . I just figured she was being paid, she needed the money.'

'That's as far as you thought about it?'

He looked at the floor, and began to rub his wrists together; when he looked up again his eyes were glistening, and he was shaking.

211

'I don't know. I . . . the other woman was Irish—Petra, Sean Moon called her, but that was bullshit, she was a hooker really, extremely coarse . . . she wasn't very happy about it either . . . I think she was pregnant . . . the whole thing was a bit of a nightmare, actually . . . '

He started to retch, and then ran out to the kitchen, where I could hear him vomit. I was giving him a hard time, bullying him, taking out on him the anger I should have used on Brock Taylor. I told myself I should have as much patience with Jonathan as I had with Emily; it looked like their family had put them both through the mill, and if I didn't find him as sympathetic, that wasn't necessarily his fault. When he came back in, his eyes burned red in his grey face.

'Are you all right?'

'What do you care? Just ask your questions and get out,' he said. 'What are you after, anyway? The Guards are dealing with Uncle Shane. Either they have enough evidence to charge him or they don't. It's pretty straightforward, I should have thought. Why are you trying to complicate it?'

'Because I'm not so sure your uncle is guilty. Because if he isn't, the question is, who did kill Jessica Howard and David Brady? Because there's more to the case than just those murders, and what there is goes back twenty, maybe thirty years.'

'Christ, you sound like David Manuel. Nothing's ever what it is, it's always bound up with something else, something that happened in the past.'

'Your mother says that's true of you. That nothing has been the same for you since your father's death.'

'So what? Does that make me special? People

212

die, life goes on. What's it got to do with you? Why are you so interested in our family anyway? You're like a little orphan boy, his face pushed up against the window of the big house. Why can't you just leave us alone?'

'I'm being paid by your mother to do a job,' I said, stung by the sense that there was a whip of truth in his words, that, for all I told myself, I didn't just make my living this way, and it wasn't just about justice; I seemed to need the chaos other people brought me so I could make a pattern from it, establish the connections they couldn't see themselves. Not from envy, but from need.

'I'd be interested in the job description. Does it include fucking her on the stairs in Rowan House? Do you think that's what a woman like my mother needs? You're a grubby man, Mr Loy. I don't think you could make sense of our family in a million years. Do you know why? Because you're not our kind of people.'

'There's a fair likelihood Wendy was being held against her will, that she was either trafficked here or kidnapped once she arrived. That she was forced to have sex with you and Emily. That's something you did, Jonathan, of your own free will. What kind of person does that make you?'

He flashed an anxious look at me, then stared at the floor again, shaking his head.

'I didn't know. I didn't know,' he said.

'Tell me what you remember about her, something, anything, no matter how trivial.'

'She wore a ring. She took it off before we started shooting. The stones were so big, they kept scratching us.'

'What kind of ring?'

213

'Red stones . . . they couldn't have been rubies, but deep red. Two big ones, coming to points, like . . . I don't know, like a claw.'

Like a crab claw. I remembered Anita's words yesterday morning: 'It's not an engagement ring. It's for protection. A talisman.'

I stood up and walked around the room and came to rest in front of the photograph of the three towers that made up the Howard Medical Centre.

'Do you think there should be a fourth tower built, Jonathan? I know that's what your mother wants.'

'Of course I do. And Denis wants it too. It's an expression of confidence in the family, of continuity, of tradition. It's the only option.'

'Jessica didn't agree. Neither does Shane.'

'Shane will come around,' Jonathan said. 'Anyway, it's hardly the day to discuss plans of that sort. Is there anything else?'

'There's one more thing I need to know. It's about Emily, yesterday, in the house in Honeypark. Did she leave the house during the day?'

Jonathan nodded.

'And when she came back? How did she look?'

He shook his head.

'I understand, you want to be loyal to your cousin. And believe me, I don't want to get your uncle off by putting Emily in the frame for her mother's murder. But the Guards aren't stupid, and if they get to her first, they'll take her down.'

'And what, you'll protect her? If she did it, if she killed David Brady, you'd try and cover it up, would you? Because that's what I'd do.'

'Is that what you did? The house in Honeypark burned down today. Was there something there? Physical evidence?'

Jonathan shook his head again.

'I saw you nearby. In the Woodpark Inn with the Reilly brothers, not long after the fire had started.'

Jonathan glanced uneasily at me and looked away.

'I . . . I needed them to keep quiet about what they knew.'

'What did they know? That Emily killed her mother?'

'Not her mother, my God.'

'You really think she killed David Brady? Jonathan?'

'I don't know. She was so angry at him. She felt she had been forced to make the film and she hated it. She went out that morning. When she came back, she was wild, distracted, like something really awful had happened. She went into the bathroom, had a shower, wrapped the clothes up in a bag and put it in the bottom of the wardrobe. Then she told me we had to have sex. In the middle of it, she started fighting, hitting me. Then crying. Then sex again. I was turned on, freaked out, all points between. I didn't know what had happened, what was happening. That went on all afternoon, until you arrived. It was too fucked up.'

'And the bag? She just left it there?'

'I think so.'

'And the fire today?'

Jonathan breathed in slowly.

'If they couldn't find any physical evidence, they couldn't link her to the murder. But I don't know anything about the fire. *I* didn't set it.'

215

He looked up at me.

'Is Wendy . . . what's happened to her?'

'The people who kidnapped her still had her tonight,' I said. 'She saw your friend Sean Moon kill your friends Wayne and Darren Reilly.'

'Oh my God.'

'But then, she got away. No thanks to you.'

I went out into the hall, feeling as if I knew less than when I had arrived.

As I opened the door to the stairs, I thought I could hear the boy sobbing.

*   *   *

I walked down Westmoreland Street to the river and stared at it for a while, envying its steadiness of purpose. Groups of drunken men and women tumbled along the quays, screaming and howling, baying at the suffocating night. It sounded like they were trying to get the party back up to where it had been on Halloween, and like they were having to work just a bit too hard at it. I envied them too, though; tonight I envied everyone who didn't know what I knew. I called Shane Howard, who told me he was at home and not in jail, and asked me did I get the little bastards and I told him not to worry about them, and that I had his money; he was pleased about that, and laughed one of his crashing laughs that nearly deafened me, and then gave me Anita Venclova's phone number and address.

Anita didn't live on the North Circular Road, she lived on North King Street, a confusion I attributed to Shane Howard's brain seizing up completely at the mere mention of Dublin's northside. The cab let me out by a dingy strip of shops, most with steel shutters on their windows and doors; Anita lived above a dry-cleaner's called Eireann Fresh. I rang her and she came down and let me in. She and her sister were on the first floor in a room barely big enough for one, lit by a bare bulb, with a sink and a two-ring stove and two plastic chairs. Maria huddled on the mattress in a grey sweatsuit, her knees drawn up to her chest, studying a television which showed an improbably coiffed James Caan doing something unlikely in Las Vegas.

Anita went over and whispered to her sister; Maria shook her head; she wouldn't look at me. I couldn't say I blamed her; if I were she, I wouldn't look at an Irish man again as long as I lived. Anita turned the volume down on the television, then came back and we sat down on the plastic chairs opposite one another.

'Mr Loy, thank you. My sister thanks you too. She is too upset to speak.'

'I'm not surprised. Are you sure you're safe here? Does anyone else know where you are?'

'Mr Howard only. And Jerry.'

'Jerry Dalton?'

'Yes. He tried to help too.'

'I need to get in touch with Jerry Dalton.'

'I should not say.'

'But you've been helping him, no? Leaving messages for me on my car?'

'Yes. I do not know what they mean.'

'Neither do I. I'd like to talk to him to find out.'

Maria made a sound, which Anita retreated to the bed to interpret.

'Maria says of course, because you helped us. He will be at the rugby club tonight, he is working.'

217

'Thanks. I don't even know . . . where are you from, Anita? Poland?'

'Vilnius . . . Lithuania.'

'Do you have papers?'

'Yes, of course.'

'I'm not with the Guards, Anita.'

Anita said nothing for a while. I could hear the sounds from the other rooms, men quarrelling, babies crying, a couple having very noisy sex; then a lull, during which I could hear, and see, Maria sobbing.

'No we have no papers. That's why I cannot ask Mr Howard to help. I am afraid he will fire me.'

'How did Jerry know to help?'

'He met me at Shane's house and talked to me. He was with Emily, but he talked with me for a while. He is interested in me, not like most Irish men, only one thing.'

'How did your sister get drawn into this?'

'She is working in a pub, went for drink with a man who comes there, she thinks she goes to other pub with him, but it is his house. Suddenly he beats her, she must sleep with other men. Anything he says.'

'An Irish man? Was that Sean Moon? Was Sean Moon or Brock Taylor the man, Maria?'

Maria's sobs had now turned to insistent, shrill wailing. Anita went to her, and they whispered together.

'No names. She is too frightened,' Anita said.

'Does he know where you live? Do any of the men who harmed you . . . do they know where you live?'

Maria looked me in the eye for the first time.

'Yes. They know.'

218

'OK. It might be an idea if you didn't stay at home tonight.'

'We have nowhere to go,' Anita said. 'If we go to the Guards, we have no papers, we get sent home. Nothing there. Not for us.'

'Nothing except pimps,' Maria spat.

I found it was easier to say it than to think about the wisdom of it:

'All right, get your stuff. You can stay at my place. I probably won't be there tonight. You go there and you lock yourselves in a bedroom, and you don't answer the door. Is that all right?'

Anita looked at Maria, but her sister was already nodding.

'You are good, Mr Loy.'

'No I'm not. I've got no choice, is all. I'll wait for you downstairs. Take everything.'

I hailed a cab, then let it go because the first remark the cab driver made was about the cushy fucking number all these fucking immigrants had round here; by the time I'd found another, the girls were on the street. Everything turned out to be a small fabric suitcase each. The cab driver promptly got out and put the bags in the trunk, which I took to be a good sign. I asked whether they needed to tell their landlord; Anita began to explain that they owed some rent; Maria, whose English was patchier than her sister's but effective, said, 'Landlord is cunt. Fuck him.' Revolutions have been fought for less. I paid the driver, tipped him well, made sure he knew exactly where he was going and gave Anita Tommy's key.

No names. She is too frightened.

17

I found the pages Jerry Dalton had left beneath my windscreen when I was looking in my pockets to pay for a pint of Guinness and a double Jameson. I was sitting on a bar stool in an old-style pub waiting for Martha O'Connor, who had called and arranged to meet me. The pages were copies of press clippings. One, from 1999, was an obituary of Dr Richard O'Connor, who it said had died suddenly. It gave a straightforward account of his medical and rugby careers (he had played for Seafield back in the pre-professional days, and was capped for Ireland 'A' teams, but never played a full international game), the violent death of his first wife Audrey and the happiness of his second marriage to Sandra Howard. The second page was a short article that had been downloaded from some kind of forensic-pathology website about how an overdose of insulin could make a diabetic look like he'd had a heart attack.

I had finished both drinks and was ordering more when a voice behind me said, 'And a pint of Carlsberg.'

Martha O'Connor was about five nine and, as Dan McArdle had said, a fine big girl, heavy without seeming overweight (at least, not unless you looked too hard at models in glossy magazines, which it didn't look like she did) in a loose cotton polo shirt and a fleece jacket and faded jeans and Timberland boots; her dark brown hair was cropped short at the back and sides, long at the front, like an English public schoolboy's; her complexion was dark, as were her eyes; her eyebrows were unplucked, and she wore no make-up. She didn't resemble her half-brother in the slightest.

'I didn't think I looked that obvious,' I said.

'You probably don't. But this is my local: everyone else here either works on the paper or is a regular.'

She sat on the stool beside me and nodded greetings to a variety of faces. The drinks arrived. Martha O'Connor looked at my whiskey-and-pint combination and smiled.

'You'd fit in here, no problem,' she said. 'Ed Loy. You worked the Dawson case, right?'

I nodded.

'Don't think we heard the real story there.'

'Doubt it,' I said. 'A lot of lawyers made sure of that.'

'How'd you like to tell it? The truth, by the man on the inside . . .'

'When I retire, you'll be the first to know.'

'If you keep on drinking like that . . .'

'Here's to drinking,' I said. 'Who wants to retire?'

I raised my pint, and she grinned and clinked hers against it.

'I'm working on a case that involves your stepmother now,' I said. Her grin took on a strained quality.

'Has she ensnared you yet? Cast her Sandra-spell? She's good at that, captivating men, inspiring them with her goodness and nobility and beauty, until the poor sods are so cuntstruck they can't see through her.'

A couple of men turned their heads in Martha's

221

direction, as if appalled that a woman should use such language, only to turn away without comment when they saw who it was.

'What should they see? When they see through her?'

Martha shrugged.

'Calculation. Ambition. Ice,' she said. 'My stepmother and I did not get along, not from day one. Understandable enough, I suppose, ten-year-old girl loses her mother, then her beloved daddy to another woman two years later, it's textbook stuff. And I didn't think of my father, that's true, what he might have needed, I just thought of myself. But you know, why not? I was the little girl who'd seen her mother stabbed to death. I needed my father to myself for as long as I felt like it. Why couldn't he have waited? I'd be an adolescent soon enough.'

The pain sounded true and clear in her voice, and as fresh as if it had happened yesterday.

'So I just withdrew. Insisted on being sent to a boarding school run by fucking nuns; then went to Oxford. God knows why I came back.'

'In the absence of His wisdom, why *did* you come back?'

'I don't know. To settle some scores.'

'With your family?'

'And with the Church. And with the whole fucking country.'

'And how's all that going for you?' I said.

'Pretty fucking good so far,' she said, and lilted, 'You're never short of a score to settle, in dear old Ire-land.'

She drained her pint, and caught the barman's eye.

'Pat, a Carlsberg, and . . . do I have to buy you two drinks? Fuck's sake, pricey date.'

'Just the pint. The Jameson's done its work.'

'And a Guinness. So, how's it looking up there anyway? Is the murder triangle theory going to hold? Are they going to charge Shane? Poor Jessica, I always liked her, she was very sexy.'

'Are you working now?' I said.

'Sources close to . . .' she said.

I shook my head.

'I can't do that, not yet.'

The drinks came and we paid them some attention.

'I wanted to ask you about Dr John Howard,' I said.

'Now that . . . *that's* a work in progress. Speaking of scores. But information doesn't come for free. If you won't show me yours . . .'

I looked at her. She was grinning, but she was a serious person, and the work she did was intense and scrupulous and valuable.

'OK, what I'm going to tell you you cannot say to anyone until this case breaks for me, do you understand?'

'Says you.'

'No, I'm serious. And then, I will tell you everything, on condition you leave me out of it. Because it's people's lives and deaths here. Including your parents.'

She looked down the bar for a moment. When she turned back, her face was set, her eyes grave. She nodded.

'OK. I spoke to a retired Garda detective today who worked the case of your mother's murder, who was promoted to inspector at its conclusion.

Now, he wasn't saying anything explicitly. But he was certainly unhappy with the outcome. What he seemed most especially uneasy about was the idea that Casey acted alone. He pointed to the disparity between your mother's and father's injuries, the fact that not only was Casey a pupil of your mother's and a player on the rugby team coached by your father but he was also the child of a servant in the Howard household whose school fees were being paid by the family.'

'Are you saying Sandra and my father . . .'

'I'm not saying anything. And neither was he. These are hypotheses—'

Martha O'Connor nodded her head impatiently, as if to say, 'I know how this works, keep the bullshit for civilians.'

'OK, so the boy seems to have been encouraged to see himself as a favourite of Sandra's. Apparently some of his classmates felt there was a good deal more than favouritism involved. So we have the possibility that Sandra is—'

'Fucking him.'

'And in the process, training him in to do as she wants. Casting her Sandra-spell, as you put it. And what she wants is for Dr Rock to become available. Which of course involves finding a way to get your mother out of the picture.'

'And in this hypothesis, is my father involved?'

'That's one possibility. He would have worked with Casey on the rugby field. He seems to have been an inspiring man, is that so?'

'People say so. For a ten-year-old girl, unless she's very unlucky, her daddy's always an inspiration, he's her entire world. But people always said, in the world of rugby particularly, Dr

224

Rock was a mighty man. A hero to the guys.'

She made the world of rugby sound like a childish place, and her lip curled with irony when she said 'Dr Rock', but, despite that, the pain she still felt at his absence was evident.

'It's not necessary though, Sandra could easily have trained him herself. She took the long view: once Audrey was dead, she'd work on Dr Rock and reel him in.'

Martha sat open-mouthed.

'You know, I had always wondered . . . not that I wished him dead, but it didn't make any sense that Casey'd kill her and let him live.'

'Afterwards, the Howards paid Stephen Casey's mother off. Bought her a house.'

'For her silence? You mean she *knew* they'd killed her son?'

'No, she knew he'd killed your mother. And had then committed suicide. They paid her off so she wouldn't ask any inconvenient questions.'

'Like why? What was in it for him?'

'Exactly.'

'And what was?'

'We have to assume—again, falling in with what is only a hypothesis—that Sandra cast some kind of spell: maybe that your mother stood in the way of Dr Rock's happiness, and only by killing her could he be free.'

'That's a bit weak, isn't it?'

'Is it? For a seventeen-year-old who went ahead and did it? It might have been enough.'

'Well, yes, I suppose, the fact that he did go ahead and do it . . .'

'Were your mother and father happy?'

Martha took a long drink of her beer.

225

'I was ten years old, remember,' she said.

'I know. A good age to think whatever you like, without censoring your thoughts. Did you ever feel glad it was just you and your father? And did that make it so much worse when Sandra came on the scene? I know you might feel like it's some kind of betrayal to talk like that, but I'm just trying to get at the logic of it, of what might have seemed plausible—to Sandra, to Stephen Casey, maybe even to your father.'

Martha stared into her drink. In a low, awkward voice that sounded like she was reading a prepared statement, she said, 'Yes, I was happy when it was just the two of us; my mother wasn't a very giving person, and resented the affection my father showed me; when he got together with Sandra, what became obvious to me was that they were sexually very attracted to each other, they were doing it all the time, and then I began to feel that hadn't been the case between my dad and my mother. Did that make Sandra's presence even harder to take? For a girl who still believes her daddy is her prince? The fuck do you *think*?'

Martha drained her pint and looked for the barman, but he was nowhere to be seen; she turned back to me and shook her head.

'I've been paying a talking-cure woman for the last five years, and I haven't come close to telling her what I've just told you.'

'She was probably too chicken to ask straight out if your da killed your ma.'

'You're in the wrong line of work, Ed Loy. Where's the barman? Pat?'

Martha's face and manner were sombre in repose, but she worked them over with a big girl's

226

forced jollity. The beer was eating into the jollity, however, and I didn't want to lose her.

'Don't get drunk,' I said. 'Remember, you promised to show me yours.'

'Drunk on beer? Not me, I have hollow legs.'

Pat materialized at the bar, a mask of jaded scepticism on his ruddy round face.

'Do you have any food?' I said.

'No,' he said. 'We have toasted sandwiches.'

I ordered two ham-and-cheese and more drinks.

'And now,' I said, 'Dr John Howard, please.'

'Dr John Howard. Actually, I was exaggerating his importance. The disappointing thing is how typical he was of the Irish Catholic doctor of the age. The Church's willing enforcers. If Ireland had been in the Eastern bloc, we would have been riddled with secret police. We'd've had more police than people. I love this thing that we're supposed to hate informers, of all things, Jesus, we'd give up our own children so long as we could do it in secret. Anyway, the Church couldn't have carried out its anti-sterilization, anti-abortion, anti-contraception policies without the enthusiastic participation of the medical profession. Just like secret police and informers, when you have the laity doing it for you, it means you don't have to keep reminding them. I guess the fact that Howard advised several ministers on public health-care policy means he's become a kind of symbol of it all, the king who must be retrospectively dethroned. But in reality, and as much as I'd dearly love to single out the head of the Howard family for particular opprobrium, he's the same as all of those guys—a stethoscope in one hand and a crucifix in the other. He was just more successful than they were. And with the Howard Clinic, he saw that private medicine was never going to die here, that there'd always be money to be made, and prestige to be garnered, from keeping the upper tier open and the comfortable class in good health.'

The sandwiches arrived, and I fell on mine. It wasn't very nice, but English mustard took care of that, and it was hot and it qualified as food, and as I'd seen two men murdered since the last time I'd eaten, it suddenly felt reassuring simply to be alive, and hungry, and able to do something about it. Martha pushed her sandwich towards me, and I slathered it with mustard too.

'What about the hysterectomies and the symphys . . . I'm sorry, I can't pronounce—'

'Symphysiotomies. Yes, well, there's no doubt these were barbaric practices, but it's not as if he was the only one, and it's not as if that just happened back in the bad old days in black and white when no one knew any better than to beat children with leather straps and bugger them in industrial schools and presbyteries. These things were going on in the 1980s, into the nineties, when the Church was losing its grip entirely. I'm not undermining the seriousness of it, or the women's lives that were ruined, just saying that at least back then when Howard was on the go, there was a context, a societal and religious context for it.'

'So no smoking gun then.'

'No smoking gun. Very amusing, erudite fellow, wrote several anecdotal books—*Doctors and Golf, Doctors and Dining, Doctors and Drink* and, would you believe, *Doctors and Smoking*. Made a broader public name for himself in the seventies when he

228

became a regular guest on the *Late Late Show*, part of a panel they'd have on to discuss the events of the day.'

'And he'd weigh in with the Catholic line, would he?'

'No, actually, he was seemingly quite deft at finessing all of that. He was funny, and ironic, and charming—like an Irish David Niven, one of the old hands on the paper told me. And of course, that did the Clinic's business no harm at all, the notion that it had almost showbiz cachet.'

My phone rang. It was Tommy; he was in the car, heading for the city. I told him where I was and he said he'd come and get me. Martha finished her drink and looked at her watch.

'Before you go,' I said, and passed her the pages Jerry Dalton gave me. After she had read the second page, about how an overdose of insulin could resemble a heart attack, she turned to me and grabbed my arm.

'My father was a diabetic. Are you saying Sandra murdered him?'

'I haven't had time to work out what I'm saying yet. Someone put those two pages under my windscreen tonight. Yesterday they left a Mass card for Stephen Casey.'

'Someone is leading you along?'

'It feels like it.'

I didn't want to tell her I knew who it was. Not until I discovered more about what Jerry Dalton was up to.

'I feel like the top of my head's about to come off.'

'Maybe I shouldn't have shown you that. I mean, there's no evidence for it, for any of this . . .'

229

'Don't worry, I'm not about to collapse, or worse, barge into Rowan House and start making accusations. I know what you're doing. Still, it is, as the Pope would say, a bit of a mindfuck.'

'I don't know if you remember the details of your father's death . . .'

'I was away at university, they couldn't get hold of me, left messages at the college, with my tutor, at the flat . . . I was having a lost weekend, actually, hidden away, getting in touch with what I had just discovered was my sexuality. So when I got the message . . . my room-mates put up posters all over the town . . . when I finally found out my father had died, I was full of guilt and shame for not being around, and so of course I blamed myself for being gay. Then I blamed him for making me gay. And my mother, for dying, and Sandra, for being beautiful and capable, it was all their fault that I was gay and therefore my father died. It was all about me, in other words.'

'So you don't know . . . was he in hospital, or—'

'Yes, he was out somewhere, taken ill, rushed to the Howard Clinic with a suspected heart attack. I know the doctor who treated him—I've interviewed him a few times on politics-of-health-care issues, he's a very sound bloke, progressive.'

Martha was summoning up a number on her phone.

'A progressive who works in a private clinic?'

'Ah here, if you judged Irish doctors' politics by public and private, you'd be in trouble.'

'Somehow I thought from the tone of your articles you might.'

'Oh yes indeed. "Somehow I thought all you socialists would live on rice and sleep in tents and give the rest of your money to the poor." Ready for the revolution, but it ain't here yet, baby.'

She strode down the bar, speaking into her phone.

I called Tommy, who said he was coming down Dawson Street. I told him I'd be waiting outside the pub. Martha O'Connor came back.

'I've just spoken to him. He has a break in half an hour, he'll talk to you then. Mr James Morgan, consultant cardiologist. I told him what it was about.'

She turned and caught sight of herself in the mirror behind the bar, pulled a despairing face and looked at the floor.

'When I left after my father's funeral, I swore it was the end. And a fresh start. That meant no contact, trying not even to think about any of it. Good luck with your lives, let me get on with mine. Even with Morgan, I never asked him about my father's last hours. Last night, the murders, all the coverage of the Howard family, Rowan House— it's just opened it all up again. Like it never really ended, like it's unfinished business.'

'That's exactly what it is.'

A text message announced itself on Martha's phone.

'I have to go, I've a pain-in-the-arse sub questioning copy for tomorrow.'

We walked out into the night. A bus advertising some green fizzy drink loomed queasily in front of us. At the traffic lights, a drunken woman in a skimpy red dress was roaring abuse at her equally drunk partner.

'Martha, do you see your brother Jonathan?' I said. 'Your half-brother, I suppose, is more accurate.'

'I try,' she said. 'I barely know him. But I've called, and written . . . I wrote him a note when he got Schol. He never replies. He . . . sad but true to say, he just doesn't want to know.'

'I think . . . I think he could do with a friend at the moment. He's in trouble.'

'What kind of trouble?'

I didn't say. But I said he was in his rooms, tonight, and she said she'd think about it. She didn't look like she'd anywhere else to go. And I was worried about the kid, as much because of how I'd treated him as anything else.

The abusive woman at the lights had started to punch her partner in the face; he deflected this after a fashion by twisting to one side, so the barrage rained on the back of his head.

Martha turned to me, tears suddenly in her eyes.

'What do *you* think happened? Fuck, I'm a mess now.'

'I'm sorry. I would be too. I don't know. I really don't know. But I will find out. And then I'll tell you.'

She wiped her eyes, and forced another of those cheerful good-girl smiles out.

'It won't just be about me, by then. Tell the world, Ed Loy. Tell the world.'

I watched her walk down the street, her head bowed, and knew that she had stored up all the pain to relive on her own; that she would continue to do so, whether I got to the truth or not.

As she vanished through the night door of her newspaper's offices, the drunk man on the corner had had enough of being punched in the head by his girlfriend; he raised his long arm high above her, then seemed to think better of it, turned and sprinted past me. As the woman subsided to the wet ground in howling sobs, Tommy Owens drove the racing green Volvo 122S up alongside me.

18

Tommy offered to drive. I wasn't feeling the drinks I'd had, but I'd had a few, so I said OK, even if penitent Tommy on his best behaviour was faintly unnerving. He had changed his clothes for an old biker jacket and jeans and black Reeboks; clean shaven and with short hair, he looked like his own long-lost brother, the one who worked in IT and read science fiction at the weekends. We drove south to the Howard Clinic. On the way, David Manuel called.

'I'd like to see you.'

'What is it? Did Emily tell you something?'

'I think she told me a lot of things.'

'What kind of things?'

'I can't really explain over the phone. Let's just say, it's looking like thirty years ago is the more significant date in the Howard family.'

'What does that mean?'

'I can't explain, I'm between clients; I had to shift three appointments so I could see Emily again tonight. I'll be free at eleven.'

'I'll be there.'

At the Howard Clinic, I gave Mr Morgan's name at the security barrier. We drove up through some pretty landscaped gardens and parked near the first white circular tower. It reminded me of the rotunda in Rowan House, and I wondered if all three towers were modelled on it. The towers rose one behind the other, and you could see the turrets of Rowan House overlooking it all. The castle looked like a fabrication, like a Hollywood set, with the modern bungalow in front an actors' trailer. Drifts of fog were blowing in again, like smoke from a machine; north and east, the city lights were cloaked in a shimmering grey blanket; the horns in the bay blared their clarion call.

The Howard Clinic had tasteful canvases and an atrium with an indoor fountain and an aquarium and glass elevators and all the other stuff upscale private hospitals had to make the patients, who they thought of as customers, feel they were really getting their money's worth. You felt like asking where the bar was; at least, I did. I passed a portrait of Dr John Howard with dark hair and a pipe in his mouth and took the elevator to the sixth level, where Morgan's offices were. All the other suites were dark; a light was on in his. He was sitting in the waiting room, and I sat down opposite him.

'Sorry if this is a bit cloak and dagger. I'd just prefer if word didn't get out that I spoke to you,' he said, in a soft, musical Northern accent, Donegal or rural Derry.

'I am working for Sandra Howard,' I said.

'Yes. Well. I still . . . this is not something she necessarily might like to be brought to public attention. So I'll trust to your discretion.'

Mr James Morgan, consultant cardiologist, was in his late thirties, with boyish blond hair thinning on top and deep-pink farmboy cheeks; he wore a grey slacks and navy blazer combination, a striped shirt and matching tie and black tassel loafers. I had the sense he'd been wearing the same clothes for twenty years, and would go on wearing them another thirty, and would never notice what colour or style they were. He had a manila file on his lap. He looked excited.

'Go on. About Dr Richard O'Connor.'

'Yes. First of all, the fact that he was diabetic . . . but this appears nowhere on the records. Even though he worked here, he had never received treatment at this hospital. I wasn't even aware of it until tonight, when Martha called.'

'You two had never discussed her father's death?'

'She never brought it up. Except to say, you know, thanks for doing your best. Anyway, he was admitted . . . it was a bank holiday.'

'You were a junior then?'

'That's right. There was no consultant on duty.'

'Even in a private clinic?'

'Don't get me started. Dr O'Connor collapsed while playing rugby. Seven-a-side, I think. Myocardial infarction, was my assumption. He was sweating profusely, I remember he stank of booze, his heart was racing, his breathing was shallow, he was passing in and out of consciousness. There was difficulty getting hold of his wife. And the friend who admitted him made no mention of diabetes. He said it must have been a heart attack. Repeated it several times.'

'And . . .'

'And the symptoms seemed to back him up: we put him on an ECG, gave him nitro on an IV, oxygen, all the standard stuff, but he fell into a coma and died within a couple of hours. His wife,

Sandra O'Connor as she was, she never showed up, it seems she was in the countryside—no signal on her phone.'

'And in your judgement, if you had known he had had an overdose of insulin . . .'

'If I had known he was a diabetic, I would have looked out for hypoglycaemia, dextrose could have been administered at a gradual rate, and he might have survived. No guarantee he would have, he went pretty fast. But he didn't have a bracelet, no one around knew him, we didn't have his records.'

'So? The friend didn't know he was diabetic. That's common enough, surely, especially among men.'

'You don't understand. The friend . . . the friend was Denis Finnegan.'

I felt as if space and time had fallen away in the brightly lit waiting room, as if I had known this lilting country-voiced doctor all my life, and had been waiting for him to say what he had just said.

'All right,' I said. 'But he didn't necessarily know Dr O'Connor well, did he? I mean, what kind of rugby did they play together?'

'They coached Castlehill College. Rock had for years, Dr Rock, he was famous. And Finnegan had started back in the eighties, when he taught at the school. I was a boarder there, so were all my brothers. Rugby may be a religion around here, but Castlehill rugby . . . that's Opus Dei, you might say. No offence, if you're—'

'None taken. And I'm not. But Denis Finnegan is a solicitor, not a teacher.'

'Aye, but he was what you might call a late vocation. He taught for about five years.'

'At Castlehill. In the eighties.'

236

The same time Sandra was there. They knew each other *before*. Before Audrey O'Connor, before Stephen Casey. They knew each other all along.

'Absolutely. And Rock was coaching even though he was a full-time doctor, they'd bring past pupils back if they could give the team something extra. Finnegan was a useful little hooker, well, I guess he was little in his school days. Nearly made the grade, played with Shane Howard at Seafield back in the day. So basically, he must have known, it wasn't just some guy you met up with for Saturday-morning sevens, they were lifelong friends.'

'You didn't know. I mean, did your brothers know?'

'It's not something you'd let the pupils in on. But a close colleague? Hard to believe he wouldn't know.'

I was reaching for a thought, but it felt like I was opening a door into a blizzard: every time I looked out, the door slammed in my face, and the sound it made was *Denis Finnegan*. Finally, I made it.

'So did Finnegan coach into the nineties there?'

'Coaching up until a couple of years back, he worked on scrummaging, front-row manoeuvres, rucks and mauls through the phases, with all sides, even the S.'

'Even the S. Even the senior-cup team David Brady played on?'

'I'd say he'd've coached all the teams young Brady played on. God that's right, David Brady.'

I had a flash of the email address David Brady had sent Emily Howard's sex film to: maul@2ndphase.ie. Rugby jargon. I was out in the blizzard now, and though the buffeting winds were

237

chill, at least I had some idea where I was going.

'So what should we do?' said Morgan. 'Should we call the Guards? I mean, this could be manslaughter at least, maybe even murder.'

Morgan's pager went off.

'Let me hang on to it for a while,' I said. 'Or not,' as I quickly saw a frown of suspicion in Morgan's face. 'I know, I'm working for the Howards, but believe me, I'm not above the law, and nor are they; the Guards wouldn't tolerate me for five seconds if I tried to help my clients cheat justice. I just . . . I'm working the case, and now I feel it's beginning to come together, and I don't want to jump before I'm ready.'

Morgan looked at me through his clear farmboy's eyes, as if I'd just asked him if I could operate on one of his patients.

'I'm going to ring the Guards.'

'Why not leave it till the morning? They probably won't get to it before then anyway: night-time Dublin, lot on their plates. Call them first thing. And remember, Finnegan may well say he didn't know about O'Connor's diabetes, and he may well be telling the truth, and even if he isn't, there's not a lot the Guards can do if he insists he is.'

Morgan considered this. And then his pager went off again, and he sprang to his feet.

'Fair enough. The morning. You'll be ready to jump by then, will you?'

One way or another, I thought, one way or another.

But I wasn't ready yet.

*　　　*　　　*

238

In the car park, Tommy said he'd remembered something else.

'When Brock Taylor worked for your oul' fella?'

'Yeah?'

'I remember the bike, the Norton, and I knew it must have been him, because he had the badger streak in his hair. But back then, he didn't go by Taylor.'

'No? What was he then?'

'It was one of the names you used. Dalton.'

'You sure? That's very good, Tommy. OK, I think it's time you went home.'

'No Ed, I'm happy to stay. To, you know, whatever. Make it up.'

'You've made it up. To me. Go home, get some sleep. It's been a big night.'

Tommy grinned sheepishly, feeling his face.

'You can call a cab from inside.'

Tommy made to go, then stopped.

'I don't have my key,' he said.

'I meant, home to your own house. You can't stay in Quarry Fields. Not tonight, anyway.'

Tommy's face flared with indignation and hurt, but he tamped it down, nodded, turned, and walked into the Clinic.

I sat in the car park and phoned Shane Howard at the house and surgery numbers and on his mobile; I went straight through to the machine each time, so I called Denis Finnegan. His office phone went straight to voicemail; he answered his mobile immediately.

'Denis Finnegan.'

'Ed Loy, Denis. I hope it's not too late to call.'

'Never too late, my friend, I've been hoping

you'd get in touch. And apologies for my vanishing act this afternoon; I'm afraid one of the hazards of my profession is that the allied guilds upon whom we must depend ply their trade in a volatile and unpredictable manner; hence my expeditious removal to advise a, a sole trader and, ah, commodities broker from Finglas on his rights and entitlements under the law, or indeed whether he had any remaining, given the quantity of refined coca bean powder he was holding when arrested.'

I'm sure this stuff went down a bundle in Blackhall Place or in the Tilted Wig or whatever those pubs near the Four Courts are called; I was only glad I was getting it over the phone, so I didn't have to applaud.

'The information that David Brady and Jessica Howard were having an affair came in the form of a phone call to Shane.'

'That is my understanding also; I gather the Guards are devoting much of their current energy to tracing a number of telephone calls made immediately prior to the murders. Unfortunately for them, they have not found David Brady's phone.'

Because I still have it. And I haven't looked at it since.

'I wonder if you're at home, and if so, could I call and see you, in the next while.'

'Liberty Hall, old chap; I am not at home just yet, but am on my way, and I work into the small hours, so by all means come and interrupt me, there are a few questions I wanted to ask you earlier, and, while they momentarily escape me, I'm sure they'll return.'

A text came through as I ended the call. It read,

'I'm waiting for you. Sandra x.'

I thought for a second, and then sent a text to Tommy Owens:

'Need some GHB urgently. Ed.'

19

I had never been in Seafield Rugby Club before, but I suppose I thought it would be like a golf club or a yacht club. Maybe the clientele was, but the surroundings were far from upscale: the place looked more like a school hall or a community centre than the playpen for south County Dublin rugby boys of all ages. There were two bars upstairs at either end of the clubhouse, one above each dressing room, with a hall in the centre that looked out over the pitch. Tonight a twenty-first-birthday party was in full swing, although to me the celebrants all looked about fifteen, the boys drenched in hair gel, the girls in their underwear, so God knows how ancient I looked to them. I suppose I could have walked past the bouncer, who was also younger than me, if a good deal wider, but I didn't want to scare anyone; nor did I want to risk losing Jerry his job by alluding to police business, so I told the bouncer I had a lecture schedule for Jerry from university, and was allowed to wade through the bubbling sea of pheromones to one bar, only to be told, inevitably, that Jerry Dalton, or JD, as he was apparently known here, was manning the other. 'Dani California' by the Red Hot Chili Peppers had suddenly brought the entire room out on the floor, which made the return journey a little trickier, but I made it with the loss of a just a few pounds in sweat.

'JD! Point of Heino!' I yelled in my best rugby voice, and Dalton pulled the pint of Heineken and brought it to me in a plastic glass before realizing I didn't have a turned-up collar or a spiked-up fin.

'Thought if you had any more pointers for me, you could give them in person. Alternatively, I've left my car down there, so if you want to slip down and stick something under the wipers, I'll hang here and watch the taps for you.'

Dalton's dark eyes flashed.

'This all some kind of joke for you, is it?'

'I think you can see from the scar on my face how much fun I'm having,' I said. 'Heard from your friend Anita Venclova?'

Dalton nodded.

'She texted me. She said you'd helped Maria to escape. You've put them up. Thank you.'

'So what about you? Do you want to try and get to the bottom of this?'

'The bottom of what? What do you think I'm looking for?'

'At a guess, your father. How'm I doing?'

Dalton looked at me, then walked up the bar to serve Bacardi Breezers to two hot, red-faced girls in plaits. More orders crammed in, and soon he had several pints on the go. He gave the girls their change, came down to me and said, 'I've a break in ten minutes' time, meet you outside, OK?' and went back about his business.

I finished the Heineken, which had no taste or purpose that I could discern, went outside and lit a cigarette. When Dalton joined me, we wandered

242

around and sat on a slatted bench outside the dressing room nearest the main exit.

'How'd you know I was looking for my father?' he said.

'You told me who you think he is, at least indirectly,' I said. 'You pointed me to Stephen Casey, who you believe was your half-brother. From him, we get to Eileen Harvey, or Casey, or, eventually, Dalton. And the boy, Jeremiah John Dalton, born March 1986. And the father on the wedding certificate, Brian Patrick Dalton. Who took off before the baby was born. That's all we know, isn't it? Well, apart from the fact that Eileen Harvey, or Casey, or Dalton, killed herself a month afterwards.'

'We believe she killed herself. The body was never found.'

'I thought . . . the priest in Woodpark, Father Massey, told me she had gassed herself in the house, the house you're staying in now.'

'No. The story I was told, they found her clothes on Seafield Pier, the East pier. She'd apparently jumped into the sea. There was an eyewitness who saw her jump, apparently, he phoned the emergency services, there was a big hunt, but they never found her.'

'And who told you this?'

'Would you believe, the same Father Massey?'

'I asked him had you been to see him and he said no.'

'Looks like one of us needs to talk to Father Massey again,' Dalton said.

'How do you know about any of this in the first place? How did you find out? I mean, what was your name, for example?'

'What do you mean, what was my name? My name was Jeremiah Dalton—'

'No, I mean, what did your adoptive parents— the ones who did the easy stuff like bringing you up—what did they call you?'

'Don't disrespect me, Mr Loy—I have full regard for what my par—I call them my parents, because they behaved like they were—full regard for what they did for me, I'm not dishonouring or disowning them—'

'All right, all right. So what did they call you? What was your name for most of your life?'

'Scott. Alan Scott. Son of Robert and Elizabeth. Robert—no longer with us: cancer—doctor, gastroenterologist, hill-walker, nice man. Elizabeth—thriving in her prayerful way— housewife, bridge, church, garden. Sutton, by the sea.'

'How did you find out? Did they tell you when you were eighteen or something?'

'This is the . . . the only bit that made me angry . . . and my father, Robert, was dead by then, and getting angry with Elizabeth, it's not a place she can go, she doesn't have the muscle. It's pointless. But apparently, the Howards swore them to secrecy, they were to do everything they could to preserve the fiction that I was their child.'

'So how did you find out?'

'I began to get this stuff in the post. Loads of stuff about the Howards, I couldn't really make sense of any of it. That went on for a while, and then one morning, I got a copy of Jeremiah Dalton's baptismal certificate, from the Church of the Immaculate Conception, Woodpark. Well, one of the things about being no good at anger is,

244

Elizabeth is no good at lying either, so as soon as I showed it to her, she told me everything, or at least, everything she knew.'

'How much further have you gotten?'

He shook his head, ran a hand through his dark, wavy hair.

'Not much. I've been trying to sound out the Howards. I proceeded from the position that they wanted to keep it a secret, so I've avoided confrontations.'

'Did you work through Emily? Do you think she might have been the person who was sending you the information?'

'No. I was the one who told her about Stephen Casey. I think I might be responsible for getting her agitated about the whole . . . family plot. I don't know. It's pretty hard to tell with Emily. She's got a lot of stuff going on herself, many issues.'

I sensed his caginess. He wanted to find out more without giving too much away. I understood that, it was practically my job description. I certainly wasn't going to tell him who Brian Dalton had turned out to be, at least not while there was the chance he could still be his father.

'So you're looking at the possibility that this mystery Dalton character—'

'Brian Patrick Dalton.'

'Was your father.'

'Jessica Howard doesn't remember him. *Didn't* remember him. She said Shane's mother didn't like her, so she avoided Rowan House. Whether she would have met him up there I don't know. And the subject of Stephen Casey was avoided by everyone.'

'Shane told me he remembers getting a lift on his motorcycle.'

Dalton nodded.

'Some of the Woodpark oul' ones, I got talking to them down the pub, the ones who remember love to rabbit on about how awful and tragic it all was, and they said he was this guy in a leather jacket with a motorbike.'

'How did you come to rent the same house?'

'Again, it was sent to me in the post, the item in the newspaper advertising it for rent.'

'So there's someone pulling your strings.'

'It feels like that. But I feel I'm ready to push hard now, to start confronting people.'

'When you say "people", you mean Shane and Sandra.'

'There's no one else, is there?'

'Emily. Jonathan. If you're a part of that family . . . Denis Finnegan . . . someone has been feeding you the information, it must be that one of them wants you to get at the truth. For their own reasons, as much as yours.'

'I guess that's right.'

The bouncer came over to where we were sitting.

'JD, Barnesy said to give you the nod, OK?'

Dalton got up.

'Two things before you go. Jonathan O'Connor ever drink here?'

'Sure. He comes in with Denis Finnegan. And I've seen him with the Reillys as well, out in the car park. Last question.'

'If your father's not Dalton, who might it be?'

He shrugged.

'Who were the available males in the Howard household at the time? Shane? Dr John Howard

246

himself? Which is why Emily and me never got it together, or at least, haven't yet.'

'Howard was a dying man.'

'Stranger things have happened. I mean, there are too many unanswered questions: why did the Howards go to the lengths they did to cover things up? Why did they buy a house for Eileen Casey? She'd been living on her own for a long time with her son Stephen, seems to have been a tough cookie. Why did she suddenly crack up and commit suicide?'

'Post-natal depression, abandonment by another partner, on top of the grief around losing her first son. It's not an impossible place to get back from, but even the toughest cookie would find it hard.'

Dalton looked out over the fog-drenched night.

'Maybe you're right. Maybe I should just think of him as a black rider, who took off into the dark, never to be seen again, and leave it at that. Is that what you'd do?'

I thought about it. I didn't have to think very long.

'No, that isn't what I'd do.'

'Well, it isn't what I'm going to do either. 'Course, the possibility that Emily and I are blood relations has something to do with it too. Because I really like her. So I'm kind of hoping the old black-rider option is true.'

'JD! People're dying of thirst here!' called the bouncer.

'All right, I'm coming.'

He turned back to me.

'The funny thing is, you're searching for one thing, and it eventually becomes about everything, do you know what I mean?'

I nodded. I knew only too well.

'So the thing is, if I were you, I'd check the graveyard.'

*   *   *

I drove through Woodpark to the Church of the Immaculate Conception. On the way, I called Martha O'Connor.

'Martha, it's Ed. Just wanted to check you're OK. Hope it's not too late.'

'I'm in the office, working. Didn't see how I was going to sleep, after the load you dumped in my lap.'

'I'm sorry. But—'

'No, it's my fault. I've dealt with it by avoiding it for so long. One of the downsides of therapy, you can make yourself feel OK, or at least, less bad, just by talking. But you don't get anywhere. I thought the only way I could survive living here was by avoiding it all. Hey, it seems to work for most Irish families, right?'

Her laugh seemed tiny over the phone, like a struck match against the night sky.

'I think maybe you were ready to head in that direction anyway,' I said. 'I mean, the investigation into John Howard, the fact that you looked at him at all . . . that could only have been the start of something.'

'Mmm. Maybe. Anyway, what's up? I value your concern for my welfare, but what the fuck do you want?'

'Two things, if you can get to them. Where's John Howard buried? Is it a family plot?'

'Can do that, it would have been in the death

248

notices. Thing two?'

'I'm looking for the name of an eyewitness to a suicide by drowning, It would have been off Seafield Pier, late April 1986.'

'Not much of a story.'

'Apparently there was a big search-and-rescue attempt, all the emergency services were out.'

'That would have guaranteed coverage. Tonight?'

'If you can.'

'Does this mean we're partners?'

'Long as you give me a co-credit when you write it up.'

'A co-credit? What kind of sick fuck are you?'

'How'd it go with Jonathan, did you see him?'

'We had a drink. He's not a happy boy. Doesn't like you at all.'

'I was kind of hard on him.'

'Do him no harm, he's a bit of a spoilt brat.'

'Did he seem, when you left him, I don't know, stable?'

'Yeah. Sure. Why? You think he's likely to top himself? Let me tell you, he's a lot more depressed about my life now than he is about his. Leave 'em thanking God they're not you. That's the therapy to give 'em. I'll call you back . . . whenever?'

'As soon as you get anything, no matter how late. Thanks, Martha.'

The lights in the church were still on, and I remembered there was a vigil tonight. There were three old ladies and two old men on their knees in the pews, and one woman hauling herself around the Stations of the Cross on a red four-wheel walker. On the altar, the monstrance was prominently displayed, with its inner circle to

249

expose the consecrated Host, which Catholics believe is the actual body of Christ, and its surrounding ring of silver spikes; I flashed on the Halloween fireworks that had lit the heavens; maybe they were both faces of the same impulse. I thought I saw the sacristy door to the right of the altar slam shut. I walked down the aisle and tried the side door, but it was locked; I genuflected at the altar and went up to the door and tried it; it was locked too. I came down off the altar, soaking up the disapproving looks I was getting from a couple of the old ladies; the old men were asleep, or rapt in devout prayer, whichever is the greater. I knelt at the side altar near the sacristy to give myself a moment to think. The altar was devoted to the Blessed Virgin Mary, and there was a statue of Mary with the infant Jesus in her arms. I reached for a prayer, but didn't get very far. I stood up and genuflected again, the old training ingrained, and set off down the side aisle when something I had seen but not fully taken in made me turn around. There was a brass plate on the wall beside the altar, and I went back and read it properly.

It read, 'The restoration of this Marian Altar was made possible with the generous assistance of the Howard Family, 1986.'

The presbytery was an old Victorian villa to the rear of the church. There were no lights on. I knocked on the door. Either Father Massey wasn't there, or he wasn't answering.

20

I approached Rowan House from the bungalow side, but there were no lights on in the modern building, so I climbed the hill and swung the Volvo down the long drive and up through the red-berried trees to park beside Sandra Howard's black Mercedes. I'm not sure what I had in mind, if I thought I was going to confront Sandra Howard with what I had learned, or try and catch her in a lie like a barrister with a defendant, or simply brief her on my progress so far and watch her reactions, but when she opened the door in a dark-green silk robe that barely reached the tops of her pale freckled legs, my mind fought a brief tussle with my blood and lost. She wore a silver chain around her neck with a bloodstone that nestled between her breasts; her nipples were red and full, as were her lips, her green eyes looked clouded with lust; her hair was outstretched on her head like a fiery halo, and between her legs a red band glowed like a tongue of flame. She turned and led me through the hall and up the dark stairs, and we might have made it to a bed this time, but her scent, the tang of sweet earth spice in my nose, and her walk, the sway of her hips and the roll of her buttocks, robbed me of everything but urgency and instinct; I pulled her to me and kissed the back of her neck and her cheeks, and the clefts below her ears, and ran my hands slowly up her ribcage to her breasts, and then kissed her back, slowly down her spine, and she wouldn't turn, just sank to her knees and raised herself in the air, and reached a hand back for me, and guided me inside, and she screamed with the first thrusts, and then steadied in rhythm, and then stopped and turned and showed our faces, and she sat above me and steadied again, and we drove and ground at each other hard and long and came, blood beating in my ears and the sweet sound of her screams.

After a while, she stood up and opened a door, and light bled through to the landing.

'We're getting closer to a bed,' she said.

I followed her into a bedroom with two arched sash windows that looked out over the three towers to the city beyond; between them stood a mahogany tallboy with a tray of booze on top; against the wall facing, the bed was brass framed; I left my clothes on a chair and joined Sandra there. She had smears of blood on her lips; she brought her hand up to mine to show me I had too. There were weals on her hips, right and left.

'How did you get those?' I said.

'Your wedding ring,' she said. 'How long were you married? You don't have to answer.'

'Not long enough. Or, too long. Isn't that how it goes?'

'I don't know. I think it goes differently for each person.'

'Are you still married?'

'Not really. Not in any of the ways that count. But I probably won't divorce Denis. He's worked hard for us all.'

I lay there for a while and thought about my wife, married to another man and about to give birth to his child, and about our child, dead and buried in the ocean, about the anger I couldn't seem to shake and the way it expressed itself, in lust for a woman who could be a murderer, my balls hardening again as Sandra rubbed a nipple against mine and held my cock firm in her pale hand.

'We need to talk,' I said.

'We need more than talk,' she said, and we took more from each other, took what we needed, or tried. Afterwards, I stood and looked out over the three great towers and the city beyond, and thought how like a king it must feel to have this view at your command, how a castle would be nothing more than your due. When I turned back, Sandra had pulled the white cover up to her neck, and there were tears in her eyes.

'If we need to talk, you'd better start,' she said. 'Tell me what you've found out, and what you think it might mean.'

'I don't know what any of it means yet,' I said. 'Maybe you can tell me.'

I thought about getting dressed, and then I thought, *If I do, Sandra is less likely to trust me, to keep her guard down*, and so I got back into bed beside her. And as I propped up some pillows to sit against and pressed a smile on to my face, I felt in need of a drink to cleanse the shame of what I'd just thought from my mind; no wonder my wife had been drifting away long before our child died; how could you live with, let alone love, someone whose every thought was double, whose cast of mind was all manipulation, calculation, whose deepest urge was not to live life, to experience moments, but to analyse them and connect them up until they reached a statement, a verdict, an indictment?

As if she could read my thoughts, or maybe

because she shared some of them, Sandra rose from the bed and pulled her green silk wrapper on and got brandy and San Pellegrino and glasses from the tallboy and brought them back to bed and made drinks and gave me one and grinned, her mascara smeared and her lips the colour of blood, high above Dublin with the brandy warming us.

I could live with this woman until the end of time, I thought, and felt it was true, and then laughed at it, or made myself laugh at it, as if it was one of those things you think on holiday, drunk: 'Why don't I drop out of the rat race, move to this island and live off the land?' But I felt it, and I thought it was true. And then I opened my mouth.

'You and Denis Finnegan and Richard O'Connor were all involved with Castlehill College around the same time, in the 1980s. I suppose you must have been involved with hiring Denis, as deputy headmistress.'

Sandra laughed.

'No, not really, there was a panel to discuss appointments, but it was the principal's call. And the board ratify that. No, all a vice-principal— that's what they were called even in the eighties, I think the only deputy headmistresses they have now are in dungeons with handcuffs and whips— all I did was, well, I'm not sure what I did, filled in gaps and held the fort, I suppose. Responsibility without power, the wrong way round. Made my mother very happy though.'

'And your father? Your father was still alive then?'

'He was dismayed neither of us was doing medicine.'

'What about dentistry?'

'Father thought you might as well be an anaesthetist, or a nurse, as a dentist.'

'It was a big step for a school like Castlehill, with its very burly rugby atmosphere, to appoint a woman to a top job.'

'That's why they did it. So people would see they had done it, and then they could just continue on the way they were. Most appointments had something to do with rugby, Denis's included. I was the exception that proved the rule. And of course, given who my brother was, I wasn't even an exception.'

'And did you know Dr O'Connor well? He just came in to lend a hand coaching, didn't he? Did you get involved at that level?'

Sandra shook her head.

'I've never cared for the game. Never attracted to the boys who played it. And the cult of it in school . . . the mother, in her fur coat, presenting the winning captain, her son, with the cup . . . it's like something from the Colosseum.'

'Not even when Jonathan showed signs of being a player?'

'That was different. That was because of how well it meant he and his father were getting on.'

'So did you know Dr O'Connor well, rugby aside?'

'When?'

'In the early eighties. In the years before his wife was murdered.'

'Did I know him . . . well . . . you mean, as more than a colleague? As a friend? As a lover?'

'Any of the above. And Denis Finnegan. How well did you know him?'

'In the period before Audrey Howard was murdered.'

'That's right. Same categories.'

Sandra drank her brandy down and pulled her wrapper across her breasts and cupped the bloodstone in her hand; I could see it flash green and red, like a barometer of the energy between us.

'In the early eighties, I spent most of the time either working or looking after my elderly parents, that is to say, nursing Father through his long final illness and keeping Mother, or my fucking mother as I exclusively thought of her back then, from alternately driving him mad, firing his nurses, taking an overdose herself, selling the house from underneath us or otherwise trying to steal the limelight. Tramping up and down those stairs at all hours, because you could be sure if he had a fever, she'd develop one too, and God forbid she should sleep in a room on the ground floor. "I couldn't sleep knowing your father was suffering so close to me," so I was the one who went without sleep. I wore navy suits and had permed hair and looked older in my twenties than I do now. I didn't have a boyfriend, didn't have time or energy for a boyfriend, and if I had, I wouldn't have chosen Denis or Rock; they were too old, and I still thought I was young, even if I wasn't getting a chance to live as if I was.'

'What did your father die of?'

'Cancer. Well, pneumonia got him at the last, but it was cancer that had weakened him, lung at first, then it spread into the lymphs. He smoked a hundred a day for years, and cigars, and a pipe. There are still rooms in the house, even repainted, sit for ten minutes and they still reek of smoke.'

'You were close, you and he.'

Sandra looked at me, her eyes clear and bright now, and nodded gravely.

'He was a great man. And funny, charming, attractive, clever, arrogant maybe, a little imperious, his way or the highway, but great men have their foibles, shouldn't they be allowed them? And that's what he was, a great man.'

'And he died in '85, isn't that right?'

'In March. And Audrey O'Connor was murdered in August 1985. So did I start a relationship with Denis or Rock during that period is your next question. No, I did not.'

'What about Stephen Casey? He was a pupil of yours, wasn't he? In your . . . what did you teach?'

'French and English.'

'In both your classes?'

'In my French class. I didn't teach him English.'

'What kind of . . . I understand you had a close relationship with Stephen Casey. Who was the son of a servant of the family, wasn't he?'

Sandra forced a tight smile.

'I'm going to have a brandy. Would you like another brandy, Ed Loy?'

'I would, yes.'

Sandra made two more drinks, gave me one, and took a deep hit of hers, which she drank neat.

'I had . . . what would be called now an "inappropriate" relationship with Stephen Casey. I could say I was in grief at the death of my father, which I was, and that in this grief my long-lost libido had returned with a vengeance, which it had, and that I was sick to death being the eldest-child good girl who always knew better, which I was, and

257

I didn't want to waste time dating the kind of twerps and bozos who would go out with a frumpy old-before-her-time deputy headmistress without the handcuffs, which I didn't; and they could all sound like excuses, which they aren't. But basically, he was seventeen, and a brilliant pupil in my French class, and our housekeeper's son, although she didn't live in, and I seduced him, and it was inappropriate, as I've said, highly so, and dangerous, and very bad, and totally unexpected, and for a couple of months both of us had an absolutely fucking brilliant time.'

She laughed then, a rueful, joyous, filthy laugh, and it was hard not to laugh along with her.

'Although, you know, maybe if he'd lived, he would have found that I'd abused him and caused him untold and unaccountable distress, even if he was fucking seventeen and we could have got married, simply because I was his teacher. Who knows these days?'

She drank some more of her brandy. I looked at mine, but I wasn't sure I needed any more.

'And then the nightmare began. Rock's wife murdered, and Stephen vanished, and then the car brought to the surface in Bayview Sound, ahhhhh . . .'

She shook her head until her hair fell forward, shook it back and forth, like a maenad, or a teenage girl headbanging into a speaker bin.

'And that was the extent of your connection with those events.'

'"And that was the extent of your connection with those events." Jesus Christ what a pencil-licking prick you sound like Edward Loy.'

Her voice sing-song and flaring with temper, her

258

green eyes flashing red.

'I am a pencil-licking prick. That is, before everything else, what I am.'

'Do you really need me to spell it out? After . . .'

She gestured around the room: the rumpled, damp sheets, the reek of sex; the brandy smoking in the glasses. *I could live with this woman until the end of time.* The blood beating in my ears, like wings.

'Yes, I need you to spell it out.'

Sandra stood then, and looked down at me, calm again, cold, in fact, and I understood, whatever happened, there would almost certainly be no way back, and I almost hoped she was guilty of it all, of anything, so the pain I was going to feel might be lessened, or justified.

'I did not have anything to do with the murder of Audrey O'Connor, either myself or in conspiracy with Denis Finnegan and/or Richard O'Connor. I didn't . . . groom Stephen Casey, isn't that the expression? I didn't groom him to kill her, or to rob her house. I didn't have a relationship with Denis or Richard. I hadn't a notion, I stumbled about in a mist the whole time, I felt I could barely see. Is that enough on that?'

I nodded. She went out of the room, and was gone for few minutes. I wondered whether I should get dressed. When she came back in, wearing jeans and a faded denim shirt, I wished I had. She sat in a chair and smiled at me. No handcuffs or whips, but I felt I'd been hauled naked before the deputy headmistress. I swallowed some brandy, and smiled right back.

'All right,' I said. 'How did you get involved with Dr O'Connor?'

She shook her head and made a pained face at the open door, as if to an invisible jury in the corridor she knew would acquit her.

'I suppose we had grief in common. We were both trying to put our lives back together . . . and he helped me to reassemble mine. He was very strong, very brave . . .'

'Did he not have reservations at becoming close to someone who had been the lover of his wife's murderer?'

'He didn't know that. He . . . who told you that anyway? Because it was far from common knowledge, it . . . maybe some people suspected, but no one could have known for sure.'

'The Garda detective who investigated, Dan McArdle, had very strong suspicions.'

'I remember him. In his three-piece suit that looked like it had been carved out of wood and an anorak over it. Couldn't take his eyes off my tits the whole time he questioned me.'

'All right then, let's assume Dr . . . Dr Rock, is that what I should call him?'

'That's what everyone else called him.'

'Let's assume Dr Rock didn't know about your affair with the dead boy. What was it, do you think, that drew you to an older man, when you said before older men weren't your type?'

'What are you, a private dick or a shrink? Why should I answer that?'

Dead boy, private dick. This was more of a lovers' quarrel than a case.

I drained my brandy and got out of bed and started to put some clothes on.

'You don't have to answer any of my questions. But it would help if you did. I'm convinced what

260

happened yesterday is linked to what happened twenty years ago, that to keep your brother out of jail, we need to solve Audrey O'Connor's murder. You say you were in a mist back then, you couldn't see what was going on. Well you're still in that mist tonight, and so is Shane, only now Emily is caught in it too, and Jonathan, and Martha O'Connor. I'm trying to clear it. I'm not trying to bully you, or pry into your private affairs. You can help me here. Or you can hold fast to a past you don't pretend to understand, and leave yourself and everyone else you know stumbling, blind, lost.'

I went to her, reached a hand to her face. She stopped it before it touched her cheek, held it to her lips and looked up at me.

'OK,' she said.

'OK,' I said, and sat on the bed.

'I guess a shrink might say . . . I didn't use one, but it seems fairly obvious . . . that having lost my father, I was drawn to another . . . father figure. But I didn't see Rock like that, or not only like that, not at first . . . I wasn't attracted to him initially, we became friends first, then the attraction grew, although it turned out he'd been nursing a bit of a pash for me . . . but he was very fit, physically, we had a good sex life, he was . . . volatile and energetic and unpredictable, he wasn't this . . . I don't know, safe harbour, that's what I always think of when I hear the words "father figure", safe harbour, like a fucking retirement home—'

'But your own father wasn't like that either, was he?'

'No, I guess he wasn't. He *certainly* wasn't. And he was inspirational, or he would have been, if he

261

wasn't so difficult to live up to.'

'You told me this, that you had no confidence, that Rock made you believe in yourself. Was that not something you had from your father?'

'Father was very . . . it was the old style, never praise, if you got a B in your exams, you should have got an A, get an A and it's no more than was expected. After a while, that wears you down, you feel you'll never do anything worthy of his attention and respect. And so you don't.'

'That's why you didn't do medicine?'

'And why Shane did dentistry. That was a real fuck you to the old man. I was angry at the time. But now . . .'

She dropped her head into her hand, pressed her eyes between thumb and forefinger.

'I'm sorry. Keep going,' she said.

'Your parents' sex life. You said they had separatex bedrooms. Was that just through your father's illness, or—'

'Oh God no, they hadn't slept together since Ma . . . since . . . I think Father had an affair, or something . . . at least I assume that's what it was, Mother never spoke about it . . . from when we were, I don't know, teenagers. It was . . . I don't know.'

She shrugged, blushing, not wanting, like any of us I suppose, to go within ten miles of her parents' sex life.

'What was that you said, "Since Ma . . . ?"'

'"Since Ma . . . found out", I suppose I was going to say. About the affair.'

'You didn't call your mother "Ma", did you? Posh girl like you?'

'Hark at the little urchin lad. No, I didn't, but

262

Stephen did. So I did sometimes. Affectation.'

'Social sliding. Below-stairs slumming.'

'Fuck off.'

'Stephen Casey. Is there any way on earth you would have expected him to do what he did?'

'I still can't believe it. Apart from anything else . . . I mean, I know he might have thought of himself as a charity case—or rather, some of his charming fellow pupils might have accused him of being one—but he wasn't chippy in the slightest. He was a brilliant rugby player—that's where I began to take a real interest in the game.'

She grinned in a hungry way.

'You said you weren't attracted to the boys who played rugby.'

'Yes. Well, that was a lie. That was before I'd decided to tell you about the affair with Stephen.'

'Now would be a good time to clear up any more lies.'

'No more lies, your honour.'

'So there's no way in which you can explain why he would do such a thing.'

She shook her head.

'I mean, say if he had harboured grudges, people have more money than me, I'm going to get me some no matter what I have to do—and then he ends up with a bag of old ornaments. What's that about?'

'He wanted to steal big money, but the presence of the child, of Martha O'Connor, threw him off, brought him to his senses, he panicked and ran. And then, realizing what a mess he'd made of it all, how he'd murdered a woman in front of her husband and child, he took the only rational course open to him, and killed himself.'

'I can't believe it. I still can't believe it,' Sandra said.

'Was there ever a time when you wondered if Rock had been the one to groom Stephen Casey? I know he wasn't happy in his marriage to Audrey—'

'How do you know that?'

'Martha told me.'

'Did she now? Well, then it must be true. Did she suggest her father had wanted his wife murdered? Nothing that woman said would surprise me.'

'She speaks very highly of you too.'

'She never gave me a chance. I went down on my hands and knees for that child, and she never gave me a chance—'

'She was just a child, a traumatized child who'd seen her mother murdered.'

Sandra was shaking, suddenly full of emotion, her burning eyes brimming with tears.

'We all had our troubles, you know. We all had our troubles.'

The emotion boiled over, sobs erupting from wherever they were stored. I went to hold her, but she shook her head and ran from the room. Down the corridor I heard her weeping, and then a door slamming. 'The teenage symphony', Sandra had called it yesterday. It seemed for the Howards, the melody lingered on long past the teenage years.

I checked my watch: I was going to be late for David Manuel. I went down the great circular stairs. I wondered whether there was anything in Emily's room worth my attention. I went back through the arch, crossed the rear hall and tried the double doors, which were open. There were no servants around, which surprised me, but in this instance, made life easier. Darkness lay ahead. I went along the white passageway that led to the bungalow, trying for lights at each corner until I found a panel and threw them all on. I knocked on Emily's door a couple of times, then tried it. The room was empty, and all her stuff was gone: no clothes in the wardrobe, no boots beneath the bed. There was a drug-company notepad, but no notes had been made, or at least, if there had, there were no indentations to tell what the content might have been. I did the usual trawl: drawers, cupboards, bedside table, mattress, bed linen, came up with nothing. All I could find was, on the window sill, a line of rowan berries spread across from edge to edge. There was another line on top of the door surround, and another layer on the carpet just inside the door stop. Maybe, like heliotrope, it had some special meaning. Or maybe Emily had just become very bored, and had left before she coated the entire room with the red and green fruit.

Back in Rowan House, all was quiet. I walked down along the rear corridor, which was hung with horse-racing prints and had a tiny marble holy-water font wall-mounted beside each door. I saw two grandly decorated sitting rooms in a Victorian style, all heavy drapes and mahogany furniture and chintz, and the inevitable portraits of John Howard, who must have had artists queuing up to paint him. A couple of doors were locked; a couple opened on musty bathrooms, there was a bedroom with a brown-leather chaise and a roll-top desk and a wall of diplomas and degrees that I imagined was Howard's, and then a room where the light didn't work. I pushed the door open and went across to the window and opened the curtains. It was a small girl's room with Sleeping Beauty wallpaper. There

265

was a beautiful old doll's house, and a teddy bear and a pig with only one ear lay on the pillow, as if waiting for the girl who owned them to come to bed. The wardrobe was full of dresses and skirts that might fit an eleven- or twelve-year-old girl, including school-uniform pinafores and kilts in red-and-green tartan; the chest of drawers was packed with tops and shorts and underwear for the same. There wasn't a speck of dust; everything was fresh and clean and smelt of lavender. I crossed the room and looked at the doll's house, which sat on a table near the window. It was a model of Rowan House, just as I had seen in Emily's room, with two differences: there was no garden plinth beneath it, and the roof opened. I turned it around and lifted the roof and looked underneath when the door flew open behind me.

'What the hell do you think you're doing in here? Who gave you permission to wander about the house?'

Sandra Howard stood in the doorway in a white cotton shift, hair pulled up and back, face drained of blood, eyes ablaze.

'I was just having a look around,' I said, working hard to get the words out. 'Was this your room?'

'Of course it wasn't my room . . . yes, yes, it was, ages ago, now come on, out of here—'

'Why is it preserved like this? It's as if—'

'It's not "preserved", I went away to school, that's all, it's not "as if" anything. Now for God's sake will you get out?'

Her voice had become a shrill, hard screech, with the grace notes of hysteria. I walked past her in the wide doorway. She wouldn't meet my eye.

In the hall, I waited for her to say goodnight, but

266

she didn't come.

I shut the great doors of Rowan House behind me, two images vivid in my brain. One was of the haunted expression in Sandra's eyes, the shadow across her suddenly gaunt face, as she said, 'We all had our troubles, you know.'

The other was what I saw beneath the doll's-house roof: Mary and Joseph and some wise men and an angel from a child's crib in a ring around a Barbie doll on all fours with a hole punched between her spread legs and red painted around the hole, and an Action Man doll kneeling behind the hole, between her legs. On the inside of the roof in red were daubed the words 'I should be ashamed of myself'.

III

All Souls' Day

He answered and said unto them, When it is evening, ye say, It will be fair weather: for the sky is red. And in the morning, It will be foul weather to day: for the sky is red and lowring. O ye hypocrites, ye can discern the face of the sky, but can ye not discern the signs of the times?

Matthew 16: 2–3

21

I drove to Hennessy's in Bayview, where everything is available at a price, and Tommy met me in the car park and gave me a small bottle of GHB.

'Be careful with it man,' he said. 'Very easy to OD, specially mixing with booze.'

'OK. Thanks, Tommy.'

'Are you sure this is the right way to go?' he said. He was so used to my being the reliable one that, whenever it looked like I was getting wayward, Tommy got very grave and paternal. It always made me smile, and I was always glad of it.

'I'll only use it in an emergency,' I said.

GHB in small doses works a little like Ecstasy; in conjunction with booze, it can knock a man out. I didn't like using it, but I could hear the clock ticking.

I drove through the night with the windows open and the damp night air blowing in, trying to breathe, trying to make sense of what I had just seen. I remembered what David Manuel had said: in regard to the Howards, it's what happened twenty, *thirty* years ago that counts; I wondered how much he knew, and what more Emily had told him: would she confirm that Sandra had been abused by her father? What might she add about herself? I called Manuel, but his phone was off; I left a message saying I was on my way, but I would be late.

When I turned into the square, I could smell the smoke clearly; no confusing it with fog this time. I

271

got out of the car and saw it pouring out the top of Manuel's house. There was no fire brigade, no ambulance or police, just a few neighbours gathering, and what appeared to be Manuel's hysterical family running up and down the garden; I recognized his wife standing in the doorway.

'Mrs Manuel, I'm Ed Loy. I saw your husband this morning. I'm a detective.'

'He's trapped up there. Please, can you try and reach him?'

A tall girl of about fifteen with the same dark colouring as Manuel's wife was crying. She turned to me.

'The flames are coming down the stairs.'

I went into the house, and started up the stairs; by the third floor, the smoke was too thick to see and the heat was unbearable; I couldn't go any further. I couldn't see the flames, but I could hear their rumbling crackle, like some infernal engine.

I went down and out through the kitchen into the back garden. An old metal fire escape ran from the first floor to the third; I shinned up on to the flat roof of the kitchen extension and climbed the spindly ladder until the pitched roof lay above me. Through the dark window of the attic room, I could see the red flames glowing like trammelled rage. I couldn't see David Manuel, and reckoned he must have passed out from smoke inhalation; the roof tiles were concrete, and I thought if I could work a few loose and hurl them at the window, I might break it, let some air in and hopefully bring him back to consciousness; I worried that the air would drive the flames higher; as it turned out, plan and worry were all in vain. I flung one tile at the Velux window; it almost bounced off the double-glazed glass, skittered down the roof and fell the long three storeys to smash on the paving stones below.

As if this was some kind of occult summons, Manuel suddenly rose up in the window, an apparition in green, arms and shoulders on fire; his hands reached for the window's release bar, and the red flames behind him danced higher as he forced the window open and there was a roar from within like a beast in torment and Manuel came out head first on to the roof above me. His back and his long hair were on fire now, his movements agonized, staccato, like an insect on a grill; I called to him, but he was beyond hearing, beyond vision. He moved on hands and knees down the roof, and looked like he might crawl right off the edge; I tried to reach across and grab him, but just then he stood up and stepped out into the night and fell like a burning angel, down into the garden below.

By the time I reached the ground, the sound of sirens filled the air, but they didn't drown out the grief of Manuel's family, who had all been watching from below; his distraught wife clutched her teenage daughter and a younger girl; two teenage boys were caught between the need to go to their father's ruined body and the natural human urge to turn away; quickly the ambulance men intervened, and then the fire service were running hoses through the house, and the family's agony was buffered by official intervention. A fireman tried to get me to stay at the scene, but I slipped away and drifted in among the neighbours and the ghouls as the Guards arrived. It would be useful to know who Manuel's last client had been, but I couldn't ask his wife; it was probable she didn't even know. All I knew was that Manuel had hoped to tell me what he had learned from Emily Howard, and now he was dead. It was hard not to believe those two facts were connected.

I caught sight of myself in the rear-view, and almost drove off the road; my face was blackened by smoke, my hair frosted with white ash; I looked like a photo-negative of myself. I pulled in at a hotel in Donnybrook, walked quickly through the lobby to the bathroom and gave myself a wash and a brush up. It was twelve ten, and I'd been on the road since six this morning; I told myself it was time to pack it in for the night.

I walked back across the lobby with every intention of listening to myself. But the bar was still open, with an extension for something they described as the 'Halloween Festival'—not just a night but an endless weekend—and I decided any man who'd just seen what I'd seen deserved a drink. The bar was thronged with people who looked like they'd been at a party for too long and needed to go home, but had forgotten where they lived. My type of crowd. I sat at the bar and ordered a cup of coffee; when it arrived, I asked for a double Jameson as if it were an afterthought. I put sugar in the coffee and added the whiskey and drank the whole thing in three draughts. It burnt my throat and warmed up my gut and made me feel half-alive again. I was doing fifty per cent better than David Manuel.

The voice in my head reminded me that I should go home, that a night's sleep and everything would look, would even be, different. I pondered this, and all I could come up with were the facts: that there was a killer on the loose, that he or she had

274

just killed again, that everyone I was working for: Sandra Howard, Shane Howard, Emily Howard, Jonathan O'Connor, Denis Finnegan, each of them was in danger of being the next victim. Equally, any of them—more than one—might be the killer. I was the only one who knew the extent of the connections and how they all joined together—to the extent that I did. The killer didn't show any sign of stopping. That meant I couldn't either. Maybe I could catch a quick nap, like the two old boys at the all-night Exposition of the Blessed Sacrament across in Woodpark. Maybe even that was unwise: neither of them had looked like he was certain to wake up.

I checked my phone to see if Martha O'Connor had called or texted with the information I'd asked her for. The phone I picked out of my pocket wasn't my phone though; it was David Brady's. I had checked the text messages before; I ordered another coffee and worked through the Received Calls and Dialled Numbers lists, comparing them to the numbers I had on my phone for the principals in the case. Several of the incoming calls were listed as 'no number'. There had been calls made to and received from Emily in the days leading up to the murder; I noted Emily's number, which came up with her name and which I didn't have. I thought of ringing her, but I didn't want to wake her if she was asleep. I sent her a text message hoping she was well, and asking to speak to her as soon as I could.

I felt like I was getting nowhere; I couldn't imagine what it would prove if David had rung anyone on my list. The green Jameson bottle behind the bar was flaunting its red crest at me again, and I was starting to give it the eye back. I thought of Tommy then, and how he had discovered the truth about his daughter Naomi by scrolling through the photographs on her phone. I wasn't used to a phone that doubled as a camera, though it struck me that it would be quite useful, particularly for all that lovely divorce work that paid the bills and left me feeling so morally uplifted and optimistic for the human race afterwards. I navigated from the menu to the picture gallery, opened the first folder and scrolled through the images. They were what I had been expecting: a series of women, including Emily and Maria Venclova, in sexual poses; there were a fair few of Brady and 'the guys', either in action on the rugby field or hoisting pints in what I now recognised as Seafield Rugby Club bar. Some images combined elements of both, though in a mildish form: girls flashing their tits for the guys; the guys flashing their bits for the girls. I experienced the kind of boredom and despair you normally associate with reality TV, and while one hand clicked faster through the images, the other was flexing itself in readiness for another shot of whiskey. So I was distracted, and three shots past the shot I wanted, and had to track back, and momentarily clicked myself out of the image gallery, and ended up having to start from the beginning and track through each image again, but finally I got to the shot I had begun to think I had imagined. There it was, two men and a boy having a pint together in the rugby club: Brock Taylor, Denis Finnegan and Jonathan O'Connor. Brock Taylor, who once worked for my da, and now had men shot to death for little or nothing, in Dublin, the city that shrank as you stared at it, until eventually, no matter who they were and what they had done, somehow, it all came back to you.

22

Denis Finnegan's offices were in Mountjoy Square, about as far from the river on the north side of the city as Fitzwilliam Square was on the south. Before I left Dublin twenty-five years ago, you would have ended the comparison there: while there had been some major demolition and deterioration among the Georgian houses on the south side, not least on the adjoining Fitzwilliam Street, Fitzwilliam Square itself had survived relatively intact, whereas Mountjoy Square had been gutted, often without the demolished houses being replaced; vacant sites and derelict houses made it look like a cross between a bomb site and Skid Row. But the gold rush had changed the fabric of the city, for better or worse. Mountjoy Square fell firmly into the former category, with the gaps having been mostly filled either with restored originals or plausible facsimiles; it now looked like a square again, and tonight, high above the river, its park dense with shedding trees, the ashes already skeletal, in the swirling fog as a church bell struck one, it gave the impression simultaneously of being absolutely real in the concrete here and now, and an illusory dreamscape from the past, an ethereal evocation of times and lives now dead and done, as if whatever actions I might take, whatever my striving, it would be to the same end.

Finnegan's house was on the north side of the square. He was as good as his word: hale and hearty, if a little drunk, he greeted me enthusiastically and led me up the stairs to a second-floor sitting room that overlooked the square and much of the city. The room was painted dark green, with a cream ceiling and a rich amber carpet; a gold chandelier with tulip bulbs hung from an ornate centrepiece; a turf fire seethed in the grate. Over chalk-stripe trousers, shirt and bow tie, he wore a peculiar-looking burgundy-velvet smoking jacket, brocaded in a faintly Turkish manner, that looked like it had last seen use in a comic opera. He offered me a range of things from a groaning drinks table by one of the big sash windows; all I wanted was a bottle of Guinness, which was good for keeping the alcohol in the blood steady while not really counting as a drink. But since Finnegan was oiling himself with a ten-year-old Macallan, which may have had something to do with his face glowing a shade or two brighter than his jacket, I asked for one as well, and commandeered the bottle on the pretext of reading the label.

I had such a number of things to charge Finnegan with that it was hard to know where to start, but I didn't think asking him how many people in total he reckoned he had murdered was a great icebreaker. And the only one I was confident he had killed was Richard O'Connor, and that would be impossible to prove. But since I'd last seen Finnegan in south Dublin, indeed looking like an exemplar of that zone, there was a time-honoured city-sensitive way of kicking things off.

'So Denis, you're here on the northside. What's that about?'

'I made a little money in the eighties. These houses were tumbling down at the time, it was a civic disgrace. But it did mean you could pick one up for a song. I had it restored, over time—living on one floor while another was overrun with builders. And of course I based my practice here.'

'During the eighties, the early eighties, while you were teaching in Castlehill College?'

'It would have been after that, about 1985.'

'You left in 1985? And what, you went back to university?'

'Oh no. I had already taken a degree and so forth, I just had to complete my apprenticeship. There weren't many of us who hung around. But I had location on my side. Back then, before we had what the newspapers insist on referring to as "gangland", we just had a clutch of ordinary, decent criminals. And the bulk of them came from within a stone's throw of my door. Although, having represented many of the gentlemen concerned, I shouldn't have considered it in the least wise prudent to throw a stone at any of them.'

'You must have known them all at that time,' I said. 'Lar and Shea Temple, the Flannery brothers, Brock Taylor.'

Finnegan nodded, as if we were reminiscing about some glorious rugby heroes of the past.

'Oh yes, Brian in particular. I brokered the settlement with the Criminal Assets Bureau on his behalf. Brian's done well.'

'He's done very well. House on Fitzwilliam Square, the Woodpark Inn, and he seems to be buying up half of the surrounding area.'

'Yes,' Finnegan nodded. His face had contracted into that oriental rictus smile again.

'Why do you think he's doing that? In that area particularly?'

'I wouldn't really know. I suppose there's council stock there still to be had relatively cheaply, he estimates that it's the coming area, just on the Castlehill/Seafield border after all.'

'And he's quite the man in Seafield Rugby Club as well.'

'Is that right?' Finnegan said.

'Is that right? Sure you know that's right, aren't you to be found there regularly? You and Jonathan? Sharing a drink with Brock?'

Finnegan put his drink down on a small mahogany side table and repositioned himself in his seat, uncrossing his legs and planting his tiny feet side by side on the amber carpet.

'Mr Loy, I'm not entirely sure where, as our American friends might say, you're going here. The fact is, I represent many people. Outside of that, I live my own life. Brian Taylor, since he seems to have become the focus of your current inquiries—although at some point in the dim and distant past, I did understand you to be working on behalf of Shane Howard, but who am I to tell a man how to do his job?—Brian Taylor appears to be a reformed character. If it turns out that he is not, I will hear about it soon enough, in the form of a phone call. Until then, what he does is beyond my control. The fact that he has chosen to move in circles, some of which are congruent with mine, is unusual but not illegal; I don't normally enjoy the society of my clients out of office hours. But then, few of Brian's coevals share his urge to . . . "better

280

himself".'

'Do you think it's a bit crass of him, Denis? A bit embarrassing? Do you and the rest of the car-coat brigade up the rugby club find yourselves sniggering into your Scotches at the presumption of the fellow?'

Finnegan's head swivelled around and his chin jutted forward, like a man in a pub ready for a fight.

'I'm a Northside boy myself, as a matter of fact. O'Connell's, then a scholarship to Belvedere. I didn't cycle up the Liffey on a fucking bicycle. I earned every penny.'

The accent had coarsened a little, but only a little; over the years, the polish had worked its way deep into the grain of Denis Finnegan.

'So you and Brock go back, do you? Back to Blessington Street?'

'I came from Wellington Street.'

'Near neighbours then.'

'We weren't friends.'

'I wouldn't have thought so. Brock's initial ideas for bettering himself were a little more short term than yours. But they seem to have worked out. Fitzwilliam Square still more fashionable than Mountjoy.'

'Once again, Mr Loy, and while it is a continuing pleasure to talk to you, of course, I must ask—'

'It's interesting, where people come from. And how they get where they're going. I didn't exactly start out with a silver spoon either. My father never really made a go of things. But for a while he ran a motor garage, quite near Woodpark. And the funny thing is he had a fellow there working for him, name of Brian Dalton. Do you know who that

281

was?'

Finnegan's face was perfectly still.

'I think—and I could be wrong—that he and Brian Taylor are the same,' I said.

'And if they are?'

'Well, I wonder if it's interesting. Since a while later he married the Howard family's heavily pregnant housemaid, and they moved into a house in Woodpark. And then he seems to have disappeared, and she was thought to have drowned herself.'

'And the child?'

'And the child was adopted. So, you see, there are connections to be made. It would be extremely interesting to know what his proper name was, Taylor or Dalton. Someone who knew him back in the day should know that, at least. Then again, maybe you're right, maybe it's not that interesting at all. Why don't we talk about property again? It's still the conversational topic of choice in Dublin, isn't it? And it's what you chose to speak to me about when we first met—can it only have been two days ago? It feels like much longer.'

'It certainly does. Can I get you another drink?'

'Here, allow me.'

I took our glasses and the Macallan to the drinks table and, seeing my reflection in the window, checked to see if Finnegan was watching. He was staring into the fire, and it was the work of a moment to snap the top of the GHB bottle, drop a capful and a bit into Finnegan's glass and replace the bottle in my pocket. As I poured the whisky and added water, I stared out the big sash window. The shutters were open, and I noted again how the windows diminished in size as the floors rose, how this one was smaller than the ground-floor window had been in Fitzwilliam Square. The congruence between Finnegan and Taylor, near neighbours as kids in a rough end of town, now residents of two of the city's great squares, was setting off flares in my brain. The light from each revealed another stop on the map; I was counting on reaching my destination before the night was out.

'What I'm interested in is the will Shane and Sandra's mother left. Remember, you were talking about it yesterday? You felt Jessica Howard was going to prove troublesome.'

Finnegan turned and looked at me as if he was surprised I was still here.

'And why should that be of any moment, Mr Loy?'

'Because it gives several people a motive for wanting her out of the way. As you reminded me, I'm working on behalf of Shane Howard, and if he's not the only one who might have profited from his wife's death, well, all the better for him.'

I gave Denis Finnegan his drink and sat down across from him.

'I spoke to the Guards in Seafield about this myself.'

'And what did you say?'

'Mary Howard stipulated in her will that Rowan House was to go to Shane and Shane alone.'

'Yes, but Shane and Sandra were locked in a dispute over what to do about the bequest. Shane told me he wished it had been split.'

'Well, in practical terms, Shane was behaving as if it had been.'

'What does that mean? That he agreed with the plan to build the fourth tower?'

Finnegan looked into his glass and made a face. I took a drink of mine and smiled. He shook his head.

'Did you mix the whisky with mineral water?'

I nodded, and Finnegan clicked his tongue.

'An unforgivable solecism, Mr Loy. An excess of sodium. Still, a sin to waste it.'

He took a good belt of his drink and sat back.

'I think *au fond* Shane was on Sandra's side, yes. I think he favoured that option. A centre for private psychiatric care. It would be the final piece of the jigsaw. But Shane was caught between Sandra and Jessica's plan for a residential development. And since she and Shane were about to separate, and presumably to divorce, you might say she was keen to maximize her settlement before she left.'

'Why do you believe Shane would have supported the plan to build the final tower? He sounded at best neutral to me.'

'He knew Sandra wanted it. Shane has always been keen to see Sandra protected, ever since they were children. To make sure she wasn't hurt. To make sure she got what she wanted. What she deserved.'

Finnegan was beaming at me now, his eyes flickering, the red dome of his brow glowing. What was he asking me to believe? That Shane Howard had been the one all along, the one to ensure that Dr Rock was free, that Finnegan was able to step forward, and now, the one to clear Jessica out of their way?

'I've tried to make that my job also, as her husband. I don't know that I can say I've succeeded. We effectively live apart now. I know

284

I've failed in many respects, although I think I have been a good father—yes, father is not too strong a word—to young Jonathan. But I know too that I've always given of my best. And I always have been, and remain, loyal to the Howard family, Mr Loy.'

He sounded like a politician giving a resignation speech. He drained his glass, made his way to the drinks table, and poured a large neat whisky.

'And that's what the fourth tower would be, would it?' I said. 'The vindication of the Howards?'

'I don't think "vindication" is the appropriate word. You might find "apotheosis" excessive.'

'I might. If I was sure just what it meant.'

'Their ascension to Olympus. Their deification. Mock all you like, but when John Howard built the first tower there was no vision in this country, nothing but piety and spite. And he saw beyond that, he saw . . . he saw the future, Mr Loy. It's not fashionable any more to laud great men, but I've seen one in my lifetime, and John Howard was that man. I remember the day I first set eyes on him. It was way back, an under-thirteen's A game. I played hooker for Belvedere; Shane was the captain of that year's Castlehill side. It wasn't much of a game, muddy pitch, kick and ruck, grind out the penalties. Castlehill won, of course, chiefly because of a great piece of opportunist play from young Howard, blindside break from twenty yards caught us napping, handed off full back and winger like they were made of straw, only try of the game. And it was a killer, but it was one of those times where you have to go, fair enough, you've got it and we don't. And that's

285

when I saw John Howard for the first time, tall, elegant, the long coat, the red-and-green paisley scarf, the black fedora. He cut a dash, you know? He really cut a dash. He looked fitter than any of the boys on the field, and he must have been knocking on seventy by then. Like Peter O'Toole, you know? And the two angel girls with him, my God. Sandra, maybe fourteen, with her hair right down her back, her eyes like jewels, her milky skin . . . my God, she looked like a princess. Like a real . . . princess.'

Finnegan stood against the window, swaying now, slopping the whisky in his glass. He leant over from the waist and let gravity trundle him towards the fire, where he slapped his crystal tumbler down above his chin on the high mantelpiece, and left his arm there, as if his glass was a peg he was hanging from. I hardly dared breathe, waiting for him to continue; from my neck to my ribcage, wave after wave of chill ice rippled; I was shaking with it. Finally, because he seemed lost to dreams, and I was afraid the drug would kick in before he said any more, I spoke.

'And her sister?' I said.

'What's that?'

'Sandra's sister. You were remembering seeing John Howard for the first time, and his two angel girls.'

Finnegan stared at me as if I had set him a riddle. Then he shook his head slowly, and gingerly lifted his glass of whisky down from the mantelpiece, brought it to his lips, and held it there a moment before moving it away from his head and holding it at arm's length. The glass seemed to have taken on a life of its own, and

Finnegan appeared mesmerized by it.

'What was she like?' I said. 'Sandra's sister.'

'No no no,' he said. 'Sandra's mother.'

'Sandra's mother? You said "two girls", "John Howard's two girls".'

'That's right.'

'Her mother was one of the girls?'

'Yeah. Fine-looking woman she was too, for her age. That's when I saw the Howards first. And you know, to this day . . . there isn't a thing I wouldn't do for them . . . to this day . . .'

Finnegan pulled the glass back in towards his face, tipped it up to his mouth and emptied it, then staggered across to pour himself another. On the way, he was intercepted by his chair, which soaked up his great bulk without a sound. He waved his glass vaguely in the direction of the Macallan on the drinks table, then dropped it on the arm of the chair, where it tumbled silently to the floor. His head came down to rest where the glass had just been. Within seconds, he was snoring.

The attic floor was full of old case files and law books. On the first floor, there was a master bedroom and two guest bedrooms, one of which looked to be in regular use. With a collection of men's magazines—*FHM*, *Loaded*, *Maxim* etc.— and a shelf full of mathematics textbooks, it wasn't too difficult to work out that Jonathan O'Connor stayed here. As with his rooms in Trinity, a portrait of John Howard and a photograph of the Howard Medical Centre hung on the wall. There was a laptop computer on a pine desk, and I wondered whether he had been here tonight. But Jonathan's laptop was silver; this one was white. I switched it on. I opened Entourage and saw that it belonged to Emily Howard—and I remembered there had been a laptop dust outline in her room. I worked through the inbox until I came to an email address I recognized: maul@2ndphase.ie. I opened the mail. It was a note of congratulations to Emily for getting a place in Trinity to study medicine, and it came from Denis Finnegan.

The other guest bedroom contained a display cabinet that was like a shrine to Seafield and Irish rugby, with photographs and press cuttings and Finnegan's own schoolboy and club medals. Shane Howard and Richard O'Connor featured prominently; there were several shots of David Brady, even a few of Finnegan himself, younger and slimmer and not quite as red.

I went next door to examine Finnegan's bedroom. I trawled through wardrobes and chests of drawers. There was nothing but clothes and shoes and volumes of political biography. I began to feel like this was a wasted trip, that anything I needed would be fast in a safe. I went back into the rugby shrine. There were two drawers beneath the glass cabinet that I hadn't noticed. The first one opened to reveal all manner of memorabilia: tickets stubs to games from the sixties and seventies; autographs of J. P. R Williams and Tony O'Reilly and other rugby greats of the past; programmes and lapel badges and so on. The second drawer was locked. I went up to the second floor to check on Finnegan: he was solid. I tipped his head to one side in case he vomited in his sleep and went down to the kitchen on the ground floor. I was looking for tools, but there weren't any; there was a lot of expensive kitchenware that looked like it was never used. I got a mallet and a pointed steel used for keeping knives sharp and brought them upstairs and, using the steel like a chisel, I smashed my way into the locked drawer, breaking off every now and again to make sure Finnegan was still asleep.

The drawer was lined with green velvet. Rugby medals were laid out on the velvet. I looked at the medals, and pocketed one of several with a name engraved on the back. I also took a silver ID bracelet. Then I pushed the drawer back in and tried to minimize the apparent damage. I took Emily's laptop and went downstairs and replaced the mallet and the steel in the kitchen. On the counter there was a block with a number of sharp Sabatier knives. There were two knives missing. As I walked to my car, I fingered the medal and the bracelet in my pocket. The name engraved on the back of the medal was Richard O'Connor's. The words engraved on the bracelet were 'Diabetic—Type 1'.

23

It was one of those old graveyards up in the mountains, with a small ruined church within the high granite walls, and an archway with a locked gate that had a sign pinned to it with the name and address of the caretaker. You'd call it an old country graveyard, except the city had come to meet it: there were red-brick cul-de-sac developments on either side, and a line of new bungalows across the road. There were no lights on in any of the houses, and no light in the sky either. But the ivy-clad wall was old and broken enough to offer as many footholds and handholds as I needed to scale it with relative ease, and I'd brought a torch from the car to check the names on the graves, limiting my search to those that looked relatively new; there were many old stones and crosses on the uneven ground, and a scurrying underfoot that might have been rabbits, or rats; I didn't want to be there at two o'clock in the morning and yet, as soon as I had received the text from Martha with the directions, I knew I had to go there at once.

The Howard plot was in a corner, shaded by yew trees and a single rowan; a big Celtic cross of black marble marked where John Howard lay; I assumed his wife had gone into the same grave; her name hadn't been added to the headstone yet. The other grave had a stone of white marble and gold lettering and a photograph that fitted into a plastic cover. The photograph was of a girl of twelve, with strawberry-blonde hair and large blue eyes and a slight overbite and a cheeky smile on her face that said she knew she had been naughty but she was sure she could get away with it. She was holding a blue pig with one ear beneath her arm; her school pinafore was red-and-green tartan. What was written on the grave was:

Marian Howard
Born May 15th 1963
Died November 2nd 1975
Requiescat in Pace

All Souls' Day. I thought of what Sandra said about her parents: that they hadn't slept in the same bedroom 'since Ma . . .' She had been going to say 'since Marian died', but had stopped herself. I thought of Denis Finnegan tonight, drunk on fine Scotch and a dream of the Howards, recalling the first time he'd set eyes on John Howard and his two angel girls. Two angel girls, only one still living.

I went and looked out the gates on to the road after that, in the hope that a car might drive by, or a truck, or a plane might fly overhead, or anything to take my thoughts away from here. But there was nothing but black cloud and mist and coal-black night. I thought that that was right, with a dead child: there is no escape from it, and there is no prayer that can ease the pain of it. Then I thought of how little my feelings were worth in the scheme of things, and how little time I had to waste if I wanted this all to end. And then I turned around and went back to work.

The cover on the photo looked new; it certainly wasn't weathered the way it should have been. And it seemed to be stuck on the headstone with glue, or resin. The grave had been visited recently; the earth was dented with marks, and there were even fresh prints in the softer mud leading up to the plot: the prints showed the kind of treads you get on motorcycle boots. There were prints small enough to be Emily's, and prints large enough to be Jerry Dalton's. And right around the child's grave, someone had spread a trail of rowan berries.

*   *   *

There were lights on in Jerry Dalton's house in

Woodpark, but I would have knocked on his door even if there hadn't been. I knocked like a bailiff about to repossess the place; it was only a matter of time before his neighbours were awake too. Emily Howard's voice came from behind the door.

'Who is it?' she said.

'Ed Loy. It's time we talked,' I said.

She opened the door, said, 'Hi Ted,' and went back inside. The door opened into a tiny hallway; a door led right into the living room. Emily sat in the middle of the floor in that knees-tucked-beneath-her way only women seem able to do. She wore indigo-blue jeans and a black sweater; her newly black hair made her pale skin appear opalescent; her eyes were panda black and her lashes were thick with mascara; her bloodstone rings gleamed in the glow from a gas fire. On the floor around her, she was surrounded by old photograph albums and journals; there was a smell of dust and worn paper in the room, of the faded and antique, of the past.

'They went through every album, picked out every photograph, and destroyed it. Even the shots of her as a baby. Isn't that weird? No, isn't that fucked up?'

'Are you talking about Marian Howard?'

'Ye-ah.'

'What about the photograph on her headstone?'

'Oh, we put that up,' Emily said, staring at me through solemn brown eyes. She seemed to have aged several years in the hours since I'd seen her; I felt as if I was meeting her for the first time: a serious young adult.

'We?'

'Me and Jerry Dalton.'

292

'You and Jerry Dalton. You're working together, are you?'

'I don't know about "together". Don't know about "working" either. We've . . . he's been getting sent this stuff about his real parents, about his background. And it crosses over with stuff about my family. So we've been, kind of, comparing notes. Trying to find out who fucked us up.'

'When I met your father, he said you'd been a perfectly normal girl, and then all of a sudden you'd had your hair dyed, broke up with your perfect boyfriend, gone off the rails entirely. Was that because you met Dalton?'

'I guess so. Jerry told me stuff, about my family, about the ways people close to the Howards keep dying.'

'People like Audrey Howard, and Stephen Casey, and Eileen Casey?'

'You've been doing your detective thing, haven't you? Yes, people like that, Ted. But you know, what my father said, about me being perfectly normal—I've been bulimic since I was thirteen, been in therapy since as long, my perfect boyfriend was a cokehead addicted to porn and that turned me on, how the fuck is any of that perfectly normal? And you know the joke of it? My parents didn't even notice. They weren't paying attention. Dad was too busy working, or lost in the land of rugby with fat Denis and all the Seafield man-boys, and Mum was obsessed with herself, with her looks or her fading looks, with her career or her fading career, with cheating on Dad with as many men as possible. I'm surprised Dad even noticed I was missing, bet if he hadn't received the ransom demand he wouldn't have.'

She said all this in a matter-of-fact tone, without any self-pity; as if she feared I might attribute some to her she quickly added, 'I'm not doing a poor-little-rich-girl routine here, it's just . . . there's something *wrong*. Something wrong with my aunt thinking it's OK for me to screw my cousin, something wrong with me for doing it, something wrong for her to put me in therapy and not tell my folks, something wrong with me for going along with it. Even if I was the child, I'm not any more. But I didn't seem to have it in me to do anything about it on my own. Jerry said, what's the problem? Something's wrong in my family. What's the solution? Well, if six years of therapy isn't telling you, maybe it isn't all in your head: chances are you need to find out for real. And I was getting somewhere, feeling better just searching, you know, looking at the Howards, at Dad, at Aunt Sandra, at Jonny even, trying to figure out what lies they were telling when half the time they didn't seem to know themselves. And dumping David Brady, who was like my sick addiction. And then this fucking porno thing comes back to haunt me, Jesus.'

Her eyes welled up and spilled over. I had a clean handkerchief in my pocket. I offered it to her, and she dabbed her eyes with it, smearing the black make-up and mascara around her eyes. She looked at the black stains on the handkerchief and made herself laugh.

'I bet I look like some girl at a debs dance now, who never wears eye make-up usually and doesn't understand you're not supposed to cry with it on.'

'You look fine,' I said. 'And you're *never* not

294

supposed to cry.'

'Is that your philosophy, Ted?'

'I wish you'd stop calling me Ted.'

She giggled then blew her nose, leaving it black on the tip. Then she went through the albums on the floor until she found something.

'So look,' she said. 'I think I'm getting closer to finding out what's wrong. Today Jerry got a photograph of Marian Howard, and a clipping. Look at this.'

She passed me an old scrap of yellowing newspaper, from the *Irish Independent*, dated 18 January 1976.

Death of doctor's child 'tragic accident'.
An inquest into the death by drowning of Marian Howard (12), the youngest daughter of well-known doctor John Howard, heard that the child was known to have a 'mischievous' sense of humour, and that she had been in the habit of 'messing around' in the large pond at the rear of the family home. Her elder sister Sandra said Marian used to hold her breath and hide underwater, fully clothed, often in one of the many crevices and breaks in the stone walls of the pond, as a practical joke, so that she and her brother and parents would panic and believe she had drowned. It was thought that in this instance she became trapped by a large or unwieldy rock, which may have snagged on her clothing. A verdict of accidental death was recorded.

'It's hilarious, isn't it? The shit you can get away

295

with if you're a big rich doctor.'

'You think they just went along with whatever the family said to hush it up?'

'It was November, Ted. I mean, it's bullshit anyway: there's barely three feet of water in that pond, how the fuck you'd get jammed down there at the age of twelve, I don't know. But say you did, and you couldn't swim or something, and you had this yo-ho-ho mischievous sense of humour. God help us, you might pull something like that in July, or August, but November? I mean, who'd think to look in the pond, who'd be out in the fucking garden in November? It's freezing, for fuck sake. Complete joke.'

'What do you think happened?' I said.

'I don't know. But listen, a childhood accident, right, a kid drowns. My *aunt*. How is it Dad never told me? How is it Sandra never told Jonny? I mean, it was thirty years ago, obviously upsetting, but they've gotten over it, right? Except if they haven't. And why haven't they?'

'Where did you get all the photo albums?'

'Granny Howard left them to me. There are journals as well. Stuff she wrote, some stuff the kids wrote. That's another thing, when Granny Howard died, she was cremated. I didn't think anything, but it would have been the normal thing to bury her with Granddad. If we had visited the grave, we would have found out about Marian.'

'Did you take them from Rowan House?'

Emily nodded.

'This morning the cops came and asked me questions about Mum, and David. They talked to Sandra too. And then David Manuel showed up, and Sandra felt it was safe to go off to the Clinic to boss people around, the way she likes. And I talked to David a while, and then he left.'

'What did you say to David Manuel?'

'Not a lot. Not then. I spoke to him again later. I forgot, before then I had another row with my cousin, because he thought I shouldn't be talking to David and I thought he should. I said it was time to tell the truth about everything. But Jonny, my God, he is a true Howard, he wants to keep it all covered up. And . . . oh, other stuff.'

'What other stuff?'

Emily rolled her eyes.

'He wanted to have sex with me. He always wants to have sex with me. And I haven't for years, except in that fucking porno. That was David Brady's idea, to spite me, or get back at me for dumping him, or something. And I suppose I thought, *Well, maybe it would be better than a complete stranger*. You see, normal again. So he stormed off in his long black coat. I always slag him, he looks like one of those guys who shoot up classrooms.'

'Jonathan said you had sex together all afternoon, in the house in Honeypark.'

'He said that? How could we have? He wasn't fucking there.'

'He what? Where was he?'

'He took off in the morning, and came back not long before you arrived. He looked in a bad way.'

'He said that's what you did. And that when you came back you showered and changed all your clothes.'

Emily stared at me, her blackened eyes widening.

'Jesus Christ. He was trying to point the finger at me.'

'Did he shower and change his clothes when he came back?'

She nodded her head, and tears sprang into her eyes again.

'Why would he want people to think I had killed anyone?'

'Maybe he was afraid I might think he had. Did you leave the house in Honeypark?'

'For a while. I went to see Jerry at the Woodpark Inn—his band was supposed to have a rehearsal. But I couldn't find him.'

'That would have been what time?'

'About midday. I had a cup of coffee there, came back around two. Still no sign of Jonny.'

'All right. Let's get back to yesterday. After you had the row with Jonny.'

'He stormed off. And I was left alone. Sandra had given the staff the day off, so I went through to the old house. Wandered about, looking for . . . you know, something wrong.'

'And you found all these?' I said, indicating the photograph albums and journals.

'I don't think Sandra wanted me to have them. Thought I'd grab them while the coast was clear. Also, I went into a room . . . a little girl's room with Sleeping Beauty wallpaper—'

'I was in that room too.'

'And a doll's-house model of Rowan House.'

'Did you look under the roof?'

She nodded, and swallowed hard.

'You must have turned the flap back to face the wall again.'

'I thought it was Sandra's room. I thought, here it is, I've found it at last, Aunt Sandra was abused by my grandfather—*that's* what's wrong . . . and I went back to my room in the bungalow, with the photograph albums, I didn't know what I was going to do, who I could tell. I mean, the idea of telling Dad, he'd just lose it. You cannot say a thing about Sandra, or about Granddad.'

'So what did you do?'

'I gathered up all the books and papers, I rang a cab, and I got out of there. I came straight here, and Jerry let me in. And before I could tell him what I had seen, he showed me the photo of Marian and the clipping. And it all fit: the girl's room preserved as if she was still alive, but frozen at the age of twelve. And we decided we should go to the cemetery—'

'How did you know where it was?'

'It was written on the back of the photograph. We'd go there and put the picture on the headstone, if there was one, and . . . I don't know what we thought after that. We were too upset—at least I was. Twelve years old. Jesus.'

'Did you tell anyone?

'I phoned David Manuel . . . and Jonathan. I thought he had a right to know. His aunt too, she would have been. He freaked out completely. Said I wasn't to tell anyone else, that this was the family's business, and it should be kept within the family.'

'You told him you had told David Manuel then?'
'Yes. Why?'

I thought about how Manuel had died, and who might have done it, and decided Emily didn't need to know that yet.

'No reason. Is there anything in the journals?'

'I'm going through them. Accounts of holidays, bridge evenings, family parties around the piano, that sort of thing. Occasionally the kids are allowed to write things. Here's one from Sandra: "Went with Dad to see Seafield play Old Wesley. Seafield won 24–16. I had a bag of Tayto and a Trigger Bar. Dad said it was a great try from Rock O'Connor. Kept warm in my new coat with fur trim hood and fur pom-poms." That was in 1968, she would have been eight or nine.'

'She sounds like an ordinary girl of eight or nine,' I said.

Neither of us looked at each other, or said what was on our minds: that she wasn't an ordinary little girl, or that if she had been, she wasn't for long.

I gave Emily my card. 'I've got to go,' I said. 'If you come across anything you think I should know about, call me. The other person you might like to talk to is Martha O'Connor, do you know who I mean?'

Emily smiled.

'Jonny's half sister? The journalist? I know who she is, I've never met her.'

'If you can't get hold of me, call her. She's good at letting people know about things.'

'You mean, she's got a big mouth?'

'In a good way.'

I left Emily on the floor, poring over the spidery writing in one of a pile of Mary Howard's journals, then turned at the front door and came back.

'Two things: the other doll's house, the one in your bedroom in Bayview—have you always had that?'

'No. No, that came from Granny Howard too, she left it to me. I've barely looked at it, to be honest. What's the other thing?'

'There's rowan berries across the threshold out

300

there. What's going on there? That was you left them up at Marian's grave as well, wasn't it?'

She nodded.

'They're supposed to ward off evil spirits. *They say.*'

'Hasn't worked out very well so far, has it?'

Emily rubbed the rings on her fingers together.

'We live in hope, Ted. We live in hope.'

24

Pat Tracy lived in one of a terrace of three small houses that opened on to the street just around the corner from the Anchor bar. Martha O'Connor's text had assured me that he stayed up late, and sure enough, his lights were on when I got there. I identified myself through the letterbox, and he opened the door and looked me up and down. We recognized each other immediately, or at least, I recognized him: he was a regular in the Anchor, where he was to be found consulting a newspaper for times of the tides, dispensing the occasional piece of information about alterations in ferry timetables, or gale warnings, or how EU fishing regulations were endangering the entire industry. Silent John called him the Captain, but I think the name was derisive in intent. He had a lined face and false teeth that didn't fit properly that he liked to work back and forth on his gums, and he wore a flat cap that shone with grime. I sat in his tiny front room at a battered Formica table, and with great ceremony he poured the remainder of the pint bottle of Guinness he had open into a grimy half-pint glass he unearthed from his scary kitchen. I didn't really want it, certainly not from that glass, but you couldn't turn down a man's hospitality. An old paperback copy of *Sink the Bismarck!* was open by his place at the table; a pale terrier slumbered in a cane basket; the house smelt of stale bread and damp dog.

'I worked the piers most of me life,' Pat announced, 'nightwatchman for coal importers, yacht clubs, lobster men, engineering works, outboard-motor sales, ships in for repairs, watched over the lot. Eyes and ears. That's what they paid me for, son, eyes and ears.'

'I wanted to ask you about a woman called Eileen Harvey. She was also known as Eileen Casey, and Eileen Dalton.'

'She had a few aliases, is that what you're telling me?' He pronounced it 'al-aye-asses'.

Something like that. You were the chief—in fact the only—witness to her disappearance.'

'Oh yeah?' he said. 'Oh, was I now?' His tone had assumed a knowing, sceptical quality, as if to warn me that he was not a man who liked to be summed up in such narrow terms. 'Was I indeed?' he said, giving equal weight to each word, like a prosecuting counsel in a television film.

'You were. According to you, she left her clothes in a pile on the East pier and took a flier into the water, and you called air–sea rescue and who knows what else, and they never found her, and that was the end of that.'

'And how do you know all this, Mr Loy?'

'Because it was in the newspapers, and on the TV as well. Because you told everyone.'

Pat sat back at this, and gave his dentures a good

302

flex, then appeared to concede the charges.

'And if I did?' he said, as if throwing the gauntlet back to me across a crowded courtroom.

'I was wondering,' I said, 'just how much the lady paid you. I take it she was pretty. What was the story, a boyfriend who beat her?'

He stared at me for a few seconds, then looked away, then stared at me again. At first I thought he was having trouble remembering who I was, and it occurred to me that I had never been in the Anchor without his having been present. That kind of intake over years leads to all sorts of short-term-memory issues, and can make the drabbest evening home alone a thrill-ride of unexpected sights (A door there? I don't remember that!) and surprise treats (A drink for me, freshly poured? Don't mind if I do!). But then it emerged that this was merely part of his adversarial strategy.

'The point is,' he began, and then paused for what presumably was intended to be dramatic effect. The pause went on for so long, however, that it began to look like he had forgotten what the point was. Even the slumbering terrier seemed to yawn in his sleep. Suddenly, and at terrific volume, Pat shouted: 'NOT! The point is NOT!' I wondered whether I'd have to go back to the beginning and start again, when, in a completely different voice, at once milder, more flexible and altogether cannier, as if Pat himself had fallen asleep and his twin brother had emerged from another room to help out, he said, 'The point is not whether I saw her, or what she paid. The point is why you're looking for her, and what's it worth to you.'

Stated as plainly as that, the comedy seemed to

bleed quickly from the scene. As often in situations like this, I found I couldn't think of anything but the truth.

'I think she can help me with the unexplained death of a twelve-year-old girl. I think she can explain how this girl came to die. I also want to reunite her with her long-lost son.'

It was nothing but the truth, yet I could see its effect on Pat Tracy in terms of the melodramas it evidently reminded him of. His eyes glowed with excitement; he rocked back and forth in his chair, his gums working his teeth rhythmically, like maracas underwater.

I produced a ten-euro note and laid it on the table. He glanced at it, then inclined himself away from me by forty-five degrees, picked up *Sink the Bismarck!*, held it in front of his nose with one hand and began to read. The effect of this move was undermined a little by his holding the book upside down. I added a twenty to the ten, which he appeared to look on with more favour, before returning to his 'reading'. I decided to employ some strategy of my own by whipping both notes away, standing up and walking to the window, as if in high dudgeon. I could see his reflection in the glass. He was peering at the table, as if the money was still there but had somehow been absorbed by the wood. I turned slowly and deliberately, and then walked back and slapped a fifty down, leaving my hand on half of it. He looked at it, tried to pick it up, looked at me and nodded. I let it go, he snaked it away in a pocket and I sat down again. Pat looked cautiously about the room, then leant in close to me.

'She was a looker all right,' he said. 'Said she was

the victim of her da. Wanted to marry her off to some fat oul' fella, so he could get the use of some land the oul' fella had. But she was in love with a young lad, and since her da wouldn't give his consent she was going to elope with him, and what's more, never see the da again.'

'It sounds very harsh on the da,' I said.

'Sure the da was beating her black and blue,' he said. 'And other things.'

'And you believed all that, did you?'

Pat looked around again, then leant in and said, 'I believed the twenty quid. Twenty year ago, twenty quid was twenty quid.'

'And what else can you remember?'

'About her? Nothing. She brought the clothes, left them in a heap, gave me the money and went off on her boyfriend's motorbike.'

'Did you see the boyfriend?'

'Not really. He had one of those crash helmets on, you know, the ones with the full-face visors.'

I got up to go. I was pretty sure I knew who it was anyway. The final thing Pat Tracy said confirmed it.

'I can tell you what make the bike was though. A Norton Commando. British engineering. Fair play to the Brits, they knew how to build a fucking motorbike.'

*　　　*　　　*

I had parked down by the pier. As I headed down towards the car, I checked my messages; seemed a sure way of getting people to call you, no matter what time of night, was to turn off your phone: Dave Donnelly had rung five minutes ago; I called

305

him straight back.

'Dave, you're working late.'

'Thought you might be up worrying.'

'Why would I be worrying?'

'That we'd get some more CCTV footage of the Waterfront apartments for the time leading up to David Brady's murder.'

'And did you?'

'We did. There's a camera across the street.'

'And how is it looking for me, Dave? Should I invest in a solicitor? Or a helmet?'

'Always wise to have both. Unfortunately, all it picks up of you is your back, just like the one inside the door.'

'Or the back of a man my height in a black coat like mine.'

'Don't get fucking smart with me Ed.'

Sooner or later, Dave always reminded you who was in charge. I was under no illusion he could run out of patience with me, and probably would if I didn't take care. But it was getting so I didn't give a damn; worse, it was getting so I wanted to bring it to a head.

'So we did get a fine look at Shane Howard, barrelling in like a man whose blood is up.'

'Yeah?'

'But before that, we have three young fellas, one lad we don't know, in a long black coat and a black baseball cap; two we do: Darren and Wayne Reilly. You know them?'

'I know who they are.'

And where they are, and how they died.

'Not sure how they avoided the camera in the lobby, maybe they went up the emergency stairs. Anyway, we have good sets of prints all over the gaff, all over the *knife*. Remember the knife, Ed?'

'Sabatier carving knife? I'm not supposed to know about the knife, Dave.'

'You're some fuckin' comedian, do you know that? How'd you like to be laughing the other side of your face?'

'And a motive? Squabble over a coke deal?'

'Something like that. Brady was a big customer of theirs. Friends of his say he was always arguing about paying them. They said Brady's father is loaded, which accounts for the flash apartment, but he had threatened to switch off the money supply if Brady's rugby game didn't improve. The old man thought Brady was too fond of the old party lifestyle.'

'So where are you, up in Woodpark waiting for the Reillys to come home?'

'We've a couple of roadblocks. Thought you should know, although fuck knows why. On a two-way street, the information has been strictly one-way for a long time. Don't suppose you've anything for me?'

How about the Reillys' dead bodies, Sean Moon, the murder weapon and Brock Taylor? How about the murderer of Audrey O'Connor, Stephen Casey and Dr Rock? How about the riddle of a dead child no one wants to remember, and a suicide that never was? Why is a father who abused at least one of his daughters commemorated like a plaster saint? And how does a burning man who fell to earth fit with it all? How about you do my job, Dave, and I sit on my arse until the Garda Technical Bureau comes up with matching prints? I looked out over the black murk of the bay, and breathed in the damp clog of the air, and nearly choked.

'Jonathan O'Connor has a black baseball hat. And a long black coat.'

'So do I. That it?'

I wanted to give him the Reillys. But I wasn't finished with Brock Taylor. And I had to keep Maria and Anita Venclova out of it; they'd be deported if I didn't.

'I've another call, Dave, I'll talk to you soon.'

I broke the connection before Dave had finished swearing at me. The other call was from Tommy. At first I couldn't make head nor tail of it because his voice was so hushed; I thought he must have gone back on the booze, if not the whole medicine cabinet.

'I can't hear a word you're saying, Tommy.'

So he said it plain.

'Sean Moon is in your house.'

I drove too fast to Quarry Fields; it was five minutes from the pier and I made it in three. And I didn't think enough about what I was doing; I probably should have bided my time. But at three in the morning, it's easier to lead with your chin than use your head. I parked across the road and up a stretch by a maroon BMW I couldn't remember seeing before and bolted across the road with my hand on the Sig Sauer compact in my jacket pocket. There was a silver SUV in my drive, and the approach light was on and the front door of my house was open. I brought the gun out as I went through the gate, and was immediately blindsided by a smash across the right side of the head. I tumbled, and the Sig clanked to the ground as my grip turned to sand. I managed to climb to my feet very briefly; my balance was shot from the

308

blow to the head; I could see that it had come from a baseball bat, although I couldn't make out the features of the man who had hit me; I probably looked pretty comical staggering around in a half-circle, trying to keep upright like a newborn colt, but it didn't seem to amuse the guy with the baseball bat; he raised it over me, and I shielded my head with my arms; my legs were spread to help me stand, so he kicked me in the balls so hard I thought I was going to die, and hoped I would. I collapsed on my hands and knees and vomited and wept and then I felt a smart of dull pain on the back of my head, more like a nudge than a pain, and I tumbled into a dark red pool.

*   *   *

In a dream, I saw a trim brunette in a black pencil skirt and a black silk blouse with hair piled on top of her head and hanging longer at the back and good legs in black stockings wandering about a room with high windows and white walls and white furniture and a white carpet, everything white, against which she seemed to sway like a dark shadow. She was busy everywhere, doing something with the shutters, lighting a cigarette, rearranging white marble ornaments on the white-marble fireplace and dabbing at the mirror that hung above it. As the growing pain in my stomach and in my head told me this was no dream, the brunette's movements started to appear agitated and fussy; after completing each action, she would sit on a long white couch opposite me and take a drag on her cigarette; sometimes she would have to relight it first. My head was slumped on my left shoulder, and I could see out of both eyes, but it felt like there was a heavy weight on the side of my head. I became convinced it was a clock, some old antique clock with heavy workings, made of lead, perhaps—did they make clocks out of lead? I could hear its ticking in my head like the driving rhythm of an old diesel train, feel it thumping in my chest, and the muck sweat on my brow and the cold sparky taste of metal, then acid, on my tongue.

I raised my head a little and the pain in my stomach slipped down into my balls and I forgot about getting sick because I thought I was going to die. I could see a white clock on the centre of the mantelpiece. For some reason, that reassured me. I could see the brunette's ankles, but I couldn't seem to raise my eyes to look at the rest of her. A wave of nausea shot up my stomach on an acid tide; I opened my mouth but it turned in my throat and hurled itself back towards my balls. A white plastic bowl, the kind you'd pack salad leaves for a picnic in, was placed in my lap, and a white hunk of something the size of a human brain was pushed carefully between my legs; it was a pack of ice wrapped up in soft plastic. After a few minutes, the pain receded to the point where I felt it would be possible to lift my head.

'Keep something down?' the brunette asked. She had a soft, mild Dublin accent. She was holding up a bottle of pills.

'What?' I said, or tried to; my voice sounded like the crackle of burning wood.

'Ponstan,' she said. 'They'll help.'

'Morphine,' I barked.

'Trust me, I'm a nurse,' she said. 'Morphine

would be if he'd cut your balls *off*.'

I was tied to a straight-backed chair. I couldn't see whether it was white or not. I didn't care much, but I seemed to care enough to wonder. The brunette stood in front of me with the pills and a glass of water; I took a drink to lubricate my mouth and throat, then she put the pills on my tongue, one by one, and I washed them down with the rest of the water. My stomach did some more rumbling and heaving, and sweat poured down my face. The right side of my head felt like a boiled-flesh poultice attached to my brain with barbed wire and rusty nails. Tears of pain rolled down my cheeks. The brunette went out of the room and came back in with a wet facecloth; she sat on a couch beside my chair and mopped my brow and wiped my cheeks and rested the cloth carefully along the right side of my face.

She must have been in her mid-fifties but she didn't look it; I'd've put her at forty-five; she was probably aiming for forty, and not falling too far short. Her face had that lush, pearly glow expensive women all seem to have these days; her brown eyes and naturally dark colouring meant she needed little in the way of make-up; her blouse had shoulder pads, and with her hair piled up the way it was, she looked a bit like a woman from the 1940s; with that thought, the whole situation seem to dissolve once more into a dream.

She dropped the facecloth in the plastic bowl and took them away some place and then sat back down opposite me and lit a fresh cigarette.

'Thank you,' I said. 'Thank you Eileen . . . is it Dalton? Or Taylor?'

She looked pleased and anxious at the same

time, as if she had finally got her wish and instinctively realized living it wasn't going to be as simple as wishing for it had been.

'Taylor,' she said. 'Eileen Taylor.'

'But Brock's name was Dalton when you married. Did he change it or fake it?'

'Let's leave Brian out of it.'

'I wish we could, Eileen. But we wouldn't be having this little chat without him and his pal Sean Moon. Do you think I might have a drink?'

She raised her eyebrows and smiled to herself, as if in praise of folly.

'Not recommended, Ed Loy. Not in the state you're in.'

'Did Father Massey give you my name?'

'He told me you were snooping around.'

'So you've kept in touch, you two. He knew all about your disappearing act, did he?'

'Not before, no. I wrote him a letter a little while after. Asking for his forgiveness.'

'He must have given it.'

'He was very good to me. Not many priests of that time would have been so sympathetic.'

'Explain something. You left a baby in the porch of the church. Father Massey brings it to the Howards, who arrange for it to be adopted. All very hush-hush. How did that work? I mean, it was 1986, in a city. He was a priest; he must have had . . . legal obligations.'

Eileen Dalton stood up and walked to the window, a fussy dark shadow once again. From there she looked around at me pityingly, reprovingly, as if I were some impossibly naive idiot she was a fool to be wasting her time on. I had a feeling she'd used that look before.

312

'I thought you'd know why.'

'I think I do. Was it because you somehow told Father Massey—'

'I left a note with the baby. A sealed envelope, addressed to him.'

'Telling him who the boy's father was.'

'That's right. So you do know.'

'I think I know. But I'd like to hear you say it.'

She looked out through the dark glass. I could see her reflection. She was shaking. When she turned, she held on to the shutter handle for balance.

'All right,' she said, throbbing with passion, as if every moment of regret for the long years of missing her son was laced through the words. 'All right then. Jerry Dalton's father was Dr John Howard.'

25

There's a moment in every case when you catch a glimmer of the end: not that you know all the answers, but you begin to see the pattern. It often comes when you're at your lowest ebb, and you've nothing but darkness in sight. Eileen Dalton telling me John Howard was Jerry Dalton's father felt like such a moment. The energy in the room seemed to split apart and flow together again in a new configuration. I was still tied to a chair in Brock Taylor's Fitzwilliam Square house, but I felt I had been given, if not quite a winning hand, at least something to play for. If Eileen Dalton had been feeding her son clues about the Howard family,

313

chances were she wanted something to happen, and that something had to involve her getting out of Brock Taylor's, and she might need some help to get where she was going.

There was a knock on the door, and Eileen left the room. When she came back in, she looked me up and down, flashed me a nervous grin, then went to what looked like a plain white wall, pressed on it and a cupboard door swung open.

'What do you drink?' she said.

'Jameson,' I said. 'Two-thirds to a third water.'

'I'll give you half and half. You've got to take it easy.'

She poured herself a whiskey too, and came over and sat beside me with both drinks.

'Who was at the door?' I said.

'One of Brian's . . . security staff. Checking to see if everything is all right.'

'And is it?'

'Have a drink and see.'

She tipped the glass to my lips and I gulped maybe half of it. She took my glass, clinked hers against it, said 'Sláinte', and drank.

'How long have you been with Brock then?'

'I said I didn't want to talk about him.'

'And then he sends a boy around to check up on you.'

'Checking up on *you*.'

'What do you think he's going to do with me?'

'Make sure you're scared, good and proper, so you keep your nose out of his business.'

'And you think that's all he'll do?'

'Brian may have robbed a few banks in his time, security vans, but that's all; he's settled with the CAB; he's moved beyond that now. And no one's said he ever killed anyone. No one's ever said that.'

The near repetition of her avowal of Brock Taylor's innocence seemed to undermine her faith in it. She fetched an ashtray and set it down beside her. She lit a cigarette, and I asked for one. When she lit mine, her hand was trembling.

'You're very frightened. Why is that?'

She drank some more whiskey.

'I was in London nearly twenty years. St Thomas's Hospital. I wouldn't have come back if I didn't believe Brian was on the level. Don't make him out to be some kind of gangster—'

'Do you know Sean Moon?'

Eileen flinched.

'There are people he sometimes has to deal with, people from the past who don't understand who he's become . . .'

'Tonight, Sean Moon murdered two criminals from Woodpark, the Reilly brothers. Brian sat there and watched.'

'I don't believe that.'

'I saw it. Afterwards, they put a Lithuanian woman called Maria Venclova in the Bentley and drove her here. Moon had been holding her against her will, forcing her to have sex against her will. Raping her, I believe it's called.'

Eileen was shaking her head.

'I took her away from them, and let her and her sister stay in my house. But they broke in and took them, and when I tried to stop them, they attacked me. Did you see the Venclova girls tonight? How was I delivered here?'

'I wasn't . . . nobody . . . I didn't see you arrive. I was upstairs. Brian came up and . . .'

315

She was having some trouble forming sentences, or organizing her thoughts.

'What did he tell you? Or are you used to entertaining, what should we call them, business clients of your husband who are beaten senseless and tied to chairs?'

'We know you're working for the Howards. He thought we might learn something from you. Said you'd been a bit obstreperous and Moon had to knock you into line.'

'Did Tommy Owens set me up?'

'I don't know who Tommy Owens is, love.'

She looked across at me, took the smoked-down cigarette from my mouth and butted it in the ashtray. Then she brushed some ash from my shirt front.

'He didn't say anything about any girls,' she said, in a low, hopeful voice.

I nodded, as if this was understandable.

'What were you and Brock hoping to learn from me? What's Brock doing out in Woodpark, buying the whole place up? Bought the old house you used to live in, did he?'

'He didn't have to buy it. It was his, and mine—except I'm dead, of course: Brian had me declared legally dead after seven years.'

'But you're not dead any more, are you? You're coming back to life now, coming back in a big way. Sending hints and allegations about the Howards to your son Jerry, the son who's never met you. What do you want, Eileen? Is it money? You look pretty well set up here, Fitzwilliam Square, hard to top that. What is it?'

'It's not the money. I want the truth about my son Stephen to be told,' Eileen said. Her voice was suddenly thick with emotion. 'I want the Howards to own up, in public, to what they did, to what they've done.'

'What have they done? Why don't you tell me what the Howards have done? Did John Howard rape you?'

All the lights and lamps in the room were controlled by a panel of switches by the door, and now Eileen stood and walked across and dimmed the lights and then stood, dark, by the nearer of the two high windows and lit another cigarette. A wash of yellow street light flowed through the etiolated off-white glow of the room; I thought of Honeypark, the way it looked in November light, like melting snow smeared with dirt. Eileen looked down into the street, and when she spoke, it was in a voice I hadn't heard her use before, a high, clear, girlish sound that seemed to come from as far in the past as the events she began to describe.

'We lived in one of the cottages along the road from Rowan House, and my father worked in the gardens there. I think at one time they were tenant cottages, and the Howards still behaved as if that's what we were, presents at Christmas, patronizing, you know? When I was seventeen, I got into trouble—a local lad, a complete fucking eejit, him and me both. My parents were furious, and there were all sorts of plans about how I should hide the baby and then pretend it was my ma's and she could raise it, or that I should be sent to a home for unmarried mothers and then the baby would be taken off me and given to a good family. Anyway, one night I had a temperature, a fever, and my parents were very scared, and my father ran down to Rowan House, and Dr Howard came up and treated

317

me, and discovered I was pregnant. The next day, Mrs Howard came and made my parents an offer: that if I went into service in Rowan House, I could have the baby safe from prying eyes, in the Howard Clinic no less, and then I could raise him while living there. I'd have my own quarters, and the Howards'd pay for everything.'

'When was this?'

'Sixty-nine. No, 1970.'

'So you would have been older than Sandra.'

'Oh yes. The idea was that I could look after the children. Sandra was ten, Shane was eight. And little Marian was six.'

'That was generous of the Howards.'

'That's what my parents thought. I suppose I thought so too. Or maybe I was just relieved I wasn't gonna be sent to some house full of nuns. I hadn't banked on a life as a servant though. I thought I could do a secretarial course, move into town, get started, you know? But how was I going to do that with a kid? So I moved in and had the baby, a boy, Stephen.'

'Was the father's name Casey?'

'No, that was my idea. That there was a father, but he died. I could be a widow at eighteen. I suggested it to Mary Howard, and she liked it. So we had his name put on the birth cert—Noel, I think it was. Noel Casey. And I was Casey to the children from then on. And that was that. Stephen grew up in Rowan House. He went to the local primary, but he was clever, so John Howard paid to have him sent to Castlehill. My own parents took a step back, it was as if Stephen was the Howard's grandchild, not theirs. And I went along with that.'

'How did the Howard children react?'

'Very well at first. I was like a big sister to Sandra. Shane was all boy, flying about the place. And little Marian was such a cutie, oh she was gorgeous. A real little princess. And they loved to play with Stephen. And then, when he was two or three, it all changed.'

'In what way?'

'In a dramatic way. Mary Howard came to me one morning and said she felt I needed to live on my own, that they had found me a small house I could live in, that I could come in daily.'

'Why did she do that? Was she afraid her husband was getting too fond of you? Did he ever make a pass?'

'Not then, no. He was a perfect gent. No, I just thought Mary was thinking of me, that I might need some independence. And the cottage was the one in Woodpark, there was a bus you could get up to Rowan House. A bit rough there, maybe, but it was nice to have my own front door. Actually, the one I thought was jealous of anyone else having anything to do with her father was Sandra, she would have been twelve, thirteen, in the first teenage flush of it all, and she took against me. Quite subtly, but making it clear I wasn't really part of the family. Remarks about my hair, my clothes, girls-school stuff, quite bitchy. Quite cruel really.'

'But Sandra and her father were particularly close?'

'She'd always idolized him. She was Daddy's little girl. And she and her mother started . . . it wasn't exactly fighting, frosting would be a better way to describe it, they avoided each other, and

319

were sharp when they had to be together.'

'It's not an unusual situation. Adolescent girl fixates on her father, rows with her mother. Happens in a thousand houses, up and down the land.'

'It's perfectly normal. I'm sure it was.'

She hadn't turned from the window. I could see the tip of her cigarette glow and fade in the glass, a tiny beacon in the night.

'I'm just telling you what I remember. I said I wanted the Howards to own up to what they did. But I still don't know the extent of it. That's why I hoped Jerry might find a way . . . and maybe now, you can help him. Help me. To get to the truth.'

'That's what I'm trying to do. I reckon I could make a better stab at it without these ropes.'

Eileen Taylor turned and looked at me, tied to the chair, and turned back to the glass and continued talking.

'The inquest into Marian Howard's death didn't make sense, I remember that. The child had been ill for months beforehand, in isolation at the end of the rear corridor. Scarlet fever, pleurisy, pneumonia. I didn't see her once. Dr Howard treated her himself, and a nurse from the Clinic came up. That was all I knew; then all of a sudden, she had been in the pool outside and drowned. In November, and with the child ill for so long. I couldn't believe that.'

'What did you believe?'

'One night, I cooked dinner downstairs for Shane and Sandra, and they went out together to the pictures or something. Marian was still alive at this point, still in her sickroom. I tidied up the meal, and I was preparing to go home. I came upstairs to the rotunda, and Mary Howard was standing there in the darkness, in a dressing gown, her hair unkempt, looking down the long corridor, tears streaming down her face. She was quite a forbidding person, and I normally would have stared at the floor, pretended I hadn't seen her, passed on by. But she was in such a state, I didn't even think, I ran to hold her. She wept on my shoulder, and kept saying the same thing, over and over. "At least this is the end of it," she said. "At least this must be the end of it." And I thought I heard . . . I still couldn't swear to it, and Mary was repeating the words in my ears, but I thought I heard a baby crying. I looked her in the eye, and she pulled herself together, and apologized, and started to fuss around Stephen, who had just come into the hall, and she shooed us both out the door.'

'You couldn't swear to it. That Marian was pregnant, not ill. That she had a baby, and it was taken off her, or it died, and she what? Killed herself? Was murdered?'

'I couldn't swear to any of it.'

'What do you *think*?'

Eileen's cigarette glowed red, and a cloud of grey smoke shrouded her dark head.

'After Marian's death, they built the new house, the bungalow. Mary wouldn't live in Rowan House any more; she wanted a clean break. But John Howard wouldn't hear of moving. He had his dream of the three towers, and while only one existed during his lifetime, he thought if he moved away now he'd lose his chance of it coming true. So they compromised by sticking one on the back of the other. And when it came to it, Mary wouldn't move into the bungalow at all, I think she felt it would somehow downgrade her in the scheme of things.

'I trained as a nurse, with Mary Howard's encouragement—and with the Howards' money. I think Mary took me on then, as a project. Sandra and Shane were older, and at university, so she asked Stephen and me to move back in. We lived in the bungalow. John Howard spent most of his time in the old house. Sandra spent a lot of time at home, and we became quite close—it seemed to me she was doing her best for both parents now, as they took fewer pains to conceal how much they loathed each other.'

'And Stephen went to school.'

'That's right, to Castlehill, and I worked in the Howard Clinic, and then when John Howard got cancer, I nursed him until he died.'

'Sandra told me she was her father's nurse.'

'Took more than one. Anyway, she had her hands full keeping the peace between him and the mother. It was fireworks every night.'

'And what happened? Did he rape you?'

'You know, all these years I've been saying yes, he did, telling myself, telling Brian. Telling the Howards. But the truth is, it wasn't rape. He was ... a very attractive man, even at seventy. Very charismatic, very powerful. And yes, he was ill, but between bouts of the illness, he'd be fit. Fit enough. And I had had nobody for the longest time. I was susceptible. I mean, it was wrong on just about every count you could think of. But we had a ... kind of an ... affair. Under everyone's noses. And I thought nothing would happen, he's got cancer, he couldn't be fertile—it's funny the way you get taken in by old wives' tales you'd scorn anyone else for believing.

322

And something happened.'

'Was Brock Taylor on the scene at this stage? Or Brian Dalton—what *is* his name?'

'He was christened Dalton. Still went by that when I met him, around this time. But his da had taken off when he was a kid, Brian never forgave him. After we got married, he started to call himself Taylor, his ma's maiden name.'

'Handy to have more than one name.'

'Sure, who are you tellin'? Brian was on the horizon at that stage, yeah. He was . . . hovering around. He seemed to know who I was. I went to see Stephen play rugby and he was there, I became aware of him that way.'

'Was it through Denis Finnegan that you met then?'

'Why would it have been through Denis Finnegan? Brian had been working in a garage in the area, he just came along for the sport. I doubt he ever knew Denis Finnegan. In fact, I'm sure of it.'

'Eileen. Brock Taylor and Denis Finnegan grew up together in the north inner city. Brock in Blessington Street, Finnegan in Wellington Street, a stone's throw away.'

Eileen Taylor whipped around and began to advance slowly on me.

'What are you saying?'

'That they knew each other, and they kept it hidden from you. Now why would they do that?'

'I don't know.'

'Stephen was a good boy, wasn't he Eileen?'

'He was growing up to be a lovely young fella. He was strong, and brave, and good to me, and very clever. He could have been a doctor, was

323

hoping to be one.'

'Do you believe for an instant, in your heart, that he killed Audrey O'Connor? Could he have done such a thing?'

'No.'

'Not even if he was under Sandra Howard's spell?'

'Not if he was under the spell of the Devil himself. And he'd never have killed himself either. I couldn't look at Sandra after she took up with Stephen—took advantage of him. But I can see how it happened. She was mourning her father, he was seventeen, how could he resist if she wanted him, she was absolutely gorgeous. I was angry about it, but I kept my head down, said nothing. I didn't want to drive him away. I saw more of Brian then. And realized I was pregnant. So I didn't know what to do.'

Eileen poured two fresh whiskeys and sat beside me, again tipping the glass to my lips. She was possessed by her past, all concentration, burrowing down, channelling it from deep within.

'Brian asked me to marry him. And I burst into tears, and explained what had happened. Except of course, I told him I had been raped. And he said that was fine, he didn't mind, he'd put his name to the child. And I said I'd have to think about it. Before I got a chance, Audrey O'Connor was murdered, and Stephen vanished. Everyone pointed the finger at him of course, even though there was no evidence, or motive. And then they found Stephen's body, on All Souls' Day. It's his anniversary tonight, twenty-one years.

'I thought Mary Howard wouldn't believe me when I told her her husband had raped me. But I barely had the words out of my mouth and she was promising this, that and the other thing. And she asked if I had a young man, and if he could be made to understand. I said he'd stick by me, and she arranged everything: the house, the wedding, the whole lot. But all I kept thinking about was Stephen. Who killed him? I had no doubt he had been killed. But everyone believed it was murder and suicide.'

'Sandra Howard didn't. She still doesn't.'

'How do we know it wasn't her? She could have worn a mask, killed the wife, maybe Dr Rock was in on it with her, and then the next day, or that night, set Stephen up, drugged him or slugged him, stuck him in the driver's seat with all the robbery junk in the boot and sent it scudding off the pier. She had the only motive I can see: to move in on Dr Rock.'

I didn't reply. Of course we couldn't know it wasn't Sandra, and there was a strong possibility that it was. But I couldn't stop thinking of Denis Finnegan, how he said there was nothing he wouldn't have done for the Howards.

'Did you know Denis Finnegan well?'

'Not really. He followed Shane around like a little dog, worshipped him. And I always used to think he had a crush on Sandra. I don't think she noticed him, to be honest.'

'And you don't think it's strange that Brock Taylor never mentioned how he and Denis Finnegan knew each other?'

Eileen took a long drink.

'Of course I think it's strange. What do you want me to do about it?'

'What is Brock up to, buying up half of

Woodpark? Joining the rugby club? What's he doing?'

'I don't know. I thought he was trying to help me.'

'You know he's been drinking with Denis Finnegan up there?'

'No, I didn't know that.'

'Why don't you put your hand in my pocket.'

'That's a pretty sleazy line.'

'My coat pocket. Go on, there isn't a gun in there, I'm pretty sure they took that.'

Eileen put her hand in my pocket and shook her head.

'Nothing here at all.'

Maybe I'd been cleaned out completely.

'Try the other one.'

She did so, and came up with a cigarette lighter and a rugby medal.

'Lucky dip. Now what?'

'What name is engraved on the back of the medal?'

'Richard O'Connor.'

'Dan McArdle told me Dr Rock's rugby medals were stolen in the robbery. And they weren't recovered in the boot of the car your son died in, with the rest of the stuff.'

Eileen Taylor's eyes opened wide.

'Where did you get it?'

'Locked in a drawer in Denis Finnegan's house in Mountjoy Square.'

'Does that mean he did it? What does that mean?'

'It means he was involved with the robbery and the murders of Audrey O'Connor and Stephen Casey, and he knew Brock Taylor at that time, which means there's a fair chance Brock Taylor was involved too, and if you want me to find out any more—and if you want to see your other son—you'll have to untie me and get me out of here. Because as soon as Moon gets back, I'm not going to be in a position to be asking or answering any more questions. They want me dead, Eileen, and they've already killed tonight; one more body's gonna mean nothing to them.'

Eileen looked at me appraisingly, then looked around as if she were afraid we were being watched. Then she crossed the room to the white drinks cabinet and found a small fruit knife and came back and cut the ropes I was bound with.

As she got me free, there was a commotion from below, the sound of raised voices and steps thudding on the stairs. I took the big marble clock from the mantelpiece, killed the lights and positioned myself behind the door. I beckoned Eileen, but a gun had materialized in her hand, looked like a Beretta 950 Jetfire; she shook her head and stood directly before the door. It flew open, and a man in a black coat swept in; seeing Eileen before him, he swung round, a Steyr machine pistol in his hands. It was Brock Taylor, badly bruised above one eye, blood seeping from a wound in his side.

Before he could turn properly, Eileen began to scream at him. 'You said there'd be no more girls, no more hookers. And what have you been running? Lithuanians? With that pervert scumbag Moon?'

'Eileen love, I'm shot. The cops . . . we have to get out of here. Where's that cunt Loy?'

'Tell me about Denis Finnegan.'

327

'What? What has Denis Finnegan to do with it? Oh fuck, I need a doctor—'

'Stephen, my son. They found the body twenty-one years ago today. And I know Denis Finnegan was involved. Now how would a soft cunt like Finnegan organize a job like that? He'd shit his pants. Except you knew him, didn't you, you grew up with the cunt.'

'Eileen—'

She shot past him, through the door.

'Tell me Brian, or I'll do it, I don't give a fuck any more, tell me the fucking truth!'

'Jesus Christ, all right. I knew him. He wanted . . . he had a big thing for the Howard girl, Sandra. But it was all fucked up, how he wanted some other man for her, someone he felt would be better for her. I couldn't follow it. All I knew was, he wanted the wife dead.'

'And then?'

'And then. Ah Jesus—'

Eileen shot again, closer this time. I didn't move a muscle; it was as if she'd completely forgotten I was there; she could have caught me with a stray bullet without thinking.

'So that was done—'

'Who did it?'

'A lad who done that kind of work.'

'Did you do it?'

'No.'

A third shot.

'No? You were a fucking mechanic who robbed the odd car. You'd never done anything, you didn't know any lads who done that kind of work. You had no fucking money, that's what you did it for, isn't it? How much did he pay you? You did it, didn't you, you did it yourself. Tell me Brian.'

'All right,' he said. 'I done it.'

Eileen hadn't really believed it until he said it; her face seemed to age in an instant; it was suddenly weary, lined with fear. When she spoke again, it was in genuine disbelief.

'How much? How much?'

'Five grand.'

'And Stephen? You killed Stephen?'

'Eileen, I'm bleeding here, it's serious, the cops are coming, we have to clear out—'

She shot at the floor near his feet.

'Ah for fuck's sake, all right! We'd've been saddled with him. We could never have done what we wanted to do, start afresh, Bonnie and Clyde.'

'You killed him? You killed my son?'

'I ran it past Finnegan; he said it would simplify things, the Howard one was carrying on with him, she didn't need that, he said.'

Eileen held one hand on her chest. She seemed to be having trouble breathing.

'And then you made me leave Jerry in the church. Both children gone . . . for this?'

She looked around at the carefully designed room in disgust. Her eyes glistened. I could hear her breathe.

'It's not just this,' Taylor said. 'It's Woodpark too, and more. When you see what we have coming to us, through the same Denis Finnegan . . . we'll be controlling the Howards before long . . . it's what we're due, what you deserve, for all the Howards done to you.'

'What did they do to me? You killed my first son. And made me abandon my second.'

'Your second son? You were raped, Eileen, raped.'

Eileen Taylor set her shoulders back and pointed the Beretta at Brock Taylor's chest.

'I was raped, yes. But not by John Howard. By you, Brock, by you.'

She shot him three times in the chest; I don't know if he meant to shoot her or if his finger hit the trigger by accident but he sprayed automatic fire around the upper end of the room and she danced briefly like a puppet in the wind and then went down beneath a hail of it.

26

I was still standing by the door with the marble clock in my hand when Tommy Owens clumped through it with a Steyr machine pistol in *his* hand. He reared back like an upright horse when he saw the bodies, swinging around so that the SMG was aimed at me.

'You can put that down, for a start,' I said.

I'd never been more relieved to see anyone in my life.

'Come on Ed, the cops are on the way,' Tommy said.

'Where's Moon?'

'Where do we go when we die, man? We can talk about that later. Right now, your chariot awaits.'

'There was a security man knocking around here—'

'He legged it when he saw this. Come *on*.'

I followed Tommy down two flights of stairs to

street level. He ducked into the violet-and-blue front room we had been in earlier and looked out at the street.

'OK, Ed, there's a maroon Beemer parked across the road. You go; I'll get your back.'

The sub-machine gun was taking Tommy over; he had started to talk like someone in an action movie. I shook my head.

'Tommy, is that the gun that killed the Reillys?'

He nodded.

'Then wipe it down and leave it here, all nice and neat and case closed for the Guards. Come on, we don't need that class of weapon any more.'

Tommy conceded with a grimace, gave the Steyr a quick clean with a hand towel from a downstairs loo and tossed it at the bottom of the stairs. We left the door open behind us and ran across to the BMW. I could hear the sirens approaching as we drove away.

*　　　*　　　*

I didn't see Maria and Anita until we were on Strand Road, the sea stretching dark and mysterious to our left, the candy-stripe chimneys of Poolbeg towering above the bay. Then the Venclova girls raised themselves from the back seat, where they'd been cowering. Neither of them said anything; they were whispering words of what sounded like comfort to each other; each cried occasionally. When I heard what they'd been through, I was surprised they had managed to stop crying at all.

I thanked Tommy for tracking me down, and silently asked forgiveness from whoever runs that department for thinking he had set me up. Looking ever more incongruous with his new face, new hair and his new seat behind the wheel of a luxury German car, and a stark, level expression on his face, Tommy Owens brought me up to speed.

' 'Course we might have been able to stop them in their tracks if you hadn't barged in like a stiff prick, not a thought to where the danger might lie—behind the fuckin' hedge, you gobshite. I was across the road in the Beemer—I got it from Brock's lock-up in Woodpark—watching and waiting. I'd gone there after I gave you the GHB. Just had a notion Moon wasn't finished with the ladies yet. I took the Steyr, and I was ready to step out and use it when Moon jumped you. But it didn't look to me like they were going to take you out there and then, otherwise, why didn't they, know I mean?

'So Brock and Moon had been in the house, they just done the locks with a crowbar: not exactly high security there in Quarry Fields, I warned you about that one, and out come the ladies, in a bad way, too frightened to scream, Moon has another sub-machine gun, Brock has one too, but he looks very nervous, like he doesn't want to be there.'

'They argue,' Anita said. 'Brock, he doesn't want to do it, he is saying leave the girls, it's too much trouble, we have no papers. Moon says girls are loose ends, we know too much, we must be dealt with. I think we are going to die.'

Anita's voice rose to a cry as she said 'die', and Maria hushed her, and then said, 'We don't die. Fat fucks die.'

'So Brock is in the SUV with Anita and Maria,

and there's a driver, some big shaven-headed heap. After Moon's kicked the shite out of you, he bundles you into the SUV and they take off, heading north. I follow, fairly close eye, 'cause there's no way Brock will recognize the motor, and it's not exactly an exotic route they're taking, Rock Road, Merrion Road, up Pembroke Road and around on to Fitzwilliam Square. They help you out and get you into Brock's gaff, then they're all back into the vehicle, and down through Ballsbridge, down towards the railway and a quick turn into this little private cul-de-sac, about a dozen town houses. They head to a house at the far end, and I drive past and park the Beemer outside a big Audi dealership. There's a laneway by the showroom that leads down to the river, couple of fences and some brambles no bother, then I'm doubling back between the wall that drops to the river and the town-house gardens, little river-view patios with paving and newly planted hawthorn and laurel. No lights anywhere except where Brock's crew have gone. I keep my distance, don't want to set off any lights, there's mud and rotting leaves and river rats underfoot but I get there, close enough to see through the big patio doors.'

'Moon is a pimp,' said Maria. 'Rape you until you do as he says. The fat-pig driver is going to run us both from the house. Brock can't refuse. He is a weakling, he keeps whining, I am so sorry. Moon has power over Brock.'

'The driver is called Bomber,' added Anita. 'Moon says each of them will fuck us and then we will behave, or they will fuck us again until we do.'

'Fat fucking pigs,' Maria said, she now on the

verge of tears.

'Then we will work in the house, and if we do well, they might let us go. But they never will.'

'Anita is crying on Maria's shoulder, and Moon is waving his hands at them, making faces, all smiles, like he's full of jokes, you know, getting them to see the funny side?' Tommy said. 'And then he just pulls Maria away from Anita, and Bomber starts pawing *her*, you know, pulling at her clothes, and she slaps him, and he hits her a dig in the stomach, and she falls to the ground. Now Maria's screaming and struggling with Moon, and he just starts backhanding her across the face, and he's shouting at her, he's got the finger pointed and he's shaking her, and Bomber's on top of Anita, ripping her clothes off like he's going to do her there and then, and Brock's in the middle suddenly, waving his hands around like some fucking vicar or something, like he's trying to keep the peace, he looked like a total fool, and Moon holds Maria to one side and points his finger in Brock's face, and suddenly Brock just opens the patio doors and comes out in the garden and slams them shut and walks down towards me. For some reason there's no security light working, maybe if you're running a knocking shop with a lot of late-night coming and going that's a good idea to keep the neighbours sweet, I don't fucking know; funny what crowds your brain when you're supposed to be on action stations, anyway, next thing I see is Bomber's trousers down and his fat arse through the window, so I don't have any more time to waste. I pull the slide on the Steyr back halfway, to semi-automatic fire—if I have to use it I don't want the

334

fucking thing cracking around like a sub-machine gun, I couldn't handle that man—and I jump up and level the gun at Brock. I don't have time to frisk him, but I haven't seen a weapon, so I'll take the chance.

' "Turn around," I said.

'He turns, and I push him forward towards the patio doors, using him like a shield. As I get closer, I can see . . . ah fuck it, it's disgusting so it was.'

'Fat pigs are raping us,' said Maria, her voice low and wavering, like an old man's. 'We live in hell.'

'I get Taylor to open the door, and then I push him in,' said Tommy, breathing heavily now. 'And I'm just standing there, like a statue, you know, because I don't want to shoot anyone. I'm not supposed to be shooting people. I'm a mechanic, for fuck's sake. And Moon says something like, "Good man, Brock, you can have the next go."

'And I shoot over him, into the wall. And he's up in an instant, his trousers around his ankles, and he's going in his coat on the chair, and he has a sub-machine gun in his hands, a Steyr just like mine, and it's him or me, and I shoot him twice, three times, centre on, hit him twice, and he gets a burst out before he goes down, he's on automatic fire, and he clips Brock in the side, and I see Bomber fumbling in his clothes and I warn him, drop it, hands where I can see them, and he comes up with a handgun—don't know what it is. I shout again, and then I shoot him twice, and that's it. He had a chance, they both had a fucking chance, now they're both dead, or they look dead, they're not fucking moving anyway, I'm not going any closer to them to check.'

Tommy was shaking now, and tears were in his

335

eyes. We had passed Seafield Harbour, and I told him to pull in at a stopping place by the promenade.

'I didn't want to do it, Ed. I didn't want to do it. I mean, they're fucking scumbags, but . . .'

I couldn't think of anything to say. Maria could though.

'They would kill you, send us to hell. Savage cunts. Better off dead.'

I looked in the rear-view. Both Anita and Maria had bruises on their faces; the misery and fear in their eyes would take longer to heal.

I put my hand on Tommy's shoulder. Sobs wracked through his body like a rolling tide. Then he sniffed and caught his breath, and took up the story.

'The girls are huddled together, weeping, I tell them to get dressed, we need to get out: the fucking noise of all the gunfire, Saturday night in Beirut, I can hear doors opening down the street. Brock is trying to lam out the front door, and I hit him on the side of the head with the butt of the Steyr. I go through Moon's coat, get your phones, and the Sig Sauer you took from the Reillys. By the time we're out the patio doors, Brock's back up and vanished. There's three of us now, and we take the route I took, back between the river and the backyards, and then round the corner, through the brambles, over the fences—a bit trickier when there's three—and made it down the lane to the car. When I passed the cul-de-sac, the Guards were already there.'

Tommy stared out at the black expanse of sea. The fog looked to be lifting, and you could see a trickle of moonlight slating the rippled surface of the water.

'You killed two men, Tommy, and I can't tell you how to feel about that,' I said. 'But I can tell you this—you did well tonight, better than I did. You saved these girls, and you probably saved my life. I think you've more than made up for everything you did, and then some.'

Tommy nodded silently.

'So you can have your key back. Now let's get going—we're not done yet.'

Tommy drove the short distance to Quarry Fields, and we took Anita and Maria inside. They were frightened about staying there, and I persuaded Tommy, whom they now, rightly, considered their protector, to stay with them. That settled, they set about washing away at least some physical traces of what had happened to them.

The answerphone light was flashing. I listened to the message, and immediately wished I hadn't. It was from my ex-wife. It was hard to make out what she was saying, as she seemed to be crying, or laughing, or both. But the gist was that she had given birth to a baby boy that morning, that she knew he could never take the place of Lily, our daughter, but that she felt happy today for the first time since Lily died, and she hoped I could share that happiness too. I couldn't. I listened to the message again, then a third time. When Tommy Owens came out I was huddled in a ball on the stairs with my head in my hands. He wiped the message, and got me up, and talked me down, and made me wash my face, and fed me coffee and Nurofen, and put the Sig Sauer in my pocket, and told me to go back to work.

27

I called Dave Donnelly and told him the reason the Reillys weren't coming home to Woodpark was because they were lying dead in the Dublin mountains. I gave him the location of the quarry and told him Sean Moon and Brock Taylor were responsible. I also told him that the murder weapon was one of two Steyr 9-mm tactical machine pistols that could be found in Taylor's house in Fitzwilliam Square. He had already heard about the killings there and in Ballsbridge. I said I hadn't heard about any of that, and didn't know anything about it either. Dave called me a few names, and I let him. Then I said he should get up the mountains fast, before the workforce at the quarry show up and some other station gets the collar. I asked him if he had traced the phone calls made to Jessica and Shane Howard on Halloween morning. He gave me one mobile number, an 087, which had called Shane Howard; the other mobile, which had called both, used a concealed number. The 087 I recognized as Denis Finnegan's. I told Dave I expected to have something for him soon on the Stephen Casey/Audrey O'Connor murders.

Before I ended the call, David said they'd uncovered something about Jonathan O'Connor: he had a record of fire-starting back when he was twelve or thirteen—schools and churches, never detained but close to it, social services were involved, went on for about a year, then stopped.

I switched on Emily Howard's iBook and read through the most recent emails, a sequence of three highly emotional notes negotiating an urgent session with David Manuel. But these emails had been sent this evening, when the laptop was in Jonathan's room in Mountjoy Square, so they couldn't have been sent by Emily. They had been sent by Jonathan masquerading as his cousin. The last message from Manuel read:

> *Dear Emily,*
> *Will cut short my scheduled ten o'clock; come at ten thirty and we can have forty minutes. But it will be all right—although let me repeat, I believe this to be a legal matter as much as it is anything else, and I am reaching the stage where I can no longer stay silent.*
> *All best,*
> *David*

When I had left Jonathan last night in Trinity, I thought I had heard him crying. Maybe he had been laughing. I called Dave back and went straight through to message: I told him why Jonathan O'Connor should be considered favourite for the killing of therapist David Manuel last night, gave him Jonathan's address in Trinity and said I considered him extremely dangerous. Then I called both numbers I had for Sandra Howard and, in my best Dave Donnelly impersonation, left the message that Jonathan was not only being sought in connection with the Manuel killing, but was also prime suspect in the murders of David Brady and Jessica Howard. It was time to stir things up.

I drove fast to Jerry Dalton's house in Woodpark. It was five in the morning, still dark, the lights in the church still on. I banged on the door and Dalton answered it as if a caller at this hour was nothing out of the ordinary. He led me into the living room. There was no sign of Emily, or of any of the photograph albums and journals she had taken from Rowan House. The room was a mess of paper though; handwritten sheets from a lined A4 pad were scattered about; an acoustic guitar lay among them.

'You writing a song?' I said.

'I'm trying. Never really sure you've written one until it's done.'

'Where's Emily?'

'She's up with her father. She said if you came back, to go up there, to Bayview. She said it was important.'

I nodded.

'May I sit down?' I said.

'Sure. What happened to your head?'

'A baseball bat.'

'Fuck me. Who did it?'

'A guy called Moon, Sean Moon.'

'I don't know him, do I?'

'You won't get to know him now. He's dead.'

Dalton picked up his guitar and fingered a little run.

'Sounds like you have something to tell me. It might be better if you just came out with it. Better for me, at least, rather than having to prise it out of you, question by question.'

So I told him everything his mother had told me, about John Howard being his father, about being persuaded against her better judgement to leave him behind, about how she had missed him, and how she wanted so badly to know the truth of what had taken place in the Howard house. And I told him how Brock Taylor had been the murderer of his half-brother, and now, of his mother. I told him how she died, I didn't spare him anything. When I was done, he sat for a while in silence, then looked around the room.

'I thought by living here, I'd pick up something . . . a clue, a hint, a sense of how she was. There wasn't a trace. How did she seem to you? My mother?' he said.

'She was very beautiful. But scared. As if she'd been in hiding the last twenty years. From you, from herself, from the world. From what she maybe feared all along. That the man who had rescued her was her destroyer.'

'Maybe it wasn't all as simple as that.'

'Maybe it wasn't all. But I think we can feel free to condemn the man who murdered her son so that he wouldn't be in his way without being confused for the lock-'em-all-up-and-let-God-sort-'em-out brigade.'

'Jesus, I've seen Brock Taylor so often, in the rugby club, in the Woodpark Inn.'

'I thought chances were, he was your father.'

'And now it turns out I'm John Howard's son. I feel like I've contracted a curse.'

He laughed then, and shook his head.

'No, that's not true. I actually feel . . . like this is a kind of dream? Like I'm still Elizabeth and Robert Scott's son, Alan, who helps out at church fetes, and is going to be a doctor. Like my life will be fine.'

'There's every chance it can be. But Brock Taylor wasn't finished with the Howards yet. He thought he had money coming to him. That can only mean through Denis Finnegan, somehow. Through the mother's will? You said Emily's at Shane Howard's now. I'd better go there myself.'

'I'll come with you,' he said, following me to the door.

I stopped him.

'This case is not going to get any safer. And if you are a Howard now, it may get very dangerous indeed for you in particular.'

Jerry Dalton shrugged.

'There's more to life than church fetes,' he said.

*   *   *

On the short journey, Dalton told me he had come up with the suspicions about Rock O'Connor's death himself; in her cups, Jessica Howard had referred to O'Connor's diabetes, and suggested it was very convenient that Denis Finnegan had been the only one with Dr Rock when he died; Jerry played a hunch and passed me the material about how an insulin overdose can resemble a heart attack. I told him if he ever got tired of medicine, he would make a fine detective: knowing what hunch to play and when was the hardest part of the job.

The narrow drive to what Anita Venclova called 'Howard Residence' ran up from Bayview Harbour. It was still dark, but the clouds had peeled away; the sky looked like it had been polished and come up shining, like a dark mirror. Shane Howard was standing in the window of the front room, looking out to sea; he saw us arrive and opened the door to let us in. Emily was sitting on the sofa, her pile of photograph albums and journals around her.

'You can put those away now, Emily,' Shane barked.

His daughter laughed at him.

'Dad, it's too late for that.'

'Your daughter's right, Shane. It's too late to keep secrets any more. Especially when you and your sister don't have anything to be ashamed of.'

Shane scowled at me.

'Who's this?' he said, pointing at Jerry Dalton.

'Well,' I said. 'There's a number of ways I could introduce him. I could say he's a friend of your daughter's from university. I could say he's Eileen Casey—you remember Eileen, your old, what would you call her, au pair? Nanny?—I could say he's Eileen Casey's son. But I think we should get it over with and say he's your half-brother, Shane. John Howard was his father.'

I thought Shane would explode, would demand proof, would wave his fists around and rail against me, against us all. Instead, he looked at Dalton, and nodded his head, and stared at the floor. He knew. He knew all along. The rage seemed to pass out of him like the fire of youth, and he slumped in a chair by the cold grate. Emily stared across at Jerry in astonishment. I looked at their faces and wondered if they'd been telling the truth, or if they had already slept together. This case was full of questions I didn't want to know the answers to.

'What else did you know, Shane? Back then, what did you know about Marian? And about Sandra?'

'I can't,' he said. 'I can't tell you . . . I made a promise.'

'To Sandra?'

He nodded.

'That must have been a long time ago.'

'It doesn't matter how long ago it was. I made it. I can't break it.'

'Not even for the sake of your own child? She's desperate to know the truth, Shane.'

'I've always tried to protect her. That's what we said we'd do, protect the kids,' Shane said in a hoarse whisper, his eyes glued to the floor.

'Did you find anything in Mary Howard's journals, Emily?' I said.

'There's no reference to Marian's death. The journal stops about six months before. And after that, it's just a stream of bile about Granddad, right up until his death. She really hated him.'

Emily leafed through a particular journal until she found a particular passage.

'Here, this must refer to Jerry's mother, listen: *"Eileen came to me tonight and told me she was in trouble, and who by. I didn't doubt it for a second, she's always been a good girl and would never lie. God damn that man to hell. The girl has found a chap to stand by her. We must do our best nonetheless. How I'd love to tell the world the truth. But Shane mustn't be hurt any more than he has been already."'*

Still Shane Howard sat with his head bowed. It was like he had begun to fear the worst. That was healthy. I needed to play on his fears.

'Shane, I want to ask you about Denis Finnegan. Tonight, Brock Taylor was killed. Before he died, he confessed to the murders of Audrey O'Connor and Stephen Casey.'

'Brock Taylor? The reformed crook? Hangs

around SRC?'

'That's right. He's the fellow you remember as Eileen's boyfriend, Brian Dalton, the one on the Norton Commando.'

'And you say he killed her son?'

'That's right. But he said he did it for someone who paid him. Someone who idolized you and Sandra, who wanted the best for her—what he thought was the best for her.'

'Dinny?'

'Denis Finnegan, that's right. And Taylor said there would be a payback coming, that soon he would be set to inherit, big time. I took that to mean, via some scheme of Finnegan's. Do you have any idea what that might be?'

'I don't. I mean, I don't have any big share portfolio or anything. I've this house, and the surgery.'

'And Rowan House.'

'That's it. And I've seen my mother's will, it's all straightforward. The property comes to me, end of story.'

'But if you were genuinely disposed towards sharing it with Sandra in order to build the last tower, in order to fulfil the Howard family dream, the completion of the Howard Medical Centre at last—'

'Who told you that?'

'Denis Finnegan. He said that's what you all wanted. For the family. But your wife was opposed to it.'

'I was opposed to it too. I didn't want to build a load of apartments, but I didn't want a fourth tower, like it was some fucking *monument* . . . Sandra wanted it . . . said she wanted to honour

345

our father, although how she could . . .'

He looked up at me, his eyes red with rage.

'What I'd like best is if the house was burned to the ground. After that, we could think about what came after. But best for everyone . . . best for Sandra above all . . . if the whole place was dust and ashes.'

'What do you mean by that?'

'You'll have to ask Sandra. I won't say any more.'

'And what about Finnegan? Do you think there's some way he envisaged getting his hands on the whole project through Sandra? If you were going to go into it on an equal basis—'

'But I wasn't—'

'What if you were in jail for killing your wife? Your resolve might not be quite so great then. You'd need money for appeals, you'd need to take the advice of your sister and your solicitor.'

'What are you saying, Dinny had something to do with Jessica's death?'

'I don't know yet,' I said. 'Try and remember. You got a call yesterday, or rather the day before, Halloween, someone telling you your wife was having an affair with David Brady. Now two people rang your number that morning. One of them was Denis Finnegan. Do you remember the call? It would have been after I left, you went back to the surgery. Your patients were getting, ah, impatient.'

Shane scowled in concentration.

'Yeah. Because it was the mobile, in my pocket. Dinny asking about you, was there anything he needed to know? Always such a fussy fucker. You can hardly say, would you ever fuck off, with some oul' one in the chair. So I said no and hung up.'

346

'Right. So the other call was the anonymous call.'

'That's right. Prissy kind of voice, I thought, but trying to sound tough. Why? Do you know who it was?'

Keep stirring, Loy.

'The Guards traced the number. It was your nephew, Jonathan.'

The telephone rang, and Emily went to answer it. Shane Howard was on his feet, and breathing like a man who's just remembered how. Jerry Dalton's eyes never left me. Emily came back into the room.

'That was Granny,' she said. 'They're at the airport. They're staying at the Radisson. I wrote the number on the pad.'

For a moment I had trouble moving my lips. Finally I got them to work in conjunction with my tongue.

'Your granny,' I said.

'Yes. Mum's mum. And Granddad. They retired to the Algarve. Awful journey, to bury their daughter's body.'

'What did Jessica's father—your granddad—do?' I said. 'He wasn't an actor, was he?'

'Oh, God no. Mum said she had the biggest rows with him when she wanted to go into the theatre. No, he ran a business, a . . . carpets? What was it, Dad?'

'Contract cleaning,' Shane said, his mind elsewhere.

Sandra's lie had been a detailed and elaborate one—about Jessica's father being a failed actor, and a widower, and a drunk; about Jessica being her father's little wife when she was thirteen, for eighteen months; about how she didn't love sex in

347

itself so much as the power it gave her. Could it have been that Sandra was talking, not about Jessica, but about herself?

The telephone rang again, and Shane answered it.

Emily was tidying all the photograph albums and journals together. I asked her if she'd looked at the doll's house in her room yet, and she made a cartoon face and said she had forgotten about it, and ran towards her room at once. Dalton followed her.

Shane came off the phone.

'No one in this family is sleeping tonight. That was Sandra. She and Denis are up in Rowan House. They're in a panic, want to talk. Will you follow me up there?'

28

Later, when it was all over—when I had been released from Seafield Garda station having been involuntarily 'debriefed'; when the identity of the man accompanying the Reillys in the CCTV footage outside the Waterfront apartments before David Brady was murdered had been established; when neighbours living close to the house Jessica Howard was murdered in confirmed that they had seen a man whose photograph they were shown arriving at or leaving the house close to the time the murder took place; when a paper trail was uncovered that linked Denis Finnegan conclusively to Brock Taylor, particularly in regard to the plans for the fourth tower at the

Howard Medical Centre; when the Guards in Seafield station had ordered the booze for their celebration party; and when I had been trailed from interrogation room to cell often enough for it to be made clear to me that if I ever conducted another case the way I had conducted this one (withholding evidence, tampering with evidence, interfering with a crime scene, lying to the Guards and, as Dave put it, generally carrying on like a total fucking bollocks who thinks he's fucking *it*) I would find it impossible to buy a dog licence, let alone pursue a career as a private investigator— when it was all over, I stood among the charred remains of Rowan House and wondered whether the sins of the fathers could ever be washed away with their deaths, or whether a legacy of tainted blood would always colour the lives of the children and the children's children. I didn't come up with any answers.

*   *   *

Shane led the way in his black Mercedes, like Sandra's two days before, once again giving a funereal feel to the cortège. I rode in its wake, and we drove in the grey pre-dawn to Rowan House. Crows had been gathering on telephone wires and poles on Bayview Hill when we left; they were massing on the turrets of Rowan House as we arrived, beating their wings and making their predatory moans.

We got out of our cars and walked through the rowan trees, and I thought about the berries, and about the heliotrope crystals, the bloodstones that Emily always wore, how Shane said Sandra had

349

been the one to introduce them to the family. I tried to remember what Emily had told me about them: how, in water, they made the sky turn red, but simply to hold one rendered the bearer invisible. The times I had worked with sexual-abuse survivors before, almost every one of them had at some point or other said that there were days her sense of self was so fragile she felt like she was completely invisible, that no one could actually see her; equally, there were days when she felt so low, so wretched and unloved and consumed with self-hatred that she wished she could simply vanish off the face of the earth, be visible to nobody, least of all herself.

The first thing I noticed about Sandra Howard that last night was that she was wearing bloodstones all over: on her fingers, in her ears and on a chain around her neck. The second thing I noticed was her drawn, anxious face, the lines around her red eyes that had softened into crêpe, the mouth set tight and hard like that of a wary animal. I don't know if she was surprised to see me, or angry, or resigned; maybe she didn't know herself. Her hair was pulled back tight, and she wore a long green wrap-around dress with red-velvet detail that tied at the waist over a pair of jeans. She still looked like the most beautiful woman I had ever seen, but now her beauty scared me; way beyond danger, it was too sad and too angry; I felt pity and fear for her.

The house was dark, the shutters and drapes closed; light spilled into the rotunda from the chandelier on the upper floor. Sandra led us down the rear corridor and into one of the sitting rooms I had seen before.

The room was lit by table lamps; it felt dark and heavy, with its mahogany side tables, dark red chairs and matching couches, dark-wood fireplace and dark-green carpet. There were antimacassars on the chairs and cushions with needlework covers on the couches; there was an upright piano and a piano stool with an embroidered cushion-cover seat that lifted off; inside there was sheet music from another time: 'Autumn Leaves', 'Night and Day', 'Last Night When We Were Young'. I had a flash of the Howard family gathered around the piano, singing together. It seemed unbearable even to imagine; what must it have been like to recall?

There were four portraits of John Howard in the room, painted at intervals between his thirties and his early sixties; in conjunction with the mirrors that hung above the hearth and on the wall opposite, it meant that wherever your eye rested, he was in sight. I could see what Martha O'Connor's colleague had meant about the David Niven comparison: there was a natural, rangy elegance to Howard which, combined with the flannels and tweeds he favoured, gave him the appearance of a classic English gentleman. But his face lacked the genial, open features needed to round that image off; his eyes were small and piercing, his nose pointed, his lips compressed in a faint smile of what looked like self-satisfaction. His children barely resembled him, although Jerry Dalton had the same carved bone structure. No, the person who most looked like John Howard was his grandson, Jonathan, who wasn't here. Denis Finnegan was, however: he rose and performed a kind of greeting in dumbshow; then he sat again, a sheaf of papers by him on a side table. I stood by the mantelpiece. With his rictus grin and a wave of his red hand, Finnegan tried to induce me to sit down. I needed to keep on my feet. In my pocket, I fingered the Sig Sauer I had taken from Darren Reilly, now dead. I was glad to have it.

Sandra stood by a chair on the other side of the room from Denis Finnegan. On a couch between them, Shane raised his gaze from the floor and looked at his sister. She in turn looked at Denis Finnegan, who spread his palms as an emperor might say, 'Let the games commence.'

'I had hoped this would just be family, Shane,' Sandra said, avoiding my eyes.

'I think it's too late for that, Sandra,' Shane said.

'I think it always was,' I said.

Sandra took a deep breath and began.

'The Guards have been in touch. David Manuel fell to his death from his attic last night. His house was on fire. The Guards believe the fire was started deliberately. By Jonathan. It seems they also suspect him of being involved in the murders of David Brady . . . and of Jessica.'

Sandra sounded like she wanted someone to reassure her that nothing she had said could possibly be true. Even Denis Finnegan couldn't stretch to that.

'What they suspect and what they can support with evidence are two different things' was the best he could come up with.

'Jonathan called to Denis late last night,' Sandra went on.

'He woke me up, with some difficulty,' Finnegan said, staring pointedly in my direction. 'At first he thought I was dead. He had to pour water on my face, and shake me hard. It was as if I had been drugged. What do you think, Mr Loy?'

I met Finnegan's gaze and shrugged. If he connected me to the GHB, I could be in a lot of trouble. But I was in a lot of trouble already. And, if I had my way, Finnegan wasn't going to be the most reliable witness the world had ever seen come the dawn.

'What did he say to you?'

'Nothing,' Finnegan said. 'He left again almost immediately, wouldn't tell me where he was going. He seemed extremely agitated.'

'There must be something we can do,' Sandra said. 'I mean, what they're saying can't be true, can it?'

'It was Jonathan who called me and told me Jessica was with David Brady,' Shane said. 'The Guards traced the calls. I think he knew me well enough to know I would lose the head altogether, that I'd lam around there to try and catch them in the act, and in the process get caught up on CCTV, which needless to say is just what I did. He tried to frame me for the murder.'

'He tried to throw the blame on to Emily as well,' I said.

'I don't believe it,' Sandra said. But she sounded, wearily, as if she did.

'Jonathan called Jessica that morning also,' I said. 'Was that usual? Did he ever have any contact with her?'

Shane shook his head.

'Not that I know of.'

Denis Finnegan sprang into action.

'I might be able to shed some light on that,' he said. 'I've been doing a certain amount of dabbling

353

in the property market. Jonathan would visit properties on my behalf, and make an assessment for me of their potential worth. In that regard, I know for a fact he has seen several of the houses Jessica was showing in recent months.'

It was impossible to tell whether Finnegan was improvising to protect his stepson or whether he was telling the truth. Before I could push him on it, Shane Howard ploughed in.

'You're a great man for property schemes, aren't you Dinny? The fourth tower, isn't that right?'

'I've made no secret of my views. They support those of your sister.'

'And isn't it very convenient that Jessica's not around any more to get in the way of your plans?'

'If you intend to level any malign insinuation regarding Jessica's murder at my door, I would advise—'

'Ah, cut the lawyer crap now, Dinny. I bet that's not the way you talk with Brock Taylor.'

'What do you mean by that?'

'I bet Brock Taylor wouldn't let a woman stand in the way of his plans. What's a nice lawyer like you doing with a crook like that?'

'Brian Taylor has paid his debt to society, has settled with the Revenue and the CAB, he is now a respectable businessman, and is legally entitled—'

I couldn't let that one run.

'Brock Taylor was a murderer and a crook, and you owed him big time. Incalculable, really, how much. At least, that's what he reckoned. I don't know what way the pair of you structured the deal, or whether he just left it up to you, but either way, he was expecting to be paid back in a major way. Was he going to be a partner? Once Shane was

354

safely stowed in jail, and you and Sandra had the running of it all, it would have been easy to cut him in, wouldn't it? Or was he already in? For what? A third? A half? It's all for Sandra, remember, so you can't cut her out entirely. Although with someone like Brock Taylor, who knows where the bodies are buried because he killed them himself, you're on very shaky ground, aren't you Denis? Maybe your loyalty to your childhood pal will have to take precedence over your veneration of the glorious Howard family.'

Sandra found her voice again.

'Denis? What is he saying? What bodies?'

Denis Finnegan had set his little feet down beside each other on the floor. I stroked the Sig with one hand, just to remind me it was there. Finnegan wasn't going to speak, so I had to.

'Denis had a crush, no, more than a crush, a kind of blind, overwhelming interest in your future, Sandra. He was benevolent, all-powerful, like God, really. And just like God, he didn't mind if a few bodies got in the way, so long as it was to serve what were considered your best interests. I don't know why he decided on Richard O'Connor—maybe he felt you needed a father figure, maybe Denis loved Dr Rock himself and hoped to channel his sublimated passion through you; fuck knows, I'm not a psychologist, what I do know is that he paid a man who called himself Brian Dalton—who we now know as Brock Taylor—to murder Audrey O'Connor and carry out a bungled robbery at Richard O'Connor's house, and then to plant the proceeds of the robbery on Stephen Casey, Eileen Harvey's first son, and murder him too. Which he duly did. And in due course,

355

presumably encouraged on both sides by Denis Finnegan, romance blooms and Sandra and Dr Rock marry, and have a son. Jonathan.'

'I must warn you that, legally, you are on the flimsiest of grounds here, Mr Loy. The law of slander—'

'Legally, I live in a cell with cockroaches and rats and no running water; when the Seafield cops are done with me, I won't have a legal bone left in my body,' I said. 'So let's just skip the legalities for a while, and continue with our nice cosy family chat. After all, Brock Taylor used to work for my father once, so I think I can consider myself part of the family too, even if I come in through the servants' entrance.'

I looked around the room. Sandra was staring alternately at me and Finnegan, her green eyes sick with fear. I took the rugby medal out of my pocket and gave it to her.

'See, Rock's name is engraved on it. The Guards never recovered Rock's medals after the robbery. I found them in a drawer in the spare bedroom of your husband's house in Mountjoy Square.'

Sandra Howard thrust the medal into my hand, flung herself off her chair and vomited into the fireplace.

'I heard Brock Taylor admit to killing Audrey O'Connor and Stephen Casey tonight. And then his wife killed him.'

Finnegan was squirming in his chair, but he seemed to have lost the power of speech. Sandra got to her feet and breathed deeply.

'Keep going, Ed,' she said. 'Tell it all.'

'So then, having set you up for marriage with Dr Rock, Denis goes off and completes his legal training and starts his practice, representing many of the prominent criminals of the day, including, of course, his boyhood pal Brock Taylor. But he keeps a hand in on the south side, the bit of coaching for Castlehill, the bit of attention paid to Sandra, and a spot of rugby sevens on a Saturday morning with the guys. Including Dr Rock. And then one Saturday morning, Dr Rock collapses, a suspected heart attack. Maybe he hasn't taken his insulin, maybe he's hungover and the exercise is getting to him. And Denis says he'll take him to hospital, which he does. Now I can't be sure—the only one who knows is Denis—but what I think happened was, Rock asks him to inject him with insulin. And Denis does, only he gives Rock an overdose. By the time they get to hospital, Rock is slipping into a coma, and Denis neglects to mention that Rock is a diabetic, and Rock is treated as if it's a regular myocardial infarction, a heart attack, and he dies in a couple of hours.'

Finnegan was shaking his head.

'I didn't know he was a diabetic,' he said. He appealed to Sandra. 'I swear I didn't.'

Sandra wouldn't look at her husband's face.

'I spoke to the doctor who admitted him. He remembers you. He'll be happy to make a complaint to the Guards.'

Finnegan got to his feet.

'I don't have to stay here and be subjected to this—'

Shane Howard pushed him back into his chair.

'Yes you do, Dinny, yes you fucking do.'

'Along with the medals in Finnegan's house, I found one other item,' I said, and produced the silver ID bracelet from my pocket. Again I gave it to Sandra for inspection. She let loose a howl of pain and sank to the floor.

'What does it say?' a shrill voice asked. It was Jonathan O'Connor, in black coat and baseball hat and wrap-around shades. I didn't know how long he had been in the room. Long enough, it looked like. Jonathan crossed the room towards his mother, who held out her arms for an embrace he avoided. He took the bracelet and examined it.

'It says "Diabetic—Type 1",' I said. 'If your father had been wearing it—'

'He took it off for the game,' Finnegan said. 'He took it off whenever we played sevens. He was in his gear when we went to the hospital.'

'How do you have his bracelet then? Where did you get it? Why did you keep it?'

'I had nothing but respect and admiration for Rock O'Connor,' Finnegan said. 'He was my friend, he was everything to me.'

Jonathan laughed, a forced, mirthless sound like static from a badly tuned radio.

'Your friend? Yes, but who are you?' Jonathan said. 'You're not who you claimed to be at all. You're a fraud, a fabrication. You're not fit to be a part of this family.'

'Everything I've done I've done for the Howards' sake. For Sandra's sake.'

Finnegan's voice was thick with a sincerity I'd never heard in it before. He looked pleadingly at Sandra, and I saw the northside boy he'd been, and the dream that had sustained him, and the ties of history and of blood that had laid him low.

'You killed her husband,' Jonathan said, his voice shrill with excitement. 'You killed my father. If that was for the Howards' sake, then so is this.'

I still don't know if Jonathan was too quick for me, or if I just stood back and let it happen. Both, perhaps. He had been inching towards Finnegan gradually, and Finnegan had risen to his feet again, and then Jonathan was upon him. The blade whipped out of his coat and sparkled in the drear and then buried itself in Denis Finnegan's chest, twice, three times, straight in the heart. By the time the Sig was in my hand, Finnegan was as good as dead. Jonathan sprang back, still holding the knife; I waved the gun at him and he tossed the bloody weapon on the floor. The knife was a Sabatier, the same as the knife that had killed David Brady; the method was the same as that used to murder Jessica Howard; the knife was probably the second of the two I had found missing from Denis Finnegan's kitchen. I wondered whether Finnegan was Jonathan's fourth victim. But the knife used to kill Jessica had not been found.

And then Shane Howard crouched by the body, and felt for a pulse, and turned to me and shook his head. It reminded me that he had a medical training, that he would have known there was very little blood when someone is stabbed through the heart, that the bleeding is largely internal. He wouldn't have asked where his wife's blood was. He would have known.

Jonathan stepped back from us all and pulled his shades off; his eyes blazed with what could have been fear, but looked like triumph. He cast around for his mother, but she was hanging one-handed on the mantelpiece now, her breath coming in quick bursts, her worn face drained of life, of hope.

'He killed my father,' Jonathan cried, as if there had been no other route open to him. 'He was nothing. Nothing but scum.'

He seemed exhilarated, almost gleeful. What I had thought was weakness in his eyes now looked like something else: a delirium of violence, a killing rage.

'How many others did you kill, Jonathan?' I said.

'No one,' he said, unable to suppress the grin that spread across his face.

'What did you say to Shane Howard when you rang him on Halloween morning? What did you tell him?'

'Nothing. I didn't ring him.'

'I have phone records that say you did.'

'You couldn't, my phone is—'

'Untraceable, I know. And now I know for sure you made that call. You told him his wife was having an affair with David Brady, didn't you?'

'No.'

'You'd already killed Brady by then. And you must have thought you were clever dodging the CCTV camera in the lobby. But there's a camera across the road, and it's got footage of the Reillys and their accomplice. That's you, Jonathan.'

Jonathan shook his head.

'And after that, you went around to Jessica Howard, whom you also rang that morning, and you went around and stabbed her to death too. Just the way you stabbed Denis Finnegan, straight through the heart. And then you went back to Honeypark, took a shower, dumped your clothes in the house in Honeypark, just the way you tried to make out Emily had had a shower and dumped her bloody clothes there—which is why you set

360

fire to the place yesterday. Now this is what I think you were doing, Jonathan. You were working with Denis Finnegan, listening to his plans, the great Howard name, the construction of the fourth tower, the grandiose achievements that separate the likes of you, great men, from the likes of the rest of us, the little people who don't have any castles or towers in our names, or portraits of ourselves on every wall. Denis knew all about the blackmail scheme involving the porn film—David Brady had sent it to him by email attachment, so he may have felt it was a way of persuading Shane Howard to play ball on the development front. But then the Reillys were involved with their crude demands for cash, and the whole thing just became too much grief. Finnegan told Brady, and Brady tried to back down—but the Reillys weren't having that. This was their chance for some long-term income, blackmailing Shane Howard. So between you and Wayne and Darren, the plot was hatched to get rid of David Brady. You didn't like him anyway, did you Jonny? All those things Emily did with him. It should've been you, shouldn't it?'

Jonathan was very still, his eyes blank now, his mouth set.

'Why you killed Jessica Howard is clearer, I think. She was actively opposed to the plan to build the fourth tower, she wanted to redevelop the site for apartments and town houses. That was bad for Denis, because with Jessica involved, there was no way he could bring Brock Taylor on board. And it was bad for you, apartments full of dreadful little people sullying the Howard name. So you went around there and you killed her. And you

361

tried to set Shane Howard up for both murders.'

I was looking at Shane as I spoke. He couldn't meet my eye.

'No, you're completely wrong,' Jonathan said. 'I didn't kill Jessica.'

'But you did kill David Brady. And you did kill David Manuel. I found Emily's laptop last night, in your room in Finnegan's Mountjoy Square house. I thought at first Emily had been emailing David Manuel. But how could she, she didn't have her computer. No, Jonathan, pretending to be Emily, negotiated an emergency late-night appointment with Manuel last night. Manuel knew too much, and wanted Emily to go to the cops. Jonathan went there, overpowered Manuel and set fire to his room. Manuel fell to his death, horribly burnt.'

Jonathan looked to his mother one last time; she seemed to be fading before our eyes, like a plant wilting for lack of water and light; she shook her head at him and turned away. He attempted a laugh, but it didn't catch; his eyes burned with hatred; he looked like a trapped and wounded animal.

'I did my best for us,' he said. 'But the only other person who gave a damn was Denis, and he should never have been allowed across the door. Now you can all go to hell.'

He bolted across the room and out the door. I thought Shane Howard might try and stop him, but he didn't. Neither did I. I put the gun back in my pocket and called Dave Donnelly and told him what had happened and who I thought was responsible and where to come.

29

A few minutes later, Emily Howard and Jerry Dalton appeared. Emily had the doll's house under her arm and an excited, urgent look in her eye. She made straight for me but Denis Finnegan's body brought her to a halt; she screamed at the sight of the dead man, and shook her head in disbelief. I led her to a sofa and calmed her down and filled her in quickly on what had taken place. I left her sitting very still with the doll's house on her lap and tears in her eyes, whatever she had been about to tell me lost to shock. Sandra stared at Jerry Dalton blankly; when Shane explained who he was, she nodded. 'Welcome to the family,' she said, with a dark smile on her face that failed to leaven the curse. I wanted to spare her any more pain. But we weren't done yet.

'Jessica's parents have arrived in the country. They're staying at the Radisson,' I said to Sandra. 'Her father, the one who isn't a dead alcoholic actor, and her mother, who didn't die of ovarian cancer.'

She looked at me as if she had hoped I'd let her off this, at least, as if what we'd been to each other should count for something. It did, but I couldn't let her see that. Not until it was all finished. Maybe not even then. She winced, as if I had hit her, then nodded, walked from the fireplace to the nearest window and began to open the heavy green-velvet curtains.

'Shut out the lights,' she said.

Jerry Dalton went round the room and turned all

the lamps off. A cold light spilled in from outside, the deep blue before dawn on a clear day, the first for a long time. There were smears of pink in the sky; the three towers loomed ahead; below them, the dark city, asleep by the bay.

'I was first,' Sandra said. 'And that made me feel important. I was thirteen, and he came to my room not long after I'd started my periods. It was exciting . . . we'd go for drives, and secret walks, and he'd always bring me to rugby matches, and of course it was very exciting having secrets from everyone, Mother especially . . . I felt the others were such babies then . . . I don't remember what I thought about the sex . . . it was messy, I remember thinking, and it seemed silly too, and then frightening when Father got so serious and intense about it all . . . but I can't remember actually *feeling* anything, or rather I felt so many different things . . . love, fear, disloyalty, the thrill of the forbidden . . . that it was hard to unravel them from each other. I suppose that's why it's been an issue for me later . . . not that I didn't enjoy it, I liked lots of things about it, but I don't think I really *felt* anything, or enough . . . except with Stephen. Even if he was seventeen, we shouldn't have been together. That was so intense. But maybe it was because it was forbidden, because I knew deep down it was wrong . . .

'Anyway, it ended with Father after two years. It got awful fairly quickly. I thought at first we might run away, that he might be mine, not Mother's. But of course, when you realize . . . when I realized what it was . . . all it could ever be . . . well, then it just became disgusting. At first he'd bring me presents,

364

new clothes, books, records . . . but then it became more about Mother not finding out than anything else . . . so after a while, he just left money under the pillow . . . I wasn't even sure what a whore was yet, but I felt like one . . . so I just wouldn't let him any more. Well, that was all right, he didn't force me . . . and then one night . . . Shane, I'm going to talk about this, is that OK?'

'Just keep going,' Shane Howard said.

'I heard screams from Shane's room. I ran in, and there he was, trying to do Shane . . . from behind, you know. I just . . . I screamed and flung myself at him and beat him and clawed and scratched until he ran off . . . and I stayed with Shane until morning. And that went on for months. Nothing sexual, we never . . . I . . . and I know, Shane, I know you thought I was protecting you, and maybe that was part of it. But honestly, I was jealous, if he wasn't going to have me, he shouldn't have you . . . I felt I had been slighted, that when I sent him away, he should have come back with a better offer, he should have taken me off on a white charger . . . I know that didn't make any sense . . . it probably wasn't even fair . . . but he started it . . . then Marian, who was precocious even by nowadays' standards, had breasts and her first period at eleven . . . and . . . and I was fifteen . . . and I just pretended nothing was happening . . . even though it was obvious, an eleven-year-old wearing make-up, eyeshadow, lipstick . . . and yet she was still such a child, in thrall to the whole princess story, the sleeping beauty, the kiss from a prince . . . but I *knew* . . .'

'I knew too,' Shane said.

'And we did nothing. I don't know what I thought.

Or maybe a part of me thought, *I had to put up with it, why shouldn't she?* Maybe that's what a very cold, cruel part of me thought.'

I looked around the room. Emily's face was a blizzard of tears. Jerry Dalton knelt by her, holding her hand. Shane had gone back to staring at the floor.

'And then Marian was suddenly, mysteriously "ill" . . . except she wasn't. We knew she wasn't, we all knew she was pregnant. We knew it from the way Mother was so unhappy, the way she'd cry herself to sleep at night . . . the way she couldn't look at Father any more, and the way he couldn't look at anyone . . . the way no one was allowed to see Marian, or if we were, she wasn't allowed to say anything to us . . . we knew she was pregnant and we . . . and I was jealous . . . and I blamed her . . . and it seemed like such a special fuss was being made of her, I wished it was me. We never . . . well, I never saw the baby . . . I don't even know what happened, it was never spoken of . . . was it stillborn?'

'Eileen Casey thought she heard a baby cry one night,' I said.

'Did she?' Sandra said. 'It's pretty bad, isn't it? For a baby to have been born into the world . . . into this house . . . and for there to be no trace of it left . . . it's about as bad as it could be . . . and we never spoke of it . . . *never* . . . who knows, did they give it away, or murder it, or what? We never knew.'

'They gave it away,' Shane said. 'That's what I always reckoned, to one of the adoption agencies, or to a home or some such. That's why Marian . . . that's why she couldn't . . .'

366

'That must be right,' Sandra said. 'That's why she
. . . *because* she couldn't. She couldn't face life
without the baby, so she walked into the pool in her
nightdress holding the heaviest rock she could find,
and laid the rock on her chest, and lay down in the
water and couldn't get up . . . at least that's how she
was when I found her, that's how I imagined she did
it . . . Oh, God forgive us, she was just a little girl,
and we did *nothing . . .*'

Sandra began to cry then. Great, wrenching sobs
filled the room. She made a harsh 'mmm' sound in
her throat and in her mouth to make herself stop.

'Keep going, to the end. The only thing we did . . .
Mother gathered Shane and me together, on the
day of the funeral, and said, "Marian's room is to be
kept like it was the day she left us. It will be
cleaned, but it must never be altered, as long as you
live in this house. Do you understand?" And so it
never has been, not a jot has been changed or taken
from it to this day.

'So what I did then, I completely denied
everything that had happened. I think it took me a
few years. I think teaching was my way of not
following in my father's footsteps. But I helped to
nurse him . . .'

'Along with Eileen Casey.'

'That's right.'

'She told me he didn't rape her.'

'Well, that makes everything all right then,'
Sandra said. 'After his death . . . and maybe it was
in getting to know Dr Rock . . . in seeing, for the
first time, a future . . . I don't know, it was as if I
decided everything had been the opposite of what
it was, everything had been perfectly fine . . . if not
for our sake, for the sake of the children we had,

that they would never know about it, or be affected by it . . . but I suppose all I was doing was living a lie, and making them live one too, crippling them under the weight of it. God, what have I done to my little boy?'

She wept again. I wanted to go to her, to hold her, to tell her what I didn't believe, that it would be all right, that we could be together. I took a step in her direction, and she turned from the window and looked at me, looked through me, and I knew that what we had had, whatever we had had, was gone, gone and best forgotten. I hadn't been straight with her, and she couldn't be straight with me; now she looked right through me and I looked right back, and she passed along to where her brother was sitting. She sat on the floor between his outstretched knees, and he slid down off the couch and cradled her in his great arms, just as she had done with him the night Emily was found, the night David Brady and Jessica Howard were murdered; just as she had been doing with him for years; now the years seemed to fall away until they were like children again in their haunted house, waiting out the dark.

Outside, the pink was filling up the sky, slices of grapefruit and salmon frothing one against the other. The sun rose over the bay like a fat blood orange. At long last, after a long long night, on All Souls' Day, some light.

30

The first petrol bomb came through the door and shattered golden against the piano. The second was smashed by hand on the inside of the door, which was then slammed shut from the outside. I could hear something being dragged against the door out in the corridor, but it wasn't necessary; the flames had shot up against the door handle, making it impossible to get out.

At the other end of the room, the drapes by the corner window Sandra had been standing at went up like tinder. Shane drew the curtains on the far window and tried to open it but it had been nailed shut, and the glass was reinforced. It might have been worse; as a ground-floor window, it might have been barred. The fire was spreading fast, and the thick smoke made it difficult to see, and to breathe. We tried to break the glass with tables and chairs, but the furniture was old and flimsier than it looked, and ended up shattering. I wondered about trying to launch the piano through the window, but it was too heavy, and now, it too was engulfed in flames. Finally, Shane Howard, Jerry Dalton and I hoisted the heaviest sofa in the room and, using it as a battering ram, together we ran it at the window and shattered the panes below the sash. This let air in, making it easier to breathe, but it also fed the flames with oxygen. It took us a while to extract the sofa from the shattered window panes, and then it was a case of kicking out the remaining shards of glass and wood. Below us there was a drop of about eight feet to a concrete path about four feet wide; beyond the path the lawn rose in a steep incline to our knee level and then swept off down the hill.

The flames reached the drapes on the second window, framing the dawn on one side in golden fire. I shooed Emily towards the open window and beckoned Jerry Dalton.

'You first, come on.'

'I'm not parting with this,' Emily said, hugging her doll's house to her.

I nodded, then grabbed it out of her arms and tossed it out the window. It bounced on the lawn beyond.

'Now go,' I said.

Emily hung from the window and dropped to the ground below. Jerry Dalton held back, waiting for Sandra to get to safety; she was huddled near the empty grate of the fireplace.

'Sandra, come on, we don't have much time,' I cried. 'We've got to get out of here.'

I took her by the wrist, and she grabbed my arm hard and looked into my eyes and shook her head.

'I don't want any more time, Ed,' she said. 'I can never leave this house.'

I released her lat once, by reflex, as you might recoil from the dead.

She smiled then, and clasped the bloodstone around her neck tight in her hand and turned and vanished into the flames. I never saw her again.

I went to the window and helped Jerry Dalton down. When I turned back to the room, it was an inferno. Whatever stuffing was in the furniture and cushions was highly inflammable; there was a circus of flame across the centre of the room.

Shane had his back to me; he looked like he was trying to find a way through the blaze. I clapped him on the back.

'Where's Sandra?' Shane said.

'She was by the fireplace,' I said.

Shane tried to head that way, but the flames were impassable; his trouser leg caught fire, and I dragged him back and beat the flames off.

'I can't go without her,' he shouted.

'Maybe she got out the door.'

'I have to go back for her.'

'Shane,' I yelled. 'Think of Emily. We can double around and try to get in some other way. But if we stay here, we're dead men.'

Shane looked me briefly in the face, his great scowl blackened with smoke. He shook his head.

'You don't understand,' he said.

'I think I do understand,' I said. 'I know you killed Jessica. I don't know why. But you would have known there would be little blood when she was stabbed through the heart. So when you rang and told me she was dead and asked where all the blood was, you were feigning some kind of shock you didn't really feel. Your wife was dead because you had killed her yourself, hours earlier.'

Shane looked at me and, for the last time, the planes of his great face shifted into a grotesque smile.

'I just couldn't take any more,' he said. 'When I saw the photographs of Emily, I blamed myself, but I blamed Jessica more. A whore breeds nothing but whores.'

The fumes were choking me now, like acid in my throat; my eyes felt like they were bleeding; the foulness of Shane Howard's words clung to the smoke like a chemical taint.

'We've got to get out of here,' I said, my words a death rattle against the flames. Shane's smile seemed garish but disembodied, as if it were the only part of him left alive.

'A father who killed her mother?' he said. 'I'm no use to Emily now. I'm better off with my sister. I always was.'

I reached out to grab him, but he pushed me towards the window and plunged back into the flames. As I let myself down on to the path, the remaining portraits of John Howard were melting off the walls.

*   *   *

I clambered up on to the lawn. When I turned back, Rowan House was burning like a tinderbox; there were flames spouting from the roof and smoke billowed from windows above and below. On the main lawn, through the smoke, I thought I saw a murder of crows assembled, thought I could hear the beating of wings; when I got closer, I saw that it was a bunch of uniformed Guards spilling over the grass. Marked and unmarked Garda cars rolled up the drive. Martha O'Connor stood by the granite-edged pool with a digital camera on her shoulder. I found out later that Emily had summoned her. Fiona Reed and Martha were in close conversation; they seemed to have a lot to talk about. DS Forde grabbed my arm and tried to have me arrested. Dave Donnelly intervened, and, if he didn't quite tell Forde to go fuck himself, he got him off my back. I told Dave I thought Jonathan O'Connor was still in the house, and I told him about Shane Howard's confession. He directed Forde to lead a squad around to see if the front entrance was still accessible.

And then I saw Emily Howard pounding across the lawn, with Jerry Dalton following. They were coughing, faces blackened by smoke, red eyes streaming; I guess I looked like that too. Emily was carrying the doll's house that had been in her bedroom, the one with the roof that didn't open. Except it was open now, the edge frayed and splintered from where it had been forced. She looked around, saw Martha O'Connor, and beckoned to her, pointing at the camera. She put the doll's house into Jerry's arms, and then she opened the roof. There were no dolls fucking this time, no 'I should be ashamed of myself', just a folded sheet of notepaper tied in red-and-green ribbon. The paper was covered with a girlish scrawl that Emily read aloud in an unsteady voice:

Cold. When she slept, she slept for a thousand years, and nobody thought or spoke or breathed, so who was in charge of her kingdom then? Not her pathetic father and mother, the king and queen of nothing. Cold as ice, cold as the spell that froze the world. Because they want to give him away. But they will not be permitted. She can see what was wrong now: everything. The wrong people, chiefly Father who is a coward and a wriggling sticky worm when she told her mother what Father did Mother couldn't make up her mind who she was angrier at maybe herself the shrivelled up old bag no one comes to visit me or talk to me as if it is All My Fault and I will be sent away to some school in fucking Galway where everyone is a fucking nun even the girls are nuns or want to be well the sky will burn the world down before that happens even if I should be ashamed of myself I am going to take the little man down to where no one can find us where we can disappear and they can wait a thousand years and even then if some prince comes and kisses her she'll slit his lips and let them run blood red all over scatter the rowan fruit in a ring that will keep the evil away that will keep them all away she has her little prince now and she and he will be invisible dark and wet and cold and safe for a thousand years

Below the writing there was a circle drawn in ink; in the top left-hand corner someone had drawn a red-and-green cross. Emily pointed to the model of the pond, with its perimeter wall of pebbles glued together; she reached finger and thumb down into the top left-hand corner, dislodged a loose pebble and extracted a small length of red-and-green tartan cloth, rolled in a small tube. She held it up, and then placed it on the surface of the model pool.

Then she kicked off her motorcycle boots and jumped into the actual pool. Martha followed her with the camera as she waded towards the spot marked on the map. Then she vanished beneath the water. Dave Donnelly looked at me, and I nodded, as if to say, it's OK. I didn't know whether it was OK or not. The flames from the blazing house burnt dark gold and blood orange; the dawn washed the sky a darker, deeper pink. Emily came up for air, and nodded to me, and almost smiled, and went beneath the dark water again.

'What's she looking for, Ed?' Dave said.

'A child,' I said. 'A dead child. A son.'

The metal cross atop the round tower stood black and indifferent against the inferno. Jonathan had told his family to go to hell, but that's where they had been living all along. He had just lit the flames. I thought of Sandra, and I felt shame at how I had used her to get to the truth, and sorrow for what might have been, and anger that she didn't trust me sooner, or at all. But it was too late for her, had been too late from the day her father touched her. I wondered in the long years she lived in Rowan House if she had sometimes envied her sister's death. I thought of Mary Howard, with her message to her granddaughter from beyond the grave. I thought of Marian Howard's child, and the dead children left in barns and church doorways and buried in fields and in gardens all across Ireland, all for the same reason, for shame, for shame. And I thought of the message last night from my ex-wife, the mother of my dead child, telling me she had given birth to a son.

When Emily came up for breath a second time, she wasn't smiling. She wiped dirt and dead leaves from her face, then reached back down into the water and lifted out a tiny sodden red-and-green bundle. As she walked towards us, the water dripping from the bloodstone around her neck, she unfolded the bundle. It was a small child's school pinafore that had been rolled into swaddling. She carefully reached a hand inside. I could see the red flames of the house burning through the trees, hear the crackle of the fire like the beating of wings. I could see the tears rolling down Emily Howard's cheeks. As she brought her hand up and threw away the pinafore and held the tiny bones of

375

Marian Howard's baby in her outstretched hands, her rings skimmed the water and the dawn flushed deep red as the sky all over Dublin turned the colour of blood.